BECOMING BELLE

BECOMING BELLE

Nuala O'Connor

G. P. Putnam's Sons

New York

G. P. PUTNAM'S SONS
Publishers Since 1838
An imprint of Penguin Random House LLC
375 Hudson Street
New York, New York 10014

Library of Congress Cataloging-in-Publication Data

Names: O'Connor, Nuala, author.
Title: Becoming Belle / Nuala O'Connor.
Description: New York : G. P. Putnam's Sons, 2018.
Identifiers: LCCN 2017033071 | ISBN 9780735214408 (hardcover) |
ISBN 9780735214422 (epub)
Classification: LCC PR6114.I23 B43 2018 | DDC 823/.92—dc23
LC record available at https://lccn.loc.gov/2017033071
p.   cm.

Printed in the United States of America
1   3   5   7   9   10   8   6   4   2

Book design by Gretchen Achilles

For Karen,

my best reader,

and

for Belle,

who lived her best life

Heart, are you great enough
For a love that never tires?
O heart, are you great enough for love?

ALFRED, LORD TENNYSON, from "Marriage Morning"

She determined at any rate to get free from the prison in which
she found herself, and now began to act for herself, and for
the first time to make connected plans for the future.

WILLIAM MAKEPEACE THACKERAY, *Vanity Fair*

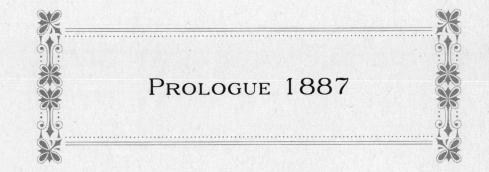

PROLOGUE 1887

Aldershot

A PROMISE

Isabel Maude Penrice Bilton.
Isabel Bilton.
Issy Bilton.
Belle Bilton.

All she could think to write was her name. She dipped her pen into the ink bowl and wrote again:

Miss Isabel Maude Penrice Bilton.

Father had taken away the pencil she had clung to and bid her practice her penmanship with ink. "A woman needs varied skills to march through this world," he'd said. "Pert figures and pretty tunes only carry ladies so far. Accomplishments, my dear Isabel. Gather a diversity of accomplishments."

"Yes, Father," she had replied, and wondered if her skills on the stage would be enough to see her adequately through the parade of life. Might they get her to London as she so desired? Lovely, wretched, teeming London, so distinct and exciting, and as far as the moon from Hampshire and her garrison home, it seemed.

Isabel laid down her pen and took her card case from her pocket; it held a single calling card—a grimy rectangle—which she took out and studied. The name upon it might determine her future. She slotted the card back into the case and snapped shut the lid. Retrieving her pen, she wrote on her page:

London. Isabel shall go to London. Isabel shall dance in London.

In the yard beyond their quarters the bugle sounded the mess call and Isabel put away her paper and pen; it was time to serve dinner. Mother and Father would dine with the regiment this evening, which meant Isabel and her two sisters would sup alone; this was a relief. Two fewer mouths to feed and no Mother to find fault with everything from the tenderness of the meat to the thickness of the potato slices.

Isabel went to the kitchen, plucked her apron from the back of the door and fastened it over her gown. She had already made their meal—a Lancashire hot pot—and it simmered now in the oven, its meaty scent filling the room.

"Flo! Violet!" she called. "I need you both. Come this instant."

Instead of her sisters, Mother appeared in the doorway, shifty as a spirit; she had a habit of gliding into view when one of her girls was doing things of which she would disapprove.

"Why must you shout, Isabel, like some Portsmouth fishwife?"

"I'm sorry, Mother." Isabel lingered by the oven, hoping her mother would leave and let her get on with dishing up the meal.

Kate Maude Penrice Bilton looked majestic in a square-collared gown with sparkling studs on the bodice; her hair was a coil of braids that looped upward like a nest of snakes. Mrs. Bilton had an austere beauty that was much admired among the soldiers at Aldershot Garrison. It had been noted, too, that Isabel, at twenty, now surpassed the comeliness of the wife of John Bilton, artillery sergeant. Isabel's beauty was a rare kind: though full of face, she had a miniature frame so she looked at once sturdy and graceful. Her lips were generous and she had lavish nut-gold hair, though her large eyes sometimes took on a liquid air that spoke of melancholy.

Flo and Violet came into the kitchen and, seeing their mother had come before them to inspect the hot pot, they set the table without prompting from either mother or sister. Flo laid three places and Violet, the youngest, trailed her and planted the cutlery discreetly by each plate—any clanking might provoke their mother's ire.

"You look very fine tonight, Mother," Flo said, and she unfurled a piece of lace on the sleeve of her mother's gown that had curved in on itself like a fern.

Kate Bilton sucked air through her nose. "I thank you, Florence." She patted her hair. "See that you girls ignore any callers," she said.

The sisters never admitted anyone to their quarters on the evenings their parents dined with the regiment, but Mother repeated this warning always, as if she feared she would one night return to find her daughters languishing in the laps of a trio of brigadiers, seduced, compromised and ruined. Kate Bilton knew what men were. And she knew that Isabel, though eldest, was the least sensible of her girls and, worryingly, the most handsome. Their father kept the soldiers at bay, but Isabel had a fanciful nature and her tender heart, combined with her lust for experience, might bring her to grief all too soon. How long would she and John be able to keep the rough culture of Aldershot from tainting their daughters?

Mrs. Bilton watched Isabel lift the dish from the oven and set it on top of the stove; her movements were swift and graceful, dancing had made her lithe and she carried herself elegantly. Kate Bilton felt a rare maternal gush; Isabel truly was the most fetching of girls, she had inherited the Penrice good looks. She went and stood beside her daughter, took up a knife and poked at the browning potato slices atop the hot pot; she sniffed approvingly.

"I rather wish, Isabel, that your father and I were supping at home tonight."

"Thank you, Mother."

Compliment given, Mrs. Bilton pulled on her shawl, rushed from the kitchen to the hall, secured her arm into her waiting husband's and left.

Flo and Violet sat. Isabel placed the hot pot onto a trivet on the table and began to serve her sisters. Only when they were fully sure that their parents were safe at the sergeants' mess, did they uncrimp and begin to enjoy their meal.

Violet spoke through a wad of lamb. "I rather think I shall have servants when I'm a married lady."

Isabel and Flo laughed.

"I rather hope you can afford them," Flo said.

Violet forked a potato slice into her mouth and looked aggrieved.

"Do not speak until you have swallowed, Violet," her eldest sister warned.

The girl chewed rapidly. "I *shall* marry a very rich man," she said, "and I *will* have oodles of servants. Shan't I, Issy?"

Isabel smiled. At fourteen Violet occupied the bottom step of their sisterly stairs and they coddled her always, tried to keep her young. "You shall certainly marry a wealthy man, Violet. And he will supply oodles, heaps and masses of maids of all work, butlers and footmen. No doubt."

"You see, Flo. Isabel says it, so it must be true."

Flo snorted. "If any one of us Biltons snares a rich man, Vi, it will be our darling Issy. Mark me." She pointed her fork from sister to sister for emphasis.

"Why do you say that?" Violet pouted. "Why not me?"

"Oh, perhaps you'll find a wealthy suitor, too, but Isabel longs for love." Flo grinned. "And she will make very sure that her love is given only to a man suitably well supplied"—she patted her gown—"in the pockets."

"That's enough now," Isabel said. "Eat your dinner. Mother's left Eve's pudding for us."

"How delicious," Violet said, and galloped the rest of her hot pot into her mouth.

Isabel rose, took her own plate and scraped the leavings into the bucket.

She thought about what Flo had said and wondered how her sister knew so much about everything when she—Isabel—seemed to know so little. She made cocoa for her sisters, pouring directly from the saucepan into three cups, as they did not own a chocolate pot. When she lived in London, Isabel decided, she would have so much money that she would own a gilded chocolate pot, blooming with red roses, and a coffeepot besides. And she would have three teapots, too, if the fancy took her.

The girls spooned the tart-sweet apples and buttery sponge into their mouths and supped their hot cocoa. They sat and talked until the bugler sounded the triumphant notes of last post. Mother would soon return; Father would follow once he had checked all his men had returned to their barracks. The three sisters moved swiftly to have the kitchen clean for Mother's inspection and they retired to their bedroom before she came in, eager to give the impression they had not lingered over their pudding. Mother said only slatterns idled away their evenings in small talk and chatter.

Kate Bilton entered her home and sighed. She longed for the day when confined military quarters would be a memory and she would have a house of her own. She slipped off her shawl and hung it in the wardrobe in her room. The kitchen was in good order when she looked it over. Her girls were not bad girls, though they tried her; motherhood was a vexatious calling, something she had not realized before marrying. Children were there to consume and drain one, it seemed. Her girls certainly confounded her at least once a day and Mrs. Bilton discerned a certain skittishness in Isabel that the girl hid well; the other two were less inflexible, more obedient. She opened the door to her daughters' room and all three were abed, Flo and Violet reading books by candlelight, Isabel tucked in but awake.

"Did you have a pleasant evening, Mother?" Flo asked.

"To be sure," Mrs. Bilton answered. "As much as one can when surrounded by men who talk of nothing but artillery and horses. Sleep now, girls."

"Yes, Mother," they chorused and the three moved as one to lift their snuffers and extinguish the candles.

Isabel lay back and felt grateful that tonight Mother was benign. Too often she forced Isabel from her bed to rescrub a pot or empty the swill can. She thought again of what Flo had said; Isabel did mean to marry for love, that was true. But wouldn't it be a lark if the one she loved had money, too? She would never meet any men in Aldershot, that was certain; her parents were too vigilant. She *must* get to London. Isabel listened to the sleep sounds of Flo and Violet—soft breathing, the odd rustle of moving limbs.

"A promise to myself," she whispered, "I shall go to London. I shall *live* in London." She put her hand under her pillow to feel the cool, pearlized shell of her card case with its lone, worn calling card. "London," Isabel said, and pushed her head into the pillow to bring on sleep.

A Card

Isabel's first taste of the stage had been as a stand-in for her mother. She was fourteen and she knew Mother's small act in the variety show from start to finish, for the kitchen in their barracks home was her rehearsal room. It was not Mother's idea to let Isabel perform—she was too ill to make such a decision—but Father insisted that Isabel take the role rather than disappoint the soldiers and locals who relished these performances.

"Isabel, you must take your mother's part tonight," her father said. "You simply must."

"If Mother wouldn't mind, Father, I should be delighted to," the young Isabel had said, worried that her mother would mind very much indeed.

"I shan't tell Mother yet, my dear; her strength is not good. But you must do it—it's the only thing, the right thing."

"If you think so, Father."

Isabel glowed inside; here was her chance to get onstage at last. She, Flo and Violet spent hours rehashing Mother's routines to the daisies and cows at the edge of Aldershot's North Camp and Isabel always took the lead. It was a little victory to get to perform in front of an audience at Farnborough town hall. What joy!

But first Isabel had to soak Mother's stained sheets in kerosene before she would scrub, boil and hang them out to dry.

"Another baby lost," Flo said, shoving the sheets into the dolly tub for her sister to deal with before attending to her own household duties.

A baby lost? How? Isabel wondered. Was Mother to have a baby? She had not said so. She did not quiz her sister, for she was not sure she wanted the answer. All she knew was that Mother would not rise from her bed for a week or more. It had happened before. Mother would moan, weep and sigh there, and eat little of the food brought to her, though Isabel planned to buy currant-studded Welsh cakes from Clement's to tempt her and make light soups that were easy to digest. When she was well, Mrs. Bilton was not an easy person; when she was ill she was intractable.

Father sat by Mother in their bedroom, held her sobbing frame and murmured, "There, there, Kate. It will come right in the end, my love, you'll see."

"It will never come right, John. I have failed you. Again."

"I am happy with my houseful of girls, you know that, my love."

Mother wailed and thrashed in his arms before slipping into a dull reverie where she neither talked nor moved; Father stayed with her, for he did not like to leave her alone. He sat on, cradling his wife, even when sleep overtook her.

Isabel had witnessed this scene before and, though the three girls knew not to crowd or harry their mother when she was unwell, Isabel hung by the bedroom door. Mother's costume was within and, in order to perform at Farnborough, she needed to get it. She waved to Father and he laid his wife back against the pillow, like a baby, and came to Isabel.

"What is it, Issy?" he whispered. "Mother needs me."

"I know, Father, but *I* need the costume and it's in the wardrobe."

"Ah." Father glanced to where Mother lay with closed eyes. The door scraped as he opened the wardrobe and Kate Bilton was roused. She propped herself up.

"John, what is it? What are you doing?"

"I, ah, that is to say, Isabel . . ." He glanced to his daughter. "Well, the fact is, my love, Isabel is going to take your place onstage at Farnborough tonight."

Mother flopped back against the pillow, her raw eyes staring at the ceiling. "So this is what it comes to, John. You mean to let her eclipse me."

Isabel knew that this was likely the beginning of a tirade and she went to close the door, but Mother saw her.

"Come, Isabel!"

"Mother?"

Mrs. Bilton wriggled in the bed, contorting her body so that she could sit. Her hair draggled down her back, a nest of knots, and she wore her oldest chemise, the one with the brown stains that no amount of kerosene would remove. She looks undone, Isabel thought. Outside, the dismiss bugle sounded its sweet notes and the girl knew she would be late if Mother pursued a row. Father had arranged for Mr. Lloyd, the variety show's director, to pick up Isabel in his brougham and take her with him to Farnborough for the show.

Her mother looked Isabel over. "Have Flo dress your hair, it needs to be up." She tugged Isabel's plait. "This is childish." She looked to her husband. "John, take the gown from the wardrobe and give it to Isabel. Hurry." Her voice was flat but at least she wasn't fighting.

A knock to the front door. "He's here, Mr. Lloyd is here," Isabel said, taking the costume into her arms with care. Mr. Bilton went to greet Lloyd.

Mother held out her arms to Isabel. "Sit," she said. Isabel hesitated; Mother looked so wretched. She seemed calm; but Isabel knew that at any second Mother might cry and wail like a virago again and, worse, lash out with her fist. "Come, come." Her mother flapped her hand.

Isabel draped the gown over one arm and sat; she took Mother's offered hand. "Do not let me down, Isabel." Mrs. Bilton squeezed her daughter's fingers hard.

"I know all the words and steps, Mother, truly I do."

"No doubt. But this is *my* role. *My* stage. Don't you dare embarrass me."

"I won't, Mother, I promise you."

Mrs. Bilton let Isabel's hand drop, lay down and closed her eyes. "Go then," she said.

At the door Isabel turned to offer further reassurance about how well she knew the part, about how she would do her very best to honor Mother's talent, but there were tears, cascades of them, sliding out from under her mother's eyelids, so Isabel took her leave in silence, closing the door softly.

M r. Lloyd had a wet mouth and Isabel disliked the way he poked out his tongue and licked his lips while looking at her. The brougham was stuffy but she daren't ask if she might open the window.

He leaned forward. "You are as fine a girl as your mother, Miss Bilton. There's that to be said."

"Thank you, Mr. Lloyd."

"You will go far if you wish." He cleared his throat. "On the stage, I mean."

"Yes, sir." Isabel hitched her gloves up on her wrists and peered out the carriage window; she did not like to look at Mr. Lloyd, for the way his eyes dillydallied over her person discomfited her. It was not like being watched at play by the barrack soldiers; this man's gaze penetrated her and made her feel murky. How Flo would laugh when Isabel mimicked Mr. Lloyd later, all roving stares and sodden lips. Isabel suppressed a smile.

They passed the Aldershot rat pit, where men had terriers kill rodents for money, and Isabel fancied she could hear shouts and squeals. When they trundled along High Street she put her hand over her nose, too aware of the smell of the slops that drained into the open sewer there; the stink could permeate even carriage doors. On the road to Farnborough, the apple farms that lined the way seemed to scurry past and she recalled the day the previous summer when she and Flo had accepted a lift on a hay cart from a young farmer who whistled beautifully for their benefit. They in turn had sung for him. Hampshire could be a glorious place at times.

The brougham hit a rut and Mr. Lloyd, who had been snoring lightly, jolted awake and smiled. He shot his tongue over his lips and began to scrabble through his coat pockets.

"I have it here someplace," he mumbled. He plunged one hand deep into his trousers and began to fumble. Alarmed, Isabel once again turned her eyes to the passing countryside. "Here it is!" he roared, and she sensed his hand hovering near her body. She looked and he was proffering a rectangle of paper.

"What is it?"

Mr. Lloyd rattled his hand at her as if she were an imbecile and Isabel took what he was holding. It was a grubby thing and she saw now that it was a calling card. She turned it over.

"'Mr. H. J. Hitchins,'" Isabel read aloud, "'Acting Manager, the Empire Theatre, Leicester Square, London.'"

"A very good friend of mine is Mr. Hitchins. A bosom comrade, one might say."

"How nice for you."

Isabel went to give back the card, but Mr. Lloyd folded his fingers around hers and pressed hard.

"Keep it, my dear. I think Mr. Hitchins would very much like to meet you, Miss Bilton. Yes, indeed. When you are older and ready for big things, contact my dear Hitchins."

Isabel pulled her hand away, glad of the protection afforded by her gloves, and nodded her thanks to Mr. Lloyd.

A HANDOUT

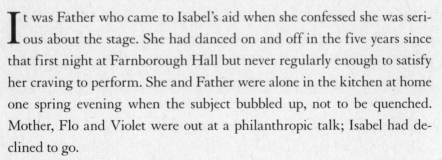 It was Father who came to Isabel's aid when she confessed she was serious about the stage. She had danced on and off in the five years since that first night at Farnborough Hall but never regularly enough to satisfy her craving to perform. She and Father were alone in the kitchen at home one spring evening when the subject bubbled up, not to be quenched. Mother, Flo and Violet were out at a philanthropic talk; Isabel had declined to go.

"Shall we drink tea, Issy, while the others enjoy listening to the Queen of the Poor?" Father grunted. He disdained altruists and could not understand why his wife liked to listen to their blather. "Yes," he said "a cup of black tea will do us nicely." As a sergeant Mr. Bilton had a generous tea allowance but, still, he was frugal with his ration; today he meant to be bountiful. "I should rather enjoy a sup. And you, Isabel?"

"Of course, Father. Sit by the hearth and I'll make it."

John Bilton watched his daughter, nineteen now and glorious, move about the kitchen; she could not cross a room without it looking like a ballet. Her movements were fluid, she was at home in her supple little body. Flo, too, loved to mince about, but she had not Isabel's grace. And Violet, well, poor Violet had a mule's feet. Mr. Bilton looked on while his daughter unlocked the caddy and spooned leaves into a scalded pot; she flitted across the flags and placed pieces of rum cake onto a gilt-edged plate. He observed her with pleasure; Isabel was a dancer through and through. But she was domesticated also, a good cook and tidy, after a fashion. He had to own, though, that there was an itch in the girl: she was giddy, always looking outward, as if for a great rescue. And skitting about like a gadfly, while singing songs, seemed to be her greatest occupation and joy. Would Isabel make a useful wife? Sometimes he thought her no wiser than a child—she could be disconcertingly naïve—and, yet, she was capable. A girl of contrasts. Was this an advantageous thing, or was it troublesome? He couldn't decide. One thing was undeniable, though, Isabel would not suffer being enclosed with the family much longer. How he was to profitably marry three daughters Mr. Bilton could not fathom. He would not brook a soldier's hand for any of them, that he did know, least of all for his darling eldest.

"Isabel, Isabel," he said, when she sat opposite and prepared to fill his cup.

"Yes, Father?"

"What will we do with you?"

She poured tea and fussed a slice of cake onto a small plate for him. "I know what I should *like* to do, Father."

Ah, here it was, there were plans abrewing. "And what is that, my dear? No doubt it involves some poltroonish young man who has snagged your heart."

Isabel lifted her eyes to meet his. "No, Father, it doesn't. I should like, if I could, to make my way in the theater."

"You wish to pursue the life of a performer?" John Bilton sighed. This was Kate's influence, though she would deny it. Why had he ever allowed *her* to take to the stage? He studied Isabel. "I confess you have the talent for it, my dear, but are you quite certain it's what you want? Your life lived by night? Your mother merely dallies with the stage, but you, I gather, mean to embrace that life. You would be mixing with all the disrespectable types who frequent theaters daily. I'm not sure I like it."

"Queen Victoria herself attends the theater, Father."

Mr. Bilton snorted. "So she does."

He gazed at Isabel. It was not possible to fully relish the idea of her taking to the stage but he didn't want a military life for her either; he had seen what it had done to his darling Kate. However, the time was ripe to put some distance between his wife and Isabel. The house could no longer contain their histrionics when they opposed each other. Well, when Kate went into opposition against Isabel, if he were truthful with himself.

"Isabel, if you are to do it all, it will entail a move to London. You do realize that?"

"Yes, Father, that's what I dream of."

"Dreams? Ah!" Mr. Bilton bit into the rum cake; crumbs and raisins scattered to his lap and he pinched them together and popped them into his mouth. He chewed and regarded her, his lovely girl. How would she fare in the city? She was still under his care and she had a heedless side that worried him, an incautious way that took over sometimes, perhaps born of her guileless nature. But the devil of it was that Isabel had a knack since a baby for triumphing, even when things did not go her way. When things toppled, she righted them.

"Well, if you dream of being an actress, Issy, you must try it out," Mr. Bilton said at last. "Dreams need courage to buoy them up and that, I think, you have. And there is no doubt that you have the ability; Mother has seen to that by letting you perform with her." He slurped his tea, then set down the cup. "Go to the wardrobe in my bedroom. There you will find an inkwell in the shape of a horse's hoof."

"Really, Father, a hoof?"

"Yes, yes. Go and fetch the thing, bring it here."

Isabel went and rummaged under folded breeches and undershirts; she found the inkwell—an odd, ugly object—and brought it to her father. He flipped open the brass lid; there was no glass well inside. Mr. Bilton stuck his fingers into the space where it should be and retrieved a roll of banknotes.

"My secret stockpile," he said and winked. He unfurled some money and handed it to her. "This, my dear, will get you to London and keep you safe for a few weeks. Until you get yourself into some theater or other."

Isabel looked at the wad of notes he had given her. "Oh, Father," she said, "it's a king's ransom." She fell to her knees before him and hugged his waist.

"There, there." Mr. Bilton patted his hand to her hair. "Enough foolishment. Sixty guineas or so will see you right in London for the time being. I'm trusting you, Isabel, to keep your head in the city; I'm trusting you as surely as I would a man. Up now, my dear, and sup your tea."

"Thank you, Father. Thank you, truly."

Isabel rose and sat opposite him again; she drank from her cup and beamed. There was a luster to her now, a more joyous cast around the eyes than Mr. Bilton had ever witnessed there. He sincerely prayed that he was doing the right thing by releasing her into the world. And he prayed further that his wife would not lose her mind over his letting Isabel go.

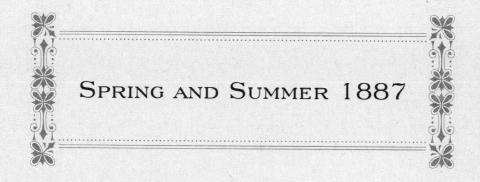

SPRING AND SUMMER 1887

London

An Audition

The door to the Empire Theatre stood under a glass awning. In his return note, Mr. Hitchins had indicated that he would meet Isabel there and not at the stage door, as she had expected. But no one waited for her and she didn't want to peer through the glass for fear of looking provincial. Isabel's hair was dressed high and she wore her best walking gown; and, though she didn't have a looking glass in her Pottery Lane lodgings, she knew she was at her finest. The cabinetmaker who kept the room below hers had stood to watch as she passed and his fulsome gawp and botched cap tip told her she looked her best. One of the lane's cat flayers, an ancient woman who stripped skins at her front doorway, spat as Isabel went by, and this, too, she took for a good sign. The women on the street were never cordial, but Isabel didn't mind much; the men greeted her and, in that way, she had some daily conversation to quell her loneliness.

It was only days since she had left Aldershot—eight when Isabel counted them up—but in that time she had moved into Pottery Lane, thanks to the assistance of a dragoon's wife at Aldershot, and she had secured this interview with Mr. Hitchins. Isabel had, too, walked London like a kind of Lazarus, newly awoken to the joys of the world. Her feet were battered from trotting the streets, but it did not cost her. She felt as if the city moved around her alone, laying out its diversions before her as special gifts. It was all beautiful: the dome of Saint Paul's, the ample parks, Buckingham Palace. And every bit of every day held new charms: a shard of city light cutting through her snug bedroom, a pink-frosted cake eaten at leisure in a tearoom, the playbills studied outside every theater on Leicester Square and the Strand. She liked to fancy her own name emblazoned there instead of Vesta Tilley and Bessie Bellwood.

Not even her solitude dimmed Isabel's pleasure at waking each day to London's racket—the din of carriage wheels, hallooing street children, the brick men's clamor—and the knowledge that she was far from her enclosed family life in Hampshire. Of course she missed Father and her sisters, but it was an extraordinary relief to be away from the crush of Mother's ill humor. It lightened Isabel, made her feel like a feather at the whim of a breeze.

"Miss Bilton?"

Isabel turned to see a spry, silver-haired man in the Empire's doorway. "Mr. Hitchins? Good morning."

Hitchins held out his hand and she shook it. "Good morning to you, miss." He smiled and studied her but she did not feel examined, as she had so long ago with his friend Mr. Lloyd. "Come, come," he said.

He led her through the mirrored foyer and up the vast staircase to the Empire's auditorium, a wonder of gilt and crimson plush. Isabel whirled, looking from the gallery to the grand circle to the boxes to the pit. The air in the theater was smoky and beery, with a bittersweet tinge like boiled onions, but there was promise in it, too. Isabel turned, finally, to appreciate the stage.

"The proscenium is thirty-five feet high," Mr. Hitchins said, as if he himself had designed and built it. He pointed ceilingward. "Look at the cornicing, how intricate it is." He swept his arm downward. "Note the width of the promenade."

This was not Farnborough town hall; this was grand and regal and proper. A thrill flushed through Isabel's body. Here she might dance.

"It's truly magnificent," she said quietly, and she meant it.

"And our players are magnificent also, Miss Bilton. Can you be that?"

Isabel squirmed but she girded herself and looked at him, full face. "Yes, Mr. Hitchins, I believe I can."

"We shall see," he said, and bid her follow him across the stage, through the greenroom, which was large enough for a spectacle, to the dressing rooms. "Change here and I shall see you onstage." He left.

Change? Into what? She had not brought a costume; it had not occurred to her. Isabel looked around, made frantic by her mistake; there was nothing to be seen: no dress, no hat, no cloak. She opened the door and peered down the corridor. Had they passed the wardrobe? She didn't think so, but she had noticed the scene-painters' room and also, she was sure, a prop room; she went there and tried the handle. The door opened and she slid inside. There was a higgledy-piggledy of thrones, armor and crockery; shelves held folded backdrops labeled with the names of shows: *Harlequin, The Forty Thieves, Robinson Crusoe.* Side by side, a huge puppet head and a lifelike piglet were eerie and still in the dim light. Isabel squeezed through the cluttered room, pushed up the lid of a trunk and, after a short rummage, found the prop she needed.

M r. Hitchins sat on a chair, downstage. Isabel had expected him to sit below, in the fauteuils; his proximity shook her. But she walked center stage, for she knew this might be her only chance, and stood before him.

"Regrettably, Miss Bilton, the piano man has not come; you shall have to improvise." Mr. Hitchins nodded for her to begin.

Isabel's blood pounded through her veins and washed into her ears; her heart bulged under her ribs. No music? That was all right—she would make it all right, she could beat it out in her head. She took deep breaths, urged herself to be calm and brought her feet together; she had removed her boots in the dressing room and the boards felt cold through her stockings, but that soothed her. She opened the Chinese fan plucked from the prop room trunk and held it up. Isabel had removed her jacket so that Mr. Hitchins might see how slender her waist was and she held her elbows aloft now to billow the fan so that he could fully appraise her form as she moved. With no music to guide her, she could set her own pace, so she began with just the fan and her eyes, coquetting for Mr. Hitchins as if it were something she did for men every day of the week. She slid the fan to cover her left ear, then briefly covered her eyes: her lover knew now that they were being observed. She switched the fan to her right hand: now he knew she had another suitor. Isabel closed the fan with a flourish and held it in her hand as she began to sway, arms above her head, her ruffled skirt swooshing with the rhythm of her hips. Mr. Hitchins's eyes on her were appreciative and she undulated slowly the better to show the slender vigor of her body. Isabel twirled on the spot twice, then performed jeté after jeté around the stage, tapping her ankles elegantly each time she jumped, and flicking open the fan in her extended hand each time she landed. Often she and Flo would do this in the barracks yard when the soldiers were drilling elsewhere. Now she conjured the air of the garrison around her, Flo flitting behind, chirping out a suitable tune, the sound of their soles on the ground.

Mr. Hitchins clapped sharply. "Thank you, Miss Bilton." Isabel stopped. "Now, sing," he said.

Again she was disconcerted; he had cut her off. She had planned a final move where she would land on one knee, fan covering her face. Isabel stood, uncertain, and tried to control the panting that consumed her. She breathed hard through her nose and heard Flo's voice telling her to collect herself *at once.*

"Yes, Mr. Hitchins," she said, "I will sing for you."

Isabel stood where she was, took a deep inhalation and released the first lines of "My Wild Irish Rose," a song her English father sang to her

Welsh mother for who knew what reason. Still, it was a beautiful air and Isabel, after a few bars, lost herself in the words:

> *"My wild Irish Rose, the sweetest flower that grows.*
> *You may search everywhere, but none can compare*
> *With my wild Irish Rose."*

"Enough!" Mr. Hitchins shouted, one hand aloft. Isabel stopped singing and looked at him, unsure. Was that all she was to do? Did he not need to see and hear her for longer than that? Had her performance been poor? "Re-attire yourself, Miss Bilton, and meet me in the foyer."

Mr. Hitchins had his back to her and she was guarded as she approached him but, when he swung around, he grinned and held his pipe aloft.

"Fifteen pounds a week to start, Miss Bilton. Rising to twenty and beyond if you please me. If you *continue* to please me." He puffed on his pipe. "Begin Monday."

Fifteen pounds a week! How Father would rejoice! Isabel stepped forward. "I thank you, Mr. Hitchins. I thank you ever so much."

"We will have Alexander Bassano photograph you, yes, that much we must do. I will arrange for you to go to his studio at Old Bond Street. Your extraordinarily pretty visage will soon be known, Miss Bilton."

"Mr. Bassano takes pictures of royalty." Isabel knew his portraits from *The Lady* and *The Evening Star* and many other publications besides.

"He most certainly photographs the royals, Miss Bilton, and very handsomely he does it, too." Mr. Hitchins studied Isabel. "Look here, girl, I mean for you to bypass the chorus. I have a role in mind for you." He pointed the stem of his pipe at her. "You are to be my Cupid."

"Isn't Cupid a boy?" Isabel blurted, and felt instantly stupid for saying such a thing.

"He is a boy, Miss Bilton, he is, ordinarily. The tiny god of large de-sires, that's Sir Cupid." Mr. Hitchins threw his arms wide. "But this, my dear, is a theater. This is bohemia. And here we do anything we please. Here we transform beautiful young ladies into Eros." He winked, strode through the Empire's front door and let it slam behind him.

Fifteen pounds! Alexander Bassano! Isabel did a quick jig on the spot, giggled into the air, composed herself and followed Mr. Hitchins out to the street.

An Appeal

March 1887

Pottery Lane, London

Darling Flo,

You will not believe what I have to tell you, but I have done it. Your incapable sister has found a job! There, do I not surprise you? You thought I would return to Aldershot like a lamb, woolly tail down, but here I am, a woman of means in London. Mr. Hitchins of the Empire took a liking to me tout de suite and I am to earn fifteen pounds a week. Isn't it marvelous, Flo? In a year I'm sure I will be richer than Father.

A bruised five-pound note will have fallen into your lap when you opened this letter and, yes, that is for you, my darling. Do please come as you so fervently promised you would, the day we parted; I'm like half a girl without you. The money will pay your fare and afford you the price of a meal at an inn along the way and you will have coins ajingle in your pocket besides.

London is even more charming to live in than it is to visit, Flo. By day it bustles with workers and by night it swarms with dilettantes and aristocrats. I now quite prefer life after dark—I sleep half the *day! I like the Empire very much, I feel at home, though the ladies of the company snub me, rather, but Mr. Hitchins says they are always begrudging and envious at first "when a new favorite arrives" and I'm not to fret, they will warm up, he says. So you see, though I'm not completely alone—the gentlemen are kind to me—I need my Flo to keep me right. I miss you, my darling, come to me!*

Your loving,
Isabel

PS Mr. Hitchins wants to audition you, he says he has "a scenario in mind" but will not tell me what it is.

PPS The cat gutters of Pottery Lane make the street smell worse than a slaughterhouse, but my room is warm and my landlady is willing to let you lodge if you share my bed. Come!

Flo stood at the far edge of North Camp, Isabel's letter in hand, and looked back at the rows of huts, the parades of men passing back and over, and the new brick barracks off in the distance. She listened to drums, the call of a trumpet, the whinnies of horses. Though it was all as familiar and comfortable as her own carcass, Flo found she no longer wanted to be in Aldershot. Since Isabel had left, things were lifeless; she and Violet conducted their days in an unusual silence, as if each had sent the sociable part of themselves away with their sister. Mother had turned her full attention to her younger daughters and, though her behavior was moderate mostly, she seemed always to dangle on the brink of rampage.

Isabel's letter was a lantern in the dark; Flo clutched it, scanned it again. Would she go? She must! Would Father let her go? Would Mother? She would no doubt be against it. And if Flo left, how would Violet fare? That Vi was Mother's favorite was a comfort. And, perhaps, with Flo and

Isabel both gone, Mother would not be as harried and, therefore, Violet would encounter few storms. There was no way to be sure, but Flo knew that she would go to London, for what, really, was there to keep her in Aldershot? There was no proper work for actresses in Hampshire, especially not ones of her slender talents. In London there would be a chorus she could muddle along with; it would not matter so much that she was more hearty than able.

And she could not be Violet's protectress forever. Anyway, Mother would surely be softer with Isabel and Flo away. Vi was a pet, an easy girl to love. She had neither Isabel's petulance nor Flo's single-mindedness. All would be well for dear Violet.

Flo held up the letter and reread Isabel's words: *I need my Flo to keep me right. I miss you, my darling, come to me!* Flo tucked the money into her pocket and resolved to speak to Father.

A Baron

Isabel only needed to be forty miles from Aldershot in order to unlock liberty. In the six weeks she spent alone in London, waiting for Flo to join her, she began to have a life. Once the curtain closed at the Empire, her nights were a whirl of the Pelican Club and the Café Royal, and wherever else the crowd was keen to spend time after the show. There was sparkling company in the form of fellow performers, directors and assorted theater folk. Aristocrats and bohemians, city men and night birds of every stripe flocked together. These were hedonists: they drank all night and slumbered by day, the better to enjoy the next night's party and the next. Along with them, Isabel began to eat in well-appointed restaurants and hotels; and she now bought her clothes from the finest of modistes. It pleased her that her life was no longer ordered by the routines of the barracks—here everything was do as you please and it stimulated her to the tips of her nerves. It all felt daring at first and then, by and by, it felt like her natural milieu. She could bend her hours to whatever shape she wished, and keep company with any motley troop, and society be hung.

On the days she roamed the city, eager to know it, Isabel took her leisure as she walked, sucking up the fetid air, rank with horse manure and slaughterhouse stenches. Despite its high smells and unavoidable filth, she grew to truly love London; she yearned toward the city even when she was in it. A view of Trafalgar Square or the Crystal Palace always whisked up within her a contented wonder that was part pride, part longing. She had been born in Marylebone and she felt in her marrow that London was the only place she ever had belonged. The years spent in the barracks in Hampshire with her family had only made her more determined to return as soon as possible to the city of her birth. Nowhere else suited her so well and, of course, London was far enough away from Mother for her not to impinge on Isabel's life. Father was another matter, but the two were entwined so Isabel had to leave him behind also. She wrote to him, of course, economical notes that told only of the sensible parts of her doings; Isabel did not want him to worry about her.

On one such day of strolling she saw a pair of ragged boys taunt a sandwich-man wedged inside his two boards.

"Where's the mustard, then?" one called, while the other poked the man around the cheeks with a straw blade. He was defenseless, ensconced like a beef slice between the heavy boards.

"Leave off, you two," Isabel shouted, and the boys, their eyes haunted with hunger, took her in, then sauntered on, as if they had better places to be.

One called back, "Spare us a bender, miss? You can surely give sixpence, a fine lady like you?"

"Get out of it!" Isabel roared and the pair scuttled off to find somebody new to bother.

The sandwich-man grinned his thanks at Isabel as she passed; she never found it hard to raise smiles from her fellow Londoners with her sybaritic looks and elegant dress. Men were drawn to Isabel even before they knew she was a dancer at the Empire Theatre. Society women were wary of her, which did not bother Isabel as she rarely sought their company. She was unguarded, cherishing conversation with fishmongers as much as blue bloods, as long as they were men.

The first time Isabel went to the Corinthian Club in Soho, she met Alden Carter Weston. She arrived to the club in a froth of Empire performers; though the other players had softened over the weeks she still did not have a particular friend among them. But soon Flo would be here and Isabel would be easy again; there was nothing like her dear sister's presence to make her feel whole.

Isabel stood to take in the scene at the Corinthian. Like most clubs, the decor was unfussy: squat brown chairs, paneled walls and soft gaslight. But there was a frisson in the air here: it was where the best and brightest night owls came to nest for hours at a time. She knew the clientele were referred to as Corinthian steamers and it was not hard to see why. Some men and their girls were already full up to the knocker, hooting and falling about. But it was all good-natured, there was little seamy about them; and Isabel giggled when one gent got tangled in his petite amie's beads and spilled champagne down her bosom.

Isabel looked away and apprehended a man's eyes trained on her; she kept his gaze and nodded when he would not break it. She turned away for a moment, then back in his direction. He held out his hand and, glancing briefly to find her companions, who had scattered it seemed, Isabel walked to where he stood. He was not handsome—Mother would have called him swarthy—but he had fine blue eyes and a commanding yet genial stance. He was old, though, probably in his thirties and, therefore, almost certainly married. A book sat open before him on the bar top and Isabel wondered what kind of person brought reading material about with them at midnight.

The man stepped forward. "Good evening to you, Miss . . . ?"

"Bilton. Isabel Bilton."

He held out his hand and Isabel took it. "I saw you laugh, Miss Bilton, at that clumsy fellow and his now sopping girl." His accent was American.

"She is doused in champagne! Was it altogether kind to snicker at her humiliation?"

Isabel looked down, unsure if the man meant to scold or tease. "Well, sir, I didn't mean to be unkind. To laugh at her, exactly." She looked at him and he was grinning. "Oh, it *was* funny," she said and laughed. He was still holding her hand aloft. "Now, do you mean to tell me your name, sir?"

"I have several names but you, Miss Bilton, may call me Alden, for I let my dearest friends do that."

"But what are your other names?"

"My, you do like to pry, young lady. Well, I am Baron Loando to some, and Alden Carter Weston to others."

Isabel chimed with his light tone. "Well, then, I shall call you Alden seeing as we are such *dear* friends."

"And I shall call you Isabel. Or Issy, when the fancy takes me."

A shiver of unease ran through Isabel's stomach but it was, somehow, welcome. This was what she had come to London for—to throw off the shackles of childhood and live as bohemians lived, wasn't it? Less than two months in the city and already, because of her performances and because of the company she kept, she had become a new person. She was emboldened, better able to push herself along. Yes, this Mr. Weston was forward but there was something divine in the way he carried himself, too; his brash confidence was alluring and it raised hers. Though he was rugged, his bearing was august. Here was a *man*.

Weston ordered wine and invited Isabel to join him at a table.

"My friends are here," she said. "I shall invite one of them to sit with us, Alden. You do understand."

"Do you really need a chaperone? I should rather like to have you all for myself."

"What would people say if I sat alone with a married man?"

"Married? I have no wife in this town!" He grinned and held her stare. Which surely only means she resides elsewhere, Isabel thought. "I only . . . it's simply that . . ." She balked at mentioning his advanced years. Flustered she said, "I thought perhaps you would have a wife. Here. In London."

"I do not." Weston leaned forward and spoke close into Isabel's ear. "And, Issy, what sort of man does not live with his wife?"

Isabel looked at him, and the grayish whiskers and brawny frame receded, all she saw were his bright eyes. She found that his strange accent and light tone were seductive beyond measure, and her faculties pooled so that she felt at once sensible and simple. Her skin expanded in his presence, it seemed, so that she became aware of every lift of her own hand, every stray curl that caressed her neck, and the slicks of sweat that bloomed in her warmest places. Isabel observed him and was very glad indeed that this night had brought her to the Corinthian Club and Mr. Alden Carter Weston. The Baron Loando.

"What say you, Miss Bilton? Will you come to a secluded corner and drink a glass with me?"

"Sir, you would not have me gossiped about. Let me call one of my companions and we shall all three enjoy some wine."

He held up one hand. "As you wish, Miss Bilton. I have no desire to compromise any young lady."

Isabel had a waiter fetch one of her Empire colleagues and, as the trio sat together, Weston said, "Well, am I not beyond lucky to be in such stylish company?"

"As are we, baron," Isabel answered, knocking her glass to his and reveling in the quake of expectation that shuddered through her bones.

An Arrival

Flo stood in the foyer of the Empire waiting for Isabel; she knew she might stand a long time, for Isabel was not always punctual. She eyed the valise at her feet and wondered if it would look ugly if she were to sit on it and read her book. Flo was tired and she wanted to devour a few more pages for, as the coach reached London, she'd had to close her novel before finding out if dear Emma Woodhouse would ever realize she really loved George Knightley. Flo didn't sit, deciding it would not do. Instead, she admired the dazzle of the foyer's black and gold decor, its sparkle of mirrors, and she watched couples and groups of men pass by, all chitchat and smart attire.

Feeling self-consciously alone, she turned to study the photographs on the wall beside her. Each picture was of an Empire player; here was funnyman Ed Looby, there Mr. Tusso and his dummy Coster Joe. Flo strolled along the gallery of photographs, stopping to read the names of actors she didn't recognize. She was brought up short by a large picture of Isabel, her eyes luminous and her name huge. This was the Bassano portrait her sister had mentioned in her last letter. How very fine Issy looked! A true star. Flo felt a whisk of pride for her sister who was not six weeks in London and seemed already to be feted. She went back to stand by her valise and fumbled Isabel's latest letter from her pocket.

*I hardly have time to breathe, dear Flo. Mornings I stay abed (how
Mother would rage!), afternoons I rehearse, evenings I dance, act and
sing. The hours after the show are for fun. Sundays I spend with
Alden Weston, whom you will meet by and by. He's an American and
a baron, too, my dear, and just as intriguing as that makes him sound.
He and I ride Rotten Row and sup at the Star and Garter Hotel. I
am really living, Flo!*

*But, you must know, I work ever so hard, too. Often we rehearse a
new show by day and dance an old show by night, and we must
concentrate mightily so as not to muddle the whole lot. Mr. Hitchins
believes in variety and we are constantly revamping and adding in
order to lure our audience back with fresh scenes. But soon you will
be in the thick of it all.*

*And I have such news! Hitchins has finally revealed to me his great
plan: we are to be a sister act. Can you believe it, Flo? He says we'll
be "like the Machinson Sisters, only fewer." He thinks it a glorious
scheme and, I have to say, I do, too. What could be better than to
share the stage with you, my darling?*

*So, now you see you must come to London ever so quickly, as Mr.
Hitchins wants us to begin rehearsing straightaway for* Babes in the
Wood and Robin Hood. *And here's the most wondrous bit, Flo—
you are to be Robin!*

Flo's breath caught in her throat. Mr. Hitchins was surely the most
trusting man alive to give her such a role without even meeting her. Isabel
had clearly talked a tempest about Flo's abilities when, in truth, they were
meager compared to her sister's. No matter. Flo could hold a tune and beat
out a dance and, if she were to get on in life, wasn't a breakneck plunge the
best way to begin? She would work like a demon.

Mother, of course, had collapsed in anguish the day Flo left, as if she
did not know the moment had come.

"Two daughters blowing loose in the London wind. Whatever am I to think?" Mother wailed and Father had soothed her, as only he could, with gentle words and caresses.

"Think on it, my dear. Life will be so much easier for you with just Violet here. Isabel and Flo are women now. They must take their place in the world. We must let them."

Mother was soon comforted, for she discerned the truth in his words—life would indeed be less fraught with two fewer mouths to feed and only gentle Violet for company.

Flo folded the letter and, feeling watched, she lifted her eyes to see Isabel, a few feet away and grinning like a lunatic. In seconds they were upon each other, in a huddle of hugs and kisses.

"I've missed you so, Isabel." Flo clasped her sister to her.

"And I you," Isabel whispered, doused in emotion now that Flo was here at last. "Come. To our lodgings firstly. Mr. Hitchins will see you tomorrow."

Flo knew that Pottery Lane would not be sumptuous in any degree, but she was surprised at quite how low the laneway was with its swills of sewerage and dejected-looking children.

"The poor, sorry mites," she said, over and over, staring at them until Isabel said the same mites would pick the ribbon off her hem if she didn't move along.

Their lodgings were bare but adequate and Flo didn't mind that they would have to share the bed—they had done so at home until recently. Isabel stowed Flo's valise in the corner, once she had unpacked, and they sat together on the bed to talk.

"I know you've been censoring your letters to me, Isabel, for fear of Mother's eyes. Luckily she didn't see the latest one. But tell me, how is it really?"

"It's marvelous, Flo. All of it. The Empire girls have tempered and my days are an endless stretch of rehearsals and socializing. Honestly, life is such a flurry that I've barely had a thought of home." She reached and grabbed Flo's hands. "Except for missing you rottenly, of course. And now we are to be the Sisters Bilton. Isn't it wondrous?"

"More than I could have wished for, perhaps more than I deserve. I hope your Mr. Hitchins won't be disappointed in me."

"Why would he be, Flo? You're marvelous!"

"Oh, Isabel, you will see good where there is little. But I thank you. I'll do my best to live up."

"I showed Mr. Hitchins your picture, Flo, and he was in raptures. He looks forward to meeting you."

"And I him." Flo softened her voice. "But what of this man you've been seeing so much of? This baron?"

"Alden? We have a grand time together. We've been half a dozen times to the Star and Garter Hotel in Richmond, a truly lovely place. And we ride the Row in his friend's barouche."

"So you've written to me. But what's he like? Is he upstanding? A decent sort?"

Isabel pushed out her chest and extended one arm. "He is commanding, a real presence. He has graying whiskers." Flo grimaced. "No, no, they make him look distinguished. He is, I suppose, a very manly man."

"And he's good to you, Issy?"

Isabel paused then gave a decisive, "He is."

Flo took her sister's hand and they both lay back on the bed. "That's all I wanted to hear."

A Performance

The first tinkle from the orchestra always made Isabel's lungs tighten, and so it was tonight. She stood in the wings and inhaled; this caused the joyous compression in her chest that meant she was fully ready to dance and sing. London's newsmen, who swarmed around her for interviews any time they fancied, always asked if she felt nervous.

"No, I do not," was ever her honest answer.

Performing took Isabel to a place outside herself; an otherworldly feeling descended once she was in costume, warmed up and waiting to go onstage. It was her body and her mind out on the boards to be sure, but she was elevated there—all cares receded when she sang and danced. She thought of neither the good nor the bad in her life but entered a conscious trance and was carried along in it by the heat of the lights, the jangle of appreciation and clapped hands and the message of her songs. All of this mingled pleasurably with the strength and allure of her own body and its movements. The first time she had ever performed at home in Hampshire brought her to a place of rapture and, now, the Empire's stage did the same, and she loved it. Isabel had become a prompt favorite with Londoners and now her sister, too, was being esteemed.

Tonight, as Maid Marian to Flo's Robin in *Babes in the Wood and Robin Hood*, she waited stage right for the silvery flash of light that was her cue.

The scene changers swiftly erected Sherwood Forest, and when they were done, swoosh, a blast of starry sparkles ushered Isabel into the dark. She rushed forward and took her place center stage. Beyond the dimmed footlights she could discern rows of heads; when green moonlight illuminated the scene, the audience broke into merry applause to welcome her. This was the moment she loved—London's adulation never failed to please her; Isabel's innards softened and calm closed in.

She faced the audience without speaking and began to flex her right leg, then she lifted it higher. As her leg rose so, too, did the hem of her gown which barely skimmed her knees as it was. Higher with her leg, arms out for balance, and a satisfying gasp erupted from the crowd. As her leg went up and up, her skirts slipped farther along her thigh; a ripple of appreciation came to her ears. She knew that Alden Weston was probably out there, savoring the sight of her; murmuring his admiration along with the rest of the audience.

The cymbals and drums built a shimmering tension that crawled into Isabel's gut and helped her to raise her leg higher and higher with what felt like the greatest of ease. Heavenward her foot in its laced slipper went, past her hip, past her breast, past her shoulder, until Isabel clasped the back of her calf in her palm and stood feeling the stretch through her tendons, the deep pull of her own muscles and, finally, the serenity that came with the knowledge that she had executed the move well and was maintaining her balance.

"Huzzah!" a man roared from the front row, and the rest of the crowd stamped and clapped in response.

"Brava, Miss Bilton!" went the cries.

Isabel raised both hands above her head, brought her leg back to earth and curtsied to cascading applause.

Flo, who had crept to the stage while Isabel completed her gymnastic feat, cried out: "Why, Maid Marian, have I come at an inconvenient hour? I seem to have caught you at your drill lesson!"

The theatergoers laughed, applauded and settled into their seats. The Sisters Bilton were a popular pair, an instant hit. Isabel turned to her would-be suitor and smiled.

"Robin Hood, why do you sneak up on me so? Have you no thieves to catch?"

"Ah, there is only one catch for me, dear Maid Marian." Flo pushed her feathered cap back, held out her hand to Isabel, and they clasped fingers and gazed at each other.

The orchestra played the opening notes and the sisters began the first of many love duets of the night.

H e's as old as Methuselah!" was Flo's first comment on seeing Alden Weston.

"Oh, Flo, why do you amplify?" Isabel had brought her sister to the Corinthian Club, for Isabel had warmed to the place immensely since that first visit just one month past. Flo, always as prudent as Isabel was naïvely impulsive, saw no reason not to speak her mind to her sister. They both stood and looked at Weston, who was holding forth among some ladies about a novelist he admired. Isabel gazed with admiration while Flo kept a skeptical heart. She noted that he had in fact seen them but allowed them to wait to greet him. Did he have appalling manners to add to his great years, or was he just a show-off?

Flo sighed. "Oh, Isabel, he's surely twice your age at least. What profit can come of that?" She did not mention her thoughts about Weston's discourtesy to them, though he was so very clearly making them wait. Flo glanced once again at him. "I presume he's married?"

"He says not."

"He says not! Unsullied by suspicion, as always, Issy. Must you see only the good in every man jack?"

"And must you catechize me, Flo? I'm your elder, don't forget."

"Then Mr. Weston is your *elder* elder."

"We're not in Aldershot now, Flo. We can see whom we please and neither Mother nor Father can tell us not to."

Flo giggled; it was freeing to be away from home to be sure. "Yes, it's true. But you don't have to let yourself be ensnared by the first man who takes an interest in you, Isabel. Discriminate a little." She looked around at the Corinthian's sloshed and groggy clientele. "Though good men may be hard to find among this lot."

"Alden's a baron, Flo. Did I mention that?"

"An *unmarried* baron. Yes, you have said little else since I got here. There's surely nothing like a title to increase ardor."

Isabel liked when Flo teased; it augmented her own good humor. She kept her eyes fixed on Weston, felt a little proud that the gaggle of girls around him were consuming his words with such attention. She murmured, half to herself, "I do love that he takes me to the best of places and in that barouche with the white horses."

"Yes, Issy, you're living as you dreamed." Flo put her hand on her sister's waist. "But, please, be alert. You mustn't dash too headlong into things, no matter how charmed. Be a little careful, darling, that's all I wish to say."

"I am careful, Flo. And, as I've also told you, Weston behaves well toward me."

"I hope so, my dear. We can never be too cautious. Life is different for ladies; we don't possess the freedoms afforded to men. Even in London."

Isabel squirmed a little. Did Alden, in fact, always behave well? Was that true in its entirety? Isabel had not told Flo that Weston's affections could be mercurial, for she barely acknowledged the fact to herself. Though she liked to consider Weston fondly when she was parted from him, she sometimes found his kindness went sour in a single moment. In her limited experience of men at Aldershot, she had never encountered such turnabout behavior. Isabel put it down to the different customs of

Americans, but it seemed to her, too, that recently Alden wooed her only on the nights she was paid, the better to borrow from her; another thing she blurred for herself as she did not like to reflect on it.

Weston at last excused himself from his mob of admirers and walked to where Flo and Isabel were, his arms aloft.

"You can only be Miss Flo Bilton. Your sister speaks constantly of your graces and I see she doesn't exaggerate. You are a beauty." He took her hand and kissed it. "Your lucky parents have at least two bewitching daughters among their brood."

"Flattery without end," Flo said. "I can see why my sister enjoys your company."

"Come," Weston said, linking arms with both ladies, "let's drink some wine and talk of literature and love."

Flo snorted and Isabel ignored her; it was like her sister to scoff at Weston even while she was allowing herself to be pursued by Willy Seymour, a city man who came to the Empire every night of the week it seemed. He had attached himself instantly to Flo. Seymour was always mooning about backstage, waiting to slip a rose into Flo's hand and tell her how marvelous she was. Isabel was sure Flo could snare a better catch than Seymour, with his gray office face and hideous bowler hat, but Flo found things to admire in Seymour and seemed determined to indulge him. Isabel was still learning that what glittered for one woman was often exceedingly dull to another. And though Weston's luster did not always dazzle as Isabel would like, he was, at least, a baron. So what if he was a little thorny at times, a little coarse? He was American and they had their own ways. She watched him swagger for her sister.

"Do you love to read, Flo, as I do?" he said. "I cannot get your sister to lift a book." He waved his hand in the direction of the Corinthian's library, the quietest room in the club.

"Oh, Isabel is not for literary pursuits, Mr. Weston. She prefers to live her story."

Weston laughed. "What a superb notion! And so superbly put."

"Flo is quite the bookworm, Alden. She reads Dickens, Mrs. Gaskell, all of it."

"A woman after my own heart." Weston slapped his fist to his chest and let out a bellow of laughter. He winked at Flo, but she ignored him and drank her wine.

Mr. Hollingshead, the Corinthian's proprietor, appeared by Isabel's side and touched her arm. "A word, if you please, Miss Bilton."

"Of course, Jack." Isabel excused herself and went across the room to stand at the end of the bar with him. She angled her body so that she could see Weston and her sister. Weston had slid closer to Flo and his hand was cupped between his mouth and her ear. Good, Isabel thought, he means that they should get along; he is being friendly and attentive.

"Miss Bilton, I must speak to you about your bill."

"My bill?" Isabel had no outstanding monies that she knew of. She guessed, though, that it might be of Weston's making. "Might you show it to me, Jack?"

Mr. Hollingshead discreetly folded out the page before her and stood by to shield it from others' eyes. There were sangarees and cocktails, punches and juleps, as well as several bottles of wine and champagne listed.

"Mr. Weston said you knew of this and I merely wanted to make sure that that was the case." Mr. Hollingshead leaned forward and trained his eyes hard on her; he was being helpful, she knew, but she felt a prickle of annoyance. She glanced again at Weston and tamped down her irritation with Mr. Hollingshead—it would not do to be discourteous to him, the club was, like the Empire, becoming another home. Isabel patted his forearm.

"Thank you, Jack. I will settle it next week, if that's all right."

"Of course, Miss Bilton."

She folded the paper, slid it into her pocket and nodded to Mr. Hollingshead. She looked to her sister; Weston was flailing his arms now, in the middle of one of his tales of derring-do, no doubt, where he was the hero against some wicked enemy. He did love to embroider and Isabel liked to listen; he had so much to say and always in such an entertaining manner. Flo, she could see, was not quite as charmed by Alden's large stories. Isabel pressed the pocket with the bill; she would not mention it now. To either Flo or Weston. Best to pay up and forget about it. What did the bill amount to but the price of a few drinks? Wasn't Alden good to her on other occasions? Didn't he pay for dinner at the Star and Garter just yesterday? It didn't matter; Isabel wouldn't let it matter, she had more money now than most girls could dream of. Wasn't it good and proper to share with the man she went around with? Mightn't she fall in love with Alden by and by? He had many fine qualities and a way of making every small outing feel like a party. He was cocksure and exciting, more so than Englishmen; and of all the women in London, he had swooped in on her. Isabel launched across the club and put one hand on Flo's shoulder and the other on Weston's.

"How lovely to see you two together at last."

"Quite," Flo said and emptied her glass down her throat.

A Coupling

Weston had begged Isabel many times to come with him into the Corinthian Club's library. Isabel knew it to be an abandoned place; some of the Empire players prattled about girls who went there because of the privacy certain men liked. They spoke of low-lit corners and fast encounters. Now that she stood inside its book-lined walls, the dim light making a den of the room, Isabel found the library to be a respite from the bar's clangor.

"See?" Weston said, "isn't it a fine place to retreat to, Issy? Didn't I tell you it was?"

She stood in the middle of the room, looking into the fireplace's glow. "You were right, Alden, of course." Some nights, after performing, Isabel was bone weary and liked quiet; the library suited her mood tonight. She moved closer to the fire.

"Are you cold, my dear?"

Isabel was warm enough, but this was the brightest part of the room; and, from the chatter of the chorus girls, she knew exactly why Alden wanted her here. One part of her thrilled to his attentions, another part was dedicated to fending him off. Flo's voice tinkled like a warning bell in her ear. Sensible Flo; she preferred the dull Seymours of this world to the glamour of the Westons and that was her right. Isabel, however, became heedless around men like Alden Carter Weston.

She had to acknowledge that Alden's kisses, stolen in a carriage or on a secluded walk, could be rough; he didn't have the tender mouth of her imagination. And sometimes she was mystified when he was capricious: he could be light and easy one moment but suddenly his mind was a broil of far-off concerns. When she asked what troubled him, he might snap; other times he was gentler. Alden Weston was a wild yet vivifying companion, that was certain.

Isabel lifted her hem to heat her ankles; perhaps she was a little cold, she was tired after all. Weston came up behind her, curled his hands around her waist and laid them on her stomach. She let her head droop to his shoulder. His lips grazed her neck, pecking softly, and, though she feared someone might enter and see them, she savored the wet trail his mouth left on her skin. Tonight Alden was sedate, and she enjoyed it when he was like this, gentle and considerate. Isabel closed her eyes and arched her neck in tandem with his kisses; his solid body, flush against hers, made a tussle of her insides. But what if Mr. Hollingshead came in? Or the fire boy to stoke the flames? She opened her eyes and straightened up.

"Somebody might see us, Alden." Isabel had meant to sound commanding but the words rasped from her throat; she was stirred and her voice betrayed her.

"Nobody will come in; I've seen to it." Weston tightened his arms around her and swayed so that they moved together, as mellow as waltzers. He murmured into her ear: "'What folly will not a pair of bright eyes make pardonable? What dullness may not red lips and sweet accents render pleasant?'"

"What is that, Alden?"

"I know you don't care for books, Isabel, but that's Thackeray. I'm telling you, with the great man's words, that you are beautiful, dear one, and that you undo me."

Isabel snuggled into his back, watched the flames lap around the coal and placed her hands atop his. When he yielded like this, fought against that stormy part of himself, he was the sweetest man alive. Here in his arms she could stay.

Weston removed one of Isabel's earrings and nibbled her earlobe. It struck her as a strange thing to do and yet and yet, the sound of his breath so close, the feel of his teeth and tongue on such a delicate part made her quiver. Her senses fused, dissolved, and she felt pulpy in his arms but oddly alert and taut, too. Her own breath began to come fast from her mouth; he moved his lips to her cheek. Isabel spun in his arms and placed her hands to his chest. Weston leaned in and kissed her; his whiskers didn't tickle her nose as they often did; tonight she didn't feel them. She pressed herself against him and Weston kissed deeper, pushing the hard length of his body into hers. His tongue seemed to fatten as his ardor rose and, with her nose crushed against his, Isabel couldn't breathe. She tried to pull away, but Weston bent her backward with the force of his bulk. Isabel wriggled hard and managed to pull her mouth from his.

"Alden," she said, and he pulled her up so that her feet didn't touch the floor.

"Oh, Issy, dear Issy." His eyes were half-closed and he looked bedeviled, as if possessed by something beyond himself. Clasping her to him with one arm, Weston grappled with the skirt of her gown, jerking it upward until his hand was under it. He snaked his fingers inside her corset and touched the small of her back; he plunged his hand into the top of her knickers and caressed her behind. Isabel gasped and blood rushed through her and flamed her skin. Desire convulsed her but she still feared that at any moment Mr. Hollingshead or somebody else might enter the library and witness their embrace. This was not the place. Isabel pushed at Weston with all her force and broke free of his arms. His eyes opened slowly and he panted.

"Not here," Isabel whispered.

"No, not here," Weston said, "quite right." But he lunged and kissed her once more, forcing his tongue around her mouth in a way that both astounded and roused her.

I sabel perched on the edge of the bed and waited for Weston. The hotel was seamy, the coverlet the color of ash. She removed her glove and touched the sheets, sure they would feel slimy, but they didn't. The hag who had let her in insisted on being paid beforehand, so Isabel gave her money. She looked around at the mildew-stippled walls; she sniffed the air and found, she fancied, the faint reek of urine and sweat.

Alden stepped through the door and grinned at her. "A place worthy of Dickens, Isabel, don't you agree?" He laid down the bag he was carrying and glanced around. "He would style it 'insalubrious' I'm sure."

"You make that sound like something fine, Alden."

"Mr. Dickens called your Pottery Lane 'a plague spot,' did you know that?"

"I think your Dickens exaggerated." She looked around again. "But this place would surely have provoked ink from his pen."

Weston leaped from the door and knelt before her. "What does it matter, Issy? We're alone together, at last." He tossed off his hat and removed his jacket; he pushed her so that she was lying back on the coverlet and pinned her arms above her head. She could taste wine on his lips when he kissed her; her heart began a skirmish behind her ribs. Weston pulled back and grinned at her.

"You are incomparably lovely, Isabel," he said and squeezed her wrists tighter.

Isabel felt the wanton thrill of being in the hotel, where nobody knew she was, with Weston. Here was what she had come to London for: experiences, freedom, a brush with unorthodox living. This was it, yes, but a rapid droop in her gut made her wonder if it was what she wanted at all. She felt dizzy. Was it safe? Weston kissed her deeper and groaned.

"We'll take our time, Issy." He sat up. "I have a tipple with me. Something to make us loose."

He shimmied his shoulders like a third-rate chorus girl and Isabel laughed. There, she need not worry. Alden was in a light mood, he was taking care of her, he meant to make sure she was comfortable and happy. He wanted her to have a pleasant, amusing time. She sat, pulled her legs under her, and covered them with her skirts. Weston retrieved the bag he had left by the door, pulled out two squat cups and handed them to her. He reached again and waved a bottle.

"Good old Madam Geneva," he said.

"Gin?"

"Exactly, my girl."

Weston uncorked the bottle and its sumpy pop sent a shiver through Isabel. He poured. "This is Old Tom, I bought it especially for you; it has cordial through it so will slip down easy."

Isabel sipped; the gin tasted of juniper and sweet lemon and it warmed her throat. It had a contradictory flavor, both sharp and nectarous, and she sipped again and let the liquid slide over her tongue.

"How do you like it?"

"I like it immensely, Alden." She gulped another mouthful.

"Whoa, whoa, Issy, don't gallop it down! It might knock you out. And we must toast each other."

She laughed. "Of course we must." Her head was woozy of a sudden and her belly warm and she wondered if this was what intoxication felt like. If so, it was a welcome feeling. "Me first. 'To a lasting peace or an honorable war!'" She giggled. "That's what my father and his comrades say."

"To British belles." Alden clinked his cup to hers and winked. "That's what I say."

The gin simmered through her and Isabel relaxed. She felt quaggy and keen; how was it possible to be both at once? She giggled and Weston lit a cigarette. He listened to her chatter about Flo and the Empire and the play they were rehearsing, and he looked at her with a languor that she enjoyed. His eyes were appreciative and her blood bloomed, the way it always did in his company, as if he created more of it to wash through her veins. Weston trailed his fingers from the cuff of her boot to her hip and kept his eyes to hers. He stubbed out his cigarette.

"You are beyond lovely, my beautiful baroness. My baroness Loando." He slid his hand through the slit at the front of her underwear, teased the hair, then slotted his finger against the slick heat of her and pressed. "Do you like that, Issy?"

"Yes." Her whole body throbbed. She licked her lips, his touch was welcome, the sweet-bitter gin delicious and the pulse through her body warmed her. Weston slid his finger over her and Isabel's breath fell in pants. "I'm stirred, Alden, but limp, too. Slack but brimful of energy." Her words came out in a staccato whisper to match the swift flick of his fingers. "A strange, stimulating way to be."

Alden kissed her and Isabel all but melted away. When she gave a long shiver he pulled his hand from inside her knickers and she tautened her body, then let it slump.

"Dance for me, Isabel."

She grinned at him and sat up. Isabel took a swig from her gin cup, set it down and stood. She wobbled a little, said "woooo" but found her balance quickly; she assumed first position.

"Take off your skirt, Issy." Weston lit another cigarette and blew smoke at her.

Her skirt, the latest London had to offer, fastened with press studs; she pulled at them and they snapped apart with ease. She let the skirt drop to the floor and kicked it away. The gin buoyed her up, made her fluid and bold. She began a varsoviana, holding her arms up for the invisible partner behind her, even nodding and smiling at him. When it came to the tiny mazurka steps, Weston roared, "Kick higher, Issy," so she inflated her movements and performed enormous leg swings and dangled her arms for comic effect. She clicked her boot heels to the floorboards in a pleasing ratter-tatter and swayed her whole body, arms aloft. Weston laughed, extinguished his cigarette and held out his hand to her. She dove on top of him, laughing, too. He pulled sharply at her knickers and they were down and gone in an instant; he rolled her under him, slid on top and, with deep grunts, took his cock in hand.

"Alden!" Isabel's alarm was belated but real. "Wait!"

"Don't fret, Issy," he whispered. "Nothing untoward will happen. There'll be no unwanted outcome. I can execute this in a particular way."

A particular way? What way? Isabel knew not, but she nodded into his shoulder to give him permission to go on and let out a cry when he entered her. Weston wheezed into her ear while he thrusted, pinching her behind with both hands as he did. It was plunge, plunge, plunge, plunge, plunge, then he bore down heavily for a moment, puffed through his nose, bucked once more and fell on top of her. His sweat drenched her corset and she felt pummeled and, oddly, guilty. Isabel lay under him, her hands hovering above his back. Was it over? Was Alden sated? He was crushing her and her breath came with difficulty. Was it over? He had not taken time to kiss or fondle her. And, now, was he snoring? Could he be?

"Alden," she whispered. He groaned and she pushed him, he flopped away from her, covering his eyes with his arm; one guttural snort from his throat and then his breathing settled into measured snores.

Isabel lay for a while, studying the mold blossoms on the ceiling. She rose, mopped between her legs with her knickers and crawled back beside him. Her mouth was sour, behind her eyes stung with pain, and she could feel that her hair was a matted nest. Well, it was done. Was it as it should have been? Some of the Empire girls spoke with ecstasy about their encounters; others were more coy and giggled much while explaining nothing. Isabel had hoped to feel blissful and buoyant, but there was nothing of that to be found, not in the final act anyway. Perhaps the first time was always so.

She stared at Weston, the solid hump of him stretched out, oblivious to her. Isabel thought of Flo, alone in their warm Pottery Lane bed. She would wonder where Isabel was at such a late hour; she might worry. Isabel got up and fixed her hair as well as she could and put her knickers and skirt back on. She looked at Alden, comfortable, it appeared, in sleep. She looked at her feet and felt forlorn and sad to realize that her boots were on, secure and laced up. That, somehow, felt like the worst thing.

A Discovery

Three days in a row Flo watched Isabel push away the saloop she normally devoured. Her Bath bun was picked clean of caraway seeds and they sat in a heap on the plate. Flo had noticed, too, that apart from being off her food, her sister's skin had taken on an opaline pallor of late.

The pair were ensconced in Twining's tearoom on the Strand, a favorite afternoon stop-off, and Isabel sat listless, poking at the saloop with a spoon.

"You're neither eating nor drinking," Flo said.

"Too much sugar in the saloop perhaps," Isabel said. "Or too much milk."

"Too much Weston, I'd wager."

"I beg your pardon, Flo?"

Her sister leaned in. "Isabel, are you altogether well these past months?"

"I know I've been out of temper, Flo. I have those headaches and my stomach churns." She leaned in. "And it's been the oddest thing, but when I sit beside a man on the omnibus, I can tell the grease of his head from the grease of his hat. Is that not peculiar?"

"It is and it isn't, Issy." Flo sighed. "Things may be as I've feared."

Isabel didn't seem to hear her and went on. "Somehow London's smells invade me as never before—the reek of horse droppings almost made me faint yesterday." She lifted her cup and took a small sip. "Even chimney smoke stinks, Flo. I'd never noticed the way coal smoke hangs in smelly wreaths; it clings all over." Isabel wiped at her coiffure as if the dark snow of soot spores was on her now. "Perhaps I've been spending too much time indoors."

"Oh, Isabel." Flo lowered her voice to a savage whisper. "Do you really not know what ails you?"

"What *ails* me? What do you mean?"

Flo leaned across the tiny table so that her forehead almost touched her sister's. "You are enceinte, Issy. I'm almost sure of it."

Isabel stared at Flo. She let out a tiny wail. "But I'm not married! How can I be?"

"Oh, for the love of the Lord, Isabel." Flo waved her hand. "Get up. Come on."

She thrust her arm through Isabel's and half dragged her out of the tearoom and along the Strand, past the Royal Courts of Justice and down toward the river. Isabel, her thoughts an insensible blare, allowed herself to be led. Could it be true? Is this why she had been gluey with fatigue? Is this why food settled poorly in her gut? Is this why her courses had dried up? She had not bled for months, when she thought about it. But how many months? Three perhaps? Four? It was never something she took much notice of. Isabel gasped. Was Weston's child growing under her skirt? She looked down, expecting to see a shadow over her shoes, some evidence that her stomach housed a growing babe. She felt heavier, yes, but hadn't she been eating a plethora of late suppers and dining on cake once too often since moving to London?

Flo steered her sister toward Waterloo Bridge and they stopped by the wall on the riverbank; she rummaged in her pocket, produced a flask and swigged from it.

"What's that?" Isabel asked.

"Gin."

Of course it was gin. Isabel held out her hand and took the flask, warm from her sister's body. She took a nip and then another. She looked into the dun stew of the Thames, mesmerized by its meander toward the sea; her mind slowed to match its slack progress. Isabel went to have another gulp, but Flo took the flask and pocketed it.

"Listen to me, Issy." Flo turned and took both Isabel's hands in her own. "You have lain with Weston how often?"

Isabel wasn't sure she wanted to speak of it, but this was Flo. "It was only once. Alden has not seemed to want to be much alone with me since then." She bunched her arms across her stomach. "We went to a hotel, Flo, that time and he said it would be all right. He said that if he executed himself a certain way, there could be no unwanted outcome."

"Is that what he said, indeed?"

Isabel nodded. In truth, she hadn't been altogether sure of his meaning. She had met him at the hotel expecting romance but, in the end, Alden proved not to be a tender lover. She never told him that she was a bit upset on leaving that night for fear he would not want to see her anymore. And Isabel had been a little glad that he had not asked her to lie with him since, for if she refused him, he might go sour. In fact, she had seen less and less of him since their encounter in the insalubrious hotel.

"The night wasn't as I'd hoped it would be, I suppose," Isabel said.

"Listen to me now." Flo softened her voice. "There are things we can do, if you're not too far along." She stepped back and looked at her sister, reached forward and smoothed her gown across her belly; it formed a small hillock. "Oh God," she said, "you're already full. I *have* been distracted." Flo frowned, doubtful. "Still, we may be able to put it right. There are people who can take care of these things. There are drafts you can purchase and swallow. Or there's a medical procedure. This can be made away with. Maybe." She eyed Isabel uncertainly. "No one need know if there is time to, well, to get rid of it. Alas, I fear there isn't." She pushed her two hands against Isabel's stomach again and they could both see the alarming protuberance.

"But, Flo, what of Weston? Perhaps he'll wish to marry now."

Flo groaned. "Isabel, do you truly wish to marry such a man?" She put her arm around her sister. "Issy, there are certain truths about Weston that you don't know. Firstly, he's not, nor has he ever been, the Baron Loando."

"What are you talking about?" Isabel pulled away.

"Isabel, I know he styles you his baroness, but it's all lies. I'm sorry to have to relate this to you."

"No. Weston *is* titled and he has large properties in America, he told me so."

"What evidence is there of this, Issy? Why does he constantly borrow money from you? And not only from you, but from everyone?"

"I don't mind paying my way."

"But you're paying *his* way, Issy, don't you see? Weston avails himself of everything that is good about you and hides his true self." Flo tutted. "And he oozes authority and power, to be sure. But wouldn't you own that everything he says has a touch of fancy about it, with only a thin seam of the bona fide sewn through?"

Isabel hung her head. The small portion of saloop she had swallowed now swirled in a sour mess inside her. She swallowed and swallowed, trying to create saliva that would not form. She whispered: "Is he really so bad, Flo?"

"Seymour has been investigating him, Isabel. He became suspicious."

Isabel's head shot up. "Well, perhaps it's Seymour who is not to be trusted."

"Why would you say that? You know Seymour is the steadiest of chaps." Flo shook her head. "Anyway, he has uncovered things about Weston. Debts. Forgeries. Your 'baron' is in England to escape several frauds perpetrated in Chicago."

"I don't believe it. Forgeries? I cannot believe it." Even while she denied it, Isabel prickled with doubt but she chose to shove it aside. "Monetary frauds, Flo?" Her sister nodded. "Weston wouldn't be *that* dishonest; he wouldn't hide such deceits from me, surely." Isabel blanched, felt a falter in her certainty. "Alden loves me, I'm sure of it. He wouldn't be able to conceal frauds from me or anyone. And why would he? He loves me."

"Does he say so, Issy? Has he made any promises to you?"

"Not exactly." Isabel felt her suspicions bloom. "But he calls me 'baroness'—you've heard him, Flo. Why would he lie? And he's so impressive, always. Isn't he? So convincing."

"He's convincing, all right." Flo stared at her sister. "Anyway, no amount of seeming genuine equals honesty, Isabel. From what Seymour has unearthed it seems the man is a wastrel, a dyed-in-the-wool fraud." She dipped forward to catch her sister's eye. "Issy, he's a devious man. I wish it wasn't so, but there it is."

Isabel frowned, she had ignored any qualms about Weston because it was simpler to do so. There were checks missing from her checkbook and, though she hesitated to suspect him, who else could have taken them? Not Flo, she had money aplenty from the Empire. Not the landlady—she never entered Isabel's room. Isabel carried her checkbook with her and Alden could easily have slipped it out of her bag when she was occupied with her friends at the club.

Flo slumped against the river wall. "When Seymour relayed his findings, I was preparing myself to talk to you about Weston's deceits. And now this!"

Isabel smoothed her hands over her stomach. "I shall go to Weston and speak with him."

"Is there any point, dearest?"

"I need to confront him, see what's what. I need to know if he loves me, Flo. I believe he does and that he will act honorably. Now we shall see."

Isabel sent a note to Weston to tell him she needed to speak with him urgently. He did not reply, so she went to his Eider Street lodgings and sat in a hansom outside, waiting for him to emerge. At last he came out, looking like a man ready for a night on the town. He stood in the open doorway, surveying the street as if choosing which way he might direct himself to find the best evening's entertainment. Isabel paid her cabman, alighted and walked up to Weston; geniality deserted his face when he saw her. He positioned himself back inside the door and held it, to bar her entry.

"You did not answer my letter, Alden."

"I received no communication from you lately, Isabel." His manner was aloof, and she wondered if news of her condition had somehow reached his ears already. Or perhaps, like Flo, he had divined it by observing her, leaving her the last to apprehend her own fate.

"May we go somewhere private to talk, Alden?"

He puffed out his chest. "As long as you don't intend to make a commotion outside my lodgings, right here suits me fine."

"Very well, if we must." Isabel moved close to him and her words emerged as a whisper: "Alden, I am enceinte." His expression did not change. So he *did* know! She looked hard at him, but he did not speak. "I am, it seems, a little too far progressed for, um, for steps to be taken." She waved her hand in front of her stomach.

"Broken things can usually be fixed, in my experience."

Such an utterance! Isabel stared at him. "Alden, I won't be able to dance for much longer, therefore my earnings will cease." He did not move or offer any kind word. Might she not expect comfort? Might she not expect a solution to her woes? "Don't you see, Alden? My reputation will be sullied by this. Destroyed."

"And what do you want me to do about it, Isabel? Do you mean to suggest the child is mine?"

Isabel felt a heart shiver; she moved closer. "Alden, of course it's yours. How can you say that?" She placed her hand on his shoulder and he jerked away, wiping at his coat as if she might have stained it.

He clicked his tongue. "You were sharp enough, Isabel, to attach yourself to me when you thought I was the Baron Loando. Your wits will help you find a way out of this predicament."

So, Flo was right, Seymour, too. Isabel blanched and stepped away from Weston. How cold he was, how indifferent. "You're not a baron, then. I had been told as much."

"I am not." He peacocked his chest. "It was said initially in jest, but you seemed to believe it, so it kept on."

Ire made her voice rise. "*You* kept it on! You lied to me. You're a scoundrel, Alden Carter Weston."

"Steady on, Isabel"—he glanced up and down the street—"they'll hear you in Hampshire."

"I know you took my money, Alden. You stole my checks. I know about your dealings in Chicago. And now you mean to deny this child is yours." She placed her hand on her stomach.

"It is yours, too, Issy. Meditate on that." He stepped back and moved to close the door.

"Alden! Is this to be the end of us?"

Isabel pushed her hand to the door, and he slammed it against her, hurting her wrist. She shrieked, but he did not open the door. She held her arm and a slick of sweat convulsed her from forehead to feet. She slouched against the wall of Weston's lodgings and tried to calm her breathing. How could he be like this? Just days ago he had called her his baroness. Now he meant to deny her completely? What kind of a man was he?

Isabel lurched forward and walloped on the door.

"Alden! Alden! Please come back. Speak to me." She knocked hard. "Alden!"

Weston did not reappear. So this was how it was to finish. Isabel couldn't believe it; she slumped against the door and wept. A passing couple stared, then turned their heads away and marched on. Isabel gathered herself—she did not want to be seen like this—and walked the length of Eider Street, nursing her wrist, small sobs rupturing her attempt at composure every few steps. She shook her head and walked more briskly. How could a man whom she thought she loved treat her this way? What wrong had she done to deserve such cruelty? And what on God's earth was she to do now?

1888

London

A Turn

Isabel chose her lodgings in Turnagain Lane because she loved the street's name. Turnagain Lane—a place that would bend her path and usher her toward a new life; a place to call her own. Flo was married now to Seymour and they had their own tiny nest; a hasty match, for sure, but perhaps Flo was the better for it. Safer from the wider world of men. In truth Isabel was happy for Flo. Seymour was not the most impressive of chaps but he was shrewd and lively in his own way, and he and Flo certainly sparked off each other, kept each other alert. He could be a little too partial at times, maybe even jealous of Flo's time with others, but this, to Flo, spoke of his love for her. And if that pleased Flo, well, Isabel might not argue.

Alden Carter Weston was gone, too, imprisoned for a series of frauds, his schemes found out at last. Weston had wronged Isabel, and she preferred not to stay living in the room where she had been so naïve; he was, as Flo and Seymour had divined, a human shambles. Isabel needed the fresh walls of Turnagain to face in order to ruminate on what she might do next, to make plans for the baby. It would soon be difficult to disguise the swell of her middle. Thankfully, though she was many months into her pregnancy, she carried small and her corset did the rest of the work.

Though it was all getting very uncomfortable. And she had yet to decide whether to get a woman in or foster the baby out.

Miss Blundell, the landlady at Turnagain Lane, was a suspicious type, wary of her tenants but prone to outbursts of inquisitive friendliness, too. There must be, Isabel thought, a college where landladies are schooled in the art of circumspection, for they all seemed to distrust their lodgers as much as they needed them. Though she pried, Blundell had not divined Isabel's lies. She had told the woman that her name was Mrs. Bilton and that her husband was with his regiment in India. And Blundell clearly did not frequent the Empire Theatre, nor did she read the *Pall Mall Gazette*, for she was unaware of Isabel's profession. The landlady's ignorance was her best feature and Blundell was often agreeable—she was accommodating when Flo needed to stay on occasion, she and Seymour being prone to frequent squabbles. Her husband wanted Flo to give up the stage but she rather liked the money.

"Your sister has not your fine features, Mrs. Bilton," Blundell said in Flo's hearing, in the hallway one February afternoon, "but she has her own charms, I daresay." This was the landlady at her best—bighearted toward poor Mrs. Bilton, who cherished her sister's company in the absence of Mr. Bilton, but still allowing herself to toss out insults.

"You are an angel, Miss Blundell," Isabel said; she held the woman's gaze before casting her eyes down. "I feel so lonely from time to time. My sister, that is Mrs. Seymour, is a balm to me." Isabel flicked her eyes to Flo, who had to turn away in case she grinned.

"I had a sister myself, Mrs. Bilton. She was my dearest companion until the gout took her."

"My sympathies." Isabel pressed the woman's cold hands in her own, nodded ruefully and rushed up the stairs with Flo, stifling giggles until the door of her room closed behind them.

"What a ghoul!" Flo said. "Watch you don't end up hacked into pieces some midnight. It could be a play: *The Tenant of Turnagain Lane*. Missing, presumed deceased."

Isabel giggled and flopped into her chair; she was frequently tired these days. "Oh, old Blundell's not so bad."

"This came for you." Flo held out an envelope. "It was left in our dressing room, but you were already gone."

Isabel took the envelope and opened it. "An invitation from Major Noah to attend a soiree at his hotel."

"Major Robert P. Noah? The American journalist? The noble Jew? Do you know him?"

"He sent me flowers last week, remember, after our performance?"

"Why do the quality always flock to you, Isabel? Where's *my* card from Major Noah, *my* flowers?"

"You should accompany me, Flo. I will send a note to the major; he will no doubt be pleased for you to attend."

"No, no, darling. Seymour would lose a kidney if I went. Best go on your own. See if you can't have a genial evening, after all that has been going on."

"If you're sure, Flo." Isabel did not mind going alone but it was always nice to have a companion at a stranger's party.

"Much as I would like to enjoy the lavish table of the excellent Jew, I decline. It will do you good to be in fine company for an evening. Keep your mind from your woes."

Isabel pulled at her fringe curls with one hand and smoothed the front of her skirt with the other. "What ever shall I wear?"

Major Noah's gathering was a soupçon more formal than Isabel had expected. She was glad of the modesty of her gown, a blue surah silk with a fichu of lace for the shoulders; it complemented her figure while hiding the hump of her stomach. Yes, she decided, she looked altogether graceful and decent. No one would divine that she was with child.

Major Noah directed his guests to the table.

"I insist on mixing the company," he said, "one lady, one man, all the way around." His American accent grated on Isabel, it was commanding and loud; Weston's was the last voice like that she had heard.

Some ladies hung back by the major while the footmen helped the rest to sit. Isabel, whose pregnancy fatigued her, sat gratefully. The table held rows of tiered silver dishes lavish with grapes and apples and, between them, the candles glimmered so that the glassware seemed to quiver. Isabel found herself with an empty seat to one side and, to the other, a man with a red-carnationed collar, a couple of years older than her, who also wore a shy smile.

"Isidor Wertheimer," the man said, and held out his lavender-gloved hand. Was everyone a Jew at this gathering? Isabel wondered. "Don't fret," Mr. Wertheimer said, "there are gentiles aplenty here."

Isabel smiled. "Ah, so you are capable of reading my thoughts, Mr. Wertheimer. That *is* an auspicious start."

They both laughed.

Isabel removed her gloves for dining, laid them in her lap and looked around. She spotted Mabel and Tilly from Drury Lane Theatre come in and they lingered, tittering, beside their host; Isabel nodded to them though she found them the silliest of girls.

Mr. Wertheimer leaned in. "And you are?"

"I do beg your pardon, Mr. Wertheimer. Miss Isabel Bilton. I'm pleased to make your acquaintance."

"Is a door. Is a bell. We have the beginnings of a house between us!"

Isabel laughed and looked at the man properly for the first time. He had dark hair and eyes the green of seawater; he reminded Isabel of a raven, sleek and neat, except that the color in his pallid cheeks rose sweetly when he spoke to her. He was not the kind of man who was attractive to her but his playful manner, in a room peopled mostly with strangers, soothed her.

"We could be 'Issy and Issy.'" She leaned closer. "What do you know of our host, Mr. Wertheimer?"

"His family and mine have long been acquainted; my father goes back and forth over the Atlantic for business. The major's pater, Major Mordecai

Noah, was a friend of my father's—'the most famous Jew in America,' Father called him. He tried to found a colony on a river island in New York as a haven for European Jews."

"An admirable venture to be sure. Is *our* Major Noah very famous?" Isabel looked to where the major, surrounded by ladies, poured bumpers of wine from a decanter while the butler stood idle. Isabel had learned through Weston that Americans liked to do things differently. Major Noah looked content and benevolent, a man sure of his own worth, as he topped up the glasses.

"Our Noah writes serious articles that bring him some notoriety. Fame, I do not know about."

Isabel glanced at her companion again. He was well-spoken, kind in his demeanor and from a wealthy Jewish line, most probably.

"And what of you, Mr. Wertheimer? What notoriety does your family possess?"

"None whatever. We are merchants. Salesmen and dealers. My father has a shop in the heart of Mayfair."

"A shop? You *are* being mysterious. What sort of shop causes him to travel so much to America? Whatever does he sell?"

"Antiques and curios."

"How charming. I do love fine, old things."

Wertheimer smiled. "As do I, Miss Bilton. And it *is* a charming business, you're quite right. I dabble in it myself. No doubt you are a lady of leisure."

"Indeed not, Mr. Wertheimer, you assume wrongly. I am an actress at the Empire Theatre; I dabble in dance, one might say."

"How marvelous. Now I'm the one who is charmed." He studied her. "You look familiar, Miss Bilton. Have you, by any chance, lately been pictured in the *Tatler*?"

"Yes, I have, just this past week." Isabel smiled. She liked that photograph, by the genius Bassano; he could make a toad look fetching. It was taken when she thought she loved Weston—and falsely believed he loved her—and she glowed rather. "Ogden's Cigarettes and Wills are currently vying with each other to be the ones to include the picture in their packets."

"A tobacco card beauty, how marvelous," Wertheimer said. "And it was a fine likeness, too."

The butler poured wine and the pair clinked glasses. "To dabbling," Wertheimer said. "And to you, Miss Bilton."

Two days after the major's party, Wertheimer collected Isabel from Turnagain Lane in a claret-colored brougham with a large *W* initialed in gold on the side.

"What a splendid brougham. Is it yours?"

"Father's. He's abroad acquiring antiques and I'm permitted to take out the carriage." He helped her in. "Where shall we go?"

"Why, Rotten Row, of course." Isabel loved to mingle with the fashionable and elite in that part of Hyde Park, everyone riding on horses or in carriages, observing one another. "We may see the Prince of Wales with one of his ladies."

"Indeed we may," Wertheimer said. "And he may see us. The Row it is." He called up their destination to the driver and on they trotted. "It's jolly nice to see you again, Miss Bilton."

"And you, sir. But you must call me Isabel."

"And you must never call me sir again. It's Isidor."

"Do you live with your parents, Isidor?"

"No, I have rooms in the Burlington Hotel."

"Along with all the other well-to-do young men of London."

"Indeed." He grinned. "As you can imagine the night antics there are rife; I may take a house somewhere for peace. The Burlington would be a finer place if women lodged there, too."

"If the Ladies' Associated Dwellings Company had their way, every working girl in the city would be locked into their religious asylums. I like the relative privacy of my Turnagain Lane lodgings." Isabel slid her hand through his elbow crook. "Tell me something terribly amusing, Isidor. I do love to be entertained."

"My goodness, am I supposed to entertain an entertainer?"

"Oh, say any old thing. I don't mind."

Wertheimer turned to her and smiled. "Well, Isabel, I went to Greek Street yesterday and paid a hundred pounds for a hundred-year-old coffeepot. A silver pot with an ivory handle. A thing of transcendent beauty."

"One hundred pounds! That's a pound for every year of its existence."

"Indeed it is, Miss Bilton, I hadn't thought of that. I want to tell everyone I meet about my coffeepot, every sweep and bone grubber that I pass on the street, such is its gloriousness. And I intend to have my coffee from it every day."

"It's an investment to be sure then."

Well, here was a man who valued finery and Isabel valued him all the more for it. She was an ardent admirer of pretty things and she put money by each week to spend when she spotted covetable items: a lace fan, a silver hairbrush, a painted parasol. Yes, she was going to like Isidor Wertheimer enormously.

Wertheimer took to meeting Isabel at the Empire's stage door each night and they would supper in the Café Royal or drink in the Corinthian Club with other revelers. She told him a little about Weston—his deceptions and frauds—but did not yet tell him of her condition. He, in turn, told her of the dull Jewish girls his parents introduced him to with the hopes that he would marry. Wertheimer had none of the sobriety of the older London Jews; he dazzled in a silk puff tie and Derby hat, and favored a plaid sack coat rather than the dark frock coat of his father's generation. And always he sported the same scarlet blossom on his lapel. Isabel loved his dash and glamour and wished ardently that she could fall in love with him, love him completely as a woman loves a man, but he did not stir her in that way. Whatever spark is ignited by a beloved man, it did not light in her when it came to Wertheimer. He was a dear man, a good friend, but love? Sadly, no.

L ove does not dole itself out in sane rations, Isabel thought as Wertheimer walked toward her on Regent Street one frosty March afternoon, his carnation bright in his buttonhole, his face luminous on seeing her. The debacle with Weston had made her cautious, to be sure, she knew now that she had been merely dazed by him but, still, it was impossible to muster love where it did not exist and it was a shame. Here was Wertheimer, perfectly wonderful, but Isabel could not ignite a fervor about him. The heart was a fickle mistress, truly. Wertheimer stepped in beside her.

"Dear one," he said and offered his arm.

"Isidor." She took his elbow gratefully and leaned on it. Isabel had not been able to eat that morning—her pregnancy offered headaches that upset her from crown to rump: she could not stomach food easily, even the smell of bread made her want to lie back down some days. Now she did not feel well; she felt overheated despite the cold air. She stopped walking and groaned, put her hand to her face which seemed to pound. Then all was gray and she was gone.

H aving an ache in her lower jaw was the last thing Isabel could recall when she came to, seated on the footpath opposite Liberty department store, with Wertheimer propping her up. She put her hand to her chin and hinged her jaw.

"My mouth," she said, and took several deep breaths to rouse herself; her skin was clammy and she felt heavy eyed. She blinked and fixed her gaze on Liberty, determined to waken and steady herself. The script underneath the clock on the shop's facade would not come into focus and she squinted. She knew it by heart anyway and murmured, "'No minute gone comes ever back again, take heed and see ye nothing do in vain.'"

"There, there, Issy," Wertheimer said, and rubbed her back. "Don't talk, rest a moment."

Isabel tried to heave forward to stand—how ridiculous to be slumped on the frozen ground like some useless sot.

"I must get up," she said, and her voice emerged as a rasp.

"You should get up, Isabel, yes, you will catch a cold. If you feel you can rise, I will lift you." Wertheimer put his hands under her armpits and pulled her to stand.

"Thank you," she whispered and looked around, hoping no one she knew had seen her. She felt weak and leaned on her friend again. "What happened to me, Isidor? My jaw hurt, I felt hot and then I was gone somehow as if a veil had fallen. I don't remember exactly."

"I'm not sure what happened. You went quiet and then swooned and fainted away, but I managed to catch you. No harm done." Wertheimer steered her toward Liberty. "Let's sit down in the café inside, give you a few moments to recover."

"Yes, let's."

Isabel allowed him to guide her up the stairs to a corner seat, where he pulled his chair close to hers. "Would you like to have something to eat?"

"Yes. Tea and shortbread. That's what I need." Isabel nodded, tried to turn over in her mind the moment when she had lost consciousness. Why could she not remember?

Wertheimer ordered, and when the food came, Isabel doused her tea in sugar and chewed two rounds of shortbread in haste.

"Do you feel a little restored?" Isidor asked.

Isabel sighed and was alarmed to find tears dropping from her eyes. "I feel much better," she said and pushed at the tears with the back of her hand. Fainting in the street and now weeping in a public place once again. The ignominy of it. Isabel swiped at her wet cheeks.

"Oh my dear." Wertheimer put his hand on her arm.

"It's nothing, Isidor, don't fret. I'm alarmed that I can't recall fainting, that's all. How embarrassing."

"There's no need to be embarrassed, no one saw."

She looked at him. "Of course everyone saw."

Isabel's tears fell fast and she wiped at her face with a handkerchief. "My head hurt this morning and I didn't eat." She sobbed. "I needed a little something to revive me, that's all." She hung her head and watched the tears waterfall into her lap; it seemed they meant to come despite her.

"Something is ailing you, Isabel. More than a headache or embarrassment about waking up on the footpath. Do tell me. You can confide in me, you know."

Isabel looked at him, so amiable and sweet. Could it hurt to tell him of her predicament? Would he disdain her if he knew she was enceinte? Despite his bohemian airs might he be as old-fashioned as so many men were? She hesitated for a moment but decided to trust him. Isidor was a good fellow; his mind was as broad as he was affable.

"The headache, Isidor, my fatigue, it's all to do with my state. You know." She looked into his eyes and willed him to take her meaning without having to say it out.

"Your state?"

"My *condition*, so to speak. A woman's state."

Wertheimer sat back and looked at her. She might lose him now. Not every man would want to be friends with a disgraced woman.

"Do you mean a monthly problem, Isabel?"

She shook her head. "No, not that."

Wertheimer lifted his teacup and sipped, his eyes trained across the room. He placed the cup back in its saucer with care and turned to her.

"Isabel. Issy. Are you trying to tell me that you are soon to be a mother?"

She raised her head and dabbed at her eyes. "I am."

"Oh my dear." He lowered his voice to a whisper. "The noble state of motherhood awaits and you are all alone." Wertheimer winced and Isabel took this as displeasure at her revelation; he was thinking, perhaps, of a way to extricate himself from their friendship. Her heart scuffled with her mind; Wertheimer was a gentleman, he must protect his own name. Isabel would have to accept it, though soon she would be entirely friendless.

"If you no longer wish to go about with me, Isidor, I understand." She said the words—gasped them—but didn't quite mean them. She relied on Wertheimer and he was available to her in a way that Flo often was not these days; Isabel had come to depend on him rather. And he was such easy company, such a kind companion compared to erratic Weston.

Wertheimer leaned across the table and lowered his voice even further. "If it's a time for disclosures, Isabel, I feel I should tell you something about myself that I've been, well, if not *concealing* from you, I've maybe been hoping you would divine for yourself. Dear Issy."

Isabel bent her head nearer to his. She watched him fidget with the carnation in his lapel. Was he sweating? Whatever could it be? She pulled off one glove and twined her fingers into his.

"Don't be afraid to tell me your heart secrets, Isidor. I'm in no position to judge man or beast. And you know that you're precious to me as a friend and I'd never peach on you if there is something you wish kept hidden."

Wertheimer nodded but looked miserable. He slipped off his glove so that their skin touched. He put his mouth close to her cheek. "Isabel, do you know what a sodomite is?"

Isabel felt relief: he did not mean to abandon her, he was confiding in her. "Yes, I do know what that is." Isidor was telling her that he preferred boys to girls. What of it? Isabel squeezed his hand. "If that's what you are, Isidor, that's your business. It means little to me and I'm not about to broadcast it to the hoi polloi. I don't think anyone we go about with in the West End would give a fig, do you?"

Wertheimer exhaled and wiped the perspiration from his top lip. He glanced around and whispered, "But you know I could go to prison for it, Isabel?"

"Yes, darling, I know it. But you're discreet, are you not?" Wertheimer nodded. "Well, then, there's nothing more to it."

"Dear girl," Wertheimer said, and lifted his teacup to his lips. Isabel fancied his eyes were full and she felt a wash of compassion for him; his life must have particular difficulties, all things considered. She had fancied him trouble-free, a flitting bird about the town. "We must band together ever tighter now, Isabel," he said at last.

"We shall, Isidor. Issy and Issy, yes?"

"Issy and Issy." Wertheimer studied her for a moment. "Considering your delicate state, I feel you must move now from Turnagain Lane. Small lodgings like that won't do anymore. You'll need a proper home, somewhere peaceful. No more Turnagain, no more Madame Blunderbuss." Isabel laughed and Wertheimer bit into a biscuit. "A decent home, yes, for you and the child. And I think I am just the man to help you with that."

A Birthing

Isabel was two months sequestered in Wertheimer's place, Fairleigh Lodge in Maidenhead, Berkshire, as far as the stars from London and its tale spreaders. She knew she was talked of, the newspapers made sly jokes at her expense without saying things outright. And when she dined out, foreheads would nod toward each other, then break apart to take her in. She kept her own head erect but, in the end, it was best to leave them to it and withdraw. Mr. Hitchins, the dear man, told people she was gone abroad and that she was welcome back just as soon as she was able to dance again.

The plum of Isabel's belly alarmed her; it poked obscenely from her front and grew larger by the hour. There was no getting away from it, unlike the false belly she had worn onstage for that daft Jack and Jill song. She had given up corsets by the time her stomach was so ripe it could not be contained, and she spent most days lounging in an armchair, for it was hard to sit upright without boning and laces to hold her erect. Who would see if she slouched, anyway, and who would care? Wertheimer took her any old way, as did Flo and Seymour. And it wasn't as if she would get a chill in her kidneys when all she did was sit about Fairleigh Lodge like a sack of potatoes in the same loose morning gown. She found herself utterly fagged by it all.

Flo had laughed when Isabel told her that her new home—courtesy of Wertheimer—would be in Maidenhead.

"My, there is sport in that, considering your predicament."

"Not much sport for me, heavy as a cow and exiled from the Empire. It will dampen me to be so removed from everything: the theater, the life of London."

"Maidenhead!" Seymour said. "There's nothing there but a Union workhouse and a clatter of low shops."

"Thank you, Seymour. That restores me utterly." Isabel tutted.

"I am sorry, Isabel. We shall come to visit you and provide diversions besides—shan't we, Flo?"

"Of course we shall. Don't fret, old girl." Flo pumped her sister's hand. "It'll all be over quick as quick and then you can make plans."

But Isabel had not realized that being in the family way would dull her, slow her body to syrup, make a quagmire of her mind. She made few plans, and forays into London were not a priority, after all. Maidenhead was convenient, somehow. The cottage hospital was close to Fairleigh Lodge if anything should go wrong with birthing; and Isabel found she did not miss the delights of town as much as she had feared. Her gaze turned inward and she generally passed her days in a sluggish, bovine trance and let Wertheimer, Flo and Seymour bring news of the city to her.

"You will be out of purdah soon, Issy," Wertheimer said often, "and then we will celebrate."

"I daresay," Isabel would answer dutifully. "Perhaps we shall have a party?"

"If you so desire, my dear. All of London is clamoring to see you."

"Really?"

It cheered Isabel to think that the world waited for her and soon she would be ready to glide her way through it again. It cheered her that Wertheimer would say it even if it wasn't fully true. Too often—and she was guilty of it herself—when a person disappeared from society, they were quickly discharged from the memory, as if they had never existed.

As her pregnancy advanced into its late stages, Isabel found it hard to breathe; she felt as if her lungs might leap out of her mouth and land at her feet. Everything inside her was pushed upward by her stomach's girth. The weight of the baby within her was a daily shock; how could an infant be so heavy? It felt as if she were carrying an anvil. The midwife said there was liquid in there, too—the babe swam inside her!—but Isabel's off-kilter heft was uncomfortable and she longed to be rid of it. Her walk had become a splay-legged, back-arched waddle. She felt ungainly and *wrong*. The midwife had only recently told her how the baby would come out and she was still shocked by it.

"It comes out the way it gets in," the midwife said.

"I beg your pardon?"

"Goodness me, haven't you ever seen a birthing cow?"

"No. Yes. No. What do you mean?"

"You push it out"—the midwife pointed between her own legs—"from here."

Isabel had snorted, thinking the woman was joking. But when it dawned on her that she was not, she chewed this information like a cud, waking in the night to work over it some more. Surely not? Surely, surely not? She questioned her sister.

"How does the babe get out, Flo?"

"Oh, Isabel, you *do* make me laugh. How can you possibly not know where babies emerge from?"

"It's true, then. But why did Mother say that babies slid through the navel like a silken ribbon? She said it more than once—many times, in fact."

"And you believed it? Despite roars that might have contradicted it? Despite the times when she lost babies and you cleaned her sheets? Come now!"

"I may have believed. Perhaps." Isabel *had* believed it in spite of the wry, wicked look her mother employed in the telling of the tale, as if daring her daughter to contradict her. "But where on earth did you learn the truth of the matter, Flo, and why did you not tell me of it? Younger sisters should not know more of the world than their elders."

"Mother told me. And I presumed she had told you before me."

"Well, then. Our mother always did favor your education over mine."

The July day the babe chose for his arrival, Isabel's head pinged with dizziness. Wertheimer had come to sup with her, as was his custom, though he rarely took more than coffee. Flo, who stayed frequently now that Isabel's time was near, was still abed. Isidor's color was as faded as Isabel's from the long hours he spent on the town with the gang of boys who were his night friends.

"You look wan, Isidor. I do wish you would take better care of your health."

"I'm all right, Issy, but if I'm wan, you're cadaverous. You look shockingly pale today."

She rubbed her temples. "I'm a little groggy, that's all. Light-headed." She dipped her face toward the table to see if it might relieve the wooziness in her brain.

"Are you all right, Isabel?"

She straightened and put her hand to her cheek. "I fear I'm even duller than usual, Isidor. I think I'll go back up and take my rest."

Wertheimer stood. "Do you need my arm?"

"No, no. Sit, read your *Times*. Go to the smoking room."

Isabel waddled up the stairs but, when she gained the landing, a sharp spasm banded her belly, and she gasped and lurched forward.

"Unh," she cried, and was rooted so deeply in the pain that all thought receded. She gripped the landing banister with two hands and leaned into it, her breath coming in broken spurts. "Ugghhhh," she groaned, the sound coming from a part of her she hadn't known existed. The pain receded, undulating away through her abdomen, so that she felt composed once more. The baby had moved suddenly, nothing more.

Wertheimer, having heard her cry out, hurtled up the stairs, taking three steps at a time.

"What is it, Isabel? Are you getting pains?"

She shook her head, but when she went to move another wave began to build. She held the banister again and stared hard at the pattern of the anaglypta wallpaper, its liver-dark sequence of raised diamonds. She made herself concentrate on it while she huffed and panted through the paroxysm in her belly. Wertheimer stood by until she seemed more composed, then took her arm and tried to steer her toward her bedroom.

"No!" she snarled and retained her crablike stance at the banister until the ragged pain had eased entirely.

"Stay there," he said, "I'll get Flo." He ran and banged on Flo's door. "The baby's coming," he shouted.

Isabel whipped her head toward Wertheimer. "Is it?" she said, but she knew, of course, that this was exactly what was happening. Another pain began to harness her body and she found she had to moan to get her through it. "Annnngghhhhhh."

Flo, hair wild and chemise half-undone, bounded to her sister's side.

"Quick, Wertheimer. She's between pangs."

Wertheimer half carried, half dragged Isabel on one side, while Flo took the other, and they got her to her room and onto the bed. As she lay back, her waters broke, a modest puddle that soaked through her dress and onto the coverlet. Flo reached up under her sister's skirts and pulled her drawers down and off. Isabel groaned as another spasm scorched its way upward through her; she began to feel dizzy again and her head lolled.

"Does the air throb?" she asked. "I'm sure it beats down on me."

"She needs chloroform," Flo said. "Mother always called for chloroform at her birthings."

"She needs the midwife," Wertheimer said. "I'll fetch her." But he stood, instead, alarmed by the creases of pain that distorted his friend's face and by her keening. "Oh, my heavens," he said, and sat to try to comfort her with pats to her arm.

"Go quickly. I can't stand this." Flo soaked a flannel in her sister's basin and dabbed at her face. "Hush now, Isabel. It will be over soon."

Isabel put her hand down between her legs and looked at Flo in alarm. "The baby will get stuck," she said. "Take off my knickers."

"They're off already."

"Maybe we should remove her gown, too," Wertheimer said. "It's constricting her."

"You do it." Flo gestured at Wertheimer and he began to undo the buttons.

Isabel batted his hand away and propped herself on her elbows. "Help me," she said, gripping Wertheimer's arm. He bent over her and she used him to pull herself onto her side; turning, she crawled toward the footboard and gripped it. She rocked and wailed as the pains thundered one on top of another, then dropped her head and grunted from deep in her throat, an alien, animal noise that alarmed Wertheimer and sent Flo scurrying for linens and hot water. Wertheimer knelt on the bed behind Isabel and rubbed her back.

"This is good, Isabel, this is right. You're doing everything you need to do."

"Am I? How do you know?" she roared.

"I don't," Wertheimer said, "but I also somehow do." Isabel needed him and what could he do but act as if he knew what he was about and encourage her? There was nothing else *to* do.

Isabel gasped and dropped her hand down between her thighs; there she felt the wet pulse of the baby's crown. "It's coming!" she roared and, leaning full into the end of the bed, she screamed and pushed.

The baby slithered out into Wertheimer's waiting hands, a grease-caked, blood-spangled bundle. He held him like an offering, marveling at the baby's rotund belly and his occidental eyes; at the gray rope pulsing from his stomach.

Isabel looked over her shoulder, tears dripping down her face. "Well?"

"A boy!"

She collapsed onto her side and Wertheimer had to carefully maneuver her leg, and the baby on its cord, to let his mother hold him. She rested her back against the footboard while opening her arms to her son. Wertheimer placed the boy in her embrace and the little one yawned and opened his creased eyelids to reveal navy eyes, glassy as a tippler's.

"He looks like he's had one too many," Wertheimer said.

"He's elephant's trunk! Drunk as a lord!" Isabel giggled and watched every unflexing of the baby's hands, every purse of his lips. His eyes, she saw as he looked up at her, were wise. She cradled him, finding his compact body exotic; he was a creature of wonder. "Isn't he magnificent?" she whispered.

"He certainly is."

"I shall name him for you. Here he is. Baby Isidor."

A Baby

Babies crawled through Isabel's dreams. Rotund ones, long-legged ones, scarlet-mawed ones—they screamed like the newly hatched and she felt stranded between half sleep and none. She drowsed, sure that she had left an infant somewhere that was unsafe and needed to recover it. Weston's face dove in and out of her sight, and she felt herself duck away from him as much as she wanted to catch hold of him and demand his help. She lay in bed and tried to escape the mewling tots of her nightmares, but they clung to her as she flickered in and out of slumber. The cries of a real infant roused her at last and she remembered that he was here now, baby Isidor, the howler. Only a day old and the boy bawled, bucked and carped for his life. And where was his father? Ensconced in a cell and, no doubt, he rested easy by night and supped like a lord by day.

Healthy lungs," the midwife had intoned the afternoon before as she plopped the last of the birthing's bloody mess into a copper bowl. Isabel turned her head; the idea that she had carried that meaty lump inside her along with the baby sickened her. What was it even for? The midwife slid a tin pannikin under Isabel's behind to catch leaks, while she prepared to clean her up.

"You managed without our Queen's 'blessed chloroform,'" the midwife said. "You're strong."

"I'm like the wreck of the *Hesperus*, if you must know. I feel absolutely wretched. As if my lifeblood has been dragged from me with the child."

"Oh come now. You're young and hardy, and there is muscle aplenty on you." She squeezed Isabel's calf. "You'll be back on your feet in no time, girl."

Isabel doubted that; she felt as if she might never walk with ease again, never mind dance. What would happen if she could not resume her position at the Empire? How would she survive? Flo could not earn well alone, it was the Sisters Bilton that everyone now wanted. "I feel lower than I've ever felt," she said, a maudlin whisper that the midwife heard.

"Lower than ever? Well, you gave birth in a rush, I suppose. It's to be expected." The midwife swabbed Isabel between the thighs and she winced in discomfort. "It's good for the child that he arrived in haste. 'The babe who is born quickly will ever quick be.' That's what my mother used to say and she escorted thousands into this world."

"Quick?" Isabel looked at the baby, swaddled and wakeful beside her. He tossed his head and frowned as if he was plotting an escape. When he slept, his mouth was a perfect red purse that he moved now and then, as if he dreamed of sucking. Would he be clever? Neither of his parents was particularly sensible, Isabel thought, or they wouldn't have ended up where they were. She, unwed and a mother; he, a fraud and locked up. None of this had been part of her dreams of London life, that was certain.

The midwife wrung out the cloth she was using to clean Isabel, and she watched the blood drip, dark and foreign.

"You enjoy a certain domestic felicity in this house, Miss Bilton. You are very fortunate indeed. There are not many men like Isidor Wertheimer in this world, truly."

"I know it," Isabel said, and thought of Wertheimer and his unassailable goodness. She thought, too, of Weston in all *his* learned, narcissistic, impoverished idiocy. He was of no use to her now, nor had he ever been. Alden

Weston had trampled on her, taken advantage of her. Flo liked to say he had corrupted Isabel, but can you corrupt someone who complies with you?

"You can recuperate nicely here," the midwife said as she shifted her patient this way and that, "for as long as Mr. Wertheimer will have you." She fitted Isabel with a sanitary towel, fixing the belt loosely across the slack jelly of her stomach. "Now, we are done. Your sister might purchase more of these towels. Tell her to buy Southall's—they're the most hygienic."

"I will and thank you. Can you also show Mrs. Seymour how to make pap for feeding the baby?"

"You do not intend to nurse him, then?" The midwife frowned.

"I'll be returning to work as soon as possible. At the theater."

"You should think more about your rest, Miss Bilton, and less about planning a dance parade."

"I have little choice," Isabel said. *A woman can't survive on air and a child certainly can't.*

The midwife gathered up the copper bowl and cloths and left the room. Isabel hoisted herself up on her elbows, hoping for a view of the garden below, its flower beds and neat lawns. But she could not see beyond the windowsill. She wondered if she would ever own such a garden attached to such premises. If she would ever meet the man who could give it to her, not on loan but permanently. A home ought to be a shrine, a solid place for all life to happen in, the joys and the sorrows. It should be a shared place for a family, not some temporary stop-off in which to lay her head, no better than the stable in Bethlehem was for Christ and his mother. It was not that she was ungrateful. Wertheimer was a dear friend, the kindest of fellows, but he was not the man she could attach herself to.

I could be happy as a lark with a hearth of my own, Isabel thought, lying back to ease her aching flesh. A garden with lawns for picnics, some nice furnishings inside: a huge Venetian mirror, Turkish carpets and a pianoforte. It wasn't that she craved grandeur or splendor. These things would not even have to be new: Isabel liked the patina of used furniture and its knowledge of earlier times. She imagined kneeling in prayer, morning and evening, with a phantom spouse and a scatter of little ones, as her own family had done. She smiled to remember Flo's deliberate mixing up of the words—invoking the Holy Goat could still make them laugh like girls.

Yes, the temporary nature of everything had begun to make Isabel feel unsettled. Now this show, now that; now this hall door, now that. A need for permanence had simmered in her along with the baby, a longing for firm habits, a home, a root-taking spot. Weston was never going to offer it; Wertheimer would like to—*he* thought—but he could not either. Isabel needed love to feel secure, it was that simple. She had realized it after Weston: she never felt safe with him—everything was always on the brink of toppling. She needed a strong love, a man to feel sheltered by but one who also leveled her out, made her feel love was a refuge for equals. Yes, some other would have to come to her, make himself known.

The midwife bustled back in, her jacket buttoned to her neck. She was dressed in serviceable navy from cowl to calf; she was a decent woman, no doubt, with an ordered life: a husband, a house, tidy children.

"I will say good day to you, Miss Bilton. I wish you well." She shifted her bag into her elbow crook. "I will return later in the week to check on you and the child."

"Thank you. Mr. Wertheimer will see to you on your way out. He's in the parlor, I daresay." Isabel hated having to mention money, but she feared the woman would look to her for payment and her funds were low.

The midwife glanced around the bedroom, at the fine decor and the sunlight from the windows that burnished the floor in fat, golden strips.

"You have everything you could want here," she said. "All you need now is a husband." She nodded and left.

Flo walked back and forth with baby Isidor in Isabel's room, trying to soothe his rigid body by rocking him, but he would not give up. Isabel beckoned her over to the bed. Flo sat, still holding Baby, and Isabel spooned pap into his outraged mouth. He burbled the pap out and she was afraid he would choke.

"Did you put enough sugar in it?" Isabel said.

"The midwife said to use but a pinch of sugar; she explained it wasn't good for him."

"What does she know? We were reared on sweet pap. Get more sugar and a dollop of butter and mix it in." She thrust the bowl at her sister. "We need to get a pap boat; it will be easier to get it into him."

"You need to nurse him, Isabel. It's you he wants." She gestured at her sister's front where two wet stains were spreading like stars across her peignoir. "Won't you just try?"

"That's not for me, Flo, and you know it." She stared at the baby, stiff in her sister's arms and red mottled from screeching. He barely drew breath between wails. Where was the quiet little sot she had held straight after birthing? Why had he been replaced by this squawler? "Wertheimer mentioned a wet nurse. Some countrywoman he knows. Quick, go ask him." Flo went to lay the baby in the bed beside his mother. "Can't you take him downstairs for a spell? My head hurts so."

"Everyone's head hurts, Issy. My addled husband has gone into town already, for he can't stand it."

"Well, poor bloody Seymour. Am I his keeper? It's not as if he has to stay here—he may come and go as he pleases, he may return home. You're both free to leave, Flo."

"I only meant that Baby can make a frightful noise when he wants to. I don't blame him, or you."

Isabel raised her voice to be heard above the boy's crying. "Ask Wertheimer about the wet nurse. I've about had it up to my gills with this racket."

Flo took the wailing baby with her and Isabel lay back, pressing her forearms to her breasts to stop the leaky tingle in them. She took her hand mirror from the bedside table and gazed at herself. There were murky crescents under her eyes and her hair was dull. It pained her, when she brushed it, to see great nut-gold clods caught in the bristles; she fluffed out her fringe but it fell flat against her forehead. She was tired of looking poorly, fed up with the fat that larded her body and the weariness that threatened to keel her over every minute. When was she going to look and feel normal again? She sighed, discarded the mirror and closed her eyes, but rest would not come when the baby had every nerve excited. She sat up and hauled the copy of Mrs. Beeton's *Book of Household Management* into her lap. It was a gift from Flo during her confinement and, at first, Isabel had thought she gave it to her for fun, knowing Isabel didn't like to read much, but Flo was perfectly serious about the book.

"You'll need it, Issy. You're soon to be a mother."

Isabel turned to the chapter near the back on the rearing and management of children. She did not like Mrs. Beeton's tone—the woman seemed at once scolding and skeptical, as if no mortal could ever be as efficient as she when it came to anything at all. Isabel softened though when Mrs. Beeton admitted that it might be presumptuous to tell a woman how to rear her infant.

"You're not presumptuous, Mrs. B., please tell me everything," Isabel murmured.

She read: "The children of the poor are not brought up but *dragged* up" in "reeking dens of squalor." Isabel began to wonder about entrusting her baby to some lowly wet nurse who might live in a repulsive hovel in Seven Dials. Might he not be better off here with her in the lovely surroundings of Fairleigh Lodge? But she had to work—how else was she to survive? She needed to dance to earn money, that was the plain truth of it. And she wanted to dance, besides. No, there was no room for a squealing infant in this house. Oh, why had she not planned all this a little better? How was one to know how demanding babies were when one had never really met one?

Isabel flicked over the pages, searching for succor concerning Isidor's endless caterwauling. Mrs. Beeton finally offered it up in the form of castigation of unprincipled nurses who issue narcotics and items to suck on.

Oh joy—there are drafts that will quieten him! Maybe we could get him a gum stick, too?

A knock to the door and Isabel arranged herself back on her pillow and called out, "Come in."

Wertheimer entered. "How are you, my dear?"

"As well as can be expected. Come sit by me."

Wertheimer sat on the bed and took Isabel's hand in his own; it looked so small in his though their pale skins blended well.

"Ugghhh. What has my life come to?"

"There are ways out of this," Wertheimer said, and he dropped to his knees so their faces were level. Isabel could smell his breath, a little porty, a little sweet. "I have been thinking most seriously and it comes to this, Isabel. We should marry. We should most definitely begin to make plans." His tone was feverish and, though Isidor had said this to her before, it was always in jest. This time, he appeared to be serious.

"Isidor, don't be a clod." Isabel tried to swat him away, but he only became more fervent.

"Listen to me, Isabel. Listen well. Would it not solve a dilemma or two? Would it not be an amiable arrangement? Do we not go well together?"

"We do, Isidor, but really, we're not a match, we're friends." Was this another banter? Isabel looked at him. His eyes were fiery. "You know this is not feasible, Isidor."

"We can make it so." He grabbed her hand and began to kiss it and before she could draw away, his lips were on her mouth in a clumsy kiss.

She pulled back quickly. "Isidor, what on God's earth are you doing?"

"I'm sorry, Issy. I merely wished to make things easier for you. I want to comfort you, to make things right." He collapsed back onto his heels and sighed. "The baby has us all overturned."

"The whole household is upside down, for certain sure; everyone is acting mad. You included. Come sit by me and stop being absurd; I have quite enough to deal with." Wertheimer rose from the floor and sat again on her bed. He looked chastened, though Isabel was not angry with him.

She knew him to be impulsive; she knew, too, that their marrying might be a solution of sorts. "Come. Talk to me, Isidor."

He sat, looking abashed. "I'm sorry I kissed you."

"Forget about it, Isidor. We're all wrong side up with the child. We're disrupted. Tired."

Wertheimer nodded. "Flo said you wanted to know about the wet nurse." He told her more about Sara, a capable young mother of Heathfield in Sussex, who would take on the care of baby Isidor for a small sum.

"How small?"

"You mustn't worry about that, Isabel. I will remunerate her until you're ready to go back to the Empire, until you're earning once more." He glanced at her. "Or we *could* just get married and that way you would never have to work again."

"Oh, Isidor, don't." She wished he wouldn't persist with this line. Isabel knew it was more selfish than truly meant. Wertheimer's mother would stop nagging him to marry and his life with his boys could continue as before. That was how he saw it. But what of her? "Isidor, I love you in my own fashion, you know this. But you also know that marriage is out of the question for us. I'm horribly romantic when it comes to men; I want a true and proper marriage. I have to believe that that waits for me. Despite all."

Wertheimer nodded. "I understand that, Isabel, I really do. But, for myself, I must try."

Isabel squeezed his hand; she understood, though it wearied her. "Tell me, is this Sara woman's home sanitary?"

"I believe it is—her own children are hardy. They spend a lot of time outdoors. The air is extremely pure in Sussex, you know."

Isabel nodded, lifted his hand higher and rubbed her cheek against it. "Whatever would I do without you, Isidor? 'Issy and Issy.' Isn't that right?"

Wertheimer smiled at their old joke. "Yes, my dear. Forever and always."

He pulled up a chair and sat by her into the night. Flo returned with a subdued baby Isidor and placed him in the mahogany cradle that had held

Wertheimer as an infant. Isabel rocked it gently with her foot and reveled in its homely creak in the new silence. Flo bade them good night and left for the theater. She did not perform as much now that the Sisters Bilton were retired for the time being, but Mr. Hitchins made room for her in the chorus and gave her a solo song on occasion, for which she was grateful.

Isabel dozed and woke, chattered softly with Wertheimer and listened for Baby's snufflings from the cradle. Together they watched a lustrous moon rise over the garden oaks and sail out of sight like a departing clipper.

"What is to become of me, Isidor? I seem to reel from one bad decision to another. Weston. Baby. What is to be done?"

"Hush now, you mustn't fret. Life seems large and unwieldy at the moment, but hummocks have a way of ironing themselves out, too. You'll see, my dear."

"I've cooked my goose this time, I think, to a pile of cinders. Who will want me now?"

"Lots of fine fellows would be happy to call you wife, Isabel." He lowered his voice. "I'd be glad to myself, as you know."

"Don't be a sheep head, Isidor." But would it come to that in the end— would she need to enter a marriage of cooperation? Wertheimer would make an adequate husband and his family were not short of brass. But did she not deserve the deep and mutual love she craved? Isabel shook her head to lose those thoughts. "We are friends and friends only. But the most cherished of friends, of course." She put her hand in his. "All will be well, will it not, Isidor?"

"Yes, dear Issy, all will be well. For you, all will no doubt be perfect in the end."

A FORAY

Neither Wertheimer nor Flo had wanted Isabel to travel alone to Lewes to see Weston, but she insisted. She left Maidenhead early and it was a relief, truth be told, to be away from the demands of baby Isidor, who remained with her while she decided what to do. Such a fretful, needy boy; he drained her gaiety as much as her strength. Eight long weeks of his caterwauling and no matter how much Godfrey's Cordial she dribbled into his mouth, she could not quiet the child. Just that morning he had wailed, the treacly concoction bubbling in his throat, and she paced her bedroom with him, singing, until she was weary of the words and of her own voice:

> "He stroked her hair—and all the rest,
> Unlaced her stays and done his best;
> Says he by this job he'll feather my nest,
> With my nice Godfrey's Cordial."

Still baby Isidor bawled and refused to sleep. "Something will have to be done with you and *soon*," she said.

The Sussex air was blithe after the stuffy train and Isabel felt scampish, walking alone outside without Flo, Wertheimer or the drone of the baby carriage for company. She felt a minuscule sense of her former self before facing again her final destination and her mission there.

Weston's abandonment of her had been cruelly done; to have wooed her, impregnated her and then to say she must have lain with another man! And, to add to it all, pilfering checks from her. Of course the fool had misspelled her name in his forgery and was rapidly found out. For all his love of words and books, Alden Weston was unable to spell.

To brace herself for seeing Weston, Isabel strayed into a gin shop near the Lewes railway station. *If,* she thought, *I could stand before every time-piece in England—Big Ben included—and roll its hands backward, I would do it. Tock-tick, ting-ting.* She would love to push through every quarter chime, every hourly strike, until she had not yet met Alden Carter Weston. To be sure, it would mean rebuilding all her successes at the Empire, but it would be worth it never to have encountered the man. Isabel sat with these imaginings in the Lamb and sipped a gin and peppermint.

The Lamb, unlike rougher London counterparts, provided seating; she could linger there in comfort and let her mind wander or settle as she chose. Two women sat nearby, slurping at cream gin and feeling no need to converse with each other; a man stood at the bar with his pennyworth, ready to leave once his throat was scalded. The proprietor lifted the basket of cakes from the bar and wiped the mahogany in a slow circle where it had rested. No one looked around or spoke. This was a place of precious peace.

A sip of gin, a thought of Weston. He—and his likes—were the pinnacle of her desires not so long ago: all she wanted was a man of some heft who would look after her in style. How little she understood of men then, of how swagger masks all manner of swinery. She was unschooled in the treacheries of those who roved all over, seeking innocents to fool and swindle.

Isabel lifted her glass, found it was empty and ordered a hot butter gin, for warmth. She swirled the cloudy mixture and drank. Gin, gin, lovely blue ruin, sweet Bryan O'Flynn. Isabel set down her drink and squinted at the gaslights until her eyes watered—their glow was mesmerizing. The business with Weston, his deceits and betrayals, must not put her off trying for a good man. She had had her brush with the brutish sort. There now, it was done. She needed a good fellow, someone with both breeding and money to recommend him. But how many of them were to be found in London or anywhere else?

Isabel found Lewes Jail was not as imposing as she had feared, until she realized she had only gained the lodge and the prison proper was farther along, inside high redbrick walls. A warder escorted her through the huge stone archway and across the yard.

When Weston's letter had come, stamped in black with "Jail of Lewes," Seymour wanted Isabel to throw it in the fire at Fairleigh Lodge.

"Let the flames have it," he said. "You mustn't read a word of what that man has to say. Give it here, Isabel. I shall burn it for you."

"No," Isabel said, "I will see what he has to say." Perhaps Weston would acknowledge his child, perhaps he would express remorse. Perhaps he meant to arrange for baby Isidor's upkeep?

Seymour tutted. "He will have nothing to say that doesn't concern himself alone."

"Seymour's right, Isabel," Flo said. "Don't concern yourself with Weston any longer."

Isabel was curious and opened the envelope. In the letter Alden Weston pleaded with her to visit, but he did not once mention her condition or ask if his child had been delivered into the world. So it was anger that propelled her to East Sussex, and, along the way, she planned the mighty bull and cow she would have with Alden, the insults that she would throw at him, the retorts she would slap down. She readied her lines as if preparing herself for a show at the Empire.

But she was not prepared for the bludgeoned look of him; it had not entered her mind that his appearance would be altered. The warder brought her to a passage and stood beside her, while Alden stood a body's length away, behind an iron-grated door. He wore a gray suit with a glengarry cap that sat, pudding-like, on his head. He was plump now, puffed-out in the cheeks. And he was subdued, as if every jot of vigor had been leeched from him.

"Isabel," Weston said, "you have really come."

"Yes, Alden. I received your letter." Isabel glanced at the warder, but he stared ahead in an attitude of indifference. "How are you?"

Weston looked at the floor. "I am well, all things considered."

Isabel bristled at the forlorn tone. Had he not committed fraud and therefore was it not his own fault that he was incarcerated? Had he not run from her when he realized she was carrying his child?

"We shall reap as we sow," she said.

"Indeed. I'm reading the Bible every day, you'll be pleased to hear. I have that, a prayer book and a hymn book. That's as much as I'm allowed for entertainment."

"You're well nourished in that case," Isabel said. She shivered, the jail felt colder than an icehouse.

"We go to chapel. And I sup well, too: a pint of gruel twice a day, meat soup, bread and potatoes." His look was imploring; he begged for a pinch of kindness but Isabel was in no humor to give it. Still he had not asked after her health or about the baby.

"Did you see the yard, Isabel?" Weston asked. "They hang men there." He agitated his hands, which were coruscated with pus-filled scabs. "I handle the rope. They have me picking oakum. See?" He held up his fingers; and she looked at the welts that decorated them and the broken, blackened nails. His hands had once been as peach soft as her own. "It's worse than the worst of Dickens," he whispered.

Isabel stifled a snort. Here he was living his own true drama and still he talked of books. Ludicrous, conceited man.

"You have not inquired after your son, Alden. Has it escaped your memory that I was with child when last we met?"

The warder cleared his throat, but Isabel was only too aware of him beside her and did not need reminding that he could hear their conversation.

"I hadn't forgotten, Isabel, but I wasn't sure whether you had, ah, taken measures."

"And you never inquired. But, no, Alden, I did not take any *measures*. If you recall, I told you that I was too far progressed for that." The warder strolled away and Isabel was grateful to him. "Your son is alive and well and, you may like to know, he flourishes despite you."

"A son." Weston rubbed his ruined hands across his face. "His name?"

"Isidor. Isidor Alden Cleveland Weston."

"I see. Isidor. He's named for your new Jewish friend."

"The only one I've had this past while." So he knew of Wertheimer; how news scuttled even into the darkest corners.

"Surely Wertheimer is too busy scollogueing at the Corinthian Club with his particular pals to be of any use."

"How dare you! Isidor Wertheimer has housed me and taken care of me when no one else would. He's paying for the upkeep of *your* son. And you mock him. From your prison cell! You who were often so drunk in the Corinthian you couldn't speak, let alone walk home unaided. Good day to you, Alden." Isabel turned to the warder. "I wish to leave."

The man extended his arm to indicate to her to walk ahead of him. "After you, miss."

"Isabel!" Weston called. "Issy! I apologize. Come back, come back. Isabel, I need money. I need money, damn you."

Isabel did not turn her head. "If you need money, Alden," she called, "I suggest you write to your wife."

"Isabel, remember this: Shylock always wants his pound of flesh! Your Wertheimer won't let you off easily." He pulled the cap from his head and whacked the grate on the door. "Isabel, I need money; I need to get out of here. Damn you, woman!"

She walked ahead of the warder through the frigid corridors of Lewes and out into the welcome glare of the Sussex sunshine. The walk to the railway station was a lighter affair than the one from it. Flo and Seymour had been right, of course; she should not have come. Weston was not worth it; he didn't care a whit about his son, his only care was for himself. Weston was beyond the help of anyone. Horrid man, she would not think of him again. That was the last time she would mire herself with a scoundrel; the next man to capture her heart would be honorable, a good man.

Spotting a row of shops, Isabel veered across the road to distract herself in admiring their wares. In the window of a modiste's stood a mannequin clad in a mauve-and-plum-striped dress, with a neat purple jacket to match. How Isabel wished to wear a gown like that, over a corset laced so tightly her breath would come in gasps. *Soon*, she thought, *soon. I will emerge from this after-baby ennui and dance again. And when I am earning again, I will build up my savings and buy everything that pleases me, everything that is au courant.*

Feeling of a sudden hungry as a raven, she accosted a passing baker's man and gave him a whole penny for a half buster. She pulled the loaf apart in great handfuls that she stuffed into her mouth as she walked, caring nothing of who saw her. The bread lodged in her throat, but she chewed and swallowed, forcing it into her as hard as she hoped to force Alden Carter Weston from her mind.

A Bargain

Isabel never did inquire exactly how Wertheimer knew Sara. When he first brought Isabel to Heathfield in Sussex, the cabin on the edge of the sleepy village seemed at once the perfect place for baby Isidor and the most miserable spot in England. The woman was sullen, Isabel thought. Not sour exactly, but wary and silent. Sara regarded Isabel with what she took to be reproachful eyes and she wished to escape the mean dwelling and its occupants as quickly as possible. Isidor squirmed in her arms and she held him in the same hopeless way she always did. He was an unruly, earthy child and, even after two months of mothering, she did not know how best to control him and his convulsing limbs. Isabel handed the baby to Sara when she felt a sneeze forming in her nose. It came in a spasm and she stepped outside into the warm September air, waving her hand in front of her face, though she was away from the smoke that engulfed Sara's room. When she came back in, baby Isidor was docile in Sara's arms and he was gazing at Isabel as if trying to remember from where he knew her.

"We shall take our leave, Sara," Wertheimer said. It bothered Isabel that his polite address to this woman was identical to the manner and tone he used with her. She had thought herself unique in his affections and assumed the gentle way he spoke to her was reserved for her alone. Isabel stared at Sara, trying to hide her annoyance.

Wertheimer pressed a pouch of money into Sara's hand and she looked at him, her expression unchanged. "Thank you, sir," she said.

Isabel stepped forward, feeling she was breaking a spell, and kissed baby Isidor on the forehead. "Good-bye, my little one," she said. She hooked her arm through Wertheimer's. "Shall we?"

The coach that would take them to the railway station came into view. On the train, Isabel stared out the window at the hedgerows, wondering if Baby would miss her and if she would miss him. She wanted Wertheimer to comfort her and he would have given his consolation gladly if Isabel had indicated she required it. But she kept her face to the passing countryside, both repelling Wertheimer and waiting for him to offer solace. She wished he would at least tell her everything would turn out tolerably, no matter if he did not know whether it would or not. When they arrived in London, Wertheimer asked if she would like to dine at the Café Royal.

"I don't feel hungry," Isabel said. She could not say why leaving Baby had affected her so miserably; she guessed it was some pang of maternal guilt and it surprised her to feel it, considering she had not adapted well to motherhood. Wertheimer took her hand, placed it on his arm and began to walk. She looked up at him. "Might we go to the bazaars instead of the Royal?" she asked.

"Of course. A splendid plan."

Wertheimer loved to frivol away his money and the bazaar stalls always threw up some trinket or gewgaw for him to buy. Every surface in his rooms in the Burlington Hotel, as well as in Fairleigh Lodge, was decorated with striated glass vases and china fairings. He owned vesta strikers shaped like bulldogs and fish, and pert courting couples fashioned from porcelain. He had trinket boxes and a rack of meerschaum pipes in the shape of lions' heads and female nudes. He was always happy to add more novelties to his collection or find bits to sell on.

They gained the street from the station, and the tumult of the traffic and the roaring costermongers assailed Isabel's ears. It made her wonder how it was she never normally noticed the noise. Though loud as Niagara, London always seemed to her a place of tranquillity and ease.

South of Oxford Street, they entered the glass doorway of the Oriental Bazaar, a fragrant, many-windowed place of aviaries and towering ferns. Isabel passed the parrots, monkeys, lovebirds and squirrels to find the cage that contained the warbling one-eyed canary she often visited.

"That fellow will never sell," the proprietor always said, "for 'oo wants a cyclops canary in their 'ome?"

The bird was stout and sunny, despite his affliction, and his one black eye seemed to Isabel so alert and attentive that she was sure he remembered her every time she visited. He trilled and sang, cocked his head and stepped madly this way and that on his pale legs. The canary's good eye had a flirty black stripe flicking away from it that gave him the air of a Chinaman. It stood out as if painted with kohl against his lemon feathers.

"That one likes you," the proprietor said, sidling up and feeding a tiny piece of apple to the canary. The bird waggled its head and stepped nearer to Isabel, lifting his face to hers as if imploring her to commune with him.

"I daresay he does like you," Wertheimer said. "Look how he gazes at you and preens for your pleasure."

"He and I know each other well, don't we, Pritchard?"

"Oh Lord, she's only gone and named the bird!" said the proprietor.

Wertheimer grinned. "You've called him after the murdering Glasgow doctor? I say, Issy, you do have a sense of humor. Who should his companion be, though: his wife Mary Jane or poor Elizabeth, the maid?"

The two men laughed. "I wouldn't want to be old Liza," the proprietor said, and mimed the strike and toss of a vesta, and a puffing conflagration.

"Pritchard is a maverick," Isabel said. "He prefers to go it alone. Isn't that right, my little one?" She put a finger between the bars of the cage and the bird reeled away, flying up and around, then returning to his perch to stare at her.

"It's a solitary bird, the canary, it's true. A sensitive species—retiring, you might say. But excellent company, especially for ladies of, ahem, expansive leisure."

"I see," Isabel said. She wanted to tell the man she worked for her living.

"They's easy to keep: a few seeds, a tidge of boiled egg, the odd dandelion. Sweetest, most mild bird in the world to 'ave round the 'ome, madam. Yes, the perfect bird for a lady, if I may say. And, ooh, you should 'ear 'im sing! Like an angel come down from 'eaven."

"We'll take him," said Wertheimer.

"Isidor!"

"A very good choice, sir, but we do 'ave two-eyed birds, sir, if you care to look over 'ere. Undamaged specimens, so to speak."

"No, my friend likes this yellow fellow, so we shall have him. And a cage. And whatever else we need."

Isabel squeaked in delight. It had never occurred to her to take Pritchard home—he was a stop-off on her trips to town, a mute comrade to call on when she was fed up with the milliners and modistes. When she was tired of people and their endless chatter and woes. But it delighted her to think that she might have Pritchard's companionship daily.

"You're such a dear, Isidor," she said, pressing her fingers into her friend's arm.

"Anything to make you happy, Issy."

The proprietor busied himself getting the canary ready: a turreted cage, food and water bowls, a mirror "for company" and "a bell for summonsing." The man whistled and laughed as he prepared the bird, telling Isabel to swathe the cage in fabric by night to "make the little fellow feel safe."

"Yes, it will keep the mite secure, to 'ave the light blocked out. They frights easy, these canaries," he said.

Isabel nodded and watched his ministrations, forgetting baby Isidor for a while, forgetting herself.

1889

London

An Encounter

Viscount Dunlo had appeared in the Corinthian with his friends after the Empire one May night and every time Isabel looked up, his eyes were upon her. It was hard not to notice the man for he was taller than most and his hair sat in golden rolls, like the seraphic boy on the Pears' Soap box. There is something shy about this one, Isabel thought. She called Lord Albert Osborn over to ask who his friend was. Osborn was one of those who liked to mingle with nonconformists by night and with his own kind by day; he had long been a patron of the Empire and the Corinthian Club and he and his tight pal Marmaduke Wood went about together. Now they had a third.

"Who is that fine, fair-haired fellow you're keeping company with, Lord Osborn?"

"That, Miss Bilton, is the Earl of Clancarty's eldest son, William Le Poer Trench—Viscount Dunlo. We were at school together. A topping chap."

"A viscount? My, my. I didn't know they made such diffident viscounts."

"He was raised in Ireland," Osborn said, "I daresay that explains it."

"Indeed it might." Viscount Dunlo? Next he would be an earl. Isabel had never encountered a viscount from Ireland and she did so like the Irish—they had a softer manner than her countrymen, were less inclined toward pomposity. And Viscount Dunlo looked to be of just that breed: a refined, titled man. Isabel took her wine in her hand and approached William Le Poer Trench, who drained his drink as he kept an eye on her advance.

"You lower that champagne like water," she said.

William stared at his empty glass and blushed. "I'm drinking heartily tonight. Tomorrow I go to Africa with the militia."

"Ah. Then I daresay you need another bottle." Isabel flicked her hand over her head and ordered more champagne from the waiter who came. "Shall we sit together, sir?" William nodded fervently and they retired to a corner table and sat. "Aren't you going to ask me my name?" she said.

"Oh, but I know who you are," William said, and there was a zealous rake to his voice.

"Then we're equal, for I know who you are, too. I've noticed you at the Empire in recent times. You are quite the regular."

William dipped his head. "Once I had seen you, Miss Bilton, I couldn't stay away," he said sotto voce.

Isabel clinked her glass to his. William's cheeks flamed, warming her to him. She was used to the bluster and swank of other men; Viscount Dunlo had a mildness about him that was most agreeable. And he was large and handsome, generous of mouth and, when they had stood before each other, she reached heart high on his chest, so that she had to tip back her head to talk to him. This was a man born to protect a woman.

They began to talk in earnest then and found that they could not stop. Any formality was lost as they flitted from one subject to the next: they touched on everything from the Plumage League who wished to ban feathered hats, to the horrible deaths of Prince Rudolf and his mistress. By and by, William asked about Isabel's childhood at Aldershot.

"Military life was too orderly for me," she said. "I longed to get away, even as a child. Though I was born here in London, I didn't know it very well—we made limited forays once we moved to Hampshire—but from what little I saw of the great city, I was determined to leave the barracks and come back."

William sighed deeply. "We are alike, Miss Bilton. I wager the martial life is not for me, either." He looked up and held her gaze.

"Oh, I do apologize, Viscount Dunlo. I was so busy jabbering that I'd quite forgotten you sail with your regiment tomorrow."

"Let's not talk of it." He swigged from his glass.

"Tell me about Ireland. I've been fascinated by your country ever since the Royal Dublin Fusiliers visited Aldershot." Isabel had just that moment remembered the Royal Dublins. "They looked very fine in their red coats and bearskin caps. And they had such pretty accents."

William's face softened. "Ireland is a wonderful country, to be sure. The people are decent and mild. Garbally Park, our home in Galway, has my heart in its grip, I don't mind telling you, Miss Bilton." He smiled and Isabel could tell that thoughts of his home moved him keenly. "It's a green and lovely place, rich with trees but with long views of the parkland. We have twenty-four thousand acres altogether in County Galway, Miss Bilton. At least, my father has."

"And do you have siblings, Viscount Dunlo?" How glorious the word "viscount" felt on her tongue.

"I have a brother, Richard, and a sister, Katherine. But I'm the eldest."

The Honorable Richard and the Lady Katherine. And Viscount Dunlo the heir to twenty-four thousand acres. Well, well. Isabel's stomach warmed and she leaned closer to her companion. "My father was not blessed with a son," she said. "I have two sisters, Flo and Violet. Father complained of being 'confoundedly surrounded' by women but, of course, it was lightly meant. In a world of soldiers he welcomed the diversity of our company."

"I'm certain he did."

William's eyes lingered on Isabel's face and she let them. He was a decidedly good-looking young man. Such flawless skin, such a neat military mustache. She wondered how it would feel brushing against her mouth.

William, for his part, was entranced. Having so long admired her on the stage, here she was before him, a thousand times more lovely at close quarters. To be sure, he had clearly seen—and memorized—the shape of her small body at the Empire: the tiny waist, her comely legs, the curve of her bosom. But, modestly attired in her evening gown, and up close, Miss Bilton was delicately beautiful, luminous, and there was a certain wistful set to her eyes that stirred him to his kernel.

They surveyed each other in this way as they talked, each appraising, each finding no fault with the other, only beauty and advantage. Isabel tamped the giddiness in her heart, she did not wish to appear too keen, but there was no mistaking Viscount Dunlo's interest. He appeared to sip her words along with his champagne and it pleased her enormously. He seemed such a sweet, good-natured man.

The Corinthian Club was almost empty when they raised their heads and it was obvious several hours had passed. Isabel was mesmerized by their easy banter and laughter, the shy glances exchanged and the bolder ones held. Their conversation never idled—it was as if they had known each other before and were merely slipping back into an old pattern of cheer. It was, Isabel thought, a singular meeting.

A Name Change

Alexander Bassano told Isabel that she was "*bella*," as he bid her to stay very, very still. He grunted, flicked his fingers and Isabel held her breath. Bassano's head wriggled under the cover and she stared ably forward. Her mind was not on Bassano's fiddling machinations but on Viscount Dunlo, William Le Poer Trench. It thrilled her that William had not gone to Africa with his regiment, preferring to stay in London to be near her. He had simply gotten up the morning after their first true meeting and decided to stay in London.

"How could I leave you?" he said, as unadorned a statement as that, when he sought her out at the Empire the next night.

Isabel had stood in her dressing-room doorway, still in her stage rig-out, and stared at him, glee ascending into her throat. "Indeed, Viscount Dunlo, I am extraordinarily glad that you did not leave."

Since that night, three weeks before, they had met daily to sup and walk, flirt and drink. And they talked, it seemed, a century's worth of words. They sought each other out like air and Isabel only felt easy when at last that part of the day arrived when they would be together. She hoped he would come to the Corinthian Club tonight and sit by her to talk. Isabel liked William's peculiar accent with its unpredictable lilt into Irishness. She enjoyed his earnest devotion—there was something quaint about his sincerity when he listened to her chatter. William would sit, his eyes round as shillings, while Isabel complained about a pianist who couldn't keep time or the bodice of a costume laced so tightly it made her want to gag. He loved to hear her talk about what it had been like to live at the barracks at Aldershot and her father's role as an artillery sergeant. William sat, mute as a lap dog, and listened. Yes, there was something tranquil and unvarying about him and the way he gave his attention. He was never showy like so many of the other men of Isabel's acquaintance. She knew William only since early May, but already there was extraordinary alchemy between them, an almost supernatural ease. It delighted her.

"*Finito!*" Bassano called, bringing her back from thoughts of William. "*Bella, bella,*" he said, though he was as London as jellied eels. "*Bella!*"

"*Bella,*" Isabel repeated. "Belle. *Belle.*" Isabel studied Bassano; they were good friends since she was in his studio so often to be photographed for shows and for the press. "Do you know, Alex, I think you've just given me an idea."

"What's that, my dear?"

"The way you said *bella*, it's made me think to change my name. I will be Isabel Bilton no more. 'Belle' seems a better one for me. Belle Bilton. *Belle!* What do you think?"

"*Eccellente!* Belle. It sums you up, Isabel."

"Belle! I like it." She blew through her lips—*pffffff*—like a kettle releasing steam and swiveled her jaw, now this way, now that. "I rather think Mr. Hitchins at the Empire will like it, too."

She concertinaed her neck and shoulders and dipped her chin to her chest, then shuddered and shook out her arms making her sleeves shush pleasantly. She let the pose roll out of her body and allowed her own self to come back, along with her new self—Miss Belle Bilton. Now, didn't that sound fine? It was a fitting name for a woman of the stage. The newspapermen would like it, too. They were hungry for her now that she was back.

Bassano removed the camera plate and fixed the image. Once finished, he sailed toward his sitter and fingered the kohled beauty mark to one side of her mouth. He ran his hand over the knot of walnut hair atop her head, then scooped her cheek in his palm.

"*Molto bella!*"

Belle lifted his hand away and cocked her head. "Would a Gainsborough suit me, Alex?"

"A Gainsborough? Now, do you mean a painting or a hat, *bellissima*?"

"A hat, of course. Silly man. With a blue ostrich feather in the band. I saw such a one on Lady Adeliza, the Countess Clancarty, and it looked ever so nice."

"Countess Clancarty? Your Viscount William's mama?"

"*My* viscount?"

"Isn't he yours? Or do you belong to Wertheimer, that dashing Jew? Perhaps the Americano, Weston, hasn't lost his hold on you? It's hard to know who is who sometimes."

"Stop it," Belle said. "Don't speak to me of Weston—he wronged me too much to hear his name said lightly."

"Mea culpa. Forgive me." Bassano tugged at one of her fringe curls.

"So, Alexander, a Gainsborough. Shall I or shan't I?"

"Well, everything suits you, Isabel, so, yes, go buy a Gainsborough. Everything and, may I say, very little at all suits you, too. Splendidly, indeed."

Isabel giggled. Bassano loved to swoon over her and admire her lavishly. She was used to such appreciation now, but Bassano was never coy about it and that pleased her.

He kissed her hand. "Go buy your feathered hat, Isabel."

"Belle, Alexander, say *Belle*."

"Belle, yes. Belle."

"Help me with my cape."

She stood still while Bassano draped the garment over her shoulders; the satin lining made her shiver from scalp to toe.

"Someone walked over your grave just then," Bassano said.

"Don't be so morbid, Alex." Belle kissed his cheek and bade him farewell.

The June air in London always hummed with heat and promise. Summer was already under way but, Belle thought, June was the month of highest possibility—anything might happen during the endless days when the song sparrow chimed his alleluia from every eave. The window-box roses of Oxford Street were shedding their puce gowns and they lay like a carpet under Belle's feet as she walked toward Piccadilly. She wanted to stoop, grab the petals and throw them like confetti to celebrate their triumph over smuts and everyday pestilence. But there were too many passersby and what would they make of her petal tossing? Instead, she toed the fallen flowers with light kicks and watched them flutter before her.

People all around were in a tearing rush: the scavengers and mud larks, dodging gulley holes on their way to the Thames; the cress and winkle sellers eager to lift their baskets to every nose. Today she felt large-hearted toward the city and everyone in it. Life was turning and she was sure to see William later, which ignited a glow of goodwill both inside and out.

Belle entered the Pantheon, her most beloved bazaar—it still held on to the flavor of the theater it once was. She liked to walk in the upper gallery and gaze down on the stage of the main hall where every kind of gimcrack and knickknack was on display and the hordes throbbed. She ran up the stairs, then paused at the railing to take in the bustle of the jewelers and toy sellers below; she watched hawkers and strollers and luxuriated in the muddled din that rose to her ears. The brassy sound of a trumpet blasted up from one of the music stalls and, as the tune settled into itself, Belle's feet itched to step in time. She turned instead to the row of stalls behind her and headed straight for Madame Gilbert's.

"I want a Gainsborough, Madame," Belle said. "Enormous and with a blue ostrich feather. What do you say?"

Madame smiled. "As you wish, Miss Bilton." She waved her hand at a slipper chair and Belle sat. "Is this Gainsborough for the stage, *ma chérie*?"

"Lord, no. I mean to wear it for all of London to see. Not just the guffs who come to the Empire."

Madame lifted a straw hat, leaving the wooden head it had sat on bald as a newborn.

"Let me try this for size." Belle tilted her head and Madame nested the hat on her hair and speared it with pins. "*Très jolie*," she said. "Now, I shall visit the plume hunters this week to find the perfect feather for you, Miss Bilton. And I have a new cake of indigo with which to attain the right shade."

"Smashing," Belle said. "I knew you would understand exactly what I wanted. You always do."

Belle liked Madame Gilbert; she was not the kind of milliner who peached on her customers, though she knew everything there was to know about them. Madame had a generous ear and a snug, discreet mouth. She had listened to Belle throughout the whole crisis with Weston and had encouraged her to take Wertheimer's help when offered. Madame un-pinned and shifted the hat, seeking the ideal jaunt for it. When she was satisfied, Belle paid a deposit on the Gainsborough and left. It felt good to be able to dress herself properly again.

She thought again of Viscount Dunlo, of his lovely face, and her stomach frisked; even imagined from air he disarrayed her. William. Weston. Wertheimer. Each one of them a *W*. Is there some sign in that, some graspable meaning? Belle wondered. She rushed down the stairs to the Pantheon's main hall to clear her mind. There she was drawn to the stalls of the Swiss and German toymakers; their baubles and trinkets were always a treat to pore over. Who could fail to delight in the whirligigs, tops and alphabet blocks, or the drumming animals who made music with the turn of a key? One monkey, in a red frock coat and yellow trousers, charmed Belle. The stallholder wound him up and Belle gazed at the animal's determined, handsome face while he drummed merrily.

"Wouldn't you like to own him, miss?" the stallholder said.

"Perhaps," Belle said, thinking what a joyful gift the monkey would make.

"Come then, miss. You surely know of a boy or girl who would treasure the little fellow. If you do not covet him yourself, that is?" He picked up the monkey and wound him tight again so that the toy frenzied. "Irresistible, I would say. Loosen your purse strings, miss. Go on."

Belle looked hard at the man, irked by his persistence. "No, thank you," she said, and walked away.

Yes, she did indeed know a small boy who might love that monkey, but thoughts of baby Isidor brought her mind around to Weston again and that would not do at all. Belle upped her pace through the bazaar, eager to regain the street and the comfort of the sunshine.

A Kiss

The horse giddied when William helped Belle off the mounting block and into the saddle, but a soothing "whoa" from him settled the animal. Belle easily fixed her right leg around the pommel and slipped her left foot into the stirrup. She had ridden at Aldershot, though as she got older Mother had forbidden it, thinking it an unseemly activity for her girls. Belle fixed her skirts, pulling the hem to her ankle, impatient for William to mount his horse that they might leave the stable hands behind and take off along Rotten Row together.

Belle's horse flickered its ears and accepted a handful of oats from the groom and a few soft words. The sweet-rotten smell of hay, mingled with manure, rose to Belle's nose and she breathed deeply, letting it bring her mind home. She watched William mount and thought of her father's love for horses, his ease with them. It seemed William possessed that same gift. He sauntered away from the Row instead of toward it; Belle nodded to the groom and urged her horse to follow.

"Where are we going?" she asked, watching the vast rump of William's horse as it moved ahead, its heavy flounce.

"We'll take a quieter path," he called back, "among the trees."

She trailed William into the wood, the gentle bob of her horse's head lulling her as much as the peace in this secluded part of Hyde Park. There was sporadic birdsong but otherwise a deep stillness among the trees.

Belle kept her eyes on William's back. He was a true horseman: he rode with confidence and his body seemed to be at one with his mount's. He was, she thought, a latter-day centaur and, with practice, she might be his centauress. She thought, too, of the chaste kiss he had delivered, half to her cheek, half to her lips when they met at Conduit Street—her latest lodgings—that morning. Even in the seclusion of the hallway, with no landlady on the prowl, his embrace was reserved. Was he afraid to kiss her more deeply? Did he long to embrace her as she longed to embrace him? Belle was sure he did. But wasn't it right that they were both cautious? Wasn't it, in fact, part of the joy of it all?

William roused her, he made her think of him constantly when they were parted, and this meant a state of apprehensive glee accompanied her by night and by day. His latest sweet words, or the curve of his mouth, loomed in her mind at random moments and made her stomach lurch and reel. Belle found she pondered often what his body would look and feel like. His bare chest—was there hair there? Might his legs be as slender as they appeared through his trousers? Might his arms be as taut? Belle conjured frequently the press of his body against hers, the lingering heat of skin on skin, a night-long entwining. All this anticipation had her wound tight as yarn on a bobbin and she found she liked it very much.

Belle brought her horse up beside William's, wanting to be near him. He looked serene when she came alongside and she did not wish to disturb his thoughts, so she didn't speak but merely observed him. He looked blissful; intoxicated by the measured movement of the animal and the calm in the air. Belle liked the mottle of leaf shade on his upturned face, the way it altered his expression though he remained undisturbed. His blond hair was neat and bounteous. He has aristocratic hair, she thought and this made her smile. They moved forward through the wood together in a cordial quiet, broken only by the soft clop of their horses' hooves. On they meandered, meeting no one on the pathway, and the equanimity between them was absolute.

William looked across at Belle, a beatific set to his face. She never felt harried when she was with him, his tranquillity was infectious. She smiled and he returned it.

"You know, Belle, I shall have the best of stables when I take over Garbally in Galway—the best horses, the finest grooms."

"I have no doubt, William."

"When Garbally's mine, I mean to work with the stewards and bailiffs every day. I'll have a firm hand in managing my own estate." William pulled on the reins to stop his horse, so Belle did the same. "I don't want to play my life away, Belle. I want to work, but it's in Ireland that I mean to do it."

Belle's horse staggered backward and she rubbed its neck to settle it. "I understand, William. Ireland has your heart, you've told me."

"I will inherit Garbally, by dint of being the eldest. But the day is far-off that the estate becomes mine, unless Papa gives it up and lets me take over sooner. Before his . . . well, before he passes on, that is." He frowned. "If I can find ways to please him, he might do that, give it to me so that he is free of it. The work of the estate, I mean. It's a younger man's job."

Belle smiled; William was thinking of the future and it gladdened her. He clearly told her these things to include her, to ensure that she saw that his fate was tied to hers. A welcome thought. His company was effortless: she felt fully like herself and didn't need to worry about how he was going to act, or about how she should comport herself. Being around Weston she often felt as if she were waiting for a cannon to fire. Viscount Dunlo was different; his inherent serenity made Belle serene, and it was a welcome feeling. And here he was telling her how life would look in the years to come.

They walked on.

"Do you ever think about Africa, William," Belle asked, "about what it might be like to be there? Do you regret not joining the regiment?"

"I honestly can't say that I do. My father likes to scheme—I never expressed an interest in army life, but he saw it as the place for me. I went along with it though I didn't want to. I would never make a soldier. Then you were before me, Belle, and I couldn't leave London. Anyway, I'd prefer to decide my own destiny, as much as I can."

"Quite."

"Let's stop here a moment," William said.

He dismounted, looped his reins around a branch and came to stand below Belle. He looked up at her, then slipped his hand under her gown and up her leg. He reached into the end of her drawers and found the top of her stocking, where he hooked his fingers under her garter and caressed the bare skin. Belle felt a welcome lurch between her thighs and she sighed. So his blood really did run as hot as her own; Belle lowered her face to his and kissed his forehead. William pulled his hand from under her skirts and grabbed her by the waist; Belle swung her leg over the pommel and let William lift her clear of the saddle and into his embrace. He slid her down his body until she gained the ground and he snugged his arms hard around her. Belle tilted her head and his mouth found hers. His tongue was large, soft, liquid, and she plunged into the kiss with a fervor to match his. Belle's insides dived and swooped and she wished that they could stay forever under the birches and limes of Hyde Park, her tongue wrapped around William's. This was what she had been waiting for.

AN ABSENCE

Every night William came to bed with Belle in her room in Conduit Street. Not the flesh and heft of him but the dream of him, the man she conjured in her fancies. He lay beside her under the covers and his reticence and timidity fell away; he was again the man who had kissed her among the trees in Hyde Park. In these invented reveries, Belle's own nature was altered, too: she didn't try constantly to entertain or worry if she looked her best or not. She and William became natural together, two bodies free with each other.

Here she had William kiss her full on the lips, his tongue flicking against hers. There she had him unlace her corset and take her breasts to his mouth. Belle swooned under the weight of these fantasies; she loved them, though they often kept her from sleep. She had had daydreams before, about some of the soldiers at Aldershot, but these thoughts seemed to have their own life: they played out inside her head like dramas, every movement accounted for. In these reveries she did things that she had never thought of before, performed acts that were new to her, and it was all a mighty pleasure.

She would drift in and out of slumber and wake with thoughts of William. He would make a proper husband, of that Belle was sure. She adored him, and with him she might reassert herself in the world—erase her indiscretions. It was a warming scene to imagine them wed. But was it impossible? The aristocracy did things in certain ways; they stood by their codes. But they were marrying millers' daughters by the dozen lately. Why not a military man's daughter, if it came to it?

Belle let her fantasies flow. She imagined how William's hands might feel cupping her behind or caressing the insides of her thighs. Sometimes, when she fell asleep, William walked through her dreams beside her. He was open and courteous, but also passionate and wild. When he came to Belle unbidden in that way, she woke content and churned up. If Flo—returned for the time being—was snoring on the other side of the curtain that divided their bedroom, Belle would slip her fingers between her legs and work them swiftly until she gasped with pleasure.

William had not come to the Corinthian Club the night before, after the show in the Empire. It was the first time since they had met two months ago, in May, that he failed to seek out her company. He had not come, though Belle was certain she had spotted him from the Empire's stage; surely she could not have mistaken his boyish quiff or that lavish mouth? But of course she might have; the dim theater and her paces through several dances skewed her view of the audience. If he *was* at the Empire, he did not look for her at the club later.

Belle peered across the bedroom; the curtain wavered, making her believe Flo was awake. It was not altogether convenient that her sister was staying—she had had another row with Seymour—but there was pleasure in having her there, too. They were as familiar as a cradle song with each other's foibles and frailties.

Belle coughed, then trilled a few notes. Flo did not answer with a matching tune.

"Still in the land of feather and flip, dearest, or are you woken?" Belle said.

Her sister groaned. "I'm asleep."

"Was William in the audience last night, do you think?"

Flo grunted and the bedsprings sang. "William who?"

"You know very well who—William Le Poer Trench. My Viscount Dunlo."

"*Your* viscount?" Flo snorted, and Belle tamped down the itch to cross the room and pinch her sister.

"Was he there, Flo?"

"How the blazes would I know? Half of London turns up to see the Sisters Bilton twirl a leg."

"And the other half don't know what they're missing." Belle laughed and Flo grabbed the curtain aside to look over at her sister and cackle along with her. It was like old times, when they had first shared digs in Pottery Lane, two sinless girls with an appetite for city luster.

Flo yawned and kicked her legs. "Isabel, I don't know what you see in that William. He's so quiet. Dreary Dunlo."

"I wish you wouldn't raise a breeze around my ears about him, Flo. You don't know him as I do. He's a darling."

"Oh but he's oppressively genial. That kind of behavior galls me to my bones."

Belle didn't like to hear her sister criticize William; it made her uneasy. It also filled her with a desire to take him in her arms and soothe him, as if he knew what was being said and she could protect him from it. "He let his regiment sail to Africa without him. For me!"

"I know that, Isabel. The *Pall Mall Gazette* knows it, too, and every one of London's rumormongers besides."

"I'll thank you, Flo, to call me Belle as everyone else now does. I've had it up to my oxters with Isabel. I hear mother's voice when you say it: Is-a-*bel*!"

"As you like, *Belle*. Belle! You astonish me the way you invent yourself anew for every situation. As if each time something happens, the life you were made for is about to begin." Flo rolled her arms forward and veed her hands under her chin. "Destiny!"

"I refashion myself for destiny—is that it, Flo?"

"Yes. And it's a skill to be proud of, for sure."

How easily her sister took Isabel apart and put her back together again. "And what do you think lies in wait for me, Flo?"

"A whole pile of hoity men with scads of bread and honey. Just imagine it—men with money dripping from their pockets like melted ice."

Belle snorted. "I've had my fill of flashy men, truly."

"So you want a steady one?"

"Maybe."

"And is your Irish viscount that?"

Belle rolled onto her side. "It's your turn to take the chamber pots down to the privy," she said. "Mind you don't spill anything."

"At least Dunlo is a blue blood, unlike your 'Baron Loando.'"

"Must Weston be a continual topic of conversation? It seems the man is more present in his absence than he ever was when I knew him." She tutted; Weston was a burr in her skin. William would have to know of him at some point she supposed. He would have to know of baby Isidor. But not yet. Not yet.

Flo got up and pissed lavishly into her pot; Belle groaned, not wanting to leave the warm embrace of her bed, but she rose and did the same. Flo took the chamber pots, one atop the other, and left the room. Belle went across the bedroom to where the canary's cage stood on its stand and pulled off the scarf she used to cover it at night. Pritchard sat on a perch in one of the cage's turrets, as still as a figure in a tableau vivant; his yellow feathers made a blazing contrast to the blue of the cage.

"The sun against the sky," Belle murmured and tapped on one of the roof finials to rouse the bird, but he didn't move. "Pritchard," she coaxed. "Pritch, Pritch, Pritch. Pritchy, my love." She poked her finger through the bars, but he did not react. "My goodness, are you altogether well? If you've gone and died on me, I'll be thoroughly goosed."

Belle opened the cage door and peered at her little friend. Pritchard turned his one eye to her and immediately began the rising warble that Belle loved so much. His song alternated between rolls, flutes and bells and it stirred her as much as any orchestra. She stood, eyes closed, and listened to the canary sing, letting her heart soar to the whirl of his crisp, ever-changing tunes. Today will be a good day, Belle thought, hoping that by willing it so, she would make it come to pass.

An Excursion

In the smoky hut on the edge of Heathfield, Sara sat in a low chair feeding baby Isidor, cradling his downy head in the curve of her elbow. She rocked him to and fro, humming a lullaby and gazing at his puckered face. Her old father, her husband and her flock of children slept around her in the dawn light.

That same July morning, Belle stepped onto a train at Victoria Station and sat alone in her compartment, plucking sleep crystals from her eyes and yawning. She was impatient for the porter's whistle to blow and to feel the rumble of the tracks vibrate through her. Smuts from the engine decorated her beryl-green bodice and she pawed at them with her glove and sighed. This outfit had cost fifteen pounds, half a week's earnings; perhaps she should have worn something less fine.

The wind wheedled its way through the birch and pine groves that crowded the slopes around Heathfield and it sent the sails of Mutton Hall windmill spinning ever faster. Thatch rippled on the huts that were falling into disrepair and everything was being blown about. Belle stepped from the coach, unbending her limbs one at a time to pull the stiffness from them. She was impatient, wanting this part of her day to be over. A soft wind rippled through her clothes and scattered brittle leaves around her skirts. Surely leaf fall had not begun so early? Were the seasons now different a mere sixty miles outside London?

Belle had found the journey tiring, first the stuffiness of the train, then the constant jolting of the coach wheels. She stepped into the roadway and stretched her back and feet with a grunt, then walked on, past the trees that slunk nearby in whispering groups. A mole burrowed out of a mound ahead of her and Belle stopped to watch his myopic snufflings.

"Hello, Mr. Moldiwarp," she said, enjoying the chance to use her father's word. "Do you search for worms?"

Belle was glad it wasn't the season for wearing her moleskin cape in case the animal could sniff out his own kin, dead and all. The mole dipped behind his hill and Belle lost sight of him. She smiled to remember that her father used to hang a mole paw around their necks to ease pain when they were unwell as children. Mr. Mole did not need to know about the paw, so eerily like a tiny human hand. Father was always so vigilant of his girls' well-being.

Belle kicked through the leaves on the springy path that led to the cottage. She wore a wool wrap against the wind and her hair was rolled in loose coils under a small felt kepi. Bassano had joked that the hat made her look like a soldier and he made her pose for him in it. Belle walked through the village, noticing how the low light filtered through the trees that lined the path. She stopped to run her fingers along the metallic bark of a birch, to feel its lines and knots. The trees reminded her of mourners standing in stillness, their branches like hands brought together in prayer. A trio of roots that bulged up through the pathway told her that she was near her destination. One root looked to her like a stern, reclining man; another a lean, writhing woman and the last a stork, its beak parted as if to deliver a message.

A leaf skeleton, a rude visitor from winter, skittled at her feet like a pup eager to play. She plucked it from the ground and examined the filigreed chambers that spread across it in an intricate map. She looked through it to filter the trees around her and then stowed it in her bag; she would show it to William if he came to the club later, as he surely would, having been unusually absent the night before. William had told her of the beautiful trees on his family's land in Galway—there was a circle of oaks he delighted in, that he vowed to show her one day soon.

When Belle reached the smoky house, she coughed to let Sara know that she had arrived. The woman opened the door, nodded a greeting and sat again to continue suckling Isidor. Her white chest gleamed against the russet fabric of her dress.

"Hello, Sara," Belle said, needing to hear her own voice in order to steady it.

"Ma'am," Sara said.

The boy's eyes strained sideways to watch Belle, while his mouth stayed latched on to the breast. He paused to frown when Belle waved at him, and a trickle of milk slid from the corner of his lips before he pressed his nose to the breast to suck harder. His eyes never left Belle's face. Sara looked at the floor, her expression serious, one hand curled around the baby's bare behind.

The smells were of boiled bone and mildew. In London Belle did not carry a vinaigrette to ward off smells. She wondered, standing in Sara's cabin—and not for the first time—if she shouldn't purchase one to take with her on each trip to Sussex. She covered her nose briefly with the back of her hand, then tried to breathe only through her mouth.

A toddler—a girl—slunk from under what looked like a heap of rags. She sidled up and stared at Belle. She went to her mother and grabbed at her breast until she managed to snatch it from Isidor, the usurper. The baby cried, but Sara was able to soothe him with soft clucking noises that Belle found both odd and enchanting.

"He is well, Sara?" Belle said, feeling out of place and unwanted in the dim room. She would have liked to sit but had received no such invitation. "Baby thrives, does he?"

Sara said, "He does, ma'am," and Belle nodded, as if this satisfied her.

"Hello, Isidor," she said. "Hello, little man." Her son ignored her and she wondered if she should hold him. But with neither muslin nor drawers to cover him up, Belle was afraid the boy might piddle on her, or worse.

"Do you want to pick him up, ma'am?"

"No. That's quite all right, Sara. Not today." Belle looked at Isidor, content in Sara's arms and growing plump in her care. No, she did not need to hold him or breathe once more of his grassy, animal scent. The boy was fat and fulsome as a distillery pig. "Isidor," she called again, feeling foolishly needy.

"We call him Dory, ma'am. It suits us better."

"I see." Dory. Well. Belle sneezed and fumbled in her handbag for her handkerchief. "The smoke," she said and waved at the fireplace, needing to explain herself. She wanted to leave; everything about Sara and her home made Belle feel miserably weak and out of sorts. She poked in her bag, unable to see anything inside it in the gloom, but instead of the handkerchief, she pulled out the paper twist of coins she had readied for Sara. Wanting to assert herself, she left the money on the table rather than placing it in the other woman's hand. "I thank you," Belle said, nodded and left.

She rushed back through Heathfield to the coach stop, noticing only the hard wallop of her heart and her thoughts that flitted from guilt to relief to justification. A wind-hooked leaf worried the air over her head. Once seated on the coach she took a swig of gin from her flask and gathered herself. So she hadn't held Isidor. What of it? The awkward bundle of him was wearisome; it was upsetting, somehow, for her to take the babe in her arms—he seemed to resist her every time, and Belle was not used to being resisted. And his mushroomy, milky smell was alien; greasepaint and London slops were the smells for her. And, anyway, what would she know of the care of babies, the soothing of them? That was best left to the motherly. Those women who had little to do but lie on their backs to birth another urchin and another. One more never bothered a woman like Sara, did it? No, the harassing burdens of motherhood were not for Belle, not right now. Not with this child, at least.

But still Belle thought of baby Isidor's sweet face. He had something of her good looks, she felt: large eyes and creamy skin. There was not much of his father to discern there. Next time, she promised herself, she would hold Isidor. She would dandle him and squeeze his cherubic thighs. The child's legs were truly enormous—surely he should be walking by now? That might make his legs less lardy, more modest looking. Oh, how did people know what to *do* with babies and their incessant needs?

After the short coach ride, Belle sat on the train, drew a long breath and closed her eyes. I will stop somewhere pleasant, she thought, and have a cannikin of hot saloop, rich with sassafras. Maybe even a wedge of plum duff if the saloop was not sweet enough. Sugary things calmed Belle, gave her the same dull satisfaction as her nips of Madam Geneva. Maybe she should forget about food and go to a gin palace, pass an hour or two on her own? Belle always enjoyed the dazzle of the dram shops' gaslights and the distant camaraderie of other drinkers. She relished the juniper tang of the gin, bitter and promising. A ditty danced through her mind:

> *I love the gin! I love the gin!*
> *And in a butt of it I could swim,*
> *Or ever live among butts below,*
> *For the juniper's taste so well, I know.*

Already Belle was feeling calmer; the train tootled out of Sussex and the farther she got from Isidor, the airier she felt. The baby was in good hands, for sure. And he had company—lots of other children to jostle and play with; Belle could never offer him that. What matter if he had little more than refuse and mud as playthings—did children need much more? He seemed a hardy type of baby; there was hope that he would grow into manhood none the poorer for living away from his mother. Yes, Isidor was fine, truly.

Belle took another swallow of gin and heard her mother's voice condemning "the devil's buttermilk": "It will get you into trouble, Isabel, if you develop a fondness for it." Too late, Mother, Belle thought, not without satisfaction. She had a last gulp, hoping it might let her snooze until the train pulled in to Victoria. Then home to her Conduit Street sanctuary.

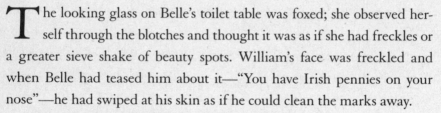

A Conversation

The looking glass on Belle's toilet table was foxed; she observed herself through the blotches and thought it was as if she had freckles or a greater sieve shake of beauty spots. William's face was freckled and when Belle had teased him about it—"You have Irish pennies on your nose"—he had swiped at his skin as if he could clean the marks away.

"There are only English pennies in Ireland," he said.

"I know that, William. I'm not ignorant."

"Oh, Isabel, I didn't mean to imply that you were." He took her hands in his. "Do you suppose, Belle, our children will have freckly noses?"

Belle liked when he talked of children; it fixed him to her in ways that no one else saw. How sweet it would be to have the child of a beloved man instead of one of a cruel one. She brushed her hair and gazed at herself, letting the strokes of the bristles act like a balm. People concluded, she knew, that theirs was one of those stupid loves, one that travels all one way. They fancied William pursued Belle and that she stood still, waiting for him to land at her feet. Implied in this was the assumption that she had lured him, exerted a spell on him with her charms. They said she was with him for reasons of rank—his—and progress—her own.

"How," the query went, "could a viscount wish to be seen publicly with an actress? Were theater people not the stuff of closed doors, of intimacies best kept hidden? What proper gentleman would harness himself to a music hall knicker flasher?"

The gossips delighted in calling her a second-rate prancer; it was all related to her by Flo, who got it from the other dancers, who got it from their highborn men, no doubt. They had proclaimed William a weak-faced, beardless boy and implied that she was duping him. As if, Belle thought, she were not woman and he were not man; as if they did not know the bray of their own desires. Their love flowed back and over between them, Belle knew. It was as if, William said once, they had drunk from the same enchanted pool as infants and the drafts they took made them one. Belle liked when William's poetic sensibilities rose up; she knew she stirred him greatly when his words spilled like nectar. And he had a title; she could not help imagining her signature rendered as "Lady Dunlo."

Flo fluttered behind the curtain, still abed though it was late afternoon, as was her custom. She grunted, stretched her limbs and hopped quickly from the bed to pull on her dressing gown. She came and stood behind Belle; putting her hands on Belle's shoulders, she spoke to her reflection.

"What's it like, down there in Sussex?"

"It's ever so green. And dark. The kind of place Jack the Ripper might fetch up."

"That old kipper?" Flo said. "I doubt he ever leaves Whitechapel—too many pickings."

Belle didn't really think that Heathfield was a morbid place and felt bad for having said it. She thought of baby Isidor, and the way he saw Sara as his one and only mother. The little Judas, Belle thought, and was instantly remorseful. But of course he took Sara for his mama—he had not known any other. Weston was the true Iscariot.

Flo picked at Belle's hair, unkinking tangles with her fingers. "How was the child?" she said. "Did he appear well? Happy?"

"His name is Isidor, Flo. You can call him that, you know. Though the woman has begun to style him 'Dory.'"

"Dory? *John* Dory—your little fish!"

"He's called Isidor."

"Very well. But try not to look so careworn when you speak of him, darling. It ages you." Belle handed the hairbrush to Flo and she worked the back of Belle's hair in long strokes until it glowed. She gouged a blob of pomatum from the pot on the toilet table and rubbed it into her palms, then let them glide over Belle's hair from crown to tips. "You always had the most beautiful Barnet Fair—like silk," Flo said, taking handfuls of Belle's hair and pressing it to her nose. "Rossetti would have painted you if he'd lived."

"Bassano does well enough."

"A cabinet card is no match for an oil painting, Belle. But maybe *your* viscount will see to that?"

"You know, the moment I heard William's voice I knew that we would be intimates. The night when I first heard him chitchatting in the foyer of the Empire, I was seduced. That soft, regal lilt."

"Oh Belle, only you could hear something majestic in Dunlo's voice." Flo pulled her sister to standing and dragged her by both hands to her bed. "Sit. Let's have a chinwag. We've been like ships crisscrossing the Channel lately—never a moment's leisure. You tell me your woes, and I'll tell you mine, and then we'll be clear of them."

"My woes are few but large, as you know, dearest."

Flo lay back on the bed and stared at the ceiling. "Begin with the most pressing."

Belle drew alongside her sister and propped herself on her elbow. "Well, it's baby Isidor, of course. And, therefore, bloody Weston. And now, of course, William."

"I take it Dunlo is unaware of baby Isidor?"

"I haven't yet found the way to tell him."

"You'll have to soon enough, Issy. It's best not to have secrets fester between you and a man."

"Why can't all men be like Wertheimer?" Belle lay back and placed her hand across Flo's stomach. "It warms me to think how deeply he always cares for me; he's such a practical friend, so efficient in his generosity. He doesn't judge. Remember how sensibly he orchestrated Baby's removal to Sussex?"

Flo, who had closed her eyes, opened them and turned her head to stare at her sister. "Wertheimer didn't have much choice, my darling. From the moment the baby was born you were set on being rid of him."

"Don't exaggerate, Flo. That's not quite the truth of it. I, perhaps, wasn't fully prepared. I misunderstood the demands of children."

"Poor Wertheimer; he idolizes you and you treat him as companion and servant, both."

Belle sat up. "I do not! Have a care, Flo. I love Wertheimer, after a fashion. In the only way I can love him. We understand each other. He's available to me in *his* way and I'm available to him in *mine*."

"He makes himself available all right—as brass clinker, as occasional landlord, as chaperone. Is there anything that man would not do for you?"

"Probably not. Like your Seymour."

"Yes, like my dear Seymour." Flo laughed. "He *is* a dear but I rather like leaving him to stew when he nags at me to give up the stage. Perhaps I shouldn't."

"Seymour is steady as an ox, Flo. You two should encourage each other's kindnesses rather than upending yourselves every time you disagree."

"Probably. But since when did the Sisters Bilton do things by halves?" Flo flipped onto her stomach. "And what of Lord Dunlo?"

"Ah now. William." Belle warmed to think of him. "He *is* a special one." A special one who would surely not be absent for a second night tonight, Belle hoped.

A Note

B elle's walk to the Empire was piebald with magpies. She counted six, then seven, then eight. She stared around frantically for another so that she would be able to say the rhyme from one to seven again without missing "two for joy." The eighth magpie was really the first—"one for sorrow." Another magpie landed on a fence ahead of her, she relaxed and chanted inside her head:

> *One for sorrow, two for joy,*
> *Three for a girl, four for a boy,*
> *Five for silver, six for gold,*
> *Seven for a secret, never to be told.*

The magpies' leavings decorated the path and she lifted her skirts to dodge them. What an extraordinary, slimy mess wild birds made! Pritchard left tiny odorless pebbles that Belle did not mind cleaning up on occasion. He was such a perceptive little fellow—not like a bird at all. Pritch seemed to have a soul the same as any person; he was a darling creature, her tiny feathered love.

Belle continued along the path, enjoying her own company; she often liked to be alone, or with only a select few, preferring that to crowds; they pressed on her rather. The stage was different: there she was in command and the throng was barely visible beyond the lights. There she felt fully alone and yet connected to her admirers; it was a contradictory pleasure. Belle tried always to walk to the theater by herself, to think out her day with her feet and get ready for the performance. Flo took a hansom; she was finicky about mud splatters and never cared to walk anywhere if she could help it.

A milk-woman trailed Belle, trying to interest her in a cup of milk.

"It's the last of it, miss," she said, "it will make a fine cream with a bit of butter added."

Belle glanced behind, feeling sorry for the woman under the heavy yoke she had shouldered for hours.

"I have no need for cream or milk, I thank you," she said. "I'm on my way to work." She wondered why in heaven she was explaining herself.

"Work, is it? Some of us work all day. Some all night, it seems." The woman hitched the yoke forward on her body. "Bloody Bunbury tart," she muttered.

Belle was about to retort when a copper who had been behind them stepped forward.

"Madam," he said, "I will confiscate your cans if you do not move along."

The milk seller pushed her nose in the air and turned away. The copper tipped his hat to Belle and she smiled in thanks and walked on, wondering why the world was determined to be at odds with her when she was doing her very best to live a smooth life. Did she not earn her own money in the best way she could? Was her son not being looked after well, as she was unable do it herself? Was she not trying to renew herself, start afresh, with a decent man? She marched on toward the Empire, stamping her cares into London's streets.

As soon as Belle was settled in her dressing room, one of the stagehands knocked and gave her a letter. Belle thanked him and tore it open. William wrote that his father had arrived unexpectedly from Ireland and he had had to leave his Burlington Hotel lodgings and pass the previous evening with the earl in his Berkeley Square house. Belle was happy with the explanation for his absence, but she fretted a little for William. Even though she had known him only a short while, she was aware that he feared his father. He had never stated it outright, but everything he said of the earl made Belle feel it was true. He had signed his note "Your loving Dunlo" and said that he would see her at the Corinthian that night. Belle's heart fluttered up into her throat, then settled.

She opened her toilet case and pulled out a jar of cold cream. Its perfume stung as she rubbed it into her forehead and cheeks, making her recall the way her mother winced every time she prepared her face for the stage. Mother always brought her case to the kitchen table—she said the light there was the best "for prinking." But the young Isabel knew, without knowing she knew, that it was all part of Mother's need to be the luminous one, to occupy the center of the family. The honeyed, floral smell of Belle's pearl powder brought back one occasion especially—the night Mother was opening as Venus in Farnborough town hall, shortly before Belle left for London.

The air in their military quarters had been taut for weeks while Mother memorized her lines and neglected all else to do so. She never relished household duties anyway and Father said they could not get a maid until they had a house of their own. Mother liked to lament loudly that her childhood in a Welsh castle, with servants galore, had been so very different from what she had to endure now. The Bilton family never once visited Wales and therefore this apparent castle of Mother's remained a blurry place, the details of which were embroidered when Mother felt particularly low. She was not a natural housekeeper; and when there was a show pending or when she and Father dined with the regiment, Mother dropped everything. It was up to the young Isabel to make sure her sisters were fed and their home was presentable.

This particular evening, Mother was performing her toilet at the table, and Isabel and her sisters stood in a row, plaiting each other's hair in preparation for going to the theater to watch Mother's play. Isabel worked on Flo's hair, and Flo worked on Violet's. The girls were excited, but they tamped down any giddiness while Mrs. Bilton was present and obediently styled their hair. When Isabel was done, she went to where Mother sat and watched her line her eyes with black and carmine her cheeks.

"May I have some powder, Mother?"

Mrs. Bilton's gaze did not move from her own reflection and she continued to dab at her face. At last she spoke.

"Who is performing tonight, Isabel, you or I?"

"Mother?"

"Who is going onstage, girl? Answer me. You or I?"

"Not I, Mother." Isabel squirmed. "That is, you are, Mother. You are going onstage."

"Correct. And for that reason, among many more, you may not have powder. Or rouge or any other item from my armory." She slapped down the lid of her toilet case and Isabel stared at it so as not to have to meet Mother's eyes.

The girls' father, hearing his wife's raised voice, came into the kitchen to see what was what.

"My beautiful ladies," he said, and he crossed the room, took Mrs. Bilton's hand and kissed it.

She rose to look into his face. "This is it, John. I can feel it. This time I will be plucked and swept up to the theaters of London. Isn't that so?"

Father didn't answer immediately, and Isabel knew he was trying to formulate the kindliest answer possible. One had to be soothing with Mother but, Isabel knew, one also had to be quick. *Speak, Father*, she urged inside her mind, *speak! Say something about how finely Mother commands the stage, no matter what you know in your heart.*

Mother stepped back from Father. "Why don't you answer me, John? I declare to the devil, I know why. It's because you don't listen to me! You never listen. You don't care! Oh, talking to you is like talking to a, to a . . . a radish."

The other girls stopped all movement and waited. Despite better sense, Isabel felt a giggle bubble from her mouth. It fell into the room and no one moved. Silence.

"A radish," Isabel said then, feeling the need to explain that the word had caused her to let loose the foolish laugh.

Before Isabel could react, her mother had rushed forward, snatched a hairbrush from Violet and slapped Isabel hard on the crown with it.

"Do not mock me, girl," Mother hissed.

Isabel's hand flew to her smarting head, but she stayed where she was and she did not cry. Mother turned and flew from the room; Father rushed out behind her. Isabel looked after them, thinking, *I will not take much more of this. Be sure of it. I simply will not.*

B elle was nestled in the Corinthian Club with a thimbleful of sweet Madeira, her muscles aching pleasantly after hours on the stage. Mr. Hollingshead had had the club's unofficial motto newly inscribed on the wall in a scrolling script: *The Corinthian Club—formed for the breaking of every law of God and man.* It made Belle smile. She looked around to see who was in. Jack Hollingshead had already been over to greet her, as had Bassano and dear Wertheimer. They congratulated her on the show—she had danced well, she knew—but her eyes continually strayed past them to see if William had arrived. She saw some of the dancers from Drury Lane and a few more from the Canterbury. The Gaiety Girls, being new, stood around large eyed with anticipation. Belle raised her glass to them and they held theirs aloft to her, then huddled to whisper that she was none other than Belle Bilton, one half of the Sisters Bilton.

It pleased Belle that the club's patrons were of such miscellaneous character: here were the braggarts and coin-tossers, there the heads-bent conferrers. Years of soldiers and regimental living had aided her love for the disorder of bohemia, the freedom in thought and dress thrilled her, the very nonuniformity of it all. And that everyone melded together in one merry band pleased her even more. There was something spicy about the Corinthian's clientele—they were a contained yet giddy crew. Fracas and disagreements happened seldom at the club; any fallings-out tended to be temporary affairs, oiled with good humor and eased with good wine. Bonhomie reigned. Belle liked that Mr. Hollingshead turned away most chance comers, for he wanted only a select society at the Corinthian. *If*, she mused, *I could set up home in the club, I most definitely would.*

Wertheimer sent over another glass to Belle; she toasted him and he colored charmingly. For such a fellow of the world, he retained a naïve grace. His ravenish looks did not stop him from appearing angelic. It amused Belle that his daily buttonhole never flagged or wilted. She accused him of carrying a tiny water spray, encased in gold, to keep it fresh. Wertheimer kept the finest of everything, and she loved him for that. She rose and went to her friend, raising her glass again in thanks. He pulled out a chair for her and she sat.

"Belle."

"Will you continue on to Cleveland Street, Isidor? You might meet some sweet fellow to spend time with."

"I'm not sure, dearest. I may retire early tonight. I can accompany you home if you'd like?"

Belle was about to say she planned to wait a while, for William, when she saw him rushing toward her across the club. His eagerness to see her was so apparent she felt at once embarrassed and thrilled.

"Isabel!" He knelt at her feet like a serf and grabbed her hands to kiss them.

Belle's eyes flicked around the club. "Sit, William, do sit."

Wertheimer had stood to welcome Dunlo, but the viscount barely returned his greeting. The chap was clearly mad about Belle, but was he a little green, a scintilla too young to truly appreciate the charms of such a woman? Wertheimer had seen William often at the Burlington

Hotel with his friends Wood and Osborn—they all had rooms there. They could be a raucous trio some nights and he had, he realized, dismissed them as puerile and somewhat beneath his notice. But if Belle liked the chap, there must be more to him. Wertheimer stood back and watched. Dunlo's large mouth hung open and his eyes were wild, drinking Belle in.

"You look ravishing," he said, and Belle nodded in acknowledgment of the compliment. She glanced around again to see if other people were watching, but most were engaged in small groups, talking and drinking their fill.

"William, do sit. You, too, Isidor. We can make a jolly party."

"Indeed we can," Wertheimer said, and he pulled out a chair for Dunlo.

"Why, thank you, Wertheimer." William smiled, a congenial acknowledgment of the other man's tight friendship with his beloved.

Belle leaned into William's sight to get his attention. "How was the earl?" she asked, though she feared to hear the answer.

"He scolded me roundly—*again*—for not getting on the boat to Africa, but I don't care a rap for what the old fellow says." William laughed and Belle knew that this was a bluff; there was something jumpy about him always when he spoke of the earl, and now he did not meet Belle's eyes fully and frowned into the distance.

"Was your father frightfully angry?" Wertheimer asked. "Does he know *why* you didn't leave with your regiment?"

William looked at Wertheimer. "I daresay he heard rumors it was over Belle, but I denied any knowledge. Said I would rather stay in town than get lost in some African jungle." William turned now to Belle. "My father complained once more about how hard he'd worked to obtain the commission for me and said he now looks an absolute fool. He tried to get Mama to agree with him, but she said not a word."

"You call your mother 'mama.' How charming." Belle wondered if baby Isidor would ever call her that. Was he, in fact, calling Sara mama at this very moment? And if he was, did it matter?

"And Father is 'papa,' of course."

"Papa," Belle murmured. William's guilelessness tickled her, but it made her realize how youthful he was, too—at twenty more than a year younger than she; he wouldn't come of age until December. But it wasn't only a matter of years, William was fresh, unplucked, if one could say that of a fellow; somehow, oddly, she realized it only endeared him to her more. And weren't men always a little behind women, always more gullible and raw? He was a dear boy, a dear man, unlike any she had known before. There was his pedigree, of course, and his handsome build, but he was softer and sweeter than other men, too. There was a genteel core to William that seemed to be of his own making, something inherently good resided in him. He was steady, despite his youthfulness, and Belle found she believed in him; she knew in her heart that he would be constant. But would he speak of her to his family? He would have to if they were to continue on. And didn't they mean to do just that?

Wertheimer stood. "I think I shall go to Cleveland Street, after all, Belle. Leave you two to catch up with each other."

Belle put out her hand and pressed Wertheimer's. "We shall meet soon, Issy."

"That we will," he said, bowed and took his leave.

"Good night, Wertheimer." William watched him go. "Topping fellow. Cuts a grand figure around the Burlington. Aloof but friendly, I always find."

"He is a dear friend to me and kindness personified."

"But what news with you, Belle?" William leaned in closer. "Did you lament my absence? I rather hope you missed me terribly."

"I did miss you, William." She dipped her head. "More than I can say."

"What have you been doing? Did you go anywhere, see anyone? Tell me how you passed the hours while we were apart, I must know everything."

Belle thought of her trip to Heathfield in Sussex and the visit with little Isidor at Sara's home. She remembered the leaf skeleton in her bag that she had saved to show William.

"I took my ease today. I did little beyond lie in my bed and eat from a box of Fry's Chocolate Creams."

"How I wish I could have been there with you," William said softly, looking at Belle to see if she would react. He sat up straighter. "Papa and I went to see some stallions in Sussex. Even though he's out with me, he asked me to come with him. Very fine horses they were, too."

"Sussex? Goodness me. What part?" An image of an encounter on the train with William and the earl skittered into Belle's mind and produced a moist tingle on her brow. "How did you travel there?"

"In Papa's cabriolet. We went to a stud farm in Godalming."

"Godalming is in Surrey, William."

"That's it, yes. Surrey. I get the names mixed up. It's so much simpler in Ireland where the place names are easy to distinguish: Ballinasloe, Athlone, Loughrea."

"Ballinasloe! Athlone!" Belle said. "Such odd, bewitching names."

"They come from the Gaelic." William took Belle's fingers in his own. "You'll know all the Irish towns and their names when you're my wife."

Belle dropped his hand and her heart jigged. If only they might marry! "Don't jest about such things, William." Was he sincere? Belle's head tingled. "It's not funny to joke about serious matters."

"I'm not trying to be funny, Belle. I'm wholly in earnest." He twined his fingers through hers. "Look here, I have a surprise for you. I mean to take you for a jaunt in Papa's cabriolet. I have something planned. What do you say?"

"Why, I say yes, of course. Where are we going?"

"That's the surprise. I shan't tell you! We will go next week when Papa is out of town and you'll see what the outing entails when we get there. You'll like it, it will be vast fun."

William leaned forward as if he meant to kiss her, right there in the middle of the club. Belle dodged his mouth and frowned a warning at him; kisses were for their secluded haunts only, it wouldn't do to cause babble for the newsmen to apprehend and report on in their sneaky way. She looked around for a suitable distraction.

"Look, there's Bassano. Alexander!" she called, waving the photographer over. He came and stood by her chair. "This is the man who inspired me to change my name to Belle, William. It's all thanks to dear Bassano."

"*Buonasera*, Viscount Dunlo," Bassano said, and William stood to shake his hand.

Belle sipped her wine and let the two men talk. There now, William was meeting all her friends and he was gracious with them. His good breeding and natural ease meant he could fit himself in anywhere. How delightful to see him earlier with Wertheimer and now chitchatting idly with Bassano. It made her want to throw off caution, hop to her feet and kiss him roundly right in the middle of the club. Belle caught his eye and winked, and the quick smile he sent back lit a beam through her. William was endearing in ways that were becoming more attractive to her by the day. What a triumph and a blessing that in the vast splay of London town they had managed to meet each other.

A REFLECTION

William lay in his bed in the Burlington Hotel, glad not to be in his boyhood room in Berkeley Square where he had spent the previous night. Sleep did not come easily there—he had always preferred his Garbally bedroom—and he passed the hours of darkness adrift between this world and the other, the drop and rise of his dreams assaulting him like the vagaries of Galway weather. He did not belong in Berkeley Square anymore; that house pertained to William the boy and he was entering the realms of manhood. Or so he hoped. It seemed to him he straddled youth and maturity in the same precarious way he was asprawl between Ireland and England. He always felt like an in-between person, someone who belonged firmly to two places and yet to no place—no tribe—at all.

Marmaduke Wood and Lord Albert Osborn, his closest friends in England, were good sports, he had to own, but they spent money like the nouveaux riches and he was having a damn hard time keeping up. He had met them at school but, as he got older, he wondered whether he really belonged with them or to them. They seemed to be snipped from a different cloth from William; he supposed it was his Irish side that made him feel at variance with his friends. They were English through and through, and liked to remind him of that, as if it was the most important thing.

Their Englishness gave them a certain poise and pluck that he knew he lacked but didn't necessarily want. There was a softer core to William that he considered to be part of his Irish heritage and he treasured that. Still, he liked Wood and Osborn's boisterous company when he was in London. They brought out his rambunctious side, made him less muted, braver, and that was to be relished from time to time.

Ireland, Ballinasloe and Galway—especially his childhood home, Garbally Park—were sewn into William, sinew and bone. Garbally was wefted through him: every acorn that fell, every splash and turn of the River Suck, every pheasant that barked in the woods. His affection for the land at Garbally, and the house that sat on it, was almost frantic. Was that bound up with the fact that he always felt on the edge of losing his connection with Galway, despite being his father's heir? Everything came back to Papa, really. Papa was the reason William could not conduct himself with grace into manhood.

William, Wood and Osborn had talked much about this business of becoming a man. At twenty years of age they were expected to *be* men but, like all their acquaintances, they retained the ineptitude of their younger years and their fathers lamented the fact often. Days before, on a horseback ride in Rotten Row, the three young men had idled their animals along the bridle way to talk.

"How does one become a man?" William had asked.

Wood hooted. "Dear Dunlo," he said, "if we must educate you on the delights of bedding women at this late juncture, all is lost."

"Does not the glorious Miss Bilton incite your manhood?" Osborn said, grabbing at his own crotch and howling.

"Do stop, Osborn." William glanced around the park to see if anyone might have overheard. "You know what I mean."

"One becomes a man by doing one's duty of course," Wood said. "Doesn't your pater say that fifty times a day?"

"Perhaps even more than that." William pulled at his mare's reins to slow her. "But what *is* my duty?"

"Your duty is whatever Papa tells you it is, my boy. That's the way for all of us."

"And I have shirked my duty by refusing to go to Africa."

"The old man will expect you to buck up now, Dunlo. Not one misstep more."

"Listen to you," Osborn said. "You sound like a pair of old milksops. Your duty, as I see it, Dunlo, is to snag that Miss Bilton and get her onto your mattress by fair or foul means. Win her, boy, you'll be sorry if you don't. Someone else will snare her. Wood and I would be happy to relieve you of the burden of the celestial Miss Bilton."

"I say." William felt a burr of anger rise to his throat. "Don't talk of Miss Bilton in that way. It's not respectful, Osborn."

"Respectful? Respectable? What the deuce, man?"

"Be careful, Osborn," William said. He would not have Belle spoken of as if she were less than. She was as fine a woman as any highborn miss they knew.

Osborn clicked to his horse to get her to trot. "Let's toss for Miss Bilton! What say you, Wood? Isn't that a first rate plan?"

Wood gentled his horse into action and cantered away, calling back, "We'll all play for her, Osborn, how's that? Wouldn't that tickle you, Dunlo?"

Osborn shouted, "Onward!" and galloped off after Wood, the sand of the track swirling up behind him.

William sat up in bed and lifted his vesta case and cigarettes; instead of lighting up, he held the case in his palm, his thumb rubbing at the mermaid's face there, as it always did in times of deep thought. Her features were worn away, which endeared her more to him rather than less. The mermaid was a familiar and he liked to contemplate her body: the flick of her scaled tail, the pronounced navel, the up-thrust of her breasts. He enjoyed always the way his flesh heated her silvered form.

William lit a lucifer, took a drag and blew the smoke out in contemplative puffs. *If you become a man by obeying your father, I'm already on a greasy path*, he thought.

"You stand in my way, Papa," he said aloud.

The earl had been mistrustful and challenging since William was a boy. Never with Katherine and Richard, his siblings, only with him. The less Father trusted William, the less he felt like being a model son. There was the business at Oxford—William had deliberately failed the exam—and now there was this other bother with the militia. Papa would not stop until he had found some place to *put* William, somewhere that would please Papa but that he, no doubt, would hate. Bloody Africa. Father had been there and swore that it had made a man of him. Ergo, William must also go there. Never mind that he had had no interest in the army in the first place. If William could only have Garbally now, he would make a good job of cultivating the estate and building it up. He loved the tenants and he loved the land, but there was a pall about the place since the Great Hunger had devastated Ireland. William felt he could make Garbally prosperous once more, as good as it had been under his grandfather's stewardship. He would expand the farm and breed horses besides. He could see himself there, clearer than he could see himself anywhere.

He lit another cigarette off the bottom of the first, enjoying the wheezy crackle as the ends met and relishing the jog to his lungs on the deep inhale. How wonderful it would be to detach from his father, though it was an impossible notion; he needed Papa like the veins need blood. He needed his money. And the earl was Garbally's master until it passed to William.

There had never been anything but unease between them though; Papa appeared to object to the very essence of William, whose solitary nature and dreaminess were a source of rage to the earl. His anger would thunder around his son—even Mama could not protect him.

William had often spent from sunrise to sundown in the deepest recesses of Garbally Park, contentedly companionless, examining every inch of the land with forensic attention. He loved to walk and admire primroses and snowdrops, then gather them in bunches for Mama. The stealthy overnight arrival of a sea of bluebells in April was enough to make tears fall from his eyes. He liked to sketch autumn mushrooms rather than pluck them; he would curl one palm over their clammy caps to congratulate them on their eccentric perfection. Winter at Garbally was a rare sight: November fogs hung above the trees like wraiths and stole their leaves as they departed. The January snows brought serenity. Every excursion around Garbally ended with a gift for Mama: a feather or twig or blossom. If Papa was home, and not in London, he glowered and complained about William's foolishness, despite Mama's defense of her son. In spring William wept over lambs slaughtered on the estate farms, and Papa's scorn was so absolute that William wondered if he might ever in his life find a way to please him.

At school in England, the other boys called William "Bogman" and rolled their *r*'s extravagantly when he spoke. William's large size and general silence fended them off, but he never felt part of the roil of boys and their endless hustle. He had never truly felt a part of anything until he met Isabel. She found him, seized him and seemed to accept him despite all his flaws. What a wonder that woman was to see anything in his gauche, sensitive self. He felt he had blossomed since meeting her; she was teaching him how to become the best man he was capable of being.

How sweet that she wanted to be called Belle! That was his pet name for her before they ever met in person, when she was the unattainable goddess he visited, night after night for months, at the Empire. He would cajole Wood and Osborn to accompany him, and they were only too pleased to sit at the feet of the Sisters Bilton and halloo their praises. William had watched Belle's performances in reverent silence, wondering if he would ever muster the pluck to speak to her after the show.

William lit the lamp, extinguished his cigarette and lunged over the coverlets to reach the jacket he had flung to the floor. In the inside pocket he located the cabinet card of Belle he had purchased before meeting her. It titillated him to think that now she was his. The likeness did not quite capture Belle's beauty; Bassano was skilled, to be sure, but this time his art had not altogether succeeded. Belle looked glorious, of course, but there was a sulky set to her face that concealed her exquisiteness. This gladdened William because other men would have bought this card and he did not want them to know that it masked the modish yet refined nature that was his beloved's true charm.

He kissed Belle's face and gazed on the curve of her form, took himself into his free hand and pumped slowly, slowly then faster and faster until he was pleasured. William released a fulsome sigh, leaned back against his pillow, the cabinet card still in his hand, and fell asleep.

A Heart-to-Heart

William met Belle outside the Empire Theatre, after a swift rehearsal that was called to help Flo catch up with her dances; she never could learn them as easily as her sister. Belle was under the awning, absorbed in buttoning her gloves as William approached and it amused him that she would do such a thing on the street; Mama and his sister would blanch if they saw it, so concerned were they for all that spoke of propriety.

"Miss Belle Bilton," he called, when he was almost upon her.

She looked up and smiled. "Viscount Dunlo, how extraordinary to happen upon each other here!" She laughed and held out her arm.

William took it and shyly fingered the lace trim at her wrist as they began to walk. "How are you today, my dear?"

"I am well, but weary a little of the city heat. Might I propose an outing to Richmond? We could sup at the Star and Garter Hotel. The pavilion is always so grand at this time of year, decked in those blowsy roses from the gardens. And the river walk is shaded."

"That would be delightful. But I'm, you see, a touch straitened, that is to say, I'm having some difficulties and, well, Papa has come down hard on me and I'm somewhat . . ."

Belle slowed her step and looked up at him. "What has your papa done, William?"

"Well, he refuses me use of the carriages for a spell and he has embarrassed me somewhat. My allowance, you know."

"William, are you trying to tell me you're a little on the floor?"

"I beg your pardon?"

Belle stopped walking. "Are you stony, my love?"

"Stony? No, not quite but Papa has concerns about me and, as good as his word, has withheld—"

"Hush now, William." Belle wanted to help him in every way she could. Love did not turn on who 'owned' money. William was not a thief or deceiver; he was not Weston. "You know I earn thirty pounds a week, William, don't you?"

"My, that's rather a healthy sum."

"And it's ours." Belle enjoyed the approving pressure of his hand on her arm. She knew how it abashed most men to speak of money troubles, but it did not embarrass her. She earned it, she spent it. It was a joy to her to share it with William in his time of want. He was certainly no Alden Weston.

Belle had William wave down a hansom and help her in. The driver opened his hatch and William called up, "The Star and Garter Hotel in Richmond."

The turrets and the canopied entrance of the hotel always lifted Belle's stomach in sweet anticipation. She loved that the gay and the famous found succor at the Star and Garter, just as she did.

"This was a favorite resort of Dickens, the author," she said, as the hansom pulled up. "And, of course, Queen Victoria herself has dined here."

"And no wonder—the prices are fit for a monarch. What was it that newspaper wrote? 'The Star and Garter is more like the mansion of a nobleman than a receptacle for the public.'"

"I daresay the newsman was cowed by too much elegance; the gray of his Fleet Street den was on his mind and he didn't like it."

William helped her down and they entered, choosing to go to the new coffee rooms over the pavilion. Belle ordered chicken baked in rice, onion custard, and raspberry-and-cream-filled cornucopias.

"I shall have the same," William said.

They did not talk much until their luncheon arrived, but the aromas of the food seemed to release not just spittle but rivers of words.

"William," Belle said, "I don't feel that money, or the lack of it, should be a point of controversy between us." Belle wanted no more upsets in her dealings with men. Everything would be open with William, it would be better that way. "Au contraire, I wish that you and I will always be frank about such matters."

"Darling Belle. You're such a generous spirit." William laid down his cutlery. "How can I thank you for easing my distress over this predicament with my father?"

Belle forked a sliver of chicken between her lips, chewed it and looked at him. "By uniting with me, William. By being true and steadfast. That's what I am asking for—that you remain dedicated to me, to us. I've been let down in the past. Be loyal, William." All young men had debts, Belle knew, that did not bother her. But she would demand William's allegiance; she could not manage another inconstant, untrustworthy man.

"I can certainly be steadfast and loyal, Belle; nothing would give me more pleasure. I should explain to you about Papa, my dear. He's a good man, an upright man, and he is, ah, perhaps a little chagrined these days by my spending habits. By the money I owe. Wood and Osborn are hard to rein in once we're out and about and, you know, a fellow must be seen to keep up. They style me Jack Thriftless from time to time." He grinned but he was subdued. "My reliance on family money is, I know, becoming old-fashioned. Men take jobs these days, in factories and in the city, all sorts of men. But my heart lies in Garbally and I'm determined to manage the land there, when my time comes. That corner of Ballinasloe will be my life's work."

"It's wonderful to have such a goal." Belle pressed his arm. "But are you sorely in debt, William?"

"Oh, no, nothing like it. Just a few pounds here and there, really. But Papa is rigorous about the family name and he doesn't want anyone to know I'm, well, as he likes to say 'a profligate.' He exaggerates but, still, I don't want to gall him."

"Might I relieve you from some of those arrears? Settle a bill or two for you?"

"Belle, you will do no such thing." He blushed. "The monies are trifling, I assure you, but, as a man of the highest honor, Papa is vexed by the business. It's nothing I can't put right. He'll see reason soon." William laughed and Belle smiled. "I rather thought you'd run a thousand miles when you found out." His debts had not shamed him until now, but he wanted to make things proper for Belle; she was worth being upright for.

"Perhaps, William, with someone else, I might have, but, you know, I've run my fill. It's time for me to stop and settle. I want only to be cherished; I want an honest allegiance. Money is not of huge importance to me." Money *was* important; but she needed William to know that because she could earn it easily, and help him with his debts if need be, that it would not come between them. Love was the greater thing now, love and loyalty, which William could offer.

"You are noble, Belle. And diligent. You earn every scrap of money you own and I salute you for it."

"My work comes as naturally to me as breathing, William. It's easy for me. I rehearse, I dance, I sing. I get paid."

He squirmed in his seat and leaned in. "I hold you in ever such high regard, Belle. You know this?"

"Yes, William, I know it. And your ardent feelings are returned."

"You were made for love, Belle."

She looked at him shyly. "Made to love you, William."

They held each other's gaze and William pressed her hand. He rattled his fingers over hers and tried to say out what was in his heart, the full burst of all it contained, but the waiter came and removed their luncheon plates, causing them to break apart. The waiter returned with the cornucopias and coffee. Belle and William giggled softly over the spurting cream and stared at each other. Both were sorry, yet a little glad, that they could not embrace, for there was a rare beauty in anticipation and, somehow, it pleased them more to wait.

A BABY SHOW

They look like oysters," William said.

"What makes you say that?" Belle stared at the babies sitting on their mothers' laps in a neat row of chairs. Why had William brought her here of all places?

"It's because of the color of their skin. No, no, I have it—this is better: they look like angels on horseback. Look—the oyster is the baby, the bacon is the blanket."

"Not all of them are swaddled," Belle said, eyeing a rotund girl in an emerald dress whose cheeks glistened like cherries. Had the mother rouged the child's skin?

This was Belle's surprise, the secret day out that William had promised: the Baby Show at the Highbury Barn Tavern. Belle fancied they might be going for a quiet walk in Finsbury Park when the cabriolet rolled toward Islington. Perhaps William had something he meant to ask her and he wished for a shielded spot. She had wondered what was in store when William told the driver to stop at Highbury. A baby show. Whatever possessed him?

A man jostled behind them and began to shout, "I bid you, ladies and gentlemen, to feast your eyes on these babes." It was the owner of the tavern, clearly delighting in the spectacle of the show. "Have you ever before seen such porky legs on an infant? Dine, if you will, on this little madam's adipose encumbrances."

Belle brought to mind the bulky limbs of her own child. She glanced at William. When would she reveal the fact of little Isidor's existence to him? It was difficult to find the appropriate moment. Every time she began to form the words "I have a son," they went to clabber in her mouth.

"Ladies and gents," the tavern man called, "pray come look. Such arms on the girl! Such legs! You will never see the likes again, no doubt."

The young mother gleefully held up her green-clad baby; the child jiggled her legs and tried to stuff an enormous fist into her mouth. "Gnnnnhh," she coodled.

The man accosted William. "Take her in your arms, sir, and guess the weight."

Before Belle could object William was holding the berry-cheeked babe by the waist and bouncing her this way and that.

"Be careful, William. I'm not sure that's the best way to hold a baby."

"Belle, you cannot know much of handling infants."

She felt mildly affronted. *I might know*, she thought, *if it had not been for Weston and for my own foolishness. I might know indeed if I could marry and raise a babe as it's meant to be raised.*

William grappled with the child who wriggled and plunged so that it looked like she might escape his arms and hit the ground. No doubt her "adipose encumbrances" and large behind would prevent serious injury. Unless she fell on her head. Belle shuddered and held out her hands.

"Give her to me, William," she said. "Quickly." Belle ached suddenly to take the girl and feel her pillowy weight. She thought of Isidor, quiescent in Sara's arms. Was there something amiss with him that he did not squirm and wobble like this baby? Was he quiet only when Belle was present? She waved her hands to get William to hand over the child.

"It's all right," he said. "Holding her is rather jolly."

"You're starting to look fatigued, William. Do let me take her."

"What say you, sir?" the tavern owner bellowed. "Is she twelve pounds, do you think?"

"I couldn't say." William bounced the baby to test her weight.

"She is not that and neither is she fourteen pounds. No, not a stone in weight. The child, this fine London lassie, is a full twenty pounds, sir, and she not half a year old!" The man grabbed the baby and stuffed her back in her mother's arms. "Come. Look at this fellow!" he called. "What do you suppose they feed him on?"

Belle followed the man's eyes to an even larger baby. "Oil cake," she murmured.

"Bartlett's Food for Cattle," a woman's voice called and the crowd laughed.

The child's mother was fat also and she sat, beaming at the onlookers, her fist wrapped around a pint of porter. Her expression seemed to say, *Are you not charmed by me and my robust child? Are we not the picture of natural good health?*

"This colossus is thirty-three pounds of infantile flesh, if you can believe it, madam. Thirty-three pounds! The sight of this young man alone was worth your sixpence fee, I daresay."

Belle took William's arm and steered him away from the babies and their grinning mothers.

"What a hobbledehoy of a chap," William said, looking back over his shoulder at the baby. "Will he ever learn to walk when he has to drag such brawn around with him?"

"Don't be unkind, William. He's just a child—blameless. He didn't ask to be put on show." Belle pulled her arm from his. "He didn't even ask to be born into this world."

"I said it in jest, my dear. No doubt he will lose the blubber when he is forking hay on his papa's farm."

"There! You did it again. Can you not see that you are insulting an innocent? Oh, you are infuriating me."

"Belle." He stopped and tilted her chin up to him. "Belle, what's the matter? I thought you would enjoy the comedy of it. I brought you out here for fun."

"Do you think those babies are having fun, being paraded like Barnum's freaks?"

"They seem perfectly fine to me. What do they know or care? And their mothers will surely enjoy the silver cups they will take away with them, not to mention the prize money."

"That makes it even worse. Babies and money mixed up together. It's disgraceful."

She stopped, for she could feel tears heating the backs of her eyes and she did not want to cry in the middle of the tavern floor. What was baby Isidor doing at this moment? Would Sara dare to flaunt him in this way? Why did she even care? She had fostered the child with Sara, as many a mother did. Why did these jabs of conscience continue to wound her? Belle tucked her arm through William's elbow crook once more and turned her back to the chain of babies and bloated mothers.

"I wish to leave. Take me home, William."

At Conduit Street William did not immediately descend from the cabriolet to help Belle out. Instead he clutched her hand.

"May I accompany you to your room?" he said.

"No, William, don't be foolish. You know I would be evicted if the landlady saw you. Besides, we must wait." Belle dipped her head. She would love to lie in William's arms, to feel the warmth from his body heat her, to have him cajole her with kisses. But she needed, also, to retain her senses. Ducking under covers with Weston had left her with baby Isidor. Her own lack of sense had compounded the problem. She could not lose her wits, but she must make William wait and she must be patient herself.

William put his finger under her chin to lift it so he could see her eyes; she stared at him. He was a beautiful man.

"We will marry, Belle, and then we shall never be parted. No room will be barred to us."

She loved to hear him say that, but his parents' undoubted misgivings could not be ignored. "And you think your mama and papa would approve of such a scheme?"

"I do not need their approval. You'll see."

"William, think of what you would lose if you went against your father." She said the words, though she hoped his love would expunge her meaning. "Be sensible."

"How can I be, when I'm with you? You make the most insensible creature of me, Miss Bilton."

Belle looked away. "We must be patient, that's all. We must keep our heads."

"I can hardly wait until the night we lie together. I yearn to hold you to me, as husband holds wife."

Belle's heart jounced and they gripped each other's hands. William glanced at the cabriolet's ceiling, hoping the driver would not grow restless and open the trapdoor. The man was tight with his father and Lord knew what news he would store up to take to Berkeley Square. William pulled Belle to his breast and found her mouth with his. His lips were soft on hers and she welcomed the urgent press of his tongue; her body went lax, everything inside her a-glide and a-glow. She opened her mouth wider to let him in and they kissed until they heard the stomp of the driver's feet which meant he wanted to get on.

"Let him go, William. I need to speak with you about something. Shall we walk?"

"Of course, Belle."

William helped her down and told the driver to leave. They walked through Mayfair to Hyde Park, Belle trying to muster the words with which to tell William about baby Isidor. She had not known whether she was going to tell him so soon but his talk of marriage necessitated it. If they were to be wed, he must know all. Belle took courage once the

Serpentine came into view—the lake's green waters acted like a salve. She kept her face forward and spoke into the air as they strolled, for it proved easier for the words to emerge that way.

"There is something you must know, William. I have been living life sub rosa and it has become unbearable to me," she said. "When it comes to you, I prefer to have no secrets. I mean, I don't want every tittle snoop knowing my business, but I simply must reveal this fact I'm holding to you, for I shall sicken myself otherwise." She glanced up at him. "It's not that I've wanted to conceal anything these past weeks that we've known each other, but it's been hard to find the right time to say it out."

"What is it, Belle? Please do tell me." William stopped by the lake the better to look into Belle's face.

She met his gaze; he looked grave and her heart plunged and pushed in her rib cage but it was time to say it. "William, what I have to tell you is that I have a child. A son."

"Ah," he said.

Belle searched his eyes. "You already knew!"

"Not exactly. I had heard something. Well, people whispered it to me at the Corinthian."

"People always seem to have plenty to say about others' lives." Belle felt a pinch in her neck and rubbed her hand over it, an attempt to swab away her anxiety. William was silent; he turned from her and faced the Serpentine. They stood, not talking, and the lap of the water and boisterous birdsong chipped at Belle's ears like an assault. William's lack of comment ground into her.

"I have shocked you, William, despite the work of the gossipers."

"I'm not shocked, Belle, no." He hesitated. "I'm wondering, I suppose, what it means. For you. For us. I'm trying to understand." William kept his eyes forward while he spoke. "I must tell you that when it was whispered to me at the Corinthian I didn't believe it. When I heard it twice more I thought maybe you did have a child but, when I thought about that, it made no difference to my ardor for you. And I didn't feel I could question you about it. When I mused on it some more, I concluded that if it was true, you would tell me in your own time."

"And all this was in your mind without my knowing. You came to me every day and we went about together and you never raised the matter. How kind you are, William." Belle was queasy with relief; she squeezed his arm where her hand lay. He had known but he did not see fit to pry.

"Nothing matters to me but that I have you, Belle. Nothing at all."

She pressed on. "I wish to tell you everything, William, the whole truth of it, though it's hard for me to talk of it. May I speak more?" He nodded. "The father of my child is a Mr. Weston, an American. He always gave the impression we would marry, or so I thought." Belle rubbed a finger across her forehead. "But that was not to be. He also led me to believe that he was a baron." She shook her head. "Weston said and did many things. His relationship with the truth was a perilous one."

"I see." William nodded.

"By the time I realized I was enceinte it was too late to fix the situation. I was naïve, William."

"It must have been a terrible time for you, Belle."

"It was but Wertheimer was extraordinarily kind to me, and Flo and Seymour, of course. They all looked after me well."

"Wertheimer's a good chap, to be sure." William poked at his quiff, his eyes distant, it seemed to Belle. "And where is your boy now?"

"In Sussex with a wet nurse. A sturdy young mother. I fostered him out because, of course, a child is incompatible with the life of an actress."

"And is he content?"

"Yes. He's part of a family in Heathfield and they do well by him. He grows stouter by the day." She gave a wan smile, thinking back to the baby show bouncers.

"And the child's father, this Weston, where is he?"

Belle watched a swan perform a serene glissade across the water. "He's in Lewes Jail, William. For fraud. He attempted to negotiate forged bonds; I don't know the exact details except that he was caught. He had already stolen checks from me."

"Oh, Belle, I am sorry. The man is a blackguard, clearly." William shook his head. "Abominable fellow."

"For a time I wanted to believe there was some decency in the man. But when I told him I was with child, he revealed just how coarse his nature was and I withdrew from him."

William was silent again. Was each new revelation pushing him farther from her? He was saying the right things, but Belle could sense a crack in William's warmth; he appeared to be mired in his own thoughts and this distance—so unlike him—made her nervous.

"Shall we sit for a moment?" she asked.

William guided her to one of the benches that overlooked the lake. "You've suffered, Belle."

"I have, William. I didn't know if I should tell you or not, but I wanted everything to be straight between us."

He turned to her. "It's better that you told me. You've been through an ordeal. Do you wish to move the boy out of Sussex to a baby nursery in town? I believe children are treated ever so well in these places. They're as happy as nestlings in them, it's said."

"Could that be so? I think of nurseries as farms, the babes no better off than penned-in swine. No, baby Isidor does well where he is. He has good air, a ready-made family."

"You named him Isidor? Ah, I see." William flicked his hand over his hair, then settled it again. "I suppose you're right, Belle, about the nurseries. They only offer day care. Where would the boy go at night?"

Belle laid her head on William's shoulder and watched a second swan skim across the water to its mate. No matter if William was quiet now and thoughtful; she had made a large disclosure and he would need time to think about it. In the meantime she would stay close to him so that he would not forget that she was still herself, despite her history. She leaned into William, glad of his bulk, of the soft core it concealed. It was his way to be pensive; he could not *be* any other way. She watched the swans dunk their heads and circle each other; the bigger one climbed onto the other bird's back for a moment, then slid off and they waltzed together, rubbing necks. Belle lifted her head to William, turned and put her arms around him.

"Thank you, William," she said, "for listening to me. You have a compassionate heart and I truly thank you."

He slid his arms around her and kissed the tip of her nose. "It cannot have been easy for you to tell me about your boy. So it is I who thank you, Belle."

They turned back to the Serpentine and sat on in silence. Belle tried to let the green waters soothe her again; but the divulgement to William had disordered her and she guessed that, despite his kindness, William's mind was alight with concerns, too.

A Proposal

Belle sipped a glass of Madeira, savoring its burned sugar and hazel-
nut heat, and watched the Corinthian's door. William came through
it at last, though she was alarmed to see him stumble as he crossed the
floor with Wood and Osborn in tow. Belle did not care much for these
two friends of William's. Like most of the club's regulars, Wood and
Osborn often paid court to Belle and tried to make themselves pets of
hers. But Belle chose her companions because they stirred something in
her. A certain flip of the heart, coupled with admiration, drew her to the
men she called her closest friends: Bassano and his talent as a photographer; dear, benevolent Wertheimer; William and his youthful openness
and splendid devotion. Wood and Osborn, though highborn and handsome both, did not disorder Belle's heart. She watched them now, grabbing and guffawing, as they made a joke of keeping William erect. He
was clearly drunk.

"Isabel, Belle, Isabel, Belle," William called. He was wedged now between Wood and Osborn and the trio were clearly holding one another up
with some difficulty as they stop-started across the floor. All three were
squiffed, not just William.

"Come and sit, William. Don't call out like a crow."

He sat hard, obviously ginned up to the gills; his eyes were bloodshot marbles rolling in their sockets. Wood and Osborn grinned and swayed like two old sots.

"Dunlo's been shooting the cat all over the lavatory floor," Wood said. "Left quite a mayhem on the tiles, didn't you, Willie?"

"Did you call Mr. Hollingshead to get it cleaned up?" Belle asked. "Someone might slip." Wood shrugged. He and Osborn were prankish fellows and William seemed to follow them into scrapes when he would be better off not to. William swiped at his mouth, and Belle looked at his wavering body as he attempted to keep himself upright. "You're in a sorry state, William, my love."

"I'm all right, Belle. Better out than in. But, yes, we have been indulging." He passed his sleeve over his lips and set his shoulders straighter. "My dear one, you'll never guess, but we've been playing lanterloo and I won. I'm in my cups, to be sure but, still, *I* emerged triumphant." William pawed at her skirt and tried to focus on her face. "I'm the winner, Belle, don't you see?"

"It was Irish loo, Miss Bilton," Wood said, "three cards instead of five, can you believe it? It made for the damnedest game." He paused as if transported. "Truly the damnedest. Oh, but excuse my language." He looked at Belle, his eyes wayward with drink, and she felt a pluck of irritation.

"Is it any wonder our Hibernian friend was victorious?" said Osborn. "He's a crafty Irish bugger."

"Manners, Osborn," said William, belching into his handkerchief.

"Dunlo pulled the jack of spades," Wood said, "before we knew what was what."

"Yes, we were very swiftly looed," said Osborn. "You've won a husband, Miss Bilton, thanks to a game of lanterloo!" He sniggered and looked between Wood and William.

"I beg your pardon, Mr. Osborn?" Belle looked from him to William, whose chin was hovering over his chest. She put her hand under it and raised his eyes to meet hers. "William, what is this? Was I the prize in some silly card game?"

He held up a finger. "It doesn't sound proper when you say it like that, Belle—it sounds a little harum-scarum, I suppose." He closed his eyes as if to think but blinked them open quickly and went on. "But, yes, yes, I won you! I won your hand. I wish to be steadfast and true, just as you want. Oh, you are a honeyed creature." He moved forward to kiss her, but Belle stood and William slithered to the floor. Wood and Osborn left him there and stared instead at Belle.

"Good night, gentlemen," she said, turned her back to them and walked away.

Belle's skin tingled with exasperation as she crossed the floor. Really, William needed to act like a man if he wished to be considered one. Why was he turning up royally drunk to meet her? How were they to talk about anything when he was potted on gin? Wood and Osborn provoked such foolery in him—they had William soused up and gambling like some gutter groveler. Did they forget who he was? Who they were? Why did he have to partake in their capers? And had he really bet for her hand? Belle shook her head in annoyance. She saw Wertheimer entering the club.

"Isidor," she called, "can you take me to some other place? Do you mind awfully?"

He held out his arm and she took it in relief. "Of course, Belle. I should be delighted. Where will we go?"

Osborn's voice blasted across the club, "I'd bet my buttons young Wertheimer is a back scuttler."

Belle did not turn to see if Osborn had directed the comment at her; she did not want to think he could be so unconscionably rude. And she did not want to look at William again when he insisted on acting like such a damned child.

A REALIZATION

The Café Royal grill room kept late hours. Its gilt-and-mirrors excess comforted Belle, for she could see that, although she was upset, she still looked well. She smoothed her hair, adjusting the beaded headband that sat behind her fringe. She looked at the garlanded ladies who held up the ceiling, at their luminous bare torsos and bowed heads. How acquiescent they seemed, how still and stoic in the labor of holding up the burden of all that gold. She wished Flo were around, to thrash out William's silliness with her, but her sister was dedicated to irritating Seymour these days by spending her nights flitting from club to club in a giddy posse of girls. And he, poor man, either followed her or sulked at home.

Wertheimer pulled out a chair for Belle and she sat. "Thank you, Isidor," she said.

"You so rarely call me by my first name anymore." Wertheimer sat down opposite her.

"I know it, my dear." She thought of telling him that she had been to Sara's to see her son. But baby Isidor provoked an unwelcome guilt in her and that made it burdensome to talk about him. She toyed with the menu and wondered if she might manage a morsel.

"How has it been, Belle, sharing such close-quarter lodgings with your sister again?"

"The sooner Flo goes back to her husband, the better for everyone. She went to the Pelican tonight with the chorus girls. She and I are beginning to grind each other to dust."

"Will she go back to Seymour?"

"Of course. He's as dull as she's sharp—they're the perfect pair. They love to squabble but their read and writes last a few weeks then they coo like doves once more."

"And you're left in peace."

"Well, something like that. I do miss her when she's not around though."

"And I miss *you*. How long has it been since we suppered à deux?"

"I'm an inattentive friend, Isidor, I'm so sorry." Belle pouted. "William occupies my time rather."

Wertheimer studied the menu. "I fancy deviled kidneys."

"Breakfast at midnight." Belle smiled. "Is it any wonder you are so dear to me, Isidor?"

"Spicy kidneys for two, then?"

"Yes, and a drop of port."

Wertheimer called the waiter and placed their order.

"Have you been reading 'Tempted London,' Belle?"

"No."

"You would positively roar with laughter. Some rigid toff was sent to a music hall to report on proceedings; he was shocked by the gallery folk as much as the acts. He said of the songs: 'When not absolutely indelicate, they are inane. When not vulgar, they are without feature of any kind.' Or words to that effect. Isn't that an uproar?" Wertheimer laughed but Belle only smiled.

"He speaks the truth, to be sure."

"You're not tiring of the music hall, surely?"

"I may be tiring of my whole life, Isidor." Belle knew she sounded dramatic, but everything was atumble. "William seems to veer between manly sincerity and juvenile absurdity. I'm not sure how I'm supposed to take him seriously. When does life follow a glassy-smooth path, Isidor? When does one know that one is on the *right* path?"

"Now I see. Dunlo. But, come, you have a jolly time, don't you?"

"I do, but I seem to have so many strands to keep straight and everything gets tangled. I told William about Baby, you know, and since then we've barely had a proper conversation. I don't know what he's thinking, truly."

"Ah. Revelations affect men in odd ways, Belle. Be patient."

"I shall have to be, I suppose."

The food arrived and Belle cut a kidney and popped it into her mouth. She considered not eating and, instead, letting the port ooze through her to make her relax and stop her troubles fouling her thoughts. Her cares encompassed William's silly actions and her capricious feelings about baby Isidor. And then there was the immovable Flo, beloved but ever present.

Once the tang of Worcestershire sauce hit her tongue, Belle realized she was hungry. She called for more bread to dredge up the sauce and barely lifted her eyes to Wertheimer while she ate. When her plate was as clean as the moon, Belle sat back, reached for her glass and drank a good gulp of port.

Wertheimer looked at her. "I would say *bon appétit*, but you appear to be finished."

Belle giggled. "I did not dine once today. Silly as it seems, I quite forgot to eat."

"I have raised a smile, at least. At last. Now, take a deep breath and tell me, what is the matter between you and the viscount? Is Dunlo acting the complete fool?"

Belle sipped her port, letting it warm her. She leaned forward and spoke quietly. "Yes and no."

"Is his interest waning?"

Belle wondered if there was a note of hope in Wertheimer's question. "On the contrary. William's as fervent as he ever was."

"Have you talked of marriage?"

"William talks of little else. It's all 'When we are wed, this' and 'When you are my wife, that' and 'You will adore Ireland once you grow accustomed to it.' I haven't thought that he was altogether serious. Well, I haven't allowed myself to think he might be, I suppose."

"Goodness. I hadn't realized you two were so far along. And so soon. I knew you regarded him highly, of course but . . ." Wertheimer paused. "What of Dunlo's family?"

"He assures me he can deal with them. He is tight with his mama."

Wertheimer lifted his port and drank. "Do you love him, Belle?"

"I do, I think. I mean, yes, I do love him. It's hard to explain."

"Love always is."

"Something about him turns my heart upside down and I don't quite know myself when I'm around him. Though he can be mightily childish at times. But, you see, he's good and steady, too." She sipped her drink and thought a moment. "I feel safe with him, but, at the same time, he makes me skittish as a colt. I don't seem to know what I comprehend when he is near; I hardly feel like *me*."

Wertheimer leaned forward and put his hand to Belle's cheek. "You do love him, my dear. You've just said it."

She looked at her friend. This *was* the effect William had on her, a topsy-turviness, and, in the end, a heated regard, a feeling of needing to be always near him, of desiring him in a needy, ravenous way.

"Yes. I think you're right, Isidor. I do love William. I love him well." She paused. "He made me a ludicrous proposal this evening. He was drunk and treated it as sport." She frowned. "He won my hand in a game of lanterloo he played with Wood and Osborn."

Wertheimer smiled. "Dunlo's original, I'll say that. So, what's to be done?"

Belle thought for a moment. William was drunk and irresponsible tonight, but she knew there was sincerity behind his shenanigans. "Well, game or no game, I believe I shall marry him."

"Brava!" Wertheimer held up his glass. "And he will make an uxorious husband—foolishly doting upon you until the day one or other of you expires. That much is clear."

"If he can only free himself from the chains of his father, he will." In truth Belle knew William had to both extricate himself from—and bond himself to—the earl if he was to inherit anything.

Wertheimer held his glass aloft. "To marriage!" he said. "To Viscount Dunlo and Miss Belle Bilton!"

Belle clinked her glass to his. "To love."

Belle stood in the wings, listening to the introduction for Mr. Tusso and his dummy. These matinee performances tired her; she felt she was only in bed, then out of it again and she had not slept well. William was no doubt still abed, sleeping off his excesses. The chairman banged his hammer and launched into his customary mellifluous oration:

"Vitally virtual variations vary valuably, vying venerably with vocalization! Ladies and gentlemen, I present to you, the world's finest ventriloquist: Miiiiiister Fred Tusso and his crafty companion, Coster Joe!"

Belle listened to the chairman go on; her corset pinched at her ribs and she tugged at it in irritation. Men always got a bigger to-do than girls, but these introductions were too much—since when had puppet masters become so popular? The crowd clapped, bellowed and stamped until Mr. Tusso settled himself onto his stool and stared them into silence; he wore a suit of amber fustian and his companion its match. The spotlight dazzled and, in its beam, dust motes descended slowly like new snowfall. Mr. Tusso conversed with Joe who sat on his lap and afterward, with the help of Mrs. Tusso, he made a whole army of dummies speak to one another.

Belle found she couldn't laugh; she longed for the act to be finished so she and Flo could get onstage, and off again, as quickly as possible. She was distracted and wanted leisure to sit and think about William's bid for her hand, about her future. Nay, it had not been a romantic proposal—in fact it had been a ridiculous one—but it was *meant*; he talked so often and so surely of them as a married pair. What matter that it was decided by lanterloo? But did William do it like that because he was upended by the news of baby Isidor? Was that why he proposed in such a silly way? But, now, had she not come to London for colorful experiences? Had she not come to meet a good man? Belle stretched her arms over her head and extended each leg in turn. Yes, it was more than possible that she would be wed before long. But William would have to do better than some drunken offer, badly executed.

More applause and soon came the cry: "And now, the dainty dames you have been waiting for all afternoon, please be upstanding, please applaud your loudest for the bountifully beautiful, the amorously artful, the one, the only, Sisters Biltonnnnn!"

Belle patched on a smile and flounced center stage, meeting Flo there. The piano in the pit struck up "My Wild Irish Rose" and the sisters linked arms and sang:

> *"My wild Irish Rose, the sweetest flower that grows.*
> *You may search everywhere, but none can compare*
> *With my wild Irish Rose."*

The audience applauded madly, then settled to listen. Belle warmed a little to their goodwill and strengthened her singing. After another verse, she waved her arm for them to join in, which they did with heart. But the clangor of the piano tried her ears and the smell of turning fruit and porter assailed her nose. Sometimes, when her mind was occupied with the bigger parts of life, she wondered at all this prancing for squawking children and drunk men. Many of the adults were more intent on their pipes, biscuits and pewter pots than the stage, and the youngsters preferred Tusso's dummy to everything else. All the while she sashayed and sweated while the footlights scalded her eyes. She loved to perform, to be sure, but day after night could be wearying. Would she need to do this much longer? Might there not be an easier life ahead?

The next part of their act was a tap dance and Belle hoped Flo had rehearsed her steps. When she and Seymour were in the thick of one of their bust-ups, Flo's head seemed to drain of everything she knew. The pianist started the tune, and Flo stepped the wrong way so that Belle had to maneuver to the other side and guide Flo back to where she was meant to be. Meanwhile Belle buck-and-winged, faced the audience and kept up her smile. She could hear that her taps and Flo's were not falling together and she silently cursed her sister and her absent husband. When Flo once again crossed to the left instead of the right, Belle grabbed her by the waist and shoved her into the correct spot.

"Go back to bloody Seymour," she hissed. "You're making a botch of this."

"Let go of me," Flo said, and wriggled away from Belle, glossing over a series of steps in an uncomplicated shuffle.

"Follow me *now*," Belle said, but Flo was elsewhere and Belle could only cover up for her by staying out in front and throwing herself into the dance with vigor.

At the end of the routine, while the audience yelped for more, Belle tried to catch Flo's eye, but her sister would not look over.

"Let me alone, Belle," she whispered.

The applause subsided and the audience waited.

Belle stepped forward. "We will leave you with our favorite song," she said, "the one set at the forge, which I daresay you know. Join in with us, please do!"

The crowd roared its appreciation and the sisters began:

"A lusty young smith at his vise stood a filing,
His hammer laid by but his forge still aglow,
When to him a buxom young damsel came smiling
and asked if to work at her forge he would go.
With a jingle bang, jingle bang, jingle bang, jingle,
With a jingle bang, jingle bang, jingle, hi ho!"

A Consolidation

William whimpered. The words "lanterloo" and "proposal" pinged inside his head like breaking billiard balls. He was tossed across his Burlington Hotel bed, still dressed, and a spit pool dampened his cheek. He hauled himself up and went to his washstand to perform his ablutions. His blood must surely be half gin today; he could feel its sour stride through his veins. The mirror spoke its own tale: his eyes were puffy and his hair sprung this way and that in an unruly show. He tried to subdue strands, but they were recalcitrant.

"Damn it to hell," he said, poked some more, then left his hair to flop about in any stupid fashion.

William went to the window; it was unbearably bright. He had not closed the shutters and he scrunched his eyes against the light and his pounding head. He had gotten drunk, he knew, not just because Wood and Osborn were debauchees who loved to divert him, but because of what Belle had told him. It didn't change his love for her, but the news of her boy had disarranged him. She was more experienced than he, vastly more of the world; Belle had lived already and knew what it was to bear a child. She had loved before, even if it had all gone sour with the chap, that shameful fellow. But Belle knew things about men and women that he was only now learning.

And then, of course, there was Papa. Papa would not be happy and that would mean strife. William shook his father from his mind and concentrated again on Belle. So she was practiced in the arts of love. Wasn't that a good thing? Didn't it meant that they would bond rapidly once married? And wasn't she utterly delightful in all ways, a woman of grace and beauty? Belle pleased William in places that he did not know could be pleased. The violence of his hangover swarmed through his brain; William rubbed his temples with force and let out a moan. "Aaahhhh."

He must go to Belle. She was no doubt furious with him and rightly so. She would be sleeping, though. Late to lie and up with the lark did not mix well. Or perhaps she had slept badly, because he had upset her? He hoped not; it pained him to think he might cause an unruly night for her. William scratched his head, pulled once again at his hair and tried to cut through the suet all the alcohol had made of him, mind and body. He must let Belle slumber, she needed her rest; later he would see her and make amends. William then remembered a promise to take luncheon with Osborn, so he dressed in haste and made his way to Verrey's.

A h, Dunlo. The condemned man has arisen!" Osborn grinned and waved his knife to beckon his friend forward. For a gentleman, Osborn had beggarly manners. "The haddock is glorious!"

William crossed the room, sat opposite Osborn and wished he had not come. He should have gone to Belle, no matter if he had to make her landlady wake her. He watched his friend shovel food into his mouth and longed for transportation at the hands of some higher power, back to yesterday afternoon. Back to the time before he had played lanterloo. Before he managed to get so vigorously drunk that he embarrassed Belle. If only some nifty Gabriel might appear and spirit him up into the sky, up through time to the hours before he, Wood and Osborn had begun their spree. Oh why was he always so easily lured into actions he later regretted? William sighed. The damask tablecloth glared into his face; the silver, too, had an aggressive glisten. He rubbed his eyes, felt his guilt smother him like a vine.

"Are you all right, Dunlo?"

"It's only that everything is so uncommonly bright today," William murmured, lifting the menu which had a pristine white cover.

Osborn stopped sawing at his food. "Have we a big head this morning, eh? A touch of delirium tremens perhaps?" He chuckled, mock-trembled his hands and recommenced his attack on the fish. "Suck a peppermint or two, Dunlo, it always works for me!"

"I need more than peppermints, Osborn."

William perused the menu and ordered poached eggs. When they arrived, the yolks were so pinkly perfect on top that he almost wept. Hangovers always made him maudlin and the sight of such magnificent eggs stirred him and, therefore, the swirl of remorse inside him rose higher. William agitated his fork and did not eat. How he regretted the fervor of his drinking; how deeply he regretted his idiotic proposal to Belle. How he wished his devotion hadn't wavered, even if only briefly. If he had remained resolutely loyal to her he wouldn't have gotten soused and he wouldn't have played lanterloo. William pushed away his plate and stood.

"What ho, Dunlo?" Osborn blinked as if emerging from a stupor. "Where are you off to, man?"

"Good day, Osborn. I have business to attend to."

Belle's landlady looked at William as if he had crawled from a thieves' den when he asked to see Belle.

"Miss Bilton is sleeping, I fancy. She's a young lady what works ever so 'ard, ever so much. Why, she's already done one performance today and is returned to 'er room for relaxation." She squinted at him. "I do not know that she wishes to be disturbed."

William should have remembered that Belle had a matinee. The land-lady was right: Belle did work uncommonly hard. But he wanted urgently to see her, to set things to rights.

"Might you tell Miss Bilton that Viscount Dunlo is below and wishes to speak to her?"

The woman sparked on hearing his name. "I most certainly will, sir. Step inside, sir. Come into my parlor, Lord Dunlo."

"That's quite all right, madam. I thank you, but I shall wait here."

"As you please, your lordship." The landlady bobbed a curtsey and disappeared up the stairwell, roaring Belle's name, lusty as a street crier.

William lit a cigarette and smoked it quickly; he stalked up and down the footpath, welcoming the harsh powder of the smoke in his lungs. He rubbed his vesta mermaid with his thumb and watched carriages clip up and down Conduit Street. On a normal day he would assess horse withers and guess horse heights, but all he was capable of now was regurgitating his remorse to chew on. He waited what seemed an uncommonly long time for Belle but took that interval as part of his punishment. She looked pensive when she opened the door, came outside and closed it.

"Belle." William offered her his arm and was relieved when she took it.

"Shall we step into the Seven Stars?" Belle said and William nodded.

There were a few quiet drinkers inside the public house, nursing their pots of ale and nips of cream gin. Belle went straight to the bar to inspect the edibles.

"Tea and Banbury cakes for two, landlord, if you please," she said.

William followed her to a corner and waited while she sat. "I want to apologize, Belle, for last night's antics."

"And so you might, William."

The barman brought a tray and poured the tea. Belle and William both reached for a cake at the same time, snapped back their colliding hands, then lifted cakes and held them without eating. Belle broke hers into bite-size pieces and William imagined licking the spicy fruit from her fingers and the look that that might bring to her face. He shook his head and gathered himself.

"Belle, I made an idiot of myself last night, but here is what you should know: I do mean to marry you."

"And you suggest that by playing cards to win my hand? By having some foolish game with your hoity-toity friends with me as the agreed prize?"

"It was very badly done, Belle. I know that now and I'm sorry. I rather lose my head when I drink too much, and Wood and Osborn, well, they like mischief of every kind."

"And they rather seem to enjoy making a fool of you."

William flinched; he was stung but only because she was right. "Yes, they often make a fool of me and it's not a difficult task." He watched Belle pop a piece of Banbury cake into her mouth and chew; she wouldn't look at him. "When you told me about your boy, I became fuddled. I wondered why you would want to be with me, so inexperienced, so callow. I may have lingered, too, on what it might mean. On what others might think."

Belle looked at him full face. "And now, William? Are you worried now for your reputation, or about mine?"

"Not in the least. I made an ass of myself and it was brattish. I have thought nothing of you and your feelings and only of my own. You are a wonder to me, Belle."

She allowed him the glimpse of a smile. "William," she said, and put her gloved hand over his. "Little Isidor is well taken care of; he is happy. His birth, and all that went with it, is something that happened to me, but I have dealt with it. It shouldn't make a difference to us. Life goes on."

"Darling, you have such strength. Can we put my foolishness behind us and make our plans now?" William leaned closer. "You know I'm insanely in love with you and I *will* make you my wife, if I have to kidnap you to do it. I long to marry you."

Belle looked into his eyes. "I would go willingly to any altar with you, William, you know that."

"And I with you." William pushed the table aside and fell to one knee. The scrape of the legs on the floor made heads turn. "Belle Bilton, will you do me the honor of becoming my wife?" He took her hands in his and smiled to see her cheeks flush.

"Yes, William Le Poer Trench, yes, I will."

A pair of gin swiggers raised their glasses to each other and clinked them, then held them up to Belle and William. Belle giggled and nodded her gratitude to the two old women, and William took the opportunity to press his lips to her cheek.

"Thank you," he whispered into her ear and sat in beside her.

Belle laughed. "When shall we marry, then?"

"Right away!" William said.

"What will your papa say? Your mama?"

"What care I for what they will say?" William lowered his voice. "We may only know each other a few short weeks, Belle, but this is what we both want, we know it is. Let's just run off and do it."

"To Gretna Green?"

"No, we'll do it here. London's our home. It doesn't take long to get a marriage license. We could be wed by mid-July."

Belle giggled. "Married by mid-July?" She nodded. "All right, William. All right, my love. Let's do it!"

A Ceremony

Belle wore her cherry-print dress; its oyster silk was the nearest she had to white. Flo traveled with her to the Hampstead Registry Office. Belle looked out the window of the hansom at the passing buildings. The bricks shimmered in the morning sun and there even seemed to be a glow coming off the costermongers and shoeblacks, the joes selling violets and roses, and the bowler hat brigade, going about their mornings. This was the most significant day of her life—her wedding day at last—and yet London dandered on as if nothing were new; only the glimmer of the early sunshine made something vivid of the city. What would Mother think, to see her now? And Father? Violet would be annoyed at missing the fun, that was certain, but it couldn't be helped. It was better to do it this way; a clandestine marriage could not be argued against by anyone. When it was done, it was done. And hadn't Flo done the same? The Sisters Bilton were not of Hampshire now; they preferred to do things their own way. How giddying it was to be covert, to pledge her love to William unobserved by the world; it was a spicy secret that they carried up until this day.

Their cabman drove as slow as treacle and Flo roared up at him, "Get a move on!"

"William will think I'm not coming," Belle said.

"The bride is always late. Don't fret, dearie."

When Belle saw William outside the registry, his top hat in his hand and his gloves on, she thought how raw he looked—how like a fledgling. His face was open and startled, as if he had woken suddenly and found himself in a place he did not mean to be. Was he about to spread his wings and fly? Had he decided this elopement was absolutely the wrong thing after all? Her heart hammered in her chest and she gasped; Flo took her hand to soothe her. William's friend Wood idled beside him, smoking a cheroot and drinking coffee purchased from a stall, as if he was about to embark on any old mundane day.

Belle turned to Flo, pulled at her fringe and shifted the pearls that nested in her hair. "How do I look?"

"You're as beautiful as ever. More so. That dress is very becoming." Flo put her hands to Belle's waist. "So neat."

"My waist is not at all neat, after, you know, after Baby stretched it." She ballooned her arms outward.

"Pishposh! You are the most shapely, beautiful woman in London. Everyone knows it, including your viscount." Flo squeezed her hand. "And Wednesday is the luckiest day to marry." Flo recited:

"Marry Monday for wealth,
Tuesday for health,
Wednesday the best day of all,
Thursday for crosses,
Friday for losses,
and Saturday no day at all."

"You see! Silly Seymour and I chose a Saturday—is it any wonder we spat like monkeys? For you, dear sister, all will be well."

Belle thanked Flo and looked again at William while the hansom pulled up to the footpath. William's face became hopeful—joyous—when he realized it was Belle arriving and relief sluiced through her body.

William helped Flo out of the cab, then offered his hand to Belle. He had removed his glove, so Belle took off hers, too, and his grip was warm and steady.

"You look wonderful, my darling."

"Thank you, William," Belle said, dipping her head.

"I have something for you." He took a small box from his pocket and handed it to her. Belle tripped the clasp to find a gold heart on a chain. "*My* heart," William said.

Belle handed it to him, turned her back, and he took it from its velvet cushion and fastened it around her neck. She lifted the cold heart so that it sat above her cleavage and she felt it warm up against her skin. Flo pressed a posy of red and white roses into Belle's hands and William put on his topper. The early sun beamed down on the four of them as they entered the registry office.

The registrar had a distant air; he seemed to Belle to look through her when he spoke and he said the required words in haste, as if he had an urgent need to be elsewhere. Still, he could not dim her happiness: her heart was swollen to the point of eruption and she could not stop her eyes from lingering on William's face. She wanted most of all to laugh with the joy that coursed through her, but she kept her head and said what was required, glad of the heat of William's hand tight around hers.

William smiled and repeated the sentences the registrar offered him. "I do solemnly declare, that I know not of any lawful impediment why I, William, may not be joined in matrimony to thee, Isabel." He produced the tiny gold band they had bought together and slipped it on her finger. "Receive this ring as a token of wedded love and faith."

Belle gazed at William when she said the words: "I, Isabel, take thee,

William, to be my husband, to have and to hold from this day forward, for better, for worse, for richer, for poorer, in sickness and in health, to love and to cherish, till death do us part, and thereto I pledge thee my faith."

Belle looked at her ring, so alien but so cherished. She twirled it with her thumb and glanced at it over and over while the registrar finished the ceremony.

"By the power vested in me, I now pronounce you man and wife." The man gave a small grimace that Belle supposed was an attempted smile. He stood staring at them and eventually nodded sharply, and said, "Yes." He flapped his hand between them.

"Oh," William said, and he gathered Belle into his arms and kissed her. She pressed her body close to his and let the warmth of his mouth linger.

"Bravo!" called Wood.

"Many congratulations, darlings," said Flo, putting her hand to Belle's back.

Belle and William broke apart but still held each other, mesmerized by the wonder to be found in each other. Belle's eyes looked liquid, William thought, almost as if she might cry, but he knew it was happiness that caused the shine; it radiated from her.

The registrar cleared his throat. "Mr. and Mrs. Le Poer Trench, please to follow me."

In a dimly lit back parlor, Belle signed the marriage certificate and wrote "spinster" and "actress" in the appropriate places. William took the pen and wrote their ages; he put "under age" for himself and "full" for her. The registrar, noting this, raised an eyebrow but said nothing.

When they joined the others, Wood slapped William on the shoulder. "Capital, Dunlo." He shook his friend's hand with such vigor that William cried out and they both laughed. "Now," Wood said, "shall we eat?"

Flo slipped her arm around Belle and they walked ahead. "You're Lady Dunlo now," she whispered and the two touched foreheads and giggled.

William stood for a moment and watched Belle move before him, the sway of her body beneath the cherry-specked gown, the upsweep of her hair that showed the pale curve of her neck. She deserved a dress of French lace, an aisle, a veil, a minister—the whole ball of wax that a church wedding meant. He hoped that in Ireland they would ascend his beloved Church Hill and in Saint John's he would give her just that. And Ballinasloe would be their honeymoon, their home, their life. He rubbed the fob of his watch that held the wording of the family motto: *"Dieu pour la Tranche qui Contre?* If God is for Trench, who shall be against?" God would see that Belle got the pomp and ceremony of the kind of wedding she deserved.

"Wait for me!" William called, and he followed the others out into the warmth of the July morning.

The wedding breakfast was a feast of stewed oysters, thick slices of chicken galantine, moist almond cake and sculpted ice cream. William had reserved a bijoux parlor in the equally tiny Victoria Hotel, but a rook's roar from the registry office.

They were a party of two halves: Flo and Wood were as merry as grigs. They drank champagne like lemonade and were soon spatting about everything from the Sudan Campaign (Wood: "We *deserve* Egypt") to bare-knuckle fighting (Flo: "Those men are lions. Heroes!"). Belle and William, though warmly content, were more subdued; they sat side by side in a complexity of bliss and contrition.

"Will your parents be terribly cross with you?" Belle said. She hadn't wanted to ask, in case William's answer sullied these moments, but her concerns had grown; and, now that the deed was irreversible, she was concerned for William, for his dealings with his parents. She put her hand on his knee and he placed his fingers over hers.

"I imagine they will be aggrieved, yes. Mama will accede, though. Eventually. Papa? Well, Papa is himself; he has his own mind about everything. But don't worry, Belle, things will be set to rights." He brushed his hand across her cheek. "How will Mr. and Mrs. Bilton take the news, do you suppose?"

"My father will be ecstatic." She smiled at her freshly minted husband, imagining her father's enthusiasm for the match. He would congratulate her—"Well done, my girl, well played!"—thinking of how Belle's position and comfort would be advanced by the marriage. Like most people, he very much approved of fine living and large inheritances. "My mother is not as easily pleased. About anything."

William put his arm around Belle. "I'm sorry we won't have a tour, my love."

"That's quite all right, William. The Empire would never spare me in high summer—we knew that already. We will have a holiday later." Until William could sort things out with the earl, secure his future, Belle would continue to work and earn for both of them. She looked across at her sister and Wood, wondered if they weren't flirting. "I do wish we could have had a larger party," she murmured. "Seymour would keep Flo in check and Wertheimer would be a comfort to me."

"You need Wertheimer no more, darling. I'm your comfort now, I'll look after you."

"Flo, will Seymour be joining us later?" Belle called across the table.

Flo looked at Belle. "His office won't spare him. Perhaps we'll see him tonight." She turned back to Wood who was enthusing about boxing gloves.

"They make the fighting more strategic," he said.

"What a load of cobbler's awls. How can a pair of bloated mittens change anything?"

Belle angled her body away from Flo and Wood and looked up into William's face. He seemed older to her suddenly, capable and in command. Could he have matured in a matter of a few hours?

"I hope we will have a church ceremony when we go to Ireland, darling," he said. "Saint John's in Ballinasloe sits atop a slope, overlooking the town—the hill of Knockadoon, they call it. You'll like Ireland. Galway is such a green and lovely place; a little wild, a little cultivated. The locals are very native but they warm up to new people. Eventually."

"Where would we stay, William? Your parents may not want me to stay at Garbally, despite the fact that we're married."

"Leave Papa and Mama to me. They *will* come around when they see how much I love you. Grandmama has a dower house in Loughrea; she rarely leaves London, so we might go there for a spell. I want to show you Galway. And let everyone see my wife."

Belle squeezed his hand and kept her doubts to herself; the Clancartys might not reside much in Ireland anymore, but they would not want Belle there, staining their name. The older generations wished everything to stay as it had been. But perhaps she and William might alter their thinking? Perhaps, when they saw how truly they loved each other, they might come round? They were married now, despite all, and no one could tear that asunder. How brave and wonderful William was to throw off the shackles of his birth and marry for love. Was he not the most courageous man? Belle's mind slithered over and around their situation, but she shook herself out of it—she did not want to fret; today was the happiest of days.

Belle lifted her glass and sipped her champagne; it had lost its froth and tasted sharp. She wished she had brought her flask—a swig of blue ruin would surely see her straight and stop her rattling thoughts. A sudden yelp from her sister bounced Belle out of her reverie, back to the wedding celebration.

"Hold your quail pipe, Wood," Flo was saying, "I've heard quite enough from you." She scissored the air in front of Wood's face as if she meant to cut out his tongue. He dodged and giggled and Belle waited for them to collapse into each other's arms, such was the intimacy of their sparring.

"You might not have any more champagne, Flo. We have to perform tonight and you know what happens when you get squiffy. You forget the words, not to mention the steps."

"Don't be such a gloom pot, Belle. And on your wedding day! You'll give everyone the morbs." Flo waved toward the window. "Look, you got the Queen's weather, you got the man, what else do you need? Let *me* have *my* fun." Flo swayed and blinked, looking first at Belle, then at Wood who, though equally drunk, appeared to sober up smartly.

"Let me order coffee," he said and, rising from the table, he tripped off to find a waiter.

Belle took William's hand in hers and kissed it. Her stomach jumped at the thought of holding him to her later. She anticipated that he would be a tender lover—his kisses were so—and she longed for the moment when they would yield to each other.

"It seems ghastly unfair that you ladies have to go to the Empire tonight of all nights," William said.

"We knew it would be this way, William."

"A girl has to earn her crust," Flo said. Deflated now that the party was over, she picked petals off the wedding roses until Belle lifted the posy out of her sister's reach.

William twisted the gold band on Belle's finger. "We have tonight, here in the Victoria," he said. "And the next few nights, too."

"That we have," Belle said, anticipating again the heat of his long body against hers.

"Oh, lord," Flo said, throwing her eyes ceilingward.

Wood bustled in, a coffee-laden waiter behind him. When they each had a cup in hand, Wood raised his.

"A toast: here's to your coffins. May they be made of hundred-year-old oaks which we shall plant tomorrow. May you both live as long as you want, and never want as long as you live. May the best of your yesterdays be the worst of your tomorrows." He tilted his coffee cup higher. "To the bride and groom."

"To the gride and broom," Flo said, hoping that Belle would laugh. She did.

They clinked cups and swallowed and Belle realized that they had not made a toast with the champagne. The thought vexed her; she knew that toasting with empty glasses was unlucky. What of full coffee cups? She looked at William's radiant face as he sipped and soothed herself. It was as Flo had said: all would be well. For certain sure, all would be well.

A Union

Flo pulled Belle's cherry-print gown over her head and helped her into her costume, a vast concoction of Venice lace and furbelows that, in truth, looked more bridal than the dress she had just taken off. Flo's own wedding to Seymour had been tiny and swift, too, but she didn't mind that—she had never enjoyed fuss. But Belle, with her fairy-tale heart, surely deserved more than a registry office and to have to work on her wedding night.

"How are you, old girl?" Flo asked as she tugged at Belle's bodice to make it sit nicely. Belle smiled like a soused pilchard and pulled herself out of some reverie, making Flo laugh. "Ah, I don't think I have to worry, it's as if you're under a spell."

Belle blinked. "I feel charmed, Flo. Full up and fevered and content."

"What about tonight? Does it vex you to be here at the theater, to have to perform?"

"No, we knew it would be this way, William and I." Belle lifted her sleeve to examine the pearl clusters sewn onto it; she shook them and they clattered pleasantly. "I will work until he can negotiate taking over the estate in Galway from the earl." She pursed her lips, "Or until he inherits."

Flo's heart plummeted. "So you really do mean to leave England?"

"Eventually, yes. Until then I will perform and we will do nicely."

Flo propelled Belle to stand in front of the mirror, the better to fix her hair and have Belle approve of what she did. She stood behind her sister and gazed at her reflection.

"We've become modern women, Belle."

"Did it occur to anyone that Kate Penrice's daughters were capable of such a thing?"

Flo giggled, thinking of their mother's strong thumb and her attempts to instill what she saw as her own noble values in her girls. Her narrow codes. "Isn't it grand that we'll soon be ushered into the eighteen nineties? What fun!"

Belle leaped to her feet, put her hands to her hips and twisted her heels outward. "The knock-kneed nineties."

Flo cavorted like a pony. "The knees-up nineties."

The two sisters laughed and collapsed into each other's arms.

Flo smelled Belle's powdered cheek, breathed deep on her skin. "You're happy, dearest?"

"I am, Flo. Extraordinarily happy."

"Then we both are." Flo hugged Belle tight. Everything was changing again, but wasn't that just the way life unfurled, mysterious and unknowable, a glorious adventure? Belle and she were married ladies now; life must prance on in whatever way it would. Yes, she and Seymour squabbled, but it went to their bones and created a welcome sizzle between them. Seymour was a good stick and Flo loved him. She had not the dreamy-eyed match that Belle enjoyed with William, but her marriage was adequate. Seymour earned a steady wage and he doted on her; she could not hope for more. Flo shook herself and held Belle away from her, keeping her hands on her sister's hips. "Come, Lady Dunlo," she said, "your public is gasping for a taste of you." She shimmied her palms up and down Belle's waist. "Not to mention your viscount."

———

The audience were responsive that night and Belle loved them for it. Every twirl she executed, every flutter of her hand, drew murmurs of admiration. She was in good voice, too, and when she sang "Come into the Garden, Maud," she imagined herself as the girl going to William at the gate for a tryst, surrounded by lilies and roses. She sang to him, knowing he watched from the fauteuils below and, like her, was ripe with impatience for their bedroom in the Victoria Hotel.

Belle's admirers did not know that she was Lady Dunlo now, though she guessed they would apprehend the fact soon enough. The tattlers were efficient—gossip grew rapidly from acorn to oak in London, this she knew. But what did she care? William was her husband and she his wife; he loved her and she loved him; and tonight he would hold her as close as man can hold woman and she would revel in it.

Their bedroom in the Victoria Hotel was warm, this was the first thing that Belle noticed; despite the late hour of their arrival and the midsummer balm, the fire blazed and made a cozy nest of the room. There was a blue chaise longue beneath the window and the bed itself was a mahogany four-poster with ocher drapes. Someone—perhaps Flo—had arranged for her wedding posy to be placed in a vase, and Belle was pleased to see that the roses still looked reasonably fresh.

Belle sat on the chaise and removed her gloves and hat. William stood with his back to the closed door, his hands hanging awkwardly and an unnerved set to his face.

"Come sit by me, William." She put her palm to the velvet of the chaise longue and patted it.

William looked at her face, illuminated by the fire's flames and, for the hundredth time that day, could not believe that she was his. How could one so beautiful, so diverting, attach herself to him? His heart careened as if it meant to erupt from his body and find a calmer settle place. He observed Belle, her open, smiling face and his jitters waned— she was here, he was here. They had done it. He walked across the room, the Istanbul rug like a hectare of ground between them, and knelt before her.

"Belle," he said, "wasn't it smashing to say those vows today?"

She put her hands to his shoulders. "It was, William."

"We've waited long but we're in the old 'orse and carriage now."

Belle giggled at his attempt at a Cockney accent. "We're proper cut and carried," she said.

William leaned in and kissed her mouth. He loved the taste of her; she was sweet as barley sugar always. She flicked her tongue against his and his passion rose. William slipped his arms around Belle and pulled her tight to him; when the kiss ended, he whispered, "I love you, darling."

"I love you, too, William." Everything inside him soared. "Shall we lie down?" Belle said.

William leaned back and swept one arm under her skirt; she locked her hands around his neck and he carried her to the bed. Belle sat while he unlaced her bodice and helped her wriggle out of it. She pulled off her corset cover herself and when William saw the blush of the corset beneath, he groaned and trailed one finger up the row of hooks to the bow that sat between her breasts. He stopped to kiss her deeply, sliding his tongue around her mouth until it felt like he would liquefy. Belle turned over and offered him the back of her skirt; he unfastened it, pulled it off and tossed it to the chaise, where it landed in a billow of cherries. Belle whipped off her underskirt, and the sight of the snow-white petticoat beneath almost undid William, the pressure in his groin making him fizzle; he put his hands to the petticoat with reverence. They were both breathing shallowly now and, realizing he was still fully dressed, William began to discard jacket, trousers and, after a minor tussle with his watch chain, waistcoat and shirt. Belle unlaced her boots hastily and knocked them to the floor, then she reached for his bare chest and looked into his eyes while running her tiny hands through the curls of hair there. He slipped out of his drawers and Belle let her eyes linger on his cock.

"Oh, William," she whispered, and he lifted her farther onto the bed so that he might slide up beside her.

He'd thought that he would feel shy when she finally saw him as he was born, but he didn't. Everything felt natural and easy, as if they had rehearsed this scene and knew exactly what they should do. Their skin broiled in the sultry room and they broke from kissing to admire each other's nakedness and then plunged again into deep kisses. William scarce knew which part of her beauty to caress first; his hands traveled from her honeyed breasts to the peach of her behind. Her skin was as soft as milk and her kisses eager and sweet. He slid one finger between her legs to find her wet and yielding.

"Are you ready, Belle?" he whispered.

"I am, William."

Afraid of crushing her with his bulk, he pushed himself up on his arms and kept his body above hers. He entered her slowly and gulped a rapid, shocked breath at the taut-soft feel of her wrapped around him. She locked her eyes to his as they moved slowly together, enjoying each thrust. They lingered over each movement, each caress; it seemed important to take their time. This is what ecstasy is, William thought, looking at the darling woman beneath him and feeling her respond to every tickle of his flesh, every rush of blood. Soon his rhythm overtook him and he no longer felt connected to his actions; they possessed him and rocked him on and on. And yet he was present, aware of each tingle on his skin; aware of the flickering fire; the heat from Belle's body; her hot, tight grip; the faraway smiles she offered him that meant she felt as euphoric as he did. He bucked faster and groaned, then spurted into her and she clung to him, scratching her fingers up and down his back so that he soared higher than he had ever done in his life.

"Oh, Belle, Belle," he said, and she responded by kissing every part of his face: eyelids, nose, cheeks and mouth, gentle pecks that spoke of her love.

William flopped sideways onto the coverlet and took her to his chest. They kissed, breathing hard, and gazed at each other, and when Belle shivered, he leaped from the bed and, pulling back the sheets, rolled her under the covers. William got in beside her and took her in his arms again. They whispered of their love and shared languorous kisses, not wanting to miss a moment of each other. As the fire fell to embers, then ash, they drowsed to sleep, snug in each other's arms in the Victoria Hotel.

An Interview

Mr. Hollingshead stopped the Sisters Bilton as they entered the Corinthian Club on Friday, placing his hand on Belle's arm. "Miss Bilton, a word if you please," he said.

"Go in without me, Flo," Belle said, and her sister bounced forward, knowing that her Seymour waited within. He had sent Flo a contrite billet-doux and she was ready, as ever, to push aside their latest contretemps. The proprietor steered Belle to one side of the vestibule and lowered his head to talk but remained silent. She looked at him. "What is it, Jack? Do be quick, I'm gasping for a bite and a tiddlywink. My stomach thinks my throat's been cut."

"There's a gentleman here to see you, Miss Bilton. An Irish gentleman."

"That will be Viscount Dunlo—William Le Poer Trench. You know the viscount, Jack—why are you being so cloak and dagger?" Belle chided him with a hip-to-hip knock.

"On the contrary, Miss Bilton, it is the viscount's pater who has come to call, the Earl of Clancarty." He lowered his voice. "Your father-in-law."

"I see," Belle said. "I don't need to wonder what he has come to say." She grimaced. "Well, I had best let the old man have an audience. Lead the way, Jack."

Mr. Hollingshead took Belle's cape and gave it to the cloakroom attendant. He nodded and had Belle follow him up a stairway to one of the private rooms. Her stomach felt as if a tram were careening through it; she gulped a quick breath and found her mouth was arid. Belle knew what the earl might say; she did not know what she might. *Courage*, she said to herself, *have courage, and do not snap at any bait*. Hollingshead knocked on the door, waited for a response, then opened it and stood back to let Belle in. As she passed him, he raised his eyebrows by way of asking if she required him to stay.

"That's all right, Jack. I'll be down again soon." Mr. Hollingshead closed the door gently.

She did not, in fact, feel all right and the sight of the seated Clancarty set her heart thudding. The earl stood up, and the swagging scarlets of the room seemed to pulse around him; he was a tall man, though not as big as his son. He looked sour, though the wave in his thick hair, and a bountiful beard, softened him. She would not have expected the earl to look anything other than cross, he no doubt wanted a blue blood for a daughter, not a dancer. But she would make him see that she was worthy of his family. She was capable, bright, well-mannered and decently brought up; yes, she had had her troubles, but everything was taken care of now. He could have no fatal objections to her. Belle sucked in her breath and set her face. *Be pleasant*, she urged herself. *Do not be cowed and do not get angry*. The earl frowned when she walked toward him and extended her hand; he stood rigid, arms tucked behind his back.

"Don't you know anything?" Clancarty said. "Unmarried ladies do not offer their hand to gentlemen with whom they have no acquaintance."

"Lord Clancarty, I *am* married, as you are aware. And surely, now that you and I are relatives, I can consider myself acquainted with you?" Belle used her sweetest tones, though her heart leaped about like a cat.

He grunted. "If you think this mésalliance between you and my son will be allowed to stand, miss, you are mistaken. The Le Poer Trench men have always made good marriages. We are known for it. My wife's father was the Marquess of Bristol."

"How pleasant for you. My husband is the Viscount Dunlo. Which means we each have a noble spouse." Despite her good intentions, the earl's tone and hostility riled Belle and she knew her ripostes would not endear her to him.

The earl hammered his walking cane against the carpet. "My son is *not* your husband." He hit the floor again. "This has been badly done and it is an abhorrent lapse on William's part."

"I do not think my husband views it that way, sir."

"You took advantage of him—he is but a boy!"

"A boy? If so then he is a boy who asked for my hand in marriage and was granted it."

The earl's voice rose. "The *Pall Mall Gazette* detailed that he won you in a coin toss. In *this* putrid place, no less."

"It was a game of lanterloo, actually," Belle said, then regretted the cheap sound of the words. "Whatever happened, it doesn't matter. William wanted to marry me as much as I wanted to marry him. The game of cards was but an opening to an appropriate conversation about our intention to wed. And we're husband and wife now. That's all there is to it."

"As long as I live you will not be a wife to my son. I am cutting him off, Miss Bilton. How do you like that? William, I might tell you, likes it not one bit." Belle was alarmed. What might have been said or decided? "He came to Berkeley Square yesterday. Did he not inform you of the details of our interview?" Belle winced. "I see by your expression that he did not. My son told me, Miss Bilton, that this so-called marriage was a grave blunder. To his credit, he asked that we—his parents—find no fault with you. 'I have played the devil, Papa,' he said. Further, he told me he was drunk at the time of the escapade and that he has been 'off his head' since he met you. You have some peculiar hold on him, young lady."

Did William really say all that? Impossible! Belle could feel confusion ring through her brain and begin to muffle it. But the earl was lying, he had to be, William would never say such things. Annoyance scrambled through her; she lifted her chin.

"Was your marriage to Lady Adeliza Hervey an escapade also? William and I are married, the same as you are married, sir." She galloped on despite reason telling her to temper her words. "I apologize that you didn't receive an invitation to the wedding, but that was how William wanted it. Had you been there, you would have seen the knot firmly tied." Belle stepped back from him. "You will excuse me now. My sister is waiting for me below."

"Hear this, Miss Bilton: we will *not* have a peasant countess among the Le Poer Trench ranks and you will not see one farthing of our family's money."

Peasant, indeed! "Sir, I do not *need* your money nor William's."

"William's money *is* my money."

"I earn enough for both my husband and myself, sir. I don't dance in some penny gaff—the Empire Theatre is a top-notch establishment."

The earl snorted. "My guess is that your Empire is a place of very low stamp indeed. You'll be in Queer Street before long, mark my words, Miss Bilton; parsimonious living may not suit you quite as well as you imagine."

"On the contrary. I will earn even more as Lady Dunlo." Belle knew she sounded coquettish and brazen but her tongue was liberated now. "The Empire is, of course, already fashioning new posters to reflect my changed status."

The earl's face expanded in anger. "You have a rare tongue in your head, miss. I do not wonder that you find yourself so often in trouble."

Belle looked at him. Was it possible he knew about Weston and baby Isidor? She went to the door and opened it. "Good evening to you, sir."

"One more detail that I may have omitted, Miss Bilton, in my haste." He furrowed his brow, but Belle saw that he did so to cover a smile. What thought was giving him pleasure? "William has begged me to arrange for him to go abroad. Not to Africa and his regiment where, indeed, he should be." Belle went to speak, but Clancarty raised his hand. "No, the antipodes are his choice. The other side of the world seems quite far enough to him."

Belle's hand gripped the doorknob harder and her chest felt muffled and tight. This could not be true. William was appeasing his father with lies, that was all. He could not be thinking of going away. It was absurd. Belle nodded at the earl and headed quickly down the stairs. Jack Hollingshead met her in the vestibule, holding a tray with a glass of Madeira on it. She grabbed the wine and tossed it down her throat.

"Thank you, Jack. My cape, if you please," Belle said.

Her mind was a maelstrom of impressions and questions, and snatches of the earl's words swirled around her brain: *I do not wonder that you find yourself so often in trouble. . . . William has begged me to arrange for him to go abroad. . . .* What did any of this mean? She stood and agitated her hands while Hollingshead went to the cloakroom. Had William not pledged eternal love to her that very morning in their bed in the Victoria Hotel? Had he not vowed to go to his family to speak of their marriage and return with his father's blessing? Had Belle not waited the entire day and presumed William had failed to find his father when he did not return? Oh, what awful muddle had he allowed himself to become entrenched in?

"William, what have you done?" she murmured while Mr. Hollingshead wrapped her cape around her and fastened it at the front. "Jack, tell my sister I had to dash away."

"Indeed. Go well, Miss Bilton," he said. "Lady Dunlo, I should say." Belle nodded and left.

A Meeting

William's rooms in the Burlington Hotel were modest in decor but large. They looked unlived-in to Belle, as if rarely occupied. Everything was neat and ordered. But, of course, a girl came twice daily to dust the furniture, adjust the drapes and make sure everything was just so. William looked discomposed, Belle thought, to find her at the door, but he pulled her into an embrace.

"My darling wife."

Belle wriggled her way out of his arms and walked to the center of the room. She was weary. Halfway to see William at the Burlington the night before she had changed her mind and gone back to Conduit Street instead. She needed time alone to think over the earl's words. But her sleep had been an undulating mess of wakefulness and drowse, and she dreamed of ships propelled on violent seas and large, stark houses with windows like empty eyes. She felt as if she had not slept for five minutes together the whole night.

Belle went to the window and looked out at Burlington Street. The brasses on the doors opposite winked in the early sunlight. She imagined the comings and goings that used to take place from Mary Boyle's house across the way, the legendary soirees, even the nefarious Lord Byron had supped there, it was said. She watched an organ grinder wheel his instrument down the street, his monkey sitting atop it like a little prince. Belle could sense William all afidget behind her, but she let him stew, for she wanted him to explain himself. When it was clear that he was waiting for her to speak, she turned to him.

"The earl came to call on me at the Corinthian Club last night." William groaned and sat heavily on the chaise longue. "He tells me you are going away. To Australia, no less." Belle walked over and stood in front of him. "He tells me that you said you were drunk when you agreed to marry me and that you were 'off your head' besides." William pushed his hands over his eyes and let his head hang. "I see by your demeanor that it's true. Is this why we did not share our bed at the Victoria Hotel last night? Is this why you requested a night apart from me? You said you needed to see your mama, to smooth things over. I didn't understand it when you asked for a night away from me, but now I see that you wanted to scheme with your father behind my back."

"I did not! No, Belle, it wasn't like that. Mama asked to see me, just as I told you, but she lured me to Berkeley Square under false pretenses. My father wishes to force me out of the country, but I have no desire to go. None! The only place I want to be is here in London with you, finding our new home, building our life. We are married."

"Yes, William, we *are* married and you have new cares now. New responsibilities. And yet you chose not to share my bed last night, so that you could go and plot with your family against me. Your father said some dreadful things to me last night. I don't necessarily believe the things he told me that *you* reportedly said, but it was painful to hear them nonetheless."

"I have no doubt. I'm sorry, Belle. Papa can be somewhat fierce and he's leaning heavily on me. He and Mama, both. I have angered them. They keep chanting, 'Propriety must be observed,' as if I care two figs for propriety."

"But we *must* care for what is right and proper, William. And at this moment, what is right is that you begin the work of setting our new lives in motion. We need to find an address. A home. We need to return to the Victoria Hotel tonight, together."

William stood and laid his hands on her shoulders. "I defended you stoutly, Belle. You must know that."

"Did you, William? Did you stand up to your father?" She could not soften the barb of skepticism that poked through. "I know he blames me entirely for our marriage, and he is mistaken in that, but I don't wish to hear the details of how I was criticized. Spare me that at least."

"I wasn't going to tell you what they said, my darling. I only want you to know that Papa will not break me. You and I are married and that is that."

"If only it were so simple, William. Do you wish to go to Australia?"

"I do not."

Belle sat beside him, shifting her bustle so that she was comfortable. What could she do but believe William's words, even though everything said, or allegedly said, formed a thick briar in her mind? Still, she knew he was hers and that he loved her well and she him. Belle took William's hand in hers and kissed the fingers, each in turn. She looked up into his face and he leaned in and kissed her. The supple press of his lips always took her by surprise; he had the most sensual mouth of any man she had known. They kissed long and deep, their tongues in a fluid dance. Belle felt the urgent swell between her thighs and she began to unbutton William's waistcoat, then his shirt. Her hand found the heat of his chest and the curled hair there that she loved so well. She ran her fingers through the luxuriant hair all the while letting his tongue explore her mouth. William made a deft job of the buttons on her bodice and Belle kicked out of her skirt with ease. She went to undo her corset.

"Keep it on," William whispered, staying her hand.

They moved as one to William's bed and into it. His mouth clamped on her breast threatened to keel her over before she was ready, so she pulled his face to hers and kissed him deeply again. His cock was hard and hot against her thigh and she shifted under his weight to guide him in. A gasp when he entered her and then they rocked together in bliss, Belle stopping and starting their rhythm so that it would not end too soon. William propped himself up and kept his eyes fixed to hers, a glazed but determined look in them. She kneaded his behind with her hands and felt the fever of his breath on her face. How she desired this man; what gusts of passion he roused in her and so easily. How she wanted to devour and swallow him, inch by inch. Each whorl of hair and blemish on his newly discovered body was sacred to her. He was *her* man. Her *man*. And nothing would separate them.

Flo arrived ahead of Belle at the Empire and was reading a newspaper in her dressing-room armchair when she came in.

"You're here already." Belle had hoped to shake the city's grime from her shoes and lungs before having to speak to anyone. She wanted to do her vocal warm-ups alone and think about everything that had happened with the earl and with William. She took off her cape and turned to her sister. "Did you return home to Seymour last night? You didn't come back to Conduit Street."

"Yes, we were close as a clam last night. Rotten with l'amour. Thank the stars!" Flo giggled.

Belle unpinned her Gainsborough and set it on a form; she gentled her palm across the blue ostrich feather, to settle it.

"Well, that's good," she said, continuing to feel the fronds of the feather with her fingers. She startled when Flo spoke.

"I see you've embraced the plume boom. Don't you care about the poor bird that was cruelly shot down for that hat?"

Belle sighed. "I'm really not in the mood for banter, Flo."

"Well, pardon me." Flo looked at her over the top of the newspaper. "But why were *you* in Conduit Street last night, anyway? Marital bliss is surely not at an end already?"

"We decided to spend a night apart. William had family business to see to."

"Ah, solemn Clancarty business to which wives are not invited."

Belle sighed. "I wonder, Flo, if I'll ever receive an invitation to the Clancarty table."

Flo shook the newspaper. "In time you will, Belle. But, listen, you must let me read this to you—this will make you laugh." She peered closer to the page. "It's ever so funny. Here it is: 'This sprig of the Irish aristocracy'—your William!—'though he will not attain his majority until December, has been for some time past an ardent supporter of the many nightclubs which have sprung up recently. The Gardenia, the Corinthian and Evans's all know him well, and it is in these festive haunts that he has laid siege to the heart of the happy lady.'" Flo looked up at Belle. "That's you, my dear. 'On Wednesday morning a bridal party consisting of the jubilant couple; Miss Flo Bilton, the bride's sister; and Mr. Marmaduke Wood ascended the hill which leads from Avenue Road to Hampstead and went through the interesting ceremony which has united a beauty of the halls to the future Earl of Clancarty.' Isn't that a royal jest?"

"'Interesting ceremony,' indeed. How they smirk at me."

"I thought it would amuse you a little, Belle. It's only silly newsmen."

"I see no fun in it whatsoever, Flo, I'm jolly well tired of prying newsmen." Belle flumped into her own armchair. "I have my own news. The earl is determined to send William away. Alone. William says he won't go anywhere, but his father has such a grip on him, I fear he'll leave."

"Leave? For where—Ireland? William won't leave! Does the earl mean for him to go to Galway, is that what you mean?"

"No." She gazed over at her sister. "Clancarty wants him to go to Australia."

"Australia! What the deuce, Belle? The earl can't make him go. William *won't* go. He's devoted to you. And you're married now. What on God's earth can his father do? He's not going to fill him up with laudanum and trick him on board a ship." Flo laughed, then looked doubtful. "Would he?"

"I don't know what the earl is capable of. All I know is that he doesn't want me anywhere near his son."

A knock to the door and a bawl of, "You've got an 'alf 'our, ladies."

Flo helped Belle out of her dress and into her costume. They were doing a sketch from *Babes in the Wood* which Mr. Hitchins had mish-mashed with a Grimm Brothers' tale. Flo was Hansel; she stuffed her hair into a cap and pulled on taffeta lederhosen. Belle battled with a dirndl and an apron and Flo helped her straighten it and tie the strings.

"Come on, Gretel," she said, "have a stout heart. William is not about to desert you, that's just ridiculous. The earl is meddlesome, to be sure, but he's only trying to intimidate you. Keep your chins up."

Belle laughed for she and Flo always worried their chins would end up like Mother's, tremulous as turkey wattle. Her mirth wavered when she thought again of the earl and his cold condescension.

"Tell me again that William won't leave, Flo. He'd never do such a thing, surely?" She paused, riddled with anxiety about the whole mess. "His father can't exert so much influence on him, can he?"

"William is, no doubt, out the front as we speak, basking in the Empire's Persian glow, waiting impatiently for his beloved wife to make her entrance." She shoved Belle toward the mirror. "Come now, do your rouge. Everything will be fine and dandy, warm as brandy, you wait and see."

Belle smiled at her sister, but could not quite believe her words. She sat, opened her pots and began to powder and pink. William's malleable quality worried her; he could be pliant in the hands of others—look at how Wood and Osborn led him astray—and Belle had experienced how ferociously the earl could exert pressure. What if he bent to his father's will? What if telling him about baby Isidor really had altered everything? She knew William had been gracious and accepting about it. But what if his niggles had resurfaced? What if, when he truly had time to appraise everything, he had decided he couldn't stomach a marriage with her after all? She stared at her reflection. It was too ghastly to think that she might lose him along with her future. William was love, yes, but he was also safety and redemption, an unspoiled life, a proper position in society. She could not lose him.

Flo finished her face, tidied wisps of hair into her cap, and rose. She began her physical warm-up, dipping into a low plié with her back straight and her arms held aloft. Belle fell in beside her in the same position, pliéed deeply, took a deep breath and began to hum.

"Mmmmmmmm," she intoned, letting the sound rise to a great height, then fall.

"Mmmmmmmm," echoed Flo. "Meeee, maaaay, moooo."

"Meeee, maaaay, moooo." Belle glanced at her sister and started on a tongue twister, though Flo struggled with them:

"To sit in solemn silence in a dull, dark dock,
In a pestilential prison, with a life-long lock,
Awaiting the sensation of a short, sharp shock,
From a cheap and chippy chopper on a big black block!"

But Flo kept her end up and repeated the verse at an even faster pace. They then recited it together while maneuvering their limbs in strong balletic motions. Once feeling limber in voice and body, the two women sat again and closed their eyes to make peace with their minds before the performance.

A TURBULENCE

Belle unlaced her boots, removed her skirt and bustle and collapsed onto the blue chaise longue.

"I'm so very glad to be seated at last." Her toes were bruised from the stage and she peeled off her stockings to knead her feet. "Fetch me the clove oil, darling, from my dressing case."

William, who paced their Victoria Hotel room, his chin worrying his collar, didn't hear her, but after a moment he felt Belle's eyes on him. "What was that, dearest? Did I enjoy the Café Royal? Yes, the Polish stew was splendid."

"I'm very glad you liked your meal, William, but that wasn't what I said at all."

"Oh, really? I do apologize." He stopped to study himself in the mirror over the fireplace and said no more.

Belle rose and got the oil herself; she sat again and massaged it into her feet, enjoying, as ever, its hot-spice scent and the relief it brought. She looked over to where William leaned on the mantelpiece, lighting a new cigarette off the end of the last one.

"You're truly elsewhere tonight, William."

"Am I?" He forced a laugh but his thumb agitated the silver of his vesta case and his brow was pleated. "Belle, it's been a long night; you've danced, you've eaten, you've socialized. You're weary and should go to bed. I, however, am horribly awake." He drew deeply on his cigarette. "I think I'll go for a walk to tire myself."

"You're exhausted, too, William, I know you are. Won't you come to bed?"

"Truth is, Belle, I need a scrap of time alone to think. My mind is churning."

"Your family has unsettled you, of course. Your father."

"I daresay."

"I understand that you need quiet to think over what your papa said." William's agitation troubled Belle; she would rather he didn't take a solitary walk for comfort. She set down her clove oil and stretched her hands out to him. "But come to bed, darling. I know the best way to ease your turmoil."

William came to her but didn't sit. He pulled her face to his stomach and caressed her neck. "I won't be long, Belle. Get undressed and nip between the covers; I'll return before the sandman can sprinkle sleep over your eyes."

She pulled her head back to look into his face; there was something concealed about her husband tonight; she divined there were things he did not wish to say to her. The mantel clock chimed midnight and William leaped as if electrified.

"If you must walk, William, then go, but please don't be long."

He leaned down and kissed her; Belle tried to prolong the kiss, to woo him into staying, but he seemed already gone. He broke away from her, took his top hat from the occasional table and left. Uncertainty twined around Belle's reason: Did William mean to return? Why this sudden need to walk alone? It wasn't altogether like him. Belle finished undressing and put on her nightgown. She lay down and tried to unpick all the earl had said, to make sense of it, but her head wasn't long on the pillow before she slept.

———

Lord Clancarty stood across from William in his Burlington Hotel room. William pulled himself up straighter and winced when the bruises across his back stretched taut. He still couldn't believe that his father had taken his cane to him. The fact that the old man delivered several blows before William had had the presence of mind to dodge away hurt him more than his injuries. He stood in disbelief and his father leaned on his stick, panting. William put his hand to his back, still shocked by the pain of the attack; the bones throbbed and the skin was tender. He took his hand away and looked at his father; he wanted to roar and scream at the man, but he knew that might provoke the earl to fresh violence. It was not the first time William had been thrashed.

"Belle Bilton is *not* the type one marries," the earl snarled. "A woman whose picture comes in every chap's Guinea Golds, so he can ogle her while he smokes? An actress and dancer? No, no. Badly done, boy."

William bristled to hear Belle once more reduced by his father. "I love my wife." He said it quietly.

"What did you say?"

"I love Belle." William said it boldly.

"Love!" The earl snorted. "Love is 'the wisdom of the fool and the folly of the wise.'"

"Papa, it's unfair and inappropriate that you talk of Belle this way."

"Inappropriate?"

"I am married. What's done is done."

The earl shook his stick. "You stain our name and how dare you do it, sir?"

"We are wed. I'm tired of repeating it. I'm married. That's all there is."

"And you want a music hall schemer for a wife, do you? A harlot? Is that how you wish to uphold the Le Poer Trench honor?"

"Don't call her those names, Papa. I love Belle and she's married to me now; nothing can alter that fact."

"We shall see about that," the earl said. He sat hard into the chair by the window and indicated to his son to lift a chair and sit opposite him. "Do you know the meaning of the word 'infatuation,' boy?"

"Of course."

"That is what this is. You are fascinated by this woman, not least because of her lowly birth. Her openness." The earl coughed hard into his handkerchief. "I own the woman has a pretty face. You may be a little obsessed with her. But this was a dalliance, William, and we do not yoke ourselves to our infatuations. The Le Poer Trench family has position and this so-called marriage is not going to undo centuries of high standing. Thankfully, unwise unions can be dissolved; you may yet escape this with your good name intact."

"I do not wish for my marriage to be dissolved."

The earl held up his hand in case his son meant to speak further. "You will go to Australia tomorrow, as arranged, and Mr. Godley Robinson will accompany you."

"For what? I have no desire to travel; I told you this already, sir. I belong here with my wife."

"Enough!" The earl thumped the carpet with his walking stick. "You will go and Miss Bilton will be taken care of. If you refuse to go, you will be disinherited forthwith. All of this has been discussed and it is infuriating to me that we are still talking of it, as if there were further decisions to be made."

"What about what I want?"

The earl ignored his son. "Your mother is made so ill by your rebellion that she has not come downstairs all day." The earl leaned forward. "William, a young man of slender talents such as yourself, and even more slender means, cannot afford to be disinherited. You have copious debts. If you proceed with this attachment, you will find yourself in complete penury. I give you my word on that."

"Belle earns enough for both of us."

The earl controlled his voice and instead of shouting, he delivered a raspy whisper: "And you would have your wife slavered over by other men in that pit of a theater, in order to support you? You would fare well married to a hoyden, is that it? Have sense, my boy. For pity's sake, have sense."

"I'm married, Papa, that's all I know and I stand by my wife."

"The woman convinced you to marry her. She is clearly skilled at cajoleries; her sort usually is. You have been duped." The earl coughed again, a deep, phlegmy affair that had him spit into his handkerchief. "You forget, William, that you are twenty years of age. Until you turn twenty-one I am in charge of you. You must do as I say."

"Yes, Papa."

"By law, you must obey me. Do you understand that?"

"Yes, I understand."

William hung his head; he supposed that much was true. And, besides, his father could not be argued with; one always ended up in the same place, for the earl would not move once entrenched. They could back and forth forever and his father would never hear him. And William knew that his position was tricky. What would he live on without Papa's support? Was it seemly for a viscount's wife to subsidize her husband? He acknowledged to himself that it was not. But he loved Belle! The smallest thought of her beautiful face and great-hearted nature made his stomach flip over and over; William did not wish to live without her. But neither could he countenance the thought of being laughed at; if Papa cut him off and Belle was forced to keep him, wasn't that likely to happen? People would titter over him and denounce Belle. He had no desire to put her in that difficult position. Why had they not realized this?

Perhaps he *should* leave for a spell. Appease Papa by going away with this Mr. Robinson, until things had settled down a bit, until he came of age. He looked at his father, at the cane he twitched as if he craved to use it once more to beat William's body until he submitted.

"All right, Papa," William said at last. "You get your way. I will travel with Mr. Robinson to Australia. I will return in December when I come of age. Five months I will stay away and no more." William could feel the wash of tears behind his eyes. "I must go to Belle now and tell her of my plans."

"William, you will not leave this room tonight and I intend to stay here to see that you do not. You set sail in the morning. If you know what is wise, you will take your rest now so that you have the energy to begin your voyage."

"But, Papa—"

"Do not argue with me, boy. If you will not steer your own course well, you leave me no choice but to steer it for you. You will go abroad until you attain your majority, thereby securing your inheritance, and then you will be your own master. Sleep now, for tomorrow you will need strength to find your sea legs. And the rest of it."

Clancarty settled back into the chair, his cane between his legs, and closed his eyes. William sat on the side of the bed and looked at his father. Did he really have William's better interests in mind? Was this trip what was needed, to cool heads on all sides? He was addled, his mind a broth of conflicting thoughts. Belle might never forgive him. He needed to get back to the Victoria Hotel, he needed to talk to her. His father's breathing did not settle and William thought he might be feigning sleep in case he should try to leave. In truth, he did not have the strength to battle with the earl again. William lay down on his bed, still in trousers, shoes and all, and wept. He woke in the small hours to find his father snoring. William slipped his coat over his bruised back and crept from the Burlington Hotel.

Steely light was already invading their Victoria Hotel room when Belle heard the door open and saw William slink in.

"Is it morning?" she asked, pulling herself up in the bed.

"It's early, Belle, half past five or so."

She put out her hand, "Come to me." William came and sat on the bed, his face knotty with distress. He winced and put his hand to his back. "Oh my love, what ails you?" Belle asked.

"My damn father ails me. The man has upset my logic, my heart. He has upset our honeymoon. Our life!" William lit a cigarette and dragged deeply. "Papa insists that I go away until I attain my majority; he won't desist from this line. He says it's the only thing to be done. He says he will have nothing more to do with me if I stay. I must go, it seems. It's the only way."

Had he been to see his father again? Why was he so freshly upset? Belle gripped his hand. "William, what am I to do if you leave? Couldn't I go with you? Do you really need to go?"

He dragged hard and blew the smoke sideways, an impatient blast. He took Belle's hand and tapped it against the eiderdown over and over until she stayed it.

"Could you keep yourself, Belle? If I had to go, that is, if I were forced?"

"Yes, I can keep myself, as I have been doing these past few years. I earn enough to live well, you know that."

"I would return in December, when I attain my majority. It'd be a matter of months, my love." He pulled her hand to his mouth and kissed it.

"Five months," Belle said, seeing the weeks elongate before her in a cold span. "Where shall I live? We have not found a home yet."

"Can't you stay at Conduit Street?"

"No, William, I already told you the landlady has indicated she wants me gone."

"Could you stop with Flo?"

"You've seen her and Seymour's tiny quarters, William."

"I'm so sorry, my darling. My papa is adamant. He says he'll cut me off if I don't go. He says Garbally Court will never be mine. I can't lose Garbally, Belle, don't you see? It's for us, it will be our home. Eventually." William put his hand inside his jacket and took out envelopes. "A letter from Papa, outlining his wishes." He opened the other envelope and Belle saw banknotes inside. "See, he means to help me clear my debts. It's all for my good. Papa says he'll give me an allowance if I leave for these few months and return in December."

William was wild of eye and he pushed one hand through his hair continuously until it stood in peaks. He winced as if in physical pain.

"But why must he force us apart, William? We're married. You love me. It's done."

He rubbed his hand over his brow. "Things are not so simple in our world, Belle. In my father's world."

Belle sensed a fissure opening, with herself on one side, William on the other. He was moving away from her; she must haul him back. She placed her hand on his thigh and stroked gently. "Come now, William, there are other ways out of this. Your mother will soften your father over time—you've said she is good at that. And, as the eldest, you're entitled to Garbally Court by law, are you not, once your papa passes on?" William nodded. "We can wait until that time, however long that may be. I earn enough for both of us; we will find our own place. We can slowly clear your debts and live in a little comfort. All is not lost, darling. We can be strong together."

"We are strong together. You're right, Belle." He kissed her face, over and over.

"You don't wish to break us apart, do you, darling?" Belle placed her hand between his legs and rubbed gently.

William gasped and kissed her deeply. "No, I never want to be parted from you, Belle. I won't go away, I won't do it. To you. To myself."

Belle felt him harden under her palm. "Stay, my love," she whispered into his mouth between kisses, "stay. We have a life to begin."

William pushed up Belle's nightgown and slid his hand into her cleft. "Papa won't harass and hound me anymore," he said while stroking her.

Belle sighed and squeezed her thighs around his hand. William kissed her neck. "Just a second," he said.

He slid away from her and undressed maniacally until he was naked. Belle yanked her nightgown over her head and William got into bed beside her. His hands were cool, but Belle welcomed the shock of them on her breasts. William kissed her with a new ferocity and in a moment he was inside Belle, but she was slick and ready for him. They made love in a fever and Belle relished every stab of William's cock inside her, she wanted to keep him there forever. She held him tightly and maneuvered him onto his back so that she was astride him. Belle moved over William and watched him watch her, the upturn of her breasts, the rhythm she perfected with her dancer's skill. His face was a stunned mask; she rocked over him and he thrust ever harder until bliss saturated his features and he cried out. She used her hand to rub herself to ecstasy with his flood while over him still and he groaned with pleasure to observe her. Belle collapsed onto William's chest and they held each other, breathing fast.

He whispered, "I love you, I cannot stand to be apart from you. My love, my love," until they both fell asleep.

When Belle woke in the morning, William was gone.

A DISAPPEARANCE

Belle stood outside the Burlington Hotel and thought of not entering its doorway. Easier by far to stand in the street to watch the early sun sneak up and sparkle off the windows. She looked up at William's quarters, hoping to see his eyes peer down at her and his hand raised in greeting, to make a lie of the morning's empty side of his bed in the Victoria Hotel.

Believing he had only gone to his Burlington room to battle some more in private with his father's wishes, Belle sat up in the bed that morning in the Victoria and wrote a note to William. She knew he was confused and she knew, also, that confused people find choice making hard. She did not wish to urge him in ways he did not want to go—against his family—but Belle meant to press the note into his hand and watch him read it. Then, she hoped, he might choose her, once and for all. Belle unfolded the page and read it hastily.

William,

Perhaps it is better for both of us that you go to Australia. Perhaps you need time to grow up and face your responsibilities. Perhaps I need time to reflect. I don't understand you, it seems. The most consistent thing about you is that you contradict yourself and yet I know you love me. It's impossible for you to be false in the feelings you show me, I believe this. Because of you, I know what love is, I know how it flows like water between man and woman, and how easeful love can be when it's mutually shared. I've thought I loved before, but I was mistaken. William, our love can't be broken apart and put aside like something worthless. I know you cherish your family but we will be a family, too—we are one already. Obey your father if you must, though I sincerely wish you would not. Whatever happens, I'm here and waiting.

Your B

Belle folded the note and clutched it in her hand. A flower seller sidled up to her.

"Roses, ma'am. Fresh red roses. You look like a woman of 'ealthful tastes, ma'am. What nicer than sweet red roses to fragrance your mantelpiece?"

Belle looked at the roses and thought of her wedding posy, pressed now under her Conduit Street mattress so she might preserve it. The dark heads of the flowers before her, the coy curve of the petals, made her shudder.

"Leave me be," she said to the woman, who hoicked her basket and trotted away swinging her hips, mock affronted.

"Red roses, two a penny!" she called, accosting another lady farther along.

Belle looked up again at William's quarters and entered the hotel. She glided across the foyer, as if she were a resident, and walked up the staircase. She did not want to have to converse with anyone, least of all the lift boy. Gaining William's door, she knocked and the door opened at the touch of her knuckles. Belle stepped in and looked around. The bed was bare of sheets; William's grooming case no longer sat on the tallboy, and the wardrobe door hung open revealing unclothed hangers. So William was gone. He had chosen other than her.

Belle sat in a chair by the window and looked to the street below. She wanted to weep, but her tears were solid as stones behind her eyes, though her chest hurt and her breath came short. So this was it. The one person she was sure would not leave her had left. Had he not vowed constancy? Had he not sworn he wouldn't go? Belle crumpled the note in her fist and tossed it to the floor; she tried to force a teary flood, thinking a hefty bawl would relieve some of her pain, but she could not cry.

Her mother's voice wavered in her ear, *There's something hard inside you, Isabel Maude Penrice Bilton. Obstinate, unruly girl. Wicked girl.*

This had been repeated often in her youth, for no punishment Mrs. Bilton could dream up ever drew forth tears from her daughter. Not beatings, not segregation, not name-calling. The little Isabel stood up to her mother in a way that enraged the older woman. It became a game for the girl who made sure never to cry, no matter what was done to her. If she was to be called hard and stubborn, then she would be those things. Was it true that she was so hard that this catastrophe with her brand-new husband would not bring tears? She cried over smaller things all the time but now, when she most needed release, her tears would not come.

A noise by the door alerted Belle to the fact she was not alone. She rose. It was Wertheimer, whose rooms at the Burlington were a few doors along from William's. Belle flumped back into the chair.

"He's gone. Not so much as a farewell note," she said.

"I am sorry, Belle."

"And I find I can't cry, Isidor. My tears are frozen. Does that make me wicked? Deserving of this turn of events?"

Wertheimer advanced into the room. "I daresay you're in shock, Belle."

"The earl won out in the end. I can scarce believe it."

Wertheimer was silent for a moment. "William will write to you from his travels. He will return. And be a better husband for his spell abroad."

"You sound so sure, Isidor." She fingered the gold heart on its chain around her neck. "I am not."

Wertheimer crossed the room and stood by her chair. "This is the window Dunlo climbed through from the roof of a cab one night." Belle looked up at him in wonder. "He was drunk and he refused to pay the cabman, until forced to at the police court the next day. Did he tell you about that?"

"No, he didn't tell me and it sounds so unlike the William I know. And yet, I wonder, do I even know him? If he is capable of abandoning me like this, perhaps I don't know him at all."

Wertheimer knelt beside her. "Dunlo loves you, Belle. You have not seen or heard the last of him."

She took her friend's warm hand in hers and stroked her own cheek with his fingers. "Why can no man, Isidor, be as constant as you?"

"Don't give in to melancholia, my dear. This is a hiatus, nothing more. His father is behind the whole caper."

"Of course he is. William is afraid of the man; he's made cowardly by him. What must his childhood have been like?" Belle stared into the street below, listened to the rhythmic clop of horses and the roll of carriage wheels. She looked across at the bed and the ticking stripes of the naked mattress. "We lay there together so recently and now . . ."

"We must get you away from that boardinghouse in Conduit Street. That should be the first thing."

"It's not some Spitalfields pit, Isidor. It's clean at least. And furnished. Though the landlady has begun to object to Pritchard—she doesn't care for his singing, apparently." She tutted and shook her head. "If she knew how much worse it could be—a bawling babe!"

"Enough now. It's clear you need a proper place to dwell. Somewhere fitting."

Belle went to rise and flopped back into the chair. "If only you'd seen the hovel I fetched up in when I first came to London. Flo called it the Stinkpot. All our neighbors were cat flayers—they made their pennies selling the skins." Belle sat up. "The best thing was we lived above a cabinetmaker who kept a blazing fire day and night, to keep his glue pliable. Our little room, in turn, was always warm as an oven. It was threadbare and the street smelled bad, but we liked it." She knew she was babbling, but it was easier to conjure old scenes than wallow in the pain of William's abandonment.

Wertheimer knelt before her. "How you have *lived*, Belle; I always feel green in comparison. But we must get you away from the cat flayers, glue boilers and so forth for good. You should not be exposed to such things."

Belle looked at him, at his slim face and high, innocent forehead. "You are nothing but good to me, my friend."

"And, as you know, it's entirely my pleasure. I'll set you up somewhere. I'll see that you are safe until William returns."

"But what will people say, Isidor? I should really try to stay with Flo and Seymour instead. Their place is tiny but they may squeeze me into a corner."

"Don't be daft, Belle. Imagine the discomfort of it. Imagine listening to Flo and Seymour bicker morning, noon and night."

Belle nodded; it was not a pleasing prospect, she had worries enough of her own. "But what will the Le Poer Trenches think if they hear you have housed me?"

"Why should you care what those people say or think, Belle? As a family, the Le Poer Trenches have been unkind to you."

"I suppose you're right, Isidor," she murmured.

"Don't addle yourself with how they think. You're my friend and I mean to help you. That's nobody's concern but ours."

"We don't live as other people live," Belle said.

"There! Quite right. We certainly do not."

She stared out the window again. Truly, how could William do this to her? Was their love not enough to fasten him to her side? She struggled to understand that he was actually gone, that he could forsake her so, with no care for how his actions would be perceived by the world. With none for his duty as husband.

"William has simply left. I can hardly fathom it."

"It's a strange business indeed. Dunlo will explain himself by and by."

Belle turned to Wertheimer. "William has not provided for me, Isidor. I earn, of course, but he has simply abandoned me."

"It's as I thought. Come now, we will evacuate your Conduit Street room and get you comfortable. We shall go to my house in St. John's Wood and you will stay there. I will keep a bedroom, but you will be mistress of the house."

"Why, Isidor, since when have you had a house in St. John's Wood? Have I seen so little of you recently that I don't even know where you live?"

"I only lately took the house; I stay there occasionally. You were right, of course—Maidenhead is only suitable for rail buffs and old biddies. Fairleigh Lodge might've been in the Scottish Highlands it was so far from life."

He put out his hand to Belle and she rose. Yes, best to follow Isidor; he seemed to know what to do. Her head was disarrayed and the ache of William's desertion bled through her. How could he do this? How inferior his family must think her to force him abroad and away from her. How tyrannized William must be to have obeyed the earl. Belle walked to Wertheimer. Arm in arm they left her husband's rooms and descended in the lift to Burlington Street.

AN APPARITION

The Juma

July 1889

My darling Belle,

I am here and I do not truly know why I am here, for my heart is in London with you. I am ill with remorse. I long to be with you and you only, I long to be away from this ghastly Mr. Robinson that Papa has entrusted me to. You are my world, Belle, you are all to me. I stand beside the ship's forecastle each day, smoke cigarette after cigarette and look at the lurching sea. The churned-up water makes me skittish; I measure the tedious progress of the ship across the blue. The hours and days accumulate and I wonder what they will make of your love for me. I wonder if Wertheimer will claim you, somehow make you his own, despite our marriage, despite his penchant for the stronger sex. I worry that he will swoop on you and bend your mind and heart away from mine. Please don't let it happen, my darling. Know that I think of you, and only you, all day and all night.

I fear my own heart will stagnate, become a sorry stone. How am I to do without you by my side, Belle, always loving, always bright? What if you cannot forgive me for leaving? What if your love wanes and you no longer want to be my wife? These are the thoughts that torment me as I sail farther away from you. I picture my heart with its four pulsing chambers and wonder if each of them holds desires that contradict the others. Do one's feelings walk from heart room to heart room—conflicting, unsettled, unknowable? Oh, how is a man to know how to do what is right? The heart, I think, is no better than an oubliette, a secret dungeon that shuns light. Or perhaps that is just my own. If you fail to understand me, rest assured you are not alone in your bewilderment. I don't much understand myself.

I'm furious with my father, at least know that. Confusion and obedience got me aboard this ship, but now I don't understand why I acquiesced. I'm a married man. A man, damn it, and Father should not dictate to me anymore. When I think of your turmoil, my love, on finding me gone, shame slicks over my body like sweat.

I might be on the ocean floor with the anemones for all I care about myself. But you! How ludicrous, Belle, that the distance between us should grow wider and that I don't know what you're doing at this very moment. Is it night or day in England now? Are you in slumber or awake? Oh, why did I leave you? Father bullied me and I let him. I wish I could stand up to him, but he's so forceful it feels impossible. I wish for a clearer hold of my own destiny and the strength to steer it. I want you, Belle, I really do, so why did I not grab on to you and hold fast and damn Father to hell?

In a clutch at comfort, I sit in my cabin and chant "The Sailor's Farewell" and it's your sweet voice I hear:

"Sweet, oh! sweet, is that sensation
Where two hearts in union meet:
But the pain of separation,
Mingles bitter with the sweet."

I never imagined the separation in the song would be ours. My mind is a bramble of concerns. When I'm not worrying about you, Belle, or the pile of debts I left behind, my mind turns over the fata morgana I witnessed last night. I was by the forecastle, smoking, when the horizon seemed to shift and distort into a cloudy mass. I squinted at the vision and, before my eyes, the clump—was it sea mist, the air?—transformed into the outline of a floating castle. As I watched, the shimmering shape gained turrets and windows. We were miles from land and as we stood and stared, Robinson and I, the apparition rose from the sea and hovered above the violet line of the horizon. The vision changed once more, turning gray and taking the form of a human head and, finally, to my mind, it took the shape of your own dear countenance! How I trembled, Belle. Did my bad conscience summon your face? Did you come to scold or forgive me?

I asked the captain later about the vision. He said there are certain conditions of the atmosphere when the sun's rays are able to form a picture in the air of objects below, like reflections one sees in glass or water. The sea warps the air and conjures phantoms that men firmly believe in, mirages. Somewhere between horizon and water things are sorcered to life. The captain said many a seaman has been driven frantic with desire or fear when he fancied he saw sea nymphs or fantastical leviathans of the deep. I said to him, "But I saw my wife's face!" The man just shrugged and I got the feeling of sailors' secrets being kept from me.

I lay on my berth last night, jarred in every nerve. And, though rattled, I fell into a profound sleep. I woke fusty and shaken in the dawn, the cloudy silhouette of your lovely head floating in my mind like a revenant. I sit now writing to you, unfed and unnerved, wishing only for your darling voice in my ear, your hand in my own. I have the curl of your hair that you gave me, I lift it to my nose and smell it; I even poke at the hair gently with my tongue to see if I can taste anything of you on it.

My only Belle, I always and forever love you, my darling, please know that. If only I could hold you now and explain, into your ear, why all this has happened. If I knew how to . . . It vexes me keenly that I have upset you and left you confounded. I do hope that you can forgive me and try to understand.

Papa has promised to take care of you in my absence, but as England gets farther and farther away, I begin to doubt him. Please write to me, my love. I will send this letter from Hong Kong where you may find me at the Hong Kong Club on Queen's Road. I will be there for a spell before sailing onward to the antipodes. Please tell me you haven't forgotten your Dunlo, who is now and ever yours. I wish that instead of the gold heart I gave you on our wedding day that my heart lay against your breast at this moment and forevermore. Thank God we are married. Nobody can part us now.

Your loving William

A Domicile

I t's not as if love can be parceled up and conveniently stored for when it's needed," Belle said. "Love is wild and wayward; it has its own way of catching hold of a person, doesn't it? Love lands where it lands, without agency—much—from the lover. And certainly not from the love object." Pritchard fussed on his perch, cocked his head fully sideways and looked at Belle with his apple-pip eye. He opened his beak and sang in fluting trills. "I love William and he loves me; that's not easily torn asunder by anyone or anything. Not the earl, not time, not distance." Belle poked her finger into the canary's cage. "You understand, don't you, Pritchy?" The bird flitted and Belle took this for an emphatic yes. She wasn't sure she understood any of it herself. William deserted her, his wife, because his father was a persecutor. Oh why could he not have stood up to the earl, refused to be tyrannized? Belle had managed to escape from her mother's oppression, but perhaps William found it harder to run. But, there, he had run from her! Ah, but he would be back. In four months, when he turned twenty-one, he *would* be back.

Belle's thoughts rose, commingled and fell, a medley of hope for the future and fear of it. She shook her head to unrattle herself and wandered from the parlor into the smoking room. It was her favorite part of the house—Sixty-three Avenue Road—and it was there that Wertheimer always seemed most at home. His beloved pair of porcelain pugs book-ended the mantelpiece, oak shelving held his favorite volumes and the wallpaper was a soothing olive color. His smoking cap and jacket, the former embroidered with autumn berries, the latter of navy brocade, lay across his chair back, waiting for him. She fingered the beautiful jacket and looked around; how grand it would be if this was her and William's house, if these were *their* things.

The smoking room held heat in a way Belle had never experienced—even when the coal was down to embers, the room was cozy and provided the warm embrace that she always craved. She had gifted Wertheimer a marble ashtray, for the cigars he so enjoyed, and it sat on the walnut table by his chair. Isidor didn't smoke in the careless manner of other men—he sipped at each cigar as if tasting a new wine. He luxuriated over them and liked to watch the smoke leave his mouth in fancy coils. Belle liked the ceremony he made of smoking and she sometimes smoked a Navy Cut, to keep him company.

Number sixty-three, nestled in St. John's Wood, wasn't as big as Wert-heimer's Maidenhead place, but its compactness suited Belle. As she was at the theater by night, she spent a large part of each day in her nightgown, strolling the rooms, stopping to examine Wertheimer's eclectic belongings or staring out at the street and thinking of William and wondering at their situation, about all the things that conspired to cause it: the Clancar-tys, William's malleability and, she had to admit, her own past.

Belle peered out the window, seeking the man she had noticed who often lurked near the house. His favorite position was behind an oak di-rectly across the road. Sometimes he jotted in a book; more often, he lin-gered and ogled like a person in a trance. He clearly thought he was being clandestine but, what with the burgundy suit he wore and his regular presence, he was hard to mistake.

Once Wertheimer had run out to him, shouting at him to declare him-self, but the man scurried off.

"That fellow is Clancarty's spy, I know it," Wertheimer said, when he came back inside.

"Would the earl go to such lengths, Isidor?"

Wertheimer snorted. "He suspects us, no doubt, of untoward behavior. And old blood will go to any lengths to protect themselves, Belle. That man is following you—following *us*—and no good will come of it."

They did not see the man for a week after that, but he spooked Belle: he was a shadow, a ghost, and she felt that his shifty presence portended something bad for all of them. She looked over at the oak now, but the burgundy-suited man was not there; the street was barren and hushed. The vibrato of London's heart seemed a long way off, though it wasn't. Number sixty-three held a muted clamor to itself as if in anticipation of a great party. But there were no parties; Belle was mostly alone, apart from the servants. Wertheimer kept a bedroom but never stayed the night, even after accompanying Belle home from the theater. He changed his clothes in his room sometimes, but the bed remained unrumpled and Rosina, the maid-of-all-work, went in there to open shutters, refresh the flowers and, once a week, to dust.

Belle had hours in which to think, to make a fine warp and weft of all that had happened, to wish for William's return. He would come back to her, she was certain, but why did he have to stay away so long? She was forlorn in a way that hollowed her out; she realized that she had never truly felt proper loneliness before, the kind that makes a listless wreck of a person. It was a cruel separation indeed.

Picking up a newspaper, Belle sat into Wertheimer's chair and flicked her eyes over the stories; little could distract her from thoughts of William, from missing him, but she had to try. Her eyes alighted on a paragraph about a woman who had drunk ammonia and perished. Her husband, the piece said, had the musical first name "Summerscales." She read that the woman's mother had died and it "weighed on her spirits" so she took her own life.

"Fool!" Belle said aloud. That ammonia-swigging twit had a husband present and willing, and she killed herself over a dead woman. And here was Belle, missing *her* husband with every ounce of her flesh, unable to see or hold him. "People know not how fortunate they are," she murmured.

A movement by the door startled her—it was Jacob Baltimore, the Negro page boy Wertheimer had hired. He had most of the duties of a footman, though he was utterly inexperienced, and he seemed to Belle to slink through the house like a stoat.

"Enter, Jacob," she said.

"Ma'am," he said, and placed the morning post on the chiffonier. He wore lavender gloves that were identical to Wertheimer's and Belle wondered idly if he had taken them or if Isidor had gifted him the gloves. Isidor had mentioned something about Jacob and a coat that went missing, but Belle could not recall the details. Still, Isidor took the precaution of not allowing Jacob a set of keys.

"Stay a moment." Belle didn't wish him to know she was lonely—he was a servant and a boy at that—but she longed for conversation. Anything to extricate herself from her own head.

"Ma'am?" he said, and there was a touch of insolence about his steady gaze that seemed to say *I know you. I know about you and your ways.*

Belle tolerated his contempt; she had no time for servants who cringed. Her preference was for audacious types—those maids and footmen who meant to better themselves and who did not hide it.

"Hand me the letters," she said, "I may need to make a reply."

Jacob gathered the envelopes and the brass letter opener, came across the room and held them out on a tray. Belle flicked through them and, finding nothing from William, dismissed the lot with a wave.

Jacob stood a moment and his gaze traveled downward to where the gold heart nested in Belle's cleavage. She put her fingers to the heart and trailed it back and over on its chain, pulling it up so that she then traced it across her open lips. Jacob's liquid eyes lingered a few seconds too long before he stepped back, bowed slightly, then turned and fled the room.

Belle sighed. He was a mere sprout, fifteen years old at most. She knew she mustn't tease, but he had started it with that unchaste glim at her bosom. Oh, Lord, she needed to do something. It was all very well performing at the Empire every night, but her daytime moping achieved less than nothing. William had promised he would come back, his letters said so, but the waiting game was not one Belle liked to play. She missed William, the gorgeous physical presence of him, his arms, his voice; it hurt not to hold and kiss him. But lounging in sorrow was too dispiriting and her urge to tantalize Jacob, no matter how brief, left her feeling unclean. She would go out; she would summon Isidor and have him take her somewhere. He would help her recapture some vigor.

FALL AND WINTER 1889
AND SPRING 1890

London

An Outpouring

My darling Belle,

   I am sending you a bouquet of lines to soothe my sorry mind and to carry my most loving wishes across the seas to you. The ache of not being with you is as fresh today as it ever was. Much as I don't have the heart for joy, being so far from you, Hong Kong is, I must own, enchanting. If only you were here to see it, too. How you would enjoy the sight of pigtailed men in smocks and trousers of blue, some pulling carts ten times their size, hung with brooms, dusters, cups, baskets, dolls and every kind of bagatelle and bauble. I wish you were here to share in each strange sight I see. I shall purchase a trinket for you, my dear, something shiny and useless.

   The peasants stare at me, interested, I suppose, in my pale coloring and height. There's novelty for me in being somewhere so alien, even if it reduces me to be removed from everything I know and love. But the heat is unmerciful and the smells, not being common, seem worse than the stink that rises off our own Devil's Acre. I try to parse one odor from another but fail; the whole effect is heady, and sometimes *nauseating, in the clammy heat. For all his efficiency, Papa didn't suggest suitable attire. My wool drawers and waistcoats are stifling. It's no wonder that some ex-patriates go native in their dress!*

Godley Robinson—he who accompanies me—is an irksome creature. He has only one tune: how noble my father is. He's somewhat relentless, deifying Papa, then plucking tirades from the air about the lower orders as if he were some great gentleman. His hat is round as a countryman's and squats on his head like an upturned bowl—he looks like a gamekeeper cut loose from the land. Where in Christendom did Papa find this man? It's demeaning, Belle, to be escorted like a child. I am disgruntled. And I miss you with every ounce of me; you are constantly in my thoughts.

I take long walks in an attempt to unmuddle my mind. I went to the shoreline today and stood before the steep granite hills, hoping to find a breeze to calm my humid body and settle my head. In Victoria Harbor, sampans crowd around; they tock against each other and the sound, blended with the lap of waves, is soothing. Women and children live on the boats; they sell fans and bananas with pressing hands. The women don't remind me of you exactly, Belle, except that everything reminds me of you. You follow me like a spirit and I even fancied I heard you cry out on Star Street, to guide me to safety when a rickshaw threatened to flatten me. Am I going mad? First the phantasm above the sea and then your voice, clear as glass in my ear.

Robinson degrades the boat people. "Smugglers and pirates, every last one of them," he said. "They reduce this colony." I wondered today how much Papa is paying Robinson to accompany me on this trip. If only I was not so encumbered with debt! If I had money of my own, I could pay Robinson off and release him from his duties. It galls me now that I frivoled away so much with Wood and Osborn. It's a pity I let them steer me so. I'm ashamed I was foolhardy. When I return to England, I'll learn to manage it all better. No more profligate spending; we will live modestly and quietly on the allowance I'll receive when I come of age; you'll have no need to perform anymore, Belle. And, when the time comes, Garbally will be mine—ours—and we'll go there and I'll run the place.

Alas, for now I'm here and I don't control the purse, Robinson does, and he takes immense pleasure in doing so. How Father must mistrust and dislike me, to let me be humiliated daily by this loquacious dolt. How am I to stand further weeks and months of Robinson's constant, hoggish chatter? Once I come of age, it will be farewell to Robinson and a welcome clearance of the man from my life.

You must forgive me, Belle, I have no one to speak with, so you get to hear every vagrant thought that occurs to me. I'm sorry for complaining—your burden is greater than mine. My darling, I will return to you soon. As soon as God allows.

Your loving Dunlo

An Exhibition

Wertheimer took Belle to the French Exhibition at West Brompton.

"Lord, it's enormous," Belle said, holding out her program. "There are twelve separate classifications. A dozen exhibits! I only want to see two: 'Vegetable Products, Stuffs, Silks, Dress and Fashions.' And I could quite tolerably do without the vegetables."

"And the other?"

"'Sculpture, Oil Painting, Watercolors, Architecture.' Doesn't that sound wondrous? French art in abundance!"

They entered the building; the walls were hung with gay banners of primrose and pale blue. From the roof swung row upon row of English and French flags. Wertheimer steered Belle to where she most wished to go and watched with approval as she exclaimed at the embroidered satins, tulles and cotton lace; he loved her appreciation of fine things. Belle pored over Venice point and guipures, table linens and knitted silk purses. She took a handful of jersey and rubbed it against her cheek, urging Wertheimer to do the same.

"Imagine the comfort of it, Isidor, against the body. By day or by night!"

After sating herself on fabrics, Belle went willingly to where her friend most wanted to go and they oohed and aahed over painted silk fans,

Morocco leatherwork, ivory cigar cases and shell soap dishes. Belle delighted in Wertheimer's shining eyes and fervor over each new treasure.

"I shall have to make my father come see this," he said.

Belle dawdled ahead of him. "Look, Isidor," she called, not wanting him to lag behind. She pointed to a flowerpot with the Eiffel Tower sprouting from it.

"How ludicrous," he said.

"I think it's rather lovely."

"The real thing is *more* than lovely, Belle." He took her arm and placed it on his. "A veritable Tower of Babel for our times."

"I long to see it myself," she said.

"Let me take you there, my dear."

Belle dropped her arm from his. "Oh no, Isidor. How could I?"

"But of course you can. I know Paris well and there are charming hotels where we could stay. Separate quarters, *naturellement*."

"But, Isidor, what if William came back unannounced and I was not here?"

Wertheimer puckered his mouth and shook his head rapidly. For the first time Belle sensed him impatient with her situation.

"Are you so very sure that Dunlo *is* coming back?" he said.

"Why, of course he is!" Belle said, astonished at Wertheimer's doubt. "Whyever would you imply that he might not return to me?" She felt the joy of their outing drain from her.

Wertheimer shrugged. "He has been away long enough to procure some wisdom, surely. He tells you he misses you and yet he does not make haste and come back."

"He *is* coming back. He writes to me—you know that, Isidor." Belle looked away from her friend through gathering tears at the stalls, the bunting, the flags. "It takes a long time to travel from the antipodes, as you're aware. He is, no doubt, making his plans to return as we speak." In that moment she questioned what she was saying—her sureness about William—and that seedling of doubt began to nestle in and take root.

How dare Isidor cause her such ill ease. "Do you really have serious qualms about William?" she asked.

"Where is he, Belle? If he truly loved you, would he not be here, escorting you around this fine exhibition, in my place?"

"We all have different perspectives on other people, Isidor. You do not know William as I do. I trust him."

Though she was moved to defend William, Belle's tears began to fall. She turned her head away so that Wertheimer would not see, dabbed at them with her glove and composed herself quickly. Isidor hovered at her back, radiating disquietude, and she felt a little estranged from him and sad because of it.

"Don't cry, Belle. Dunlo is not being a man about all this."

She faced him. "William will come back; he promised me. This trip abroad was not made of his own free will—you know that. His father coerced him. But William means to return and he will."

Wertheimer exhaled sharply. "Dunlo is a dullard. He wants for brains if he chooses not to honor you. That's all I am attempting to say."

Belle turned from him again; she felt the glances of people who passed while she tried to catch her tears in her handkerchief.

"Shall we peruse the pictures?" Wertheimer said at last.

"If you wish."

Belle let him lead her to the far end of the hall. They passed bronzes by the dozen and every size and class of painting. Belle glanced at them but did not see them properly; she couldn't muster interest. She stopped by Delaunay's *Madame Toulmouche*, lured by the sitter's frank stare and buttermilk complexion. Belle studied the pink roses at the woman's waist, the shadow of a building behind her. The woman looked content to Belle, a person in charge of herself.

"What devotion does this woman know?" she murmured, but Wertheimer did not choose to answer. If only Madame Toulmouche—a wife, like Belle—would break free of the frame and stand before her to give her advice. What would she say? Might she urge Belle to go after William, to book a passage and set sail? Or perhaps she would tell her to wait, to be patient and trust in her man. When Belle thought about William, she felt she wanted to crack him open and climb inside him; that way she could be with him always, tucked inside his skin. Whatever his pull on her was, it made Belle want to have and own him in the profoundest way. His absence, and missing him, was now a savage burden.

T hat night, in her bed, the corner shadows of Belle's room pulled the chairs and bureau in and seemed to swallow them whole. She had gotten Jacob to open the windows to alleviate hanging smoke from the fire and the curtains soughed against the floorboards, sounding to her ears like discontented sighs. She lay awake hour after hour, listening to the susurrations of the house and mulling over Wertheimer's words: *Are you so very sure that Dunlo is coming back? . . . If he truly loved you, would he not be here, escorting you around this fine exhibition, in my place? . . . Dunlo is a dullard. He wants for brains if he chooses not to honor you. That's all I am attempting to say.*

Would William return to her? Did he really mean to come back at all? And if he did, would Belle ever possess him as she longed to?

A Counsel

Sydney, Australia
December 1889

My darling Belle,

I long to be away from the sprawling antipodes. I am sated on the world now, I've seen enough to satisfy me that the planet is large and that it is diverse. I need see no more. Last night I tried to obliterate myself with brandy, to stop the endless rotation of thoughts that make my head circle back and over to the other side of the globe. To you. So now I'm thickheaded and sad. I could wallow in this pit for the entire day, but I know it would be pointless to do so. So instead I write to you, my darling, to let you know I miss you and that I'm more sorry than ever to have bowed to my father's will. It's a fault of mine that I'm easily led and sometimes I don't know how it happens or why I surrender to others' wishes.

I'm sick and heartsore. Melancholy, I fear, is making me ill, for I find it hard to rise each morning and my head and stomach fight with each other all day. It's not only brandy that has me this way, in case you fear I've become a habitual inebriate—last night was the first night that I drank too much. Mostly my stomach shuns even the smallest of tots, for it's so agitated; I may seek out a physician.

Speaking of agitation, Robinson is the queerest chap. Last night he burned like hellfire to say something to me and I had to poke him to get it out. I will report our conversation here as much as I remember it, for it was curious and upsetting.

"Do you know the wording on your family's coat of arms, Dunlo?" was his opener.

"'Consilio et prudentia.' 'By counsel and prudence.'"

"And do you ruminate on it much?" Robinson asked.

"Not really. That is, I used to. I would read it every day as a boy, where it hung in the hall in Garbally, and think what it might mean."

"And what does it mean?"

"I suppose it means that one gains wisdom through listening to others."

"Precisely, Dunlo. The Bible tells us: 'Without counsel purposes are disappointed: but in the multitude of counselors they are established.' Now, is that not appropriate to our situation here?"

"It may be," I said, "except that I haven't the devil's notion of what you're blathering about, Robinson."

He went on to say that Papa had appointed him "a counselor of sorts" and asked if I took his meaning. I did not.

"Your father means to get you to give up your wife. That is why you are here."

I was outraged and I told him that Papa said he would look after you until my return, but Robinson continued, mentioning a private inquiry agent who is supposedly following you (??). He began to talk of that scoundrel Weston and then of Wertheimer (referring to him as "that bric-a-brac Jew") and he called St. John's Wood "a coven of infidelity" at which I laughed. But, Belle, the more he talked his nonsense the more uneasy I became. I felt a morbid stab of homesickness, a pounding ache for you, but also, I confess, a wreath of worry landed around my neck. My father began to loom large in my mind and, also, his dealings with Robinson, his employing of this particular man as my escort. His ability to wheedle and needle and cause a contretemps within my head.

I confess, Belle, I also began to obsess about you and Isidor Wertheimer. Now, I know that you and Wertheimer have an unusual friendship—you are close, very warm indeed—and I know, too, that he has been exceedingly kind to you. But I also know that he has asked you to marry him. Whether you felt it was a serious proposal or not is of no consequence. I've begun to think Wertheimer may mean to have you. Should I worry, Belle? Have I cause for concern? Isidor has been wonderful to you, of course, and I'm glad he's able to protect you in my absence, but might you not move in with Flo and Seymour instead? St. John's Wood has a certain reputation—you know this— for being a place where men keep women. I wouldn't want the gossips at their miserable work. Will you stay with Flo awhile? It would ease my heart and perhaps stop Papa from alighting on conclusions.

You're a dazzling woman, Belle. You hold yourself as if you were the moon and the rest of mankind were the earth below you. You're as lustrous as that orb, as waxing and waning in your light and dark. As irresistible. How I love you. How I need to return to you as soon as possible. Damn Robinson and his insinuations. Damn my father, damn the man to Hades and back. And damn Wertheimer, for being where I cannot be. (I do not truly mean that—I am grateful to him, but I am agitated beyond reason, my love. Forgive me.)

I'm weak now, Belle, from the outpour above. Please excuse me. I wish only to write pleasant things to you, but, somehow, my worries accumulate like a rain cloud and burst onto the pages I write to you. Know that I think of you always with a brimming heart,

Your loving William

Sydney, Australia
December 31, 1889

My darling,

Have you ever in your life done something that seemed so right in the moment but that later—or, perhaps, almost instantly—you realized was the wrong thing? I hope that you have, for then you may understand me and my actions, though I feel I beg too much of you with that because, truly, I fail to understand myself.

I am not attempting to spin you a riddle, Belle, I am merely full of remorse at my latest folly; I have been an utter fool yet again. Please absolve me, though I know your patience may, by now, be worn as thin as gossamer. I would not blame you, Belle, if your faith in me yet evaporates entirely.

Soon you will know all. But know this the most: I do love you, body and soul, and God will see that we are united in the end. Let us hope that this new year that is upon us brings better things to us both.

William

A Writ

Belle was between theater engagements. For a chance to leave London briefly and breathe different air, she had accepted a pantomime run in Manchester over Christmas. But it had felt long and, now, with too much leisure time, and February stretching endlessly on, she was listless. William's letters were infrequent and she had not had one in weeks; the last one was cryptic in the extreme and she knew not what to make of it. Belle yearned to hear from him, to know how he fared and when he would return. Her mind was a constant fret over William's absence and, more recently, his health. Had his small stomach complaint escalated into something worse? Was his mind made wretched by misery? Was he, perhaps, bedbound and unable to write?

She sat in a chair by the window and watched Jacob arrange the table for her breakfast—it was midday—and she longed for company, someone with whom to cogitate over her worries. Why did Seymour and Flo have to be so united, just when Belle needed her sister the most? It was inconvenient, though she could never truly begrudge them their happiness. It was good that one Bilton sister, at least, did not make a continual turmoil of life.

Flo and Seymour insisted, when Belle did see them, that William would return.

"Do not wither yourself to a crone over William's long absence," Flo had said the previous day on a visit to number sixty-three. "She shouldn't be so dejected, should she, Seymour?"

"You know Dunlo will be back, Belle," Seymour offered. "Take courage, old stick."

"But December has been and gone, Seymour. William is twenty-one now. What holds him in the antipodes?" Belle had watched the months tick by in dismay: now December, now January, now February. "He's almost eight months away and I haven't had a letter in weeks."

Flo squeezed her hand. "But don't you see?" she said. "Dunlo can't send a letter from a sailing ship. Can he, Seymour?" Flo's husband gave a vigorous head shake. "William is between ports and, no doubt, almost home."

Belle was grateful to Flo and Seymour for trying to keep her vivified, but once she was alone again, her doubts attacked and sorrow took over. She leaned farther into the window and looked along Avenue Road to see if the burgundy-suited man was prowling, but it occurred to her that she had not seen him for a fortnight or more. She turned back into the room.

"Jacob, bring my canary to me."

"As you wish."

Belle went to the table and chewed on a piece of bacon and buttered a small breakfast roll while she waited for Jacob to return with the blue cage. He carried it in, and Pritchard agitated from perch to perch inside, discombobulated, as always, by the movement of his home from its sheltered corner in the parlor.

"Hello, dear one," Belle called, to settle her pet. "Coo, coo. Hello, Pritchy, my love. Bring him right here to me," she said, pointing to the floor beside her chair.

"Why don't you release it?" Jacob said, setting down the cage. "Let it fly around a bit?"

She looked at him. "Pritchard does not wish to take off about the room like some wild thing."

"He was wild once, I'll wager. And what bird does not wish for freedom? For space to stretch its wingspan?"

"You are loose with your opinions, Jacob Baltimore. Canaries are sedate birds; you know nothing of them."

"I know they like to fly." Jacob shrugged and kept his eyes fixed on Belle's.

She stared back and found a thought forming, *What is beneath his clothes?* And the reply, *More coffee-dark flesh. Yes, but what more? What more, Baltimore?* Belle blushed and turned back to Pritchard so Jacob would not see the rise of color to her cheeks. The sooner William returned to her to resume their connubial rites, the better. She feared she was becoming lewd and libidinous without him.

A key in the front door meant Wertheimer had come and Belle leaped from her chair to greet him. He took off his hat and she hugged him hard and kissed his cheek.

"What a vast welcome!" he said.

"Isidor, you should allow the page boy to admit you—he has little enough to keep him occupied." She kissed him again and dragged him through to the dining room. "Rosina has made Devonshire junket, I know you enjoy that. Lay another place, Jacob."

"No need." Wertheimer nodded and the page boy left. "I shan't eat, Belle. My appetite won't catch up with me until late this afternoon." He yawned.

"Were you late at the Pelican? Or the Corinthian? You're tired."

"Sleep is for simpletons. Blue o'clock in the morning is my favorite hour—I hardly see my bed in the Burlington."

"Well, sit now and keep me company. You will drink some tea, no doubt."

"I've come to take you out, Belle; I know you've been feeling gloomy without Dunlo. About the lack of letters lately."

"Of course I have," she murmured. "But, how lovely. Yes, let's go somewhere. Shall we walk in Regent's Park? I would like a chance to flaunt my new parasol. Madame Gilbert called it a 'husband beater' when she sold it to me. I felt tickled when she said it, but now it makes me lachrymose—if only I had a husband *to* beat." Her tone was rueful; she glanced at Isidor, unsure now of his feelings about William, unsure if she should mention him so breezily.

"We won't be melancholy today, my dear. Wear your sky-blue dress and flowered bonnet and you'll feel gay. Come, take your sup and then we shall go."

"You are a dear, Isidor." She looked at him and felt moved once more by his constancy, his kindness. He was the best of friends. "Whatever would my life be without you?"

"Come now, Belle. Don't embarrass a fellow."

The cab traveled at a fair clip and Belle felt her spirits rise. It was good to be out; and today was one of those days when London enchanted her anew, as if she were visiting for the first time. Everything seemed wondrous: the dove-gray buildings, the trees in bud, the mélange of queer smells it offered—manure, riverweed, soot, sewage and the Lord knows what else. All she needed was a bit of variety in her day, some dear company, a bit of air—tainted air, maybe, but welcome nonetheless. Her father always said that if one leaves the house, good things happen. She was too much alone, too much in the dolorous stew that William's absence caused. This was what she needed: diversions, pleasant things to elevate her mood. The cab stopped and both Belle and Wertheimer startled when the door opened.

"Occupied!" Wertheimer roared and went to pull the door to.

The door opened wider and a man stuck his head through.

"Mr. Isidor Wertheimer?"

"I am he. Who asks?"

The man placed an envelope in Wertheimer's lap. "A writ, sir," he said. "The notice of action in the case of Dunlo versus Dunlo and Wertheimer. Served by Misters Lewis and Lewis."

"Now look here," Wertheimer said. He lunged toward the door, knocking the envelope onto the cab floor. The horses trotted forward and the door snapped shut. Belle stared at the envelope and stooped to retrieve it, but Wertheimer opened the cab door and kicked it out onto the street.

"Isidor! What did you do that for? Shouldn't you have opened it?" Belle's voice rose. "I don't understand what just occurred. Who was that man?"

Wertheimer grimaced. "He's a process server, Belle."

"And what did he want with you?"

"Didn't you hear him, woman? That was a summons. A divorce petition. William means to dissolve your marriage. And I am to be the reason for it."

A Den

Belle's agitation was physical; it did not abate, rather it stormed her in ever increasing floods until she felt she would be carried off by it. She stayed in bed, aggravating the covers into humps with her toss and turn; she wailed and cried and could not get a fix on one hopeful thought. Wertheimer summoned Flo, who could not come as she was visiting Seymour's family in Devon. He had Rosina brew tisanes of lavender and mint that Jacob brought on a tray and Belle could not stomach. Wertheimer sat on her bed and held the steaming cups to her nose so she could at least breathe the vapors. Her eyes were two aching slits, her nose was rimmed with scarlet and sodden handkerchiefs lay about the eiderdown and on the carpet.

Theories rode pell-mell through her mind. William had had an accident—an injury to the head, perhaps, that upset his thinking. Someone had, in fact, forged his signature; that man his father had sent to accompany William—Robinson. William had said he was an odd, pressing fellow; yes, *he*—Robinson—had signed the petition. And the earl was behind everything, of that she was certain.

"I will write to Lord Clancarty. Plead my case." Belle sat up in bed, her hair in scraggly tails from lack of care.

"I wonder if it would help," Wertheimer said. "I'm not sure."

"He knows something. He's the cause of it, no doubt."

"Or perhaps your Dunlo changed his mind: has decided he does not wish to be married to you after all." Wertheimer glanced at her.

Belle glared back. "How can you say that, Isidor? William loves me and I him. Ours is not a love that can be dissolved."

"I'm sorry, Belle, but Dunlo has been gone a long time. Eight months. And now this!"

"Is our friendship a masquerade, Isidor? Do you pretend to love me and want what is good for me when really you wish to undermine me?"

Wertheimer reached out his hand to her. "No, Belle. Ease yourself. Let me go to Ely Place, to the offices of Lewis and Lewis, and see what they have to say about the writ. Perhaps there has been some blunder or mistake."

Belle rubbed her hands over her face and through her hair. "You know that's not true—there has been no blunder. No mistake. But thank you for trying to animate my spirits. Yes, go and see what the Lewises have to say. I'll try to sleep." She curled into the mound of sheets and put her head to the pillow. Her whole body ached with terror about what might be about to unfold. *She* knew that Wertheimer was merely a friend, but she also knew how people's minds worked: they would gladly misconstrue things since she lived at a house he had taken.

"Jacob is on hand should you need him and Rosina is below stairs."

Belle nodded and did not watch Wertheimer leave her room; she heard him murmur for a spell with Jacob, who was acting as sentinel on the top landing. She wished the boy would go away—how could she weep in peace with him listening? Now that her tears came more than freely, she wished to indulge them. Her fingers found the gold heart around her neck and she held it and sobbed as noiselessly as she could, forming William's name on her lips over and over until she fell asleep.

She woke to a gentle knocking and called "Come in" before she knew who wished to enter her bedroom. Jacob came through the doorway with a tray.

"Rosina commanded me to bring you this." He set it on a side table.

Belle pulled the eiderdown up to her throat. "She might have brought it herself."

"She was afraid to disturb you, ma'am, but I know you haven't eaten in a whole day."

Belle eyed the boy and he stared back. "That is kind of you, Jacob. Is it morning? Has Mr. Wertheimer returned?"

Jacob folded back the shutters. "It is morning, ma'am, and my master is not here." The boy stood and Belle was piqued once more by his tendency to linger.

"That will be all, Jacob. Tell Mr. Wertheimer I'm awake when he comes."

"If it pleases you, ma'am, there are common remedies for agitation. I suggested one for you to Mr. Wertheimer that might help."

Belle looked at the boy. "I thank you," she said, continuing to hold his gaze until he bowed and left.

She got up and poked at the scrambled egg Rosina had sent up and poured some tea. This loss of appetite was not customary—Belle loved to eat—but the toast she bit into tasted of nothing. She sipped the tea and was disappointed to find it lukewarm; she had hoped it would scald her mouth so that she could feel an alternate pain, one that did not center on William's betrayal.

"Oh, William," she said, churning up once again the agony of the previous day's news.

Rosina helped her to dress: petticoat over corset, skirt over underskirt. She was efficient with the bodice buttons—much faster than Belle herself. Her skin, she knew, had the curdled grease-and-dust aroma of one who has spent too many hours in bed. She should have washed—it would make her feel better—but she had not even the will to dab water under her arms or between her legs. Belle did not want to put on clothes or leave the house; there was comfort in lying under the covers to sob.

Wertheimer waited for her in the smoking room. He rose when she entered.

"I want to take you to a place that will ease your nerves." He wanted to aid Belle to rise out of herself, so she could feel less troubled. "This trip will help you forget your cares."

"But I don't want to forget! There are things I must do."

"There is nothing to be done today, my dear. Mr. Lewis says the date for the trial is not yet set. Nothing can happen anyway until Dunlo returns from the antipodes."

"I suppose that is so." William would be back! The court case would go ahead, that was certain, for once in train it could not be reversed, but at least she might talk to William face-to-face and see what exactly had pushed him into this chaos. Had pushed both of them.

Wertheimer pressed Belle's arm. "We must get you feeling settled, a little more like your gay self. We will bring you succor and then you can work on regaining your strength. Trust me."

Belle did trust Wertheimer—was he not her closest ally and dearest friend? She linked his arm and let him lead her to the waiting cab. Jacob came to open the door for them and Belle noticed that his customary impudent smile was replaced by a softer look.

"Have Rosina ready the goods for mustard poultices, Jacob, in case Lady Dunlo needs them on our return."

"Very well, sir."

They sat into the cab and Wertheimer called out "Pennyfields" to the cabman.

"Limehouse?" Belle said, settling her skirts. "You are being mysterious, Isidor. Whatever might we do there?"

Wertheimer lowered his voice, though the cabman would need a bat's ears to hear anything. "I have arranged, with an acquaintance of mine, that we should visit a den. We will be the only people present, so you must not be alarmed."

"A den? Couldn't I just drink some poppy tea or down a swig of

Sydenham's laudanum? What if someone should see me enter a den and carry news back to Clancarty?"

Wertheimer leaned into her side and took one of her hands in his. "Our spy has flown, Belle. You need not worry about the earl. And this place will delight you."

"Are ladies even permitted in such establishments?"

"Certain women frequent them, to be sure, but my friend Chi Ki—a Chinaman—is affording us privacy today. Don't fret, all will be well."

Belle looked out at Regent's Park, at the trees that were stripping off their winter dark for March clothing. The horse's hooves drummed in her belly, causing a soporific lull through her that was assisted, no doubt, by lack of food. It seemed no time at all until she could divine the reek of the Thames in her nostrils.

The den was accommodated above a shop and was not the low haunt of Belle's imagination. It was a large, bright room with couches and tables; the walls held dragon hangings and stringed instruments. Chi Ki served a bitter tea that Belle did not finish and he began to prepare two bamboo pipes with bowls like pigeons' eggs. She watched as he dipped a needle into the gallipot of treacly opium and let it fizzle over a lamp flame; he stuck the needle into the bowl of the pipe and handed it to Belle. The smell of burned sugar and laudanum alarmed her and she passed the pipe to Wertheimer.

"You first," she said.

He took it, grinned and drew rapidly on the pipe, which burbled as pleasantly as Pritchard when he was content. Wertheimer sucked harder and two wisps of black smoke escaped his nose. Belle watched perspiration rise rapidly on her friend's brow; his cheeks slackened like collapsing dough. He grunted, lifted his chin and settled back into the couch like a man unboned after love.

"The lady now," Chi Ki said, and he began his ritual once again.

Belle wondered if she really wanted to be made insensible. Wertheimer opened his eyes and gave a faraway, languid smile that seemed to Belle to come from another realm. Yes, that was a place she wanted to go to herself, she concluded. She held out her hands to take the pipe from Chi Ki, but he held it for her instead; she wrapped her lips around the mouthpiece and took rapid pulls as she had seen Wertheimer do. Immediately she felt her face loosen and the moist push of sweat on her forehead; her heart slowed to a dull thud and she even fancied that she could feel her pulse become lethargic in her wrists. Then her arms and legs did not feel a part of her body anymore—they appeared to float above her, ghost limbs. And her mind unraveled and sagged into a dull trance.

"How are you, my dear?"

Wertheimer's face hovered over her and he was smoking a cigarette. Someone placed a cigarette between her fingers, too, and she smoked it obligingly and it seemed to take an hour to finish it. She saw that Wertheimer was having another opium pipe. She found that her thoughts were neither hers nor not hers—they directed themselves without her bidding. One moment she was scolding William, the next she was fully in the room, listening to Wertheimer who was now mumbling who knew what to nobody in particular. Mostly, Belle seemed to have no thoughts at all and she floated, instead, in some cloudy elsewhere. Her eyes felt veiled and hazy. She flapped one hand in front of her face, sure suddenly that it was made of smoke or, at least, that the hand did not have a thing to do with her arm.

"We have sailed through the gates of paradise," Wertheimer said, and then repeated the words quietly, as if spellbound by them: "We have sailed through the gates of paradise."

"How poetic you are, Isidor," Belle murmured, looking at her slumped friend who seemed to be on the other side of the room though his hot hand was in hers. "William is poetic, too."

Chi Ki materialized at Belle's side and proffered another pipe, but she knew that a second blast of opium would flatten her.

"No, I thank you."

He went to the other end of the couch and held the pipe while Wertheimer smoked it. Chi Ki smiled benignly at Wertheimer, who was in a stupor, though his eyes glistened. The next time she felt roused, Belle knew by the slant of light from the window that it was late afternoon. Hours had idled past without her being sensible of them marching by. She squeezed Wertheimer's hand and, though his eyes stayed slitted, he spoke coherently.

"We must go now, yes," he said, and he hunched forward and pushed himself to stand.

Belle rose, too, and looked at her skirt to see if her legs knew enough to propel her across the room and down the stairs.

"My wife hail a hansom for you," Chi Ki said, and Belle was surprised to see an English girl enter the room on some unknown signal. "Cab for Mr. Wertheimer and friend," the Chinaman said and she nodded and left.

"An unlikely marriage," Belle said to Wertheimer, once in the cab. "But a solid one perhaps."

He slid against her shoulder and his head found rest there. She did not tell him that his carnation was getting crushed, for it would fuss him. Belle looked out at the passing streets and wondered if a fog had descended or if her eyes were still clouded from the opium. Once at the house on Avenue Road, Isidor insisted he must use the boot scraper before entering, but he could not lift his foot. He tried and it flopped and he snorted, tried again. Jacob had to help Belle escort Wertheimer up the staircase to his bedroom.

"My legs feel utterly uncooperative," Wertheimer murmured. "Now, why should that be?"

They pitched him onto his bed, and Jacob straightened his master's clothing and put the pillow under his head.

"I'll have Rosina prepare a mustard poultice, sir," he said. "It cures any kind of ache or ill."

"Quite," Wertheimer said; his eyes were shut but he was clear of voice.

Jacob followed Belle out of the room and stopped behind her at her door until she turned to see if he wanted something.

"I trust you had a pleasant day out, ma'am?" There was a smirk on his lips and Belle did not like it; he was little more than a tea boy, after all.

"See to your master, Jacob. I wish to be left alone."

Belle entered her room and laid her sluggish body on the bed without undressing; she wanted to rise and remove her corset, which cut into her flesh like teeth, but she did not have the will to move so much as a pinkie. A dream-riven sleep followed, a world awash with seawater—number sixty-three, the whole of Avenue Road, her bedroom there—all were salty with brine. Objects floated by—the ormolu clock, her coal hod and shovel, the detestable porcelain pugs—but everything she reached out to escaped her grasp.

When Belle woke in the night, the moon was a silver coin framed by her window; she slipped under the covers in bodice, skirt and stockings. She wondered if the same moon hung like a lantern over Australia or Hong Kong or wherever William was now; she watched its ride, graceful and easy against the navy sky. *The moon does not struggle to gain its place above the world*, she thought, *above the oceans. Tomorrow I will write to William and my letter will sail safely across the waves to his hands.*

In the morning Belle was clapperclawed with tiredness, but her resolve to write to William was fresh. She rose to fetch her writing slope and bring it back to bed with her. Passing the mirror she saw salty tracks staining her cheeks. She wiped at them. Had she been crying in her sleep? Impatient with her disheveled reflection, Belle turned her back on it and gained the bed. Propped against pillows she took up her pen, dabbed it in ink and began:

63 Avenue Road, London
March 18, 1890

My darling William,

　You will see by my address that I am still at Avenue Road.
Isidor has been such a friend to me and I know that you will
thank him for seeing to my safety and well-being. He jokes with
me that you are over there to capitalize on the gold rush, but I cannot
laugh, for I miss you so. The antipodes are so terribly far away;
another planet, almost. You may as well have flown to Jupiter,
William.

　Why must you accept, and act on, everything your father says? I
am saddened beyond belief by your actions; it is difficult for
me to comprehend what has occurred. I know you love me still, as I
love you, I really believe this. My heart tells me there has been some
horrible mistake, that you would never sign a petition to divorce
me and, yet, according to Messrs. Lewis and Lewis, you have
done so. Is that what you were trying to warn me of in your last,
incoherent note? Have you been threatened with something to
do it, my love? Please tell me what has led to this; I am all
bewilderment.

　My appetite has fled, William, and my eyes bulge from weeping.
Flo and Seymour tell me to keep my heart out but, if I do, I fear it
will land on the floor. They assure me you will come back and set
everything straight. Their faith in you is touching, all matters
considered. Wertheimer tries to cheer me with outings but I am rent
asunder; I still cannot quite believe that you've done what you've
done. Or why.

　William, whatever anyone may say of me, don't believe them. I
love you dearly. I do so wish that people would leave other people's
business alone. If your father dispossesses you of whatever he can keep

from you, what of it? I earn enough for both of us; we will not starve, of that I am certain. I wait for you, London waits for you.

                                        Your loving wife,
                                        Belle

A Reunion

Belle had been neglecting her correspondence. Any letter that did not come from William was of no interest to her and she had allowed a pile of unopened envelopes to build up on the chiffonier. Some were for Wertheimer, but most were for her. She looked across at the stack and was made guilty by it.

"Bring me the post, Jacob," she said.

It was eleven o'clock and she had just sat at the breakfast table, jaded finally by the four walls of her bedroom. Jacob piled the letters on the tray and kept one eye on the quivering tower they made as he walked to where she sat. Belle stacked them against the silver syrup cup and sighed. She lifted the first one and sliced it with her letter opener. The bill for her parasol from Madame Gilbert. Overdue. She tossed it onto the floor. Next, a note from Sara to say that baby Isidor needed new clothing. Did Sara write it herself or did she ask her husband to pen it? Either way the hand-writing was appalling. Down to the floor with it.

Belle lifted another envelope; the curl of the writing jigged something in her recall, but it was not until she had taken out the paper and was as-saulted by the smell of violets that she realized it was from her mother. The letter was weeks old and, when Belle examined the envelope, she saw by the marks on the rear that it had tried to find her at the theater in Manchester in December before finally arriving at Avenue Road. It consisted of a single sheet.

My dear Isabel,

 I shall be in London to attend a doctor in March, from the 21st, for one week. I will take luncheon each day at the Star and Garter Hotel and trust you and your sister will join me at least once.

              Mother

"Succinct as ever," Belle said, forking a wedge of apple dumpling into her mouth though she had not yet started on her porridge. She needed the sweet dumpling to calm her; today was the twenty-fifth of the month and she would meet her mother. "Jacob," she called, rising from her place, "send Rosina up to me, I need to get dressed; I'm going out." She took a plate of Pearl biscuits upstairs with her to eat while dressing.

As the hansom climbed the hill to the hotel, Belle wondered if her mother was staying at the Star and Garter or if it was merely convenient to the hospital she was attending. Was there a hospital in Richmond? She knew not. The pavilion rose out of the trees as the cab approached the front entrance and Belle knew it was there that she would find her mother for, even though Mrs. Bilton was frugal, she liked the finest of surroundings to eat in. The Thames passed pea-soupily by in the grounds below the hotel and the country quiet assailed Belle's ears in a way that eased her. Would it be pleasant, she wondered, to hear nothing but birdsong and the snap of twigs at night, instead of rolling wheels and the cries of night shifters and the fallen?

The many-paned roof and gas chandelier made a glittering dome of the pavilion's ceiling; it beguiled Belle always. She stopped in the doorway to admire the glow and when she dragged her eyes downward they fell on her mother who was standing by a small table, as if waiting for her. Mrs. Bilton had the same regal posture as ever, accompanied by the same vanquished set to her jowls, as if the whole universe were set against her. Her mother sat when she knew her daughter had seen her and Belle advanced.

"Hello, Mother."

"Your sister failed to come."

"Flo is busy; she is rehearsing a new show."

"One should never be too busy for family." Mrs. Bilton waved her hand and a waft of bergamot filled Belle's nostrils—this fruity-sweet spice was the aura of Mother. "And you are not in this show?"

"I declined to take a part. I have needed to rest lately."

"I see." Mrs. Bilton made no inquiry after Belle's health, a fact that did not pass her daughter's notice. "It has been some time, Isabel, since we broke bread together."

Belle sat opposite her. "Several years, Mother."

Even though Belle did not care for her mother's good opinion, the older woman's bellicose manner still unnerved her. Mrs. Bilton had always done well as an artillery man's wife by being as combative yet self-possessed as any soldier. Her father put it down to his wife's Welsh upbringing, though how childhood in a castle had made her so pugnacious, Belle failed to see. She studied her mother's face—inscrutable as ever—and waited for her to explain the exact reason for this meeting.

"How is Father?"

"Yes, you *should* ask how your father is for you have not seen him in so long. I am happy to say that he is in good spirits. As robust as he ever was."

"I'm glad to hear it."

"Violet is also thriving."

"We correspond."

Mrs. Bilton grunted, a noise Belle presumed represented distaste for her and Violet exchanging letters. Belle ignored the disapproval and scrutinized the menu, though she knew it by heart from frequent visits to the Star and Garter. She looked across the table to her mother and took in the gray that was salted through her upswept hair, and the further sag of her chin. She was in her forties now, Belle supposed—an aging woman. "You look well, Mother," she said at last, tired of waiting for the conversation to continue.

"I am not well, but there it is."

"Nothing too serious, I hope?"

"Is that your hope, indeed?" Mrs. Bilton squinted at her. "I am not mortally ill, but I am told my condition is grave. It debilitates me certainly."

"You will, no doubt, outlive every one of us, Mother." Silence then, for Belle did not want to press her mother about the nature of her complaint when specifics were not on offer. "The shin-of-beef soup here is extraordinarily fine," Belle said, and nodded to the waiter who had hovered for some time nearby.

They both ordered the soup. Mrs. Bilton asked for plain toast and Belle said she would have hers with Gentleman's Relish; she loved the pep of the spicy anchovies as a foil to the beef. Her mother asked for portions smaller than the hotel's usual ones for herself.

Mrs. Bilton talked then of people they knew at Aldershot—those who had died; those who had gone abroad with their regiments; those whose daughters had married, well and badly. Belle found it hard to match faces with the list of names her mother recited, no matter how she concentrated; lack of sleep began to overtake her and she yawned. Blood roiled around her eardrums making a far-off murmur of her mother's speech; Belle blinked and when she focused again, she realized she had missed some important statement.

"I beg your pardon, Mother, I didn't hear what you said."

"I said that we read newspapers in Hampshire." Mrs. Bilton frowned, put out by Belle's lack of attention.

"Yes?" Belle affected innocence but guessed what would come next.

"*Lloyd's Weekly* takes a particular interest in your affairs."

"You were on the stage yourself, Mother, you know how they love to gossip about theater folk."

"And as you well know, Isabel, I am not referring to your music hall engagements. I speak of your marriage."

Belle looked out the window, down to where the river snaked past; she could see several ladies walking the towpath. She thought how grand it would be to stroll there with them, drawing river-weedy air into her lungs and prattling, perhaps, about this milliner or that dressmaker. How grand it would be to be a normal married lady with few cares.

Mrs. Bilton coughed, drawing Belle's eyes back to her. The atmosphere was torpid between them; her mother made a show of not speaking again. Their food arrived and Mrs. Bilton kept her eyebrows raised when she lifted her spoon to taste the soup. Her portions were small, as she had requested: a porringer of beef soup and one slice of toast—it looked a minuscule amount of sustenance to Belle.

"There's a Welsh plate if ever I saw one," Belle said.

Her mother grimaced. "I am not, I must say, Isabel, alarmed by your hasty marriage. Rather I am perturbed by the reports that have come after it. It seems you have managed to both snare and sacrifice a husband almost instantaneously."

"William has had to go abroad on business, Mother, nothing more. You mustn't believe every tittling gossipmonger who speaks."

"But, my dear Isabel, I did not hear these reports from tattlers. Your uncle—my brother—happened to stop at a club called the Corinthian, I do believe, when he was in London before Christmas. An acquaintance there told him the details of the sorry tale."

"Well, then, you know everything." Belle threw her napkin over her soup bowl; her mother's words churned up her anger. "I am shamed by my own husband. There it is. Under the influence of his dominant father, Lord Dunlo left for the antipodes mere days after our marriage."

Her mother buttered her toast carefully and bit into it. "You *are* having a thin time."

"Oh, it will please you that the story has moved on, Mother. It gets ever more dreadful. My husband now means to divorce me!"

"Well. What a performance you have managed to mire yourself in, what an extraordinary pickle."

Mrs. Bilton continued to chew her way through the bread at a slow pace; she looked straight at her daughter as if trying to fathom how she could be hers, then she cast her eyes down to the food she was laboring so hard over.

The very way her mother ate riled Belle. Her own appetite, such as it was, had collapsed. As she sat and watched Mrs. Bilton eat, she remembered childhood scenes where her mother would ram unwanted food into Belle's mouth. On one occasion Mrs. Bilton had held her daughter's nose and spooned an entire creamer of semolina between her lips. When Belle had sicked it up, her mother had forced her to eat it again. Yes, out in the world Kate Maude Penrice Bilton was the beautiful Welsh wife of Sergeant John George Bilton, but at home she was her children's oppressor. She very much resented the drudge of maternal duties.

"No doubt you are aware, Mother, that because of this there will be a court hearing." Belle adjusted her gloves, pushing her fingers firmly into them. "But I'm sure of William's love for me. Though he has acted abominably, I'm certain that everything will turn out for the best."

"You clearly never took it upon yourself to learn the first rule about husbands, Isabel: they must fear you. The coy, winsome woman does not make a good wife. If your spouse is not somewhat frightened of you, you have failed." She snorted. "And you think all will be well?" Mrs. Bilton put her hand to her face; her shoulders shook, and it took Belle a moment to realize that it was mirth that was causing her to convulse.

"Do you mock me, Mother?"

Mrs. Bilton waved her hand. "I married down, Isabel, and you married up, but a fat lot of good it did either of us." She chortled and laughter tears filled her eyes.

Belle stared at the rocking, rollicking form of her dour mother. Before the waiter could jump to assist her, Belle pushed back her chair and stood.

"Good day to you, Mother," she said, and walked away.

She heard Mrs. Bilton's voice call after her, "And good luck to you, my dear!"

Belle did not turn around.

A Report

"Lady Dunlo," Bassano said, as Belle entered his studio. "I do so love to call you that."

"Enjoy uttering it while you can, Alexander, for it may not be my name for too much longer."

"I read about your predicament in the newspaper this morning, my dear."

"Good heavens, it has been reported on already? Those newsboys are like starved urchins picking over scraps." Belle flopped into an armchair and Bassano fetched another and pulled it to her side. "There's no privacy in this town, none whatsoever."

"Well, that's true. But it's a short piece; I daresay no one will notice it wedged between 'Floods in Mississippi' and some nonsense about a liberal majority in the Stoke-on-Trent election."

"You may as well read it to me."

"Are you sure you want to hear it, Belle?"

"My life has been one bizarre turn upon another lately, Alex, I am sure I can bear the words of a journalist. Read, please."

He lifted the newspaper and thumbed through the pages. "Here we are: 'Viscount Dunlo, son of the Earl of Clancarty, is bringing an action for divorce against his wife who was Belle Bilton, one of the Sisters Bilton, the music hall artistes.'"

Belle started forward. "What do they mean 'was'? I'm still here, am I not?"

Bassano lowered the paper. "It merely means that since your marriage your name has changed to Lady Dunlo."

"Yes, quite. Carry on."

"'The co-respondent is a relative of a wealthy dealer in bric-a-brac. Lewis and Lewis are acting for Lord Dunlo and the papers were served on the co-respondent at the Lewis and Lewis offices in Ely Place. An attempt was made to serve the co-respondent on Tuesday in a hansom cab . . .' Oh, this next bit is fantastical, you will love it, Belle: 'The process server threw the papers into the cab, but the co-respondent *kicked them out again.*' Is that not wonderfully silly?" Bassano chuckled.

"It may well be silly but it's exactly what happened. I was there. How do these newspapers know every fiddle-faddle of a person's doings? It's very unfair."

"But why on earth did Wertheimer punt the papers out of the hansom?"

"We were confused, caught off guard. Isidor reacted and the first thing that shot out was his foot."

Bassano raised his eyebrows. "Shall I read the rest?"

"Go on."

"'The papers were found by the police in St. James's Square and brought to the offices of Lewis and Lewis. The co-respondent subsequently went to Ely Place and was served with them properly.' Gracious, you have been having adventures, Belle. Is it any wonder I hardly see you? I must be far down on your list of daily activities."

"I don't avoid you on purpose, Alexander. I've been addled, my head a fug of thoughts and schemes. And when I get like that, my skin suffers, my smile droops and the last thing I desire is to titivate myself for the camera."

"No doubt there is some coven of women that you turn to for blowing off rages."

"Alex, you know perfectly well that Flo is my only female friend and I only tolerate her because I'm related to her." Belle stretched her legs and studied her ankles, turning them this way, then that. "Women don't altogether like me, Bassano, and I don't care for their company much either. Men are easier, somehow." Belle puckered her mouth in concentration. "Though men *do* seem to bring me endless strife."

"*Ma bella* Isabella, you're one of those extraordinary women who craves—and deserves—happiness, but it seems to come to you embroidered with botheration." He let down the newspaper, reached over and put his hand under her chin. "There's something tragic in your eyes, Belle. You are tragic and prone to self-sabotage but nonetheless magnetic. Yes, my dear, your charms are total. Perhaps your tragedy is beauty."

"Alex, you do talk perfect rot." Belle let a sharp laugh and took his hand from her face. Self-sabotage? It was probably true.

"It's understandable, my dear, that you don't wish to hear yourself dissected. I've been reading too much Thomas De Quincey, perhaps." He stood and held out his arms. "Come, you're here now and we should get to work. Augustus Harris doesn't invite any old matron to take the stage as Venus at Drury Lane, after all. You're a cause célèbre and you must capitalize on it."

"It *is* delightful to be asked to dance in Drury Lane, I'm happy for it. And it's time for me to rise above my worries and earn some money again."

Bassano went to his prop cupboard; he balanced what he took out of it on his palm and crossed the room to Belle.

"Your Mr. Harris has sent over this *piccolo* crown for your new likeness. Is it not the prettiest little ornament you've ever seen?"

Belle took the tiny golden coronet in her hand and studied it. "How dainty. But it's so miniature it may get lost in my curls," she said.

Bassano rushed back to his cupboard. "But the venerable Augustus Druriolanus sent this one, too!" He held up a tiara with seven tall crests that shot up from the circlet like icicles.

"That's the one!" Belle said. "If the newsmen want to notice me, then notice me they shall." She reached for it, and Bassano led her to the mirror and fixed the tiara into her hair. "Isn't it formidable and gay?" She twisted her head and admired the sparkle of each of the columns; the central one had the largest stones and its crystal glow was mesmerizing.

"Now, take it off, change your gown and we shall reassemble you for the photographs."

Belle did as she was asked and was soon seated in a throne-like chair by Bassano's much-employed palm fronds. Her dress had a deep neckline, petal-ragged layers, large bows on the shoulder and the bodice was embellished with dog roses; Mr. Harris's costumier had designed well.

As Bassano worked they chatted and, during rest periods, Belle rolled her arms and neck to loosen her muscles.

"My mother summoned me to the Star and Garter lately, Alex, for a tête-à-tête."

Bassano inspected her. "Really? And what did Ma Bilton want with you?"

"She wished me to know that news of my marriage had reached her. *'We read newspapers in Hampshire.'* Though it was my uncle, of all people, who provided the juiciest morsel—the fact that William had gone abroad." Belle moved her hands from her lap to her neck, letting the gold heart rest in her palm for a moment. "She met me to shame me, really, that being her natural inclination."

"Mothers are queer creatures, are they not? They love us madly until we display the signs of our true selves, until we're no longer malleable. Then they *choose* whether to love us anymore. Or not."

Belle rose from the chair and paced the studio. "When I came to London, there were none of the ancient grudges to deal with; I was free to be a new self. But now there are different animosities, new adversaries. Every person I meet brings so much with them and everything becomes a gallimaufry of this intrigue and that. It's tiresome."

Bassano came to her and put his hand on her arm. "Life is hard, Belle, that is an immutable fact. And people only make it harder."

Belle looked up at him. "My mother should be glad I didn't end up in a bawdy house, with a thousand other Hampshire lasses. Flo and I have made a success of ourselves, but Mother gives us no credit for that."

"Might she be envious?"

"Undoubtedly she is. She had ambitions as an actress herself. But it would be pleasing if she'd celebrate our accomplishments. Even a little."

"And what of your father?"

"Poor Father. He is lamb to mother's wolf."

"It's often the case." Bassano clapped his hands and drew Belle back to her seat. "Come, let us attempt this pose one more time, my dear. We have to keep Augustus Harris happy. Now, try to look less dejected, if you can."

"I will try, but when things are topsy-turvy in my life, my whole body reacts from brow to boot. I'm fatalistic, Alexander, it has always been so."

"Well, if that's true—and I'm inclined to think that it is not—you're an optimistic fatalist and they're the best kind."

"You're so sweet to me, Alex, and I neglect you terribly."

"Come now, let us press on. You're the queen of the West End, Lady Dunlo, and you have the headgear to prove it." Bassano pushed his upper body under the camera's cover and told Belle to hold her pose.

She breathed in, attempted to empty her mind and tried—and failed—to look serene. Bassano had not the heart to tell her that in her Drury Lane Theatre poster she would look dashed and dispirited. But, then, wasn't there always something a little toxic about Venus?

A SEVERANCE

Little Isidor scuttled away from Belle and hid his face in Sara's skirts. Her infrequent visits made her a stranger to him. It was April already and she had not seen him since before Christmas. Belle smiled at the child, but, it seemed, he was disinclined to engage with her.

"It's all right, Dory," Sara said. "Say hello to the lady." She tried to grasp the boy, but he ducked farther behind her. "She's your mother." Belle wondered if Sara said that with some reluctance.

Isidor groped his way around Sara's legs and stared up at Belle; a snail trail of snot silvered his upper lip. He made no move to wipe it away and neither did Sara, and Belle did not want to ruin her lawn handkerchief by going at him. What to do?

"His nose is dirty," Belle said.

Sara bent low and pulled the back of her hand under the boy's nose; she gawked at Belle as if she were absurd to have pointed out such a thing. Belle still clutched the parcel with the flannel shirts, cape and knickers she had brought for Isidor. On the train she had vowed to herself that once seated in Sara's cottage, she would gather the boy onto her lap and talk to him. He might even answer her—at almost two years of age children could talk, she presumed. Belle would show him his new clothes and maybe even dress him in the red wool cape, so he would remember it was from her when she was not there. She would cuddle Isidor, pet his hair and sing him a ditty:

> *Bobby Shafto's gone to sea,*
> *Silver buckles at his knee;*
> *He'll come back and marry me,*
> *Bonny Bobby Shafto!*

But the unaccustomed fact of her son, his physicality, tumbled her from her good intentions. The boy looked bedraggled and feral in a long, shapeless shirt—a replica of Sara's own children. Where was the braid-trimmed shirt Belle had so recently sent? This was a baby's garment he had on; it was time he was in something shorter with knickers to match.

She watched Isidor move about the room; he reminded her of a mouse, watchful and silent, but swift when it was needed. Belle did not now feel any desire to touch the boy, or sing to him, or rock his body on her knee. And she did not want to dress or undress him; if she did, she would see whatever grime painted his naked body. He looked as though he might be sticky as a newt all over.

It was easier, it seemed, to be a mother in her imagination than in fact. Her own mother's disdain for *her* flooded Belle of a sudden, and she did not like that little Isidor raised similar contemptuous feelings in her breast. She would not become Kate Maude Penrice Bilton, not in this world or any other. Belle was capable of being a loving and gracious mother, she knew it. Something must be done. She dipped to the floor and brought her head close to her son's. He jinked away from her, quick as quick.

"Dory," one of the older girls warned. She knew, no doubt, that Belle's visits were important.

Belle moved closer to the boy and he slunk back. "Would you like to take a walk with your mama, Isidor? With me? *I* am your mama."

Sara pushed him forward. "Go out with the lady, Dory. Show your mother the trees and flowers. Show her the pond."

"Is it far, the pond? Does he know how to get there?" Belle asked, all amazement that one so young might have knowledge of such a thing as a route that led somewhere.

"It's only down the way, ma'am. He plays there most days." Sara scooped up the child and looked into his eyes. "You want to go to the pond, don't you, lad? Eh, Dory?"

Isidor nodded, struggled out of Sara's arms and ran for the door. Belle followed.

The pond was a scummy, dark pool beside a derelict cabin. Belle had followed Isidor's short, sturdy strides along a mud track to get there; she lifted her hem to avoid gathering a rim of dirt. The air felt sweet in her nostrils, as refreshing as post-cigarette air.

"What a superb day, Isidor, to be surrounded by nature. How fortunate you are to live in such a place, are you not?" She rocked in her shoes which were seeping now on the boggy bank.

Her son ignored her; he fell to his knees at the pond's edge and dragged rushes and twigs into a roundel, as if he meant to make a nest for himself. His back was to Belle, and she felt his avoidance of her as a deliberate rejection of her voice, of her touch. Belle had never in her life been fond of children; she was not a clucky cooer like Flo who, since a child, had loved opportunities to be with babies of all kinds. Belle's own son made her feel inadequate; her maternal feelings—those she thought she should have—would not rise. Around her the trees crackled and she felt as if a hundred pairs of eyes judged her ineptitude as much as her discomfort. A rustle from the track they had come by made her stare that way. She was not sure if what looked like the figure of another child was real or fantasy. It was a bush perhaps, the branches hung like limbs. Belle squinted but could make no sense of the form at this distance.

Little Isidor continued to erect his twig burrow, some sort of refuge, perhaps, from the other children. Maybe he came here so often to get away from them and the smoky hut. Belle was disquieted by his lack of attention to her; his absorption in choosing the right stick, and the perfect clump of moss, irked her. And yet she admired his stout concentration on his task— he struck her as a fully formed, tiny man going about his day's work. How did babies suddenly become people? When exactly did that occur?

"Look, Isidor," Belle called. "Dory, look over there—daffodils." She pointed to the flowers that stood in a sunny cluster at the base of a tree near the water's edge.

Dory lifted his head, turned and fixed her with a stare that seemed to encompass every ounce of Belle's neglect—it was at once a look of sorrow, indifference and, she was sure, contempt. It was as if the boy knew full well that she was his mother, but spurned the fact violently. Such a small person, such malice. Could one so young really have such *feeling*? But, oh, didn't Belle perhaps look that way when she, as a girl, stared at Kate Bilton? The boy continued to glare at her and it jarred her insides. What was amiss that she could not control the men in her life, even one as unfledged as her son? For years she had witnessed her mother lord it over her father, and he had obeyed without question. Belle could not make her own husband stay by her side, and now this child she had labored into the world would not respond to her. Was her agitation and sadness over William warping her, or was it a fact that she would never be able to engage satisfactorily with men? And, further, would she ever become a loving mother to treasured babes?

"See, daffodils," Belle called out, trying to be amiable, and waved her hand again.

Little Isidor turned his head toward the flowers, rose out of the muck and went to them. He plucked each stem; when one dropped to his feet, he scooped it up. He stood with the bunch of daffodils wrapped in his small embrace.

"Well now," Belle said, "you are a gentleman after all. Come, give the flowers to Mama."

She held out her arms and fixed what she hoped was a cordial smile to her lips. But Dory did not come; instead he walked back to the water's edge and laid the flowers by it. He hunkered down and plucked off the daffodils' golden heads, then tossed them bloom by bloom onto the murky surface of the pond. He gathered the stems, went to his nest and began to weave them through it.

"You little Podsnap," Belle said, but the boy did not look her way. "Isidor Alden Cleveland Weston, turn to face me when I speak." He did not shift. "I'm talking to you, boy." She could not understand her noxious anger, it rose through her and swathed her, and she could not seem to tamp it down. "Isidor!"

Dory stopped his work, but did not turn and did not move. Belle stared at him, at his composure, his stubbornness. The small body and the back of his head seemed an affront to her.

"Turn!" she shouted. Her voice echoed into the trees and across the pond. She was as mad as hops; the child was an intractable little shit! Weston had made him so; Sara had made him so. "Turn to me!" Belle roared.

The boy stayed where he was, his gaze toward the pond. The very stillness of him enraged her. How dare he deaf ear and cold shoulder her, how bloody dare the child?

"Turn your face to me, Isidor." Her voice was low and steady now.

The boy remained a statue; Belle inched forward. "Turn!"

He would not move and his mulish stance made her furious. She went up right behind him and grabbed at his arm, but Isidor had sensed her and he jerked himself away. He toppled then and Belle watched, stunned, as he fell forward into the pond. A heavy splash and, swift as a stone, he was gone. Wavelets rippled from where he had sunk and Belle watched them flutter outward, then disappear. Daffodil heads bobbed away from the bank.

A crack and shuffle nearby made Belle turn her head and one of Sara's girls stepped out and gazed at her.

"You!" Belle shouted and the girl turned and ran back up the track toward the cottage.

All was silence. The trees seemed to hold their breath along with Belle. For a moment the hush deafened her. She could feel the shush of air at her fingers where Isidor had missed her grasp. Had she been about to hit him? She knew not. Belle looked up through the trees at cloud fragments ragging across the sky. What had she become? Was she going mad?

The thrash of wings and a click-and-shift movement among the trees woke her from her trance. At the same moment Isidor burst through the surface of the water, whooshing air into his lungs in starved gulps. He was farther from the bank now and, arms flailing, he once again fell below the surface. Reason and remorse flooded Belle and she lunged into the pond; she knew where he had been, and she got to that spot and groped through the dank water to find him. Nothing. She plunged sideways and moved her arms frantically under the water. One hand caught something and she yanked it surfaceward. His ankle! She pulled on the leg until she was able to grab the boy's waist and heave him up into her arms. Belle stumbled, but she stood in the water and held him, terrified he would slip from her, swift as an eel. Isidor coughed and dragged breaths into his lungs; he did not struggle.

"I have you," Belle gasped. "I have you, Dory."

You're sodden, ma'am."

Sara met them on the path and lifted the boy from Belle's arms and handed him to one of her older daughters. They entered the cottage and Belle saw the small girl who had been at the pond; she stared at her and the girl eyed her back and said nothing. Isidor did not fuss or sob, and Sara's older daughter stripped him deftly and wrapped him in a blanket. Sara pulled Belle by the arm to the fireplace and bade her sit. The whole family stood around, watchful, as Belle tried to explain.

"He fell. He fell in the pond," she stammered. She glanced at Isidor, who sat in the girl's lap, shivering, and kept his eyes fixed to Belle's. "I . . .

we were picking daffodils and we must have gone too close, for he lost his footing and—"

"No!" said a small voice. The younger girl stepped forward.

"Hush, Mabel," said her sister. "The lady is speaking."

Belle looked around and continued. "I went in straightaway. I grabbed Dory; he wasn't in the water for long."

"You both got a fright, no doubt, ma'am." Sara glanced at the boy. "No harm done. Come, Miss Bilton, let me take your gown and dry it for you. You may lie on the bed in the room beyond until you're recovered."

"No, no, it's quite all right, I have inconvenienced you enough today. My clothes will dry on the train. I must get back to London now." She wanted to say *It is not Miss Bilton, it is Lady Dunlo,* but did not. She felt a stab of guilt at the thought; she could be as imperious as Kate Bilton and no mistake. And as deliberately cold.

"Sit a while, miss. Dry your skirts at least." Sara beckoned to her eldest girl. "Annie, make cocoa for Miss Bilton and a round of bread and treacle for Dory."

The girl nodded and set about her tasks; Belle pushed her feet in front of the grate and stared into the fire. She tried not to think about what had happened by the pond and she deliberately kept her gaze away from her son.

The cup was veined with dirt and the cocoa tasted bitter, but Belle drank it and was thankful for its heat. Mabel, the smaller girl, stood where she had been since they had arrived back and would not unfix her eyes from Belle. She was made uneasy by the girl as much as by the conflicting feelings that mauled her breast and mind.

"I will thrash you, Mabel, if you do not find a way to occupy yourself," Sara said, lifting the poker and shaking it at her daughter.

Dory unpeeled himself from the blanket and climbed out of the chair he had been placed in. He walked toward Belle, naked, and stood before the fire. Belle thought he was going to speak, but he only stared at her. She held his gaze; he had Weston's eyes, not hers. Would little Isidor eventually end up like the pretender that his father was, his whole life built on deceit? Or would he be more like Belle—unruly in every choice? Perhaps he would live as simple a life as Sara and her family. Whichever path he followed, she could see no fine future for him.

Sara came over and put a long shirt on the boy and rolled up the sleeves. When she was done she kissed the top of his head and pushed him away. He took a twig from the pile by the fireplace and scuffled on the floor with it. Belle watched him and realized she felt mostly indifferent to the boy; he did not fill her with love, though she rather wished he did. He bore the taint of Weston, that was the problem. But the child was safe, well and at home. It occurred to her that she might feel more affection for her canary than for her own child; the bird raised *feeling* in her, something akin to love. Could this be true? The thought was both horror and balm. Was she the worst mother to have lived? A replica, in fact, of her own mother? Weston had soiled the boy for her; she could not get over the circumstances of his birth. Belle was not proud of these feelings, but how was she supposed to muster love for little Isidor? But then, she reasoned, if she did not care for the boy, she need feel no true maternal burden. If motherliness toward him was not naturally awoken in her, she was surely not to blame. This new rationale made a sigh of relief erupt from her mouth and the boy lifted his eyes to hers at the sound.

Belle stood up. "These are for Isidor, Sara." She indicated the parcel she had placed on the table when she went to the pond. "For Dory. Perhaps there is something in the package that would fit Mabel, too." She smiled at the girl.

Belle fished in her bag and tucked a brooch, which she had intended to pin to the boy's shirt, under the top layer of paper. It would keep him safe, or so the woman at the bazaar had said. It was heart-shaped, golden, and no doubt Sara would keep it for herself. What did it matter? Beside the parcel, Belle placed the twist of coins for her son's upkeep.

"I thank you, ma'am."

Belle nodded. "I really must go now."

She looked down at Isidor, busily scraping the mud floor with the twig. He released a babble of sounds—*mumu-dudu-mumu*—and seemed to take pleasure in gouging the hard mud while he yapped to himself. No harm done, then. Surely no harm done. Belle rubbed her forehead as if trying to erode her shame. Why could she not just love the boy? And if that was impossible, why could she not let him go with ease?

"Good-bye, Sara. Thank you for your help."

Belle stuck her parasol out the door ahead of her and opened it; she stepped out into the fragile Sussex sunshine. This, she decided, is the last time I will see this place.

A Rejection

ow was the boy?" Flo asked, plunging low to the right, the better to
elongate her left leg. She kept eye contact with herself in the
dressing-room mirror. "Is he now a hardy little fellow?"

Belle fell in beside her and began her stretches; sweat rose on her forehead though she had only begun. "He's as rough as his companions; he has
become one of Sara's savage brood."

"Well, you know what they say: 'A wild goose never reared a tame
gosling.'"

Belle humphed. "I can't see him ever making it in society."

"Isidor may be his father's son, then. 'Baron Loando' did not last long
in London. Seven years in Lewes for his trickery around the town."

"Quite." Belle rolled her head in a slow arc, taking care to keep her
shoulders still. "But enough of Weston, Flo, I truly never want to hear his
name again. He's my past." Belle stretched her arms wide, then pushed
them high over her head. It was good to feel the lengthening of her muscles, to switch the focus from her tangled thoughts to her body and the
performance ahead.

"And baby Isidor, what is he?"

Belle sank into a plié and kept her gaze forward. She saw little Isidor, wet and shivering and accusatory. "He's also from a time I wish to leave behind."

"But, Belle, he's still your son."

"He's Weston's son, too," she snapped, "and what is he doing about it? Enough, Flo. I said I don't want to speak of it."

Belle sat and snatched up the poster which Mr. Harris had left for her to add to her collection. Her crowned head—her face a touch mournful, she saw—took up most of the page. The lettering was curlicued: "Drury Lane Theatre presents Lady Dunlo as the venerable Venus, Goddess of Love, in Yardley, Rose and Harris's burlesque *Venus; or, The Gods as They Were and Not as They Ought to Have Been.*"

"Mother played Venus," said Flo, coming over to lay her palms on Belle's shoulders.

She put one of her own hands over Flo's. "She did. And she was magnificent."

"Yes, she was."

"Mother is ill, you know."

"She won't die of it, whatever ails her. The woman is made of Welsh flint."

"Welsh coal," Belle said.

"Daffodils," Flo said, making her sister giggle.

"Bloody leeks!" Belle hooted and they both laughed madly.

"She's the red dragon though, isn't she?" Flo said. "You know, Seymour has never believed Mother's childhood-in-a-castle story."

"Well, nor did we, by the by," Belle said.

"But you know Seymour—he loves to poke about, fancies himself a detective. Well, through some acquaintance in Wales, he found out that Kilvrough Castle was owned by a Penrice all right, but the man lived and died there without ever marrying."

"Seymour missed his true calling."

Flo gave a fond smile. "He is certainly fond of unearthing things."

"We've long suspected there was an amount of fancy behind Mother's claims. Still, I almost feel sorry for her."

"I don't," Flo said. "Come, enough palaver, let's get started."

The sisters rose as one to begin their voice warm-ups.

"Mmmmmmmm," they chanted. "Meeee, maaaay, moooo."

When their call came, Belle and Flo hurried along the cold passageways to the stage. As always, the wings were black as hell and they picked their way carefully so as not to snag a foot on a stray rope. The dark was absolute: it pressed on Belle's eyes and skin. She was washed with that familiar preperformance tentativeness: part elation, part fear. Things were magnified suddenly; the shadows loomed and unnerved her. She was upturned by everything: William, little Isidor, the constant pluck and pull of life's demands. Irritation coursed through her; and Flo's breath, as familiar to her as her own, seemed suddenly to spurt as large as the spume of a whale and it increased Belle's annoyance.

"Stop breathing so loudly, Flo. You're panting."

"I am not!"

Belle's cue—Vulcan waxing jealous over Adonis—had her leap to the stage first. She soon forgot about all upsets and Flo and the oppressive darkness of the wings. The footlights were as ardent as a dear friend's welcome and, as Venus, she warmed up in their glow. Belle minced under the adoration of Vulcan and a small army of gods.

It came to the moment where Mercury was threatened by Jupiter about the damage to his reputation by a newspaper article, if it were not contradicted.

Mercury bawled, "Well, why don't you marry the girl?"

The house agitated with laughter and Belle turned to them and winked, acknowledging her own predicament. This made them cheer and whoop, and Belle, in the yellow haze of lights, felt suspended for an instant in a place of perfect peace. A stray thought flew: *if only I could stay here forever.*

A DELAY

A letter from William sat on the credenza in the hallway of Avenue Road. Jacob had placed it at the top of the pile and Belle snatched it up. She pulled off one glove with her teeth and broke off the seal. She walked up the stairs, pulling the pages out and unfolding them, hungry for William's words. She sat on her bed and began to read.

S.S. Orient
February 2, 1890

My darling Belle,

By now you will know what has occurred and I must try to explain it to you, though I'm weak in limb and spirit today. You may be livid with me and you must certainly be mortally upset and I'm sorry for that. For my part, though I'm ill at present, I feel some amelioration of my anxiety about the whole business because I'm now one ocean closer to England and to you.

Hong Kong
February 10, 1890

*Some days have passed, my darling, since I began this letter. I've
been bedbound and unable to hold a pen. I spent many hours on the
voyage from Australia in my cabin in feverish half sleep, broken only
by excessive chills; I couldn't eat and as a result I arrived to Hong
Kong weak from crown to rump. My depletion in mind, spirit and
body is an encompassing disquiet, a giddiness in the limbs and brain
that I can't soothe. Onboard ship, my heat imbalances and jitters, I
was certain, were caused by a bad conscience, nothing more. I didn't
like to meet myself at the mirror each morning, for my guilt dwelled
like a spirit in my eyes. In sleep I could forget myself and the scratch of
my nib on the divorce papers, but morning reflected my idiocy back at
me when I stood to shave. Water. Badger brush. Lather. Fool. That
was my daily ritual.*

*Now I'm a little brighter, but I can't unkink the huge gnarl of
remorse over what I've done. In one way I felt it was the right thing to
do, the only course possible, for it would release you, Belle, and I, too,
would be liberated—from debt. That is how it was put to me by
Father, via Godley Robinson. The point was pressed hard on me and,
in my weakened state, it did make sense.*

*But I also want you, Belle, with my whole heart, that has never
changed. Never have I felt more ardent toward a woman. You know
this. I do so wish our letters didn't skirr past each other, out of time,
and that we could converse in a cohesive way. This inharmonious
communication doesn't help either my conscience or my malady. I do
not even know when you will read these words and I so wish that they
were with you now, so that you might somehow understand.*

*I got worse in my sickness some mornings back, waking with
nausea, a broiling fever and sweat excreting from my skin in torrents.
A dream had startled me out of sleep. In this dream I stood in a*

cemetery and realized, for the first time, that the dead outnumber the living; while the thought formed, corpses burst from the ground like ripening bulbs. My overheated body and the residue of the dream fuddled my brain. I got up to pour a glass of water, but fell to the floor and found I was too stone limbed to regain the bed. The boy who attends me found me slumped on the rug and a physician was immediately summoned.

"Malaria, as sure as eggs," the doctor said. A disease of tropical lands, Belle, and I managed to contract it. Robinson has had to change our berths, for I can't travel while in the grip of malaria which, the doctor says, is a singular illness that takes its leisurely time; apparently you may think it's over and then, snap, it returns. I take quinine and total rest.

The last few days I've lain marooned in bed, afloat on the fever, though I could sense the hubbub of Queen's Road below my window, but it was a far-off, hushed hum that came and went. I could hear people speaking a coddle of languages; and my boy brought thin gruel, but a few spoons were all I could stomach. I will not tell you, Belle, the horrid intricacies of the illness and I probably shouldn't mention either that Robinson cheerfully informed me this morning that quinine can paralyze a man. "It can kill you, too," he said. (Be assured, I have no plan to die.)

Today I'm calm. I've even found a slitch of hope to cling on to. I will return to you, Belle, and make right the wrong I've done. If you won't accept my apology, I'll harry you until you do. I'll neither give in nor give up. I'll fight for what I want and that is you, dear Belle, forevermore. Nothing endures, my darling, and soon I'll be well and will return to you. "Consilio et prudentia," Belle. By counsel and prudence we will get it all done and continue with our life.

Your loving Dunlo

Belle curled onto her side on the bed. William was ill and it was a serious condition. Malaria. She had heard her father say it decimated troops in the colonies. Would William survive it? Perhaps the letter was proof enough that he had rallied and thrived. How did he fare now that April was almost over? His letter was weeks old. Distress and worry simmered. Was William sincere, did he truly mean to come back and set things right? She held the letter up and read the last lines again: *"Nothing endures, my darling, and soon I'll be well and will return to you. 'Consilio et prudentia,' Belle. By counsel and prudence we will get it all done and continue with our life."*

She supposed by getting "it all done" he meant the court case and that it would go ahead as soon as he was able to come home. It was, of course, unstoppable now. And every scintilla of their lives would be reported on by those Fleet Street daubers and picked over afterward by the whole of London. There would be no more slyness or hints about her private life: everything could be legitimately reported on and sized up from whatever angle the writer chose while he—the journalist—remained incognito. And Belle would just have to endure it.

SUMMER 1890

London

An Encounter

When she beheld the back of William's head in the Café Royal—it was he, she was certain—Belle's first thought was how uncanny it is that even the rear aspect of one's beloved is so familiar. Her second thought was that it was true, he was back, and yet he had not contacted her. His last letter had been contrite, he knew he had wronged her, but here he was, the full, de facto flesh of him across the room and he had not seen fit to let her know, in person, that he was in London. What fresh eccentricity was this? Belle's gut twisted in confusion: she felt a surge of love for William, but twined about it like a serpent was deep annoyance. Still, she must get to him, she must see his face; maybe then she would be able to divine why he behaved in such contrary ways. With heart jolting, she galloped toward his table, where he sat alone.

"William," she said, putting her hand on his shoulder.

Dunlo turned and, when he stood, she saw that he was rawboned and scraggy; he was swamped in his clothes, as if they belonged not to him but to a bulkier man.

"Belle." It was a solid, assured utterance, as if he had fully expected to see her there, as if they had arranged to meet. His eyes widened, but he did not reach for her.

Her bewilderment grew, but she steadied her voice. "So, William, you *are* back. I heard it whispered but I didn't believe it. I was so sure you'd come to me first." How perplexing to stand before the man she loved—her very husband!—and yet to feel like an interloper. Did she not belong to him? Did he not belong to her? Belle wanted to put her arms out to him and have him enwrap her in his. Instead, her mouth formed into a thorny smile. "Your silence has been earsplitting, William."

"They forbade me to contact you since I got back, Belle. I dearly wished to."

Fury rose. "Who forbade you, William? A short note to tell me you were safely returned would have sufficed." But it would not! Why did he avoid her person when his letters spoke of loyalty and love? "Really, William, a visit, no matter how brief, to let me see that you were safe and improved in health, would have been proper. People have no right to keep us apart. What say has anyone else in the communications between man and wife?" She bristled. "William, to contact me would have been the *loving* thing to do."

He held out his hands, not to touch her, it seemed, but to lay himself bare. "Lewis and Lewis, Papa's legal people, they said it would not be wise to see you before the case—"

Belle interrupted him. "Lewis and Lewis! And Papa himself forbade you, too, no doubt. And you obeyed him. He is, after all, your god." William glanced away and Belle, following his gaze to the doorway, apprehended that he was not planning to dine alone. "Ah, the earl is here with you. And you don't wish him to see me."

"I'm with my mama."

Before Lady Adeliza could return, and no doubt make a pantomime of ignoring her, Belle spoke rapidly to her husband.

"William, I'm painfully flummoxed by you. Your letters say you love me, but your actions contradict it; I know not what to think anymore. You've done a terrible thing and now you compound it by ignoring me. What am I to make of you? How am I to believe the words of your letters that seemed so sincere?"

William's hand flew to his mouth and Belle was relieved that he at least was injured; he *was* capable of remorse.

"I know I've done wrong, Belle. I know I continue to perplex you, but this will be put to rights. I give you my oath on that."

Belle could feel Lady Adeliza behind her without having to turn and see her. "You might leave us now, Miss Bilton," the countess said.

Her son stepped forward. "Mama—"

"Good day to you, William," Belle said, and she brushed past Lady Adeliza, avoiding the other woman's gaze.

The mirrored walls blurred as she moved toward the café's door; she walked with care, keeping herself erect. Of course all eyes trailed her, but she did not glance to see who was staring. Salivating gossip hounds, every one of them. Belle's heart pummeled her ribs. So, William gave her his oath. He would put it to rights. How exactly would he do that? Tears began to burn behind her eyelids and she could feel the scald of her cheeks. She gulped back a sob and exited onto Regent Street. If life threw her one more obstacle or upset, she knew not how she would go on.

Belle hailed a hansom, screeched "Avenue Road!" at the driver and got herself into the cab. She slumped in her seat and whimpered. Why did every damn thing in her life have to upend itself? Could one thing not go right? She daubed at her face with her handkerchief and put her hands together. Unaccustomed to prayer, she prayed anyway: "Dear God, please let William be true to his word. Please, I beg you, Lord. Amen."

A Case

Belle lifted her veil for a moment, the better to study William who sat at the other end of the solicitor's bench. His return glance was sheepish but earnest, and they locked eyes for a beat. Belle's heart bulged into her throat. She was angry with him still, and hurt by him, but there he was—handsome and big, the man she loved. Belle found she couldn't be completely displeased with William; his presence moved her so. She wanted to go to him and climb into his arms; she wished they could get up and run from the courtroom, the two of them, run to some covert place where nothing might assail them.

Belle smoothed the skirt of the new gown she had had made, a pink silk with white braid trim. Her outfit was a message to William: pink for love and white for her stainless state; she hoped he would divine that.

The judge, Sir James Hannen, entered the court and people began to rise. Mr. Lockwood, Belle's solicitor, nodded in her direction and she and Flo stood. When the judge was settled and the case announced, Mr. Russell, representing William, rose. He looked around the court, letting his gaze linger on Belle as he began to speak.

"I will first read to you the petition for the dissolution of this marriage. 'This is the humble petition of William Frederick Le Poer Trench, commonly known as Lord Dunlo.

"One: on the tenth day of July 1889 he was lawfully married to Isabel Maude Penrice Le Poer Trench, formerly Bilton, at the register office in the district of Hampstead in the County of London.

"Two: that since the said marriage the said Isabel Maude Penrice Le Poer Trench has been daily in the company of Mr. Isidor Wertheimer and has continuously and habitually committed adultery with the said Isidor Wertheimer at Sixty-three Avenue Road, St. John's Wood, in the County of London and at diverse other places in the said County of London.

"The petitioner therefore humbly prays that your lordship will be pleased to decree that the said marriage be dissolved and that he have such further and other relief in the promises as to your lordship seems meet. Signed by the petitioner."

Mr. Russell once again focused on Belle and continued, his voice more conversational now.

"Lord Dunlo is a *young* man; he attained his majority only in December last. Miss Isabel Maude Penrice Bilton, the respondent in this case, is not only his senior in age, it must be noted that she is also his senior in point of experience of the world. She is a lady of considerable attraction as well as of considerable talent, being a doyen of the music hall. The acquaintance between the petitioner and the respondent began in May 1889 in the Corinthian Club and they hastily became intimates, leading to their marriage. Lord Dunlo's father's assent was not obtained, as it should have been, the petitioner being under age."

Belle watched Mr. Russell as steadily as he watched her. He meant to unnerve her it was clear, but she was determined to appear imperturbable, no matter what he said. Flo had fed her Pepper's Quinine and Iron Tonic for days and she could feel the vigor it afforded her. Seeing William again had also energized Belle. Yes, he appeared to have been made delicate by his recent illness but he looked older, more manly because of it, too. It had been a wrench to continue to avoid him, but all advice had been in that direction. When she queried Mr. Lockwood, her solicitor, he had been most firm about it.

People had wrestled with one another to gain entrance to the court and the room was packed. Belle looked around and wondered what spectacle they hoped to witness. The vindication of the aristocracy? Her downfall, maybe? But many of them were surely on her side. She certainly had a loyal following at the theater, but it was hard to know if those people were here. There was a varied crowd, between nobility and pauper. The poor who frequented the theater also loved to gawp at these kinds of cases. They were invariably in awe of the gentry; they aped the rich as much as they disdained them. It occurred to Belle that they might be on Lord Clancarty's side rather than hers. Belle let Mr. Russell's speech become a burr outside her ears while she looked around. *Did* these people of London hope to see her humiliated? Her eye caught on a smart woman in a check suit and it took her a moment to realize it was her mother. Mrs. Bilton nodded. So she had come. What did Mother hope to see and hear? Belle whipped her head away and returned her attention to Mr. Russell, who was now addressing the jury—an unreadable cohort of men.

"This lady," he said, "wrote to Lord Dunlo saying that she felt it better, in the circumstances, that he should go to Australia as arranged by his father. 'Better for both of us,' she wrote. Better for *both* of us." Mr. Russell was skewing Belle's meaning, taking it out of context; that note had been a test for William but, of course, he had never read it because she had discarded it in his Burlington room. How on earth did it end up here? Mr. Russell shook the papers he was consulting and held them aloft. "The respondent is charged with adultery. It is alleged that she entered into an adulterous relationship with Mr. Isidor Wertheimer, her co-respondent, the son of a well-known bric-a-brac dealer on Bond Street."

The word "adulterous" clanged around the room and, Belle thought, it was probably heard along every corridor of the Royal Courts of Justice and out on the Strand, so loudly did Mr. Russell exclaim it.

"But we must go back now to July 1888 when the respondent was living under the protection of Mr. Wertheimer. During that month, on the twenty-fifth to be exact, she was delivered of a male child. Mr. Wertheimer made arrangements for Miss Bilton's accouchement. The child was regis-tered as the son of Mr. Alden Carter Weston, then (and now) in prison for fraud. Mr. Wertheimer kept this lady and her child; he saw her constantly, he paid her expenses."

Mr. Russell cleared his throat and let his latest statement hang in the air. Belle looked at the jury to see how they had reacted to the news of baby Isidor and of Wertheimer's support of her but, to a man, they re-mained impassive of expression. She could not divine if this was a good or a bad thing. Her stomach began to babble softly and she put her hand to her abdomen to try to calm the strain there. She felt Flo grapple for her and she took her sister's fingers and pressed them, unsure who was com-forting whom. Belle did not look to where her mother sat.

"In the late spring of 1889, Miss Bilton was introduced to Lord Dunlo by Lord Osborn, at the Corinthian Club, as we know. But, to Lord Dunlo, Wertheimer was merely a name. He was unaware of the huge impor-tance of this man in the lady's life. To this day, gentlemen, Miss Bilton is protected by Mr. Isidor Wertheimer. To this day she lives at a house he rents at Sixty-three Avenue Road, St. John's Wood. Miss Bilton is con-stantly in the society of Mr. Isidor Wertheimer: he meets her at stage doors, they convene at the house on Avenue Road, he traveled to Manches-ter at Christmastime to see her perform." He paused. "They have been watched."

Belle conjured the burgundy-suited man who had hovered around Av-enue Road for so long. She bent forward in her seat to see Wertheimer, and he grimaced at this confirmation of their being spied upon.

Mr. Russell swiveled on his feet. "I call William Frederick Le Poer Trench, Viscount Dunlo."

William glanced at Belle, rose and went toward the stand. He looked, Belle thought, hunted and gray. When he was settled, Mr. Russell began his questioning. William confirmed where he had met Belle, the date of their marriage and that his father did not know about their union. He acknowledged that he had left for Australia days after the marriage and that Belle had not wanted him to go, but that she gave "a sort of blessing," knowing if he went that he would return.

"Lord Dunlo, Miss Bilton earns in the region of fifteen hundred pounds per annum. Would you consider that enough for two, nay *three* people, to live on?"

"It is adequate."

"Do you have an income, Lord Dunlo?"

"My father provides for me."

Mr. Russell indicated Belle with one hand. "Do you believe the charges contained in the petition against your wife—that she had an adulterous affair with Mr. Isidor Wertheimer?"

"I have never believed them. I only signed the papers because my father, through Mr. Godley Robinson, insisted."

"And yet you did sign them. Of your own free will you put your signature to a petition for divorce that called your spouse an adulteress."

"Mr. Robinson worked on me on the voyage we took; he led me to believe at first that my father intended to disinherit and disown me. Later he said if I signed the divorce petition that those things would not occur." William paused, and Mr. Russell nodded to indicate he might go on. "Robinson pressed upon me that it would be better for my wife also, that she would escape my 'foolishness' without blemish. He also said that Papa promised to write off my debts if I consented to sign. I was beginning to get ill, my brain was fuddled. I hardly knew up from down." William dropped his head, then raised it again. "I didn't realize either that there would be immediate consequences. Robinson impressed upon me that I had erred in my life and endangered my whole family's reputation. Who was I to diminish the Le Poer Trench name? I thought. Perhaps, I reasoned, it would be better to set Belle—that is, Lady Dunlo—free."

A vibration of sweat ran over Belle's body. Set her free, like some sort of unnecessary encumbrance, when there was so much love between them? It was difficult to listen to William tell how Robinson had cajoled and undermined him. Belle wanted to crush Robinson and shake William.

Mr. Russell held up a bundle of envelopes. "I have letters here, correspondence from your wife to you while you were abroad. In one she admits she is 'out with you.'"

"That may be. We were newly married and I had left her."

"Yet, she gave her blessing to your journey. Do you see the contradictions here, on both sides?" Mr. Russell opened one envelope and took out the pages. "Let me read an extract for the court. This is the voice of Miss Bilton, I remind you, gentlemen: 'Wertheimer is the last person in the world I would misconduct myself with, you know that. And, for the sake of the tongue waggers, I am only ever with him on the street. I do hope, William, that you are as true to me as I am to you.' But was Miss Bilton not spied under many a roof with Mr. Wertheimer? Should Lord Dunlo and his father, the Earl of Clancarty, suffer in silence while Miss Belle Bilton, a dancer, struts around all London and beyond with Mr. Wertheimer? I say *no*, they should *not*." He threw down the letter. "No further questions, Your Honor."

Mr. Lockwood, representing Belle, stood.

"Lord Dunlo, is Miss Bilton excessively fond of Mr. Wertheimer?"

"She has told me he pesters her with his affections, but she likes him nonetheless."

A ripple of laughter from the public gallery made Belle glance that way.

"Did you know that Wertheimer had offered to marry her?"

"Yes, I knew that. It was a long time ago; he meant it to help her out of a poor situation."

"And when did you offer your hand to Miss Bilton?"

"Ever since I met her."

More laughter.

"Did some of your friends try to discourage the marriage?"

"Some of them; they hinted that she had been living with Mr. Wertheimer. They told me about Mr. Weston."

"I have a letter here that you wrote to Miss Bilton from Sydney,

Australia. You say, I quote: 'Now, Belle, I don't believe a word of it.' This was in relation to the rumors of her intimacy with Wertheimer?"

"That is correct."

"Lord Dunlo, was it your father who gave instruction for the commencement of this suit?"

"Yes."

"You never gave any instructions for its commencement?"

"I did not."

"Did you believe the charges made against your wife?"

"No, never."

"Did you know that when you signed the papers your father says he began to pay off your debts?"

"No. Through Mr. Robinson he said he would help with my debts, but I was not sure if I believed it. That is, I wanted to believe this, but my mind was rather addled. I could not think clearly."

"Do you owe a lot of money?"

"My debts are, unfortunately, as plentiful as the hairs on my head."

"So you signed the papers?"

"I was confused. I did not realize that the papers would be acted upon at once. The divorce papers and the debts became entwined in my reason. Mr. Robinson led me to believe I would be imprisoned; he talked of the debtors' jail. My position was not clear to me." William rubbed his forehead with one hand. "I was muddled, my mind was agitated."

"Is it true that you were in fact coming down with a serious illness, perhaps already severely tainted by it?"

"I contracted malaria on my travels, yes."

"Lord Dunlo, has your father, in fact, cleared the monies you owe?"

"Not to my knowledge, no."

Mr. Lockwood smiled, a small curl of the lips. "No further questions, Your Honor."

A Tip

Belle stood outside the Royal Courts of Justice, watching the dark rags of jackdaws being tossed up on the wind above the building's turrets. It's a castle of a place, she thought, and quite as imposing as one. How often had she passed it and admired its long, fortresslike stance? Little she knew then of the painful stories that unfolded behind its gates. Walking through the gothic vault of the Great Hall early that morning, the space looming above her grand as any cathedral, she had felt like a condemned queen stepping toward her execution. She did not share the thought with Flo who, she guessed, would have pooh-poohed such morbid fancies.

"A wearisome day," Flo said now, standing by Belle outside the court, while Wertheimer flagged down a hansom.

"We will all three fit," he assured the ladies.

A cab, Belle knew, would be tight with three in it, but it would get them away quicker than a coach, for the cabdrivers liked to move fast, to dip and dodge around larger vehicles. She did not want the faces from the public gallery gawking at her afresh on the street.

Belle kept her eyes on the doorway of the courthouse, hoping that William would step out and speak to her. But, as she watched, Mrs. Bilton emerged on a tide of stragglers; she stopped in front of her daughters.

"Florence," she said, nodding to Flo, before turning to Belle. "Isabel."

"Mother. You are here."

"I am, Isabel. And now that it appears you have a child of your own, you surely understand why I came. Children pull on their parents. I am drawn to you, despite everything." Mrs. Bilton adjusted her parasol. "I may never have been a model mother to you, Isabel, but I can no more turn from you than scrape the marrow from my bones."

Belle eyed her mother, tried to digest her words. "I had no notion of your coming, Mother. Of your hearing everything."

"Nor I," Flo muttered.

"When do you take the stand, Isabel?"

"I know not. I simply have to wait my turn."

"Be plain. Be truthful. You can do no more."

"Yes, Mother."

"You have always had an elastic disposition, Isabel. No doubt you will survive this. And prosper."

Wertheimer stepped forward. "Ladies, our hansom is waiting." He lifted his hat to Mrs. Bilton. "Madam, may I offer to hail a cab for you?"

"I wish to walk," Mrs. Bilton said and, without offering a farewell, she turned and set off down the Strand, her august carriage causing other pedestrians to make way for her.

"The woman is astonishing," Flo said, as Wertheimer helped her into the cab. "As impudent as a goat. She is 'drawn' to Belle! What about bloody *me*? I put up with plenty from her, too."

Wertheimer held Belle's hand while she climbed up, then got in himself. "Perhaps, Flo, if you generated a bit more theater in your life—off the stage, of course—your mother would be equally drawn to you."

"Oh do be quiet, Wertheimer," Flo said, but she smirked at him and he smiled.

Belle laid her head on Wertheimer's shoulder. "I'm glad that part of the day is over, at least."

Wertheimer lifted the trapdoor in the roof. "Drive on, man!" he shouted, and the hansom lurched forward.

Jacob let them in at Avenue Road and, when they were settled in the smoking room, Wertheimer ordered him to bring tea. "And tell Rosina we need cake. Shall we have some wine, too?"

"Neither you nor Belle should get tipsified this week, Wertheimer. Keep your heads clear."

"True. No wine, Jacob. Tea and cake." Wertheimer nodded and the page boy left, leaving the door hanging open.

Flo closed it and plunked into an armchair. "Your Master Baltimore has something of the scamp about him. There's disquiet lurking there."

"Jacob often speaks in a way too large for his position," Belle said. "Isidor lets him forget who he is."

"He's a fine fellow—leave him be."

"Isidor," Belle said, "might you bring Pritchard to me? I want to see his sweet face."

"Of course." Wertheimer rang the bell; by and by Jacob returned. "Miss Bilton wants her canary in here. Fetch the cage from the parlor."

"Yes, sir."

Jacob was back moments later; the bird flitted mightily, disordered by the movement of his home.

"There you are, Pritchard," Belle called, and she waggled her hand to have Jacob bring him to her quickly. Jacob set the cage on the floor beside her. "But I can't see him properly," she said.

"Put the cage on a table," Wertheimer said. "Come along, boy."

Jacob lifted a table to set beside Belle's chair and once again scooped up the cage. Belle watched him for signs of his usual audacity of manner, but Jacob benignly obeyed his master. When the canary was ready before her,

Belle pressed her face to the bars of his blue home. Pritchard hopped from perch to mirror to bell.

"What do you seek, little one?" Belle said. "You're upset from being tussled about, isn't that right?" She whistled to him, a roll of notes meant to soothe him.

"'A whistling woman and a crowing hen are neither fit for God nor men,'" Flo said.

"Ah, but 'Be she old, or be she young, a woman's strength is in her tongue,'" Belle replied. "Mother was fond of *that* saying, too, Flo."

"She was when it was her own tongue."

Wertheimer sent feathers of smoke ceilingward where they joined to form a wispish cloud; he threw back his head, making the tassel of his smoking cap swirl over one eye. He puffed on his cigar and watched the smoke whorl away from his mouth.

"Your mother is a very fine-looking woman. You've led me to expect a crone."

"Don't be fooled by her grand exterior, Wertheimer," Flo said. "She's sly as a badger. And has the entirety of Hampshire in her lap, convinced she's a marvel. Meanwhile, at home, it is nothing but peppery exchanges and raised fists."

Rosina came in with a tea tray with plates piled with cake and biscuits.

"You always have the best eatables, Wertheimer," Flo said.

"Isidor keeps me in Pearl biscuits and every other delicacy I wish for."

Flo turned to Wertheimer. "You spoil her, you know. She'll remain a child forever under your guidance, if you don't take care."

"Nonsense, Belle's the most capable woman of my acquaintance. Like your mother said, she has a gift for fortitude. I do believe she could survive anything."

Belle listened to them discuss her and let the hot tea warm her gullet; it was restorative after the long first day in court. She picked a piece of candied lemon peel from her slice of plum cake; she thought about giving it to Pritchard, so charmingly did its color match his feathers, but she feared he would choke on it.

"I so wish I could hold and pet you," Belle said, peering in at the bird.

"Why can't you?" Flo asked. "My pal Iris takes her budgerigar out on walks."

"Pritchard is a canary, Flo. They are not as brash as budgerigars." She wiggled a finger through the cage bars. "I should like you to sleep on my pillow at night, darling Pritchy."

"You're daft when it comes to that bird," Flo said.

"It was unexpected, I daresay, your mother turning up like that." Wertheimer puffed on his cigar. "But a ruddy fine thing for her to do." Both sisters turned to look at him; Flo cast her eyes heavenward. "What? What have I said?"

"Have you understood nothing of what I've related to you about our mother, Isidor?" Belle said.

"I only mean she didn't seem harsh, when she spoke to you outside, Belle. Rather, she gave you some useful advice."

Flo sipped her tea. "She came to gather ammunition against Belle for future use. There's no doubt about that."

"She has plenty now, to be sure," Belle said. She thought of her mother's words to her outside the Courts of Justice: *Be plain. Be truthful.* Belle intended, of course, to be both those things in court, but Wertheimer was right. Though it was unlike her mother to be cordial, she *had* offered guidance. There was decency in that, for sure.

Pritchard frenzied at his seed bowl as if starved—he sent seeds scattering about and Belle could already hear Rosina muttering darkly about waste and uncleanliness. The bird took a short flight around the cage and stopped to admire his mirror image. The canary had a sweet life, no doubt about it, Belle thought. He burbled and sang blithely to himself.

"Oh to be as innocent and free as my darling Pritchy, so unaffected by life's tribulations. Why is my life so tangled?" Belle looked away from her pet to her sister. "All my days—ever since I met Alden Weston—have been days of adversity. Everything disintegrated the moment he began to pursue me. I swear I haven't known a peaceful twenty-four hours since that time."

"Every long lane has a turning," Wertheimer said.

"I'm blessed if I ever heard such nonsense, Belle," Flo said. "Do you mean to let Weston color your life? I will remind you that since you met him you have acquired a dear friend in Isidor, a son, and a husband. You have danced and delighted people. Weston is a person of no consequence. A criminal. He's nothing, forget him. You must gather your courage, Belle. Never allow yourself to be a misery merchant."

"I have both acquired a husband and lost one. You didn't mention that."

Flo slapped her hand on the arm of her chair. "Stop it. Nothing's decided. Your William has acted like a true fool, but it's not over yet. You must retain a stout heart, Belle. That's vital."

Belle nodded, glad for the balm of Flo's optimistic pragmatism. She sat back into her chair and fingered the gold heart at her throat.

Wertheimer sipped his tea and looked from Belle to Flo. "I so often feel like Christ between the thieves when I'm with you two."

The sisters burst into laughter and turned to him.

"What on earth are you talking about?" Flo said.

"One never knows what mad subject you will latch on to next. I feel I hover in the center of you and learn much."

"Christ between the two thieves. From you, Isidor!" Flo said. "Well, I never."

Belle looked from her sister to Wertheimer. "What on earth would become of me if I did not have you both?"

A Witness

Belle ate a few scraps of cold pork before court; she chewed and stared at the jig of dust motes by the window. Rosina had tried to tempt her with hot rolls and kippers, but hunger seemed a thing of the past. The boom of thunder had woken Belle that morning and the rotten-egg smell it left still hung in the air; a huge downpour would break any second she was sure.

Flo came to her side of the table. "Open your beak," she said, and spooned in a measure of Pepper's Tonic.

Belle swallowed it and stuck out her tongue. "Ugh, it tastes as if I had licked a fire iron."

"Don't be juvenile," Flo said. "It helps."

"I know it does, thank you." She put her arms around her sister and placed her head against her stomach. "Seymour must miss you terribly at home."

"He gets along fine. Come now, Belle. Our hansom will be here soon, Jacob is outside hailing one."

The July sun burnished the front of the courthouse and Belle thought how pleasant it would be to take the hansom past the building and on up the Strand to the heart of the city or back to Covent Garden.

Anything but to have to go inside and listen to further assaults on her character.

When all were settled in their places, Judge Hannen emerged, dapper even under his periwig. Mr. Russell, William's solicitor, looked like a weary owl, myopic and harmless, in comparison. It wasn't until he began to speak that one understood Russell's somnolence was illusory; the man was spear sharp.

"I call Mr. Jacob Baltimore," said Mr. Russell.

Belle turned to Flo. "Jacob? Whatever for?" She sought out Wertheimer and mouthed *Did you know?* whereupon he shook his head.

Jacob sauntered to the stand and took his oath. He wore his lavender gloves and Belle thought how fearless he looked, how jaunty and at ease.

"You were first employed in this country, Mr. Baltimore, as a program distributor for the Bohee brothers, whoever they may be. Were you not?"

"No, sir. I was a corner man."

The public gallery erupted in titters and Jacob looked their way and smiled.

"He is having a rare old time," Flo whispered to Belle.

"And who was your employer after that?"

"Mr. Isidor Wertheimer, sir. I was his stable boy until he wrongly accused me of stealing a coat and I left him after that, sir."

"And who is your employer now, Mr. Baltimore?"

"Mr. Wertheimer, sir. I am his page boy."

"At Sixty-three Avenue Road, the address of Miss Bilton?"

"Correct, sir."

"Does Mr. Wertheimer live at that address also?"

"He comes and goes, sir. He passes the night at his hotel in town. But he and Miss Bilton dine alone together there. In Avenue Road, I mean."

"Not in the company of the respondent's sister and her husband, Mr. Seymour?"

"Sometimes, sir, but more often alone. Together, that is, on their own in Avenue Road."

"So they dine and servants come and go. I see." Mr. Russell looked bored. "Do they, Mr. Baltimore, frequent other rooms in the house?"

"They favor the smoking room, sir. Though they like to play piano-forte together in the parlor, too; they lay their heads on each other's shoulders when they do so. One time, when they had left that room, I observed that the key was on the inside of the door. Another time, while Miss Bilton was in her bedroom, I saw Mr. Wertheimer go up the stairs."

Mr. Russell did not seem satisfied with Jacob's testimony and he left way for Mr. Lockwood to step in.

"You were discharged by Mr. Wertheimer for stealing a coat, but you are employed by him again. Correct?"

"No, sir. I was wrongly accused of stealing and I left. But now I'm back again."

"I see. So Mr. Wertheimer employs you out of pity." He held up a hand to indicate to Jacob that he did not require an answer. "Now, as to the occasion when Mr. Wertheimer went upstairs. You recollect it well?"

"Yes, sir," said Jacob, a swagger to his certainty.

"What time of day was it?"

"In the middle of the day. I daresay Mr. Wertheimer might have been going out; he might have gone up to his bedroom to fetch a hat. Or a coat."

"And where was Lady Dunlo?"

Jacob bit his lip. "She may have been in the parlor."

"You say Mr. Wertheimer might have gone up to his bedroom to fetch a hat. Or was it a coat? And you say Lady Dunlo *may* have been in the parlor. Yet, Mr. Baltimore, you told Sir Charles Russell and this court, mere moments ago, that she was upstairs. No further questions."

Jacob stood and rucked his forehead; he looked to Wertheimer, shrugged and left the stand.

Flo squeezed Belle's arm and whispered, "Mr. Russell is sorry he summoned the fellow now. He doesn't know his head from a hole in a bucket."

"Mr. George Clarke, private inquiry agent, is called to give evidence, your lordship."

Belle watched the burgundy-clad sentry take the stand; she listened to him tell the court that he was employed to follow and observe her and Wertheimer from July 1889. She was annoyed that Mr. Russell did not immediately ask whom he was employed by.

"'On the nineteenth of July, respondent met co-respondent outside the Empire Theatre,'" Clarke read from a notebook. "'I tracked them that night to Conduit Street, where the lady had lodgings. They walked up and down the street for some time, then Miss Bilton went inside and Mr. Wertheimer left the scene.'" He turned a page. "'Another night they seemed to be larking by the window.'"

"Larking? Do you mean they embraced?"

"They may have."

"Did they or did they not, Mr. Clarke?"

"It's hard to say. I was seventy feet from the house."

Report after report from his notebook took this form: Miss Bilton and Mr. Wertheimer were seen leaving the Café Royal together at midnight on August the third. Miss Bilton and Mr. Wertheimer on the eighth of August dined at the Continental Hotel with another gentleman. On the twenty-ninth of August Miss Bilton went to live at Sixty-three Avenue Road; Mr. Wertheimer left the house at half past one that morning. Clarke saw them go shopping together at the bazaars. He witnessed the pair smoking cigarettes by the window in Avenue Road. On the sixteenth of September they were in Miss Bilton's bedroom together, by the window, overlooking Norfolk Road. (Gasps in the courtroom.) And on and on until Belle felt ill with hearing her own life being played out like scenes on a zoetrope, she and Isidor whirring round and round, animated shadows.

"It will be over soon," Flo murmured.

Mr. Russell left Clarke to Mr. Lockwood.

"Mr. Clarke, what was it that struck you as *most* important in all of what you say you saw take place between the respondent and the co-respondent?"

"Him caressing her. He pulled her to him inside the window. They kissed."

Mr. Lockwood raised both eyebrows and looked to the jury, then back at Mr. Clarke. "There is nothing of this in the book."

"These points I always carry in my memory."

Several hoots of laughter from the gallery and Lord Hannen lifted one hand. "I will not have an atmosphere of feeling created on one side or another."

Mr. Lockwood resumed. "Mr. Clarke, is this book you have been quoting from the original notebook?"

"No."

"Ah, it is not. Where is that first book, the real one?"

Clarke looked at the floor. "I destroyed it."

Judge Hannen roared across the court, making everyone jump. "This examination has proceeded under the impression that the notebook you hold is the original!"

"That was *my* understanding," said Mr. Lockwood.

Mr. Russell stood. "And mine."

"Why, Mr. Clarke, did you destroy your firsthand reports?" asked Mr. Lockwood.

"The book contained other entries about other cases. I had what I needed. When my notebooks are full, I always burn them."

Judge Hannen turned to the jury. "I am obliged to tell you, gentlemen, that the notebook which Mr. Clarke holds is no corroboration. He has deliberately destroyed that which would have *been* corroboration. And he substituted it with nothing of the sort. You will disregard his litany of sightings."

Mr. Lockwood asked two more questions of Clarke. "Did you know, sir, that your inquiries were made on behalf of the Earl of Clancarty; that you were in fact acting on his behalf?"

"I did not."

"From whom did you take instruction?"

"Misters Lewis and Lewis."

"No further questions, my lord."

Clarke stood down, pushed one hand through his hair and avoided looking at anyone. Belle watched him walk to his seat and felt a small spurt of hope. Clarke said he didn't know the earl was behind his surveillance. Then, there was the burned evidence and inconsistencies in his reports.

Flo nudged her sister and leaned in to whisper, "None of this looks good for Clancarty."

Belle nodded and pressed Flo's hand. Indeed it did not look promising for the earl. And for a man for whom appearances were all? Well.

Mr. Russell rose once again. "I request the swearing in of Richard Somerset Le Poer Trench, fourth Earl of Clancarty, my lord. The earl is not well and wishes to proceed now, though he attends this court against medical advice."

Judge Hannen nodded and Belle watched the earl try to correct a stoop as he took the stand. He was a shade of the man who had bellowed at her upstairs in the Corinthian Club: thinner, less regal, but still somewhat noble because of his height, she had to own. Her heart contracted when she looked at him. He was a man of power and he wished to crush her. Sitting so close to him and, now, looking straight at him, made her feel dizzy. Belle's breath came fast and she had to swallow spit over and over, so dry was her mouth.

The earl confirmed that the petitioner was his eldest son and that he intended him for the army. William had failed to pass the examination for Oxford, he said.

"I obtained a position for him with the Herefordshire Militia but that was distasteful to the boy, so I looked out for—and found—a person to accompany him abroad. This was with my son's full approval, you understand. I engaged Mr. Godley Robinson on the fourth of July."

"And when," asked Mr. Russell, "did you book two berths to Australia?"

"The twelfth of July."

"And when did you first know of the marriage of Lord Dunlo to Miss Bilton, which took place, we remember, on the tenth of July?"

"I read it in the *Pall Mall Gazette* on the thirteenth."

"What did you do?"

"I summoned my son and told him he must go abroad until he attained his majority and then he would be free to act for himself."

"When did you first engage the services of Misters Lewis and Lewis?"

"The twentieth of July."

"Are you aware your son is in debt?"

"I believe he is."

"Is it true you undertook to pay his debts if he agreed to sign the petition in this case?"

"There is not one word of truth in that statement."

"My lord," said Mr. Russell and he sat.

Had not Mr. Robinson led William to believe that that was the case, that the earl would relieve him of his debts if he signed? The earl was lying and Belle found herself glad that he was. He would be found out and Mr. Russell would rue the very hour he agreed to represent him.

Belle's Mr. Lockwood stood and faced the jury; he indicated Lord Clancarty. "Be aware that this man did not tell his son that if he went away and returned when he was of age, that he could live with his wife at that point. He did not *believe* in the marriage that had taken place." He turned to the earl. "Is it true that you told your son that if he stayed in London with his wife, and refused to go abroad, that you would have nothing more to do with him?"

"Yes, I did."

"Did you think that Miss Bilton might go wrong if left by her husband?"

"No."

"Will you swear to that?"

"Yes."

"Did you *expect* that Miss Bilton would go wrong?"

"Well, now you put it in my mind, I think it extremely probable."

"Well, did you care if she went wrong?"

"Not much. I did not believe the marriage a valid one and I did not trouble my head about it."

"Did you answer a letter from Miss Bilton begging for an interview in order that she might refute certain rumors? Did you ever give her a chance of meeting the charges against her?"

"No, I did not."

"Did you approach the lady with a view to making some arrangement as to what she was to do?"

The earl sighed. "No."

"It did not occur to you that it would be a chivalrous and generous thing to see your son's wife?"

"I was under the impression that the marriage would not be valid until he turned twenty-one."

Mr. Lockwood paused. "When did you first determine to have Miss Bilton watched?"

"The twenty-second of July."

"Was this because you had discovered that the marriage was, in fact, a valid one?"

"Yes."

"Is it your opinion that your son was anxious to have his marriage annulled?"

"I should think he was. He wrote in a letter to me that he believed himself truly married. And that he must now get out of it."

"What did your son say when you informed him that you knew of his marriage?"

"He sneered at it. The marriage."

Belle flinched. This was invention: it had to be. She did not like to hear this version of William trotted out before the gawpers. The earl was not to be believed, but how would the throng in the public gallery know that? Would Judge Hannen believe him?

"Your son is educated, I presume?"

"Of course."

"Is your son sane?"

"He is now."

The public gallery rippled with laughter and Belle looked at William who seemed unmoved. The earl was determined to act the fool, it seemed, and his son was determined to remain stoic in the face of his father's nonsense. Bravo, William!

Lockwood waited for quiet and pressed on. "Did you promise your son a good allowance if he stayed abroad until he turned twenty-one?"

"No, and if my son has said that, he is wrong."

"Did you show your son a newspaper article that hinted that Lady Dunlo had had three children out of wedlock?"

"I may have."

"Did you say if she was left alone she would have another?"

"I do not recall saying that, but it is possible." The earl chuckled, and a rumble of mirth rose from all sides of the court.

Judge Hannen banged his gavel. "I will not have laughter."

My God, Belle thought, *the earl truly hates me*. Flo took her hand and petted it. She was rubbing so hard that Belle's skin felt raw.

"Let me read to you, sir, from a letter your son allegedly wrote to you in July of last year. 'My dear Papa' etc. . . . 'Why I got married, I do not know. I have no excuse, I am not sure I was drunk. I don't think I was but I believe I must have been rather off my head these last few months. Several of my friends have been most kind—Mr. Wood, Mr. Osborn—and have gone to solicitors without my knowledge and have done their level best to see if there was a flaw in my marriage. I know, of course, that I have acted the devil. I am very sorry for it. I care not a rap for myself but I do care for Mama. No one is to blame but myself; truly no blame attaches to the girl. All is my fault. I cannot expect to get forgiveness from you. Please understand I want to know your wishes.' Did you deduce from those words that your son wanted to get rid of his wife?"

Belle listened and cringed. If William wrote those words—*if*—he did so with fear in his soul. What kind of a man was Clancarty who would bully his son and then lie about it all in the Courts of Justice? Did he think he was above the law?

"That was my understanding, that he regretted the marriage."

"Do you mean to say that you held no inducement for him to go abroad?"

"None. He perfectly agreed to go."

Belle wanted to rise and shout, "He did not! You coerced him, sir!" but she knew she could not.

Mr. Lockwood strode on. "Did you know that your son wrote affectionate letters to his wife from his travels?"

"Yes. I gather he believed her to be the most immaculate woman in the world."

"Until you and Mr. Robinson decided to undeceive him?"

"Yes."

"Did your son know you had his wife shadowed?"

"Yes."

"And do you say that this suggestion to have Lady Dunlo watched came, in fact, from your son?"

"Certainly."

Belle knew this to be an outright lie; William was not the man his father was and would do no such thing. How could the earl sit and concoct such stories? Was he losing his mind? She shifted in her seat until Flo hissed at her.

"You mustn't wriggle about, Belle. Think how it looks."

Belle stopped agitating and sat rigid backed instead, hands anchored together to stop herself twisting them.

Lockwood let the earl's precise word—"certainly"—hang in the air before continuing. "Did you, Lord Clancarty, tell your son, in a letter, that it was possible to get a divorce without being present in court?"

"Yes, I believed so then. I understood if I acted as his representative he might remain abroad."

"You put the matter in the hands of Misters Lewis and Lewis, did you not?"

"I did."

"You knew they sent the divorce petition to Australia for your son to sign?"

"Yes."

"But you feared if your son returned to England to act for himself all might not go as you wished. Is that correct?"

Lord Clancarty opened his mouth to speak but nothing emerged. Belle watched him attempt to answer, but his thoughts seemed unable to connect with whatever it was his tongue wished to say.

"No further questions, Your Honor," Mr. Lockwood said.

William rose from his seat in the courtroom and everyone swiveled his way.

"I have a question," he said.

Belle put out her hand as if she could press William back into a sitting position. What was he about to say? Murmurs flew about the room.

"What is Dunlo doing?" Flo whispered.

"I know not," answered Belle.

Mr. Lockwood turned to William, then to Judge Hannen, who flicked his hand in William's direction to indicate he might speak. William stood up straight and turned to face his father.

"My question is this: Why do you dislike me so, Father?"

The judge banged his gavel. "No," he shouted, "not in my court. Take your seat, Lord Dunlo."

But William had been goaded to life by his father's blasé, glib testimony and he refused to sit.

"How can you come here, Papa, and act the jester about matters as serious as my future happiness? How can you take the character of my wife?"

"Be seated, sir. I tell you," the judge called. "Order! Order!"

The earl tried to pull himself erect to face William, but he was weakened by his illness and, instead, he hung on to the box and swayed in an ungainly crouch. He opened his mouth but, once more, no words emerged. Mr. Russell rushed to his side, but the earl batted him off.

"You think that I have brought shame on the Clancarty name, Papa." William lifted his arm and pointed. "You have shamed yourself here today. Firstly by lying and then by laughing about it." He glanced at Belle and she smiled her encouragement.

"Remove that man. Remove him!"

William turned to the judge. "I will remove myself." He left his seat and stalked out of the courtroom.

"Very well done, William," Belle murmured, looking after him.

"*Bravissimo*, Dunlo," Flo said, taking Belle's arm and pulling her to stand, "and about time, too."

A Pause

Belle stood by the window of the smoking room and watched the downpour wash Avenue Road. Obese drops fell from the leaves and puddled underneath the trees. The cloudburst had come late in the day and the city had waited for it, steamy and sulfuric beneath the threat. It was a release when the rain finally fell, though Belle felt as churned up as ever within herself.

"Why can't something happen? Something large that would lessen people's interest in us," she said.

"Is that what you want—indifference?" Wertheimer said.

Belle shrugged. She did not know what she wanted. Did she really wish disaster on some other person to divert attention from Dunlo v. Dunlo and Wertheimer? A raging fire? A murder? A lightning strike to Buckingham Palace?

It alarmed her to see the surge of newspapermen at each day's end, their undignified rush out of the court toward their Fleet Street dens, mouths dribbling ink. She knew, too, that the Pig and Goose across the Strand was most likely wedged each evening with those who had listened all day. No doubt the most succulent tidbits of the case were chewed over along with plates of pickled snout and foie gras, slugged back with pots of ale.

"Strangers are so hungry for crumbs of my life." Belle went from the window to a chair and flopped into it. "I'm a mouse in a nest of vipers when I sit in that courtroom. And the place is full to suffocation."

"London loves a scandal, Belle, you know that. All the better if the parties are already known as you are. And if the people can ingest it in court, even better."

"But there is no scandal here, Isidor, isn't that the very point? We are not lovers and never have been. We're not at fault!"

Wertheimer came over and squatted by her chair, his smoking jacket swung out behind him like a peacock's train. "Of course that's the point and it will be proven. Already Clancarty has made himself look extremely foolish by his actions and testimony. Don't fret." He pressed her arm. "And Dunlo was splendid in standing up to his papa at last, was he not? Marvelous!"

"He *was* splendid. But seeing William at court every day stirs me up— he's there, so close, yet he may as well be in the antipodes still. He hardly glances my way. What can it mean?"

"I suppose he's trying at last to do the right thing. It will be over soon. And then you might talk to William properly and see what's what."

"I had rather hoped to catch him today. Where did he get to? Did he even leave? I think he may have concealed himself inside the building afterward. Perhaps his father tries still to face him and get under his skin." Belle rolled her shoulders to unleash some of the disquietude of the day. "I'm so utterly fatigued."

"Then we must help you to shake off that fatigue."

Wertheimer rang the bell and ordered Rosina to prepare a hot bath for Belle.

Though unaccustomed to taking baths—like most people she preferred a stand-up wash—when Belle sank into the tub she was grateful to Wertheimer; the water lulled and comforted her. The buoyancy it afforded was both freeing and gentle. Taking the bar of lilac soap that Rosina had left for her, she skimmed it up and down her arms and legs, enjoying its slithery silk.

After a time, the bathwater made prunes of her fingers and Belle examined the puckered pad of each digit as if it were a map that might yield a followable path. She thought of William and his betrayal. *Am I to be his scapegoat?* she wondered. *He ties himself in knots displeasing to his father and unravels them by condoning lies told about me. How could he do it?* But perhaps his squaring up to the earl today, his defiance in court, augured well. It was so hard to know what was what when William would barely look at her, much less speak to her, day after day. He was a confounding man. What was she to think?

Belle laid back her head and closed her eyes. A vision of little Isidor came to her, followed immediately by the splosh as he was swallowed up in the Heathfield pond. Then the trees in judgment around her and a ticking silence. And the girl—Mabel, was it?—staring stupidly. The horrid quiet, the one-second action of her hand shooting out to grab at him, the soaked clothing. Belle squeezed her eyes tight to unpick the scene. *Am I,* she thought*, to lug this guilt about with me forevermore, awkward as a third leg? The boy was not harmed, he lives yet. It's not as if I discarded him on the street. My son belongs to another time now and to another world entirely.*

Belle slid lower in the bath, determined that the heat should take her cares and float them away. She held her palms above the water and marveled at how strange they looked, how ghostly and *other*.

"What a brew my life is," she said.

She looked at her bobbing breasts and at the hill of her belly released from its corset cage; she ran her hands over its softness. Would it ever grow plum ripe again, the temporary home to another babe, one that could be cherished, one born of a man she loved? Belle drowned the thought and plunged even lower to let the warmth engulf her; she had had enough thinking to last her a decade. It was better, for now, to allow herself to lie in the scented water and let all concerns, conjectures and conclusions float away. Life would unfold in its own messy way and she had to let it.

An Examination

Mr. Lockwood was puffed out like a pigeon when Belle, Flo and Wertheimer entered the court to take their places. He came to where Belle sat and pressed her fingers with his own.

"Courage," he said.

She nodded her thanks and placed her hands in her lap, entwined together to stop them shaking. She was glad of the veil on her hat, for it protected her a little from the eyes that continuously sought her out from the gallery. Her mother had not appeared after the first day, fatigued, perhaps, by the drab testimonies of various landladies of Belle's and Wertheimer's. None of them had found fault with their behavior, thankfully; it would have been just like some vindictive old fool to grab a little infamy for herself by telling lies. But, to a woman, they had observed no stain on Belle's character, though one claimed she had not known Belle was a dancer when she lodged at her house. Had Belle not made her a gift of theater tickets at least once? She was positive she had.

Marmaduke Wood, too, gave his evidence in an unappealing way—his stance was louche and he kept a sardonic tone to his voice that seemed to irritate everyone, not least Judge Hannen. To think Wood had had the privilege of being one of their two wedding guests! He said in evidence that he recalled meeting Belle at the races in Brighton and asking her if she thought it fair that she should "go about" with Wertheimer so much while Lord Dunlo was away. Wood said she had given the impression that she would rather be with Wertheimer than anyone else. He went on to say that Belle had also told him she missed William and asked him to use his influence to stop the suit proceeding against her.

Mr. Lockwood said, "Do you mean to tell me that in the conversation in which she asked you to use your influence to prevent the divorce proceeding, she said she was devoted to Mr. Wertheimer?"

"I will not swear she used the word 'devoted,' but it was the impression I got."

Belle shuddered to think of Wood's recounting of the conversation. Were those really his impressions of what passed between them that day? She had thought their exchanges pleasant and Wood amicably on her side. He was most attentive and stayed by her for quite a spell. Despite Wood's usual long tales about nothing, in her mind the part of the conversation about William and the impending proceedings was mutually friendly and supportive. Oh, but how was one supposed to remember exact words uttered months before? It was impossible.

Belle let the din of the waiting courtroom fill her ears; it reminded her of the background noise to a nightmare—a horrible, far-off scuffling and muttering that clotted the mind. When Judge Hannen entered the court and gained his seat, the noise abated and, Mr. Gill, acting for Wertheimer, began.

"Lady Dunlo has never, before or after her marriage, been the mistress of Isidor Wertheimer. It might be said by men of the world that no man could do what Mr. Wertheimer did for Lady Dunlo without having some return for it. But I assure you, gentlemen, no guilty relations subsisted between my client and the respondent. As to the evidence regarding Lady Dunlo's residence at Sixty-three Avenue Road, might I remind you that the page boy, Jacob Baltimore, was formerly discharged by Mr. Wertheimer. Would a discharged servant have any motive for saying favorable things? Would a private inquiry agent, who had destroyed his evidence and was being paid to shadow my client and the respondent, say favorable things?"

Mr. Gill paused and his whole body seemed to twitch as he let his questions linger.

"These people saw the lady and gentleman dine together, take cabs together and walk together. They saw no deep familiarity between them. One witness says he saw Mr. Wertheimer's arm around Lady Dunlo's waist, another that he saw him kiss her. But it has been established that these events took place prior to Lady Dunlo's marriage, at a time when Mr. Wertheimer may have hoped she might be *his* wife. Surely human nature is not so degraded that this might be done without it being inferred that *of necessity* a guilty relationship existed?

"Mr. Lewis, solicitor to Lord Clancarty, wrote to Lord Dunlo in Australia to tell him his wife was frequently in the company of Mr. Wertheimer. This, he supposed, was told to Lord Dunlo as a surprise. However, Lady Dunlo frankly and frequently told her husband, in letters to him, that she kept company with her friend Mr. Wertheimer. Mr. Lewis's letter continues thus:

"You have had time to think over your unfortunate marriage and I hope you now see how sad a step you then took, having regard to the previous history of your wife. It is now open to you to do justice to yourself and your family by taking proceedings for a divorce. And, if you are prepared to follow the wishes of your family, I enclose a petition for your signature.

"Who do these proceedings belong to, gentlemen? The person who seeks relief in the court is usually the person who is injured. But in this case, the proceedings are those of the Le Poer Trench family. Lord Dunlo is invited to do justice to the *family*.

"Why did Lord Dunlo sign the petition? Gentlemen, I have no good answer for that. But let us remind ourselves that the aristocracy enjoy great advantage over other people, however I have yet to learn that they can perjure themselves with impunity. In his petition Lord Dunlo swore that his wife committed adultery. Yet he wrote to his wife that he did not believe the statements against her. No man has a right to swear to anything he does not believe. I ask again, how was it he was induced to sign this paper? Remember Lord Dunlo contracted a grave illness in the antipodes. Remember, he says himself that he was 'confused,' that he was 'muddled.' His mind was 'in a stew.'

"Let this suffice, gentlemen: in all of these matters, Lady Dunlo has been treated in an infamous and disgraceful manner. She was under the misery of perpetual observation. Her name was discredited."

On and on Mr. Gill went, outlining that private inquiry agents were paid by results and that it was not in their interest to find no evidence of misconduct. He deplored the burning of the notebook; he asked the jury to believe there had been deliberate lying. He said that Lady Dunlo *would* have worked out of necessity to support her husband, but she could have expected generosity from the highborn Clancartys, or at least some sort of nobility of conduct.

"Protection is the duty of the husband," he said, "and in his absence, it is the duty of his family."

Belle squirmed in her seat and Flo put a steadying hand on her.

"It will not do," Flo said sotto voce, "to look fidgety directly before you are called. You know this."

But Belle could not help it; nerves had choked off her airways and she pulled wayward breaths through her lungs to try to calm herself. She lifted her veil and dropped it again; she pulled off her gloves and wiped her sweaty palms on her skirt. Her head bent, she examined her nails and began to push back the cuticles with each thumbnail. Flo was pucking her; Belle lifted her head to see all eyes on her. Mr. Lockwood looked expectantly in her direction. He lifted his hand and indicated the box. Belle turned to Flo.

"Look sharp," her sister whispered. "It's your turn."

Belle pulled on her gloves, rose and walked across the room, the only sound the clack of her heels upon the parquet. She stepped up into the box and looked around. Belle had been in courtrooms before but only as a watcher, never the watched. Her heart trounced in her chest—surely its terrible pummeling was audible? She stood and looked around at the faces that seemed to gloat from the public gallery. One man was scarred so badly that he had a clown's lips and he seemed to permanently sneer. A woman in a flounce-bodiced dress was like a remnant from a long-ago ball. When the woman saw Belle's eyes on her, she grinned to reveal a gumful of mossy teeth. Was this what loving William had come to? Was her marriage to be rendered to nought with these indigents as witnesses?

Flo had urged her that morning to keep her eyes on Mr. Lockwood alone.

"Don't look at William, Belle, or you might falter. Or worse, cry." She spooned Pepper's Quinine and Iron Tonic into her sister's mouth. "Don't look at Wertheimer or you may appear guilty." Belle began to protest, but Flo shushed her. "Certainly don't look at Mother if she deigns to turn up. Or at Clancarty. Keep your eyes on Mr. Lockwood and he will help you along."

"And when Mr. Russell is upon me?"

"Keep your head, darling."

Mr. Lockwood flicked open his watch and studied the dial, then put it away. He cleared his throat and began.

"The petitioner is the son of a peer of the realm. And although my learned friend Mr. Russell is indirectly representing Lord Dunlo, he is, in fact, directly representing his father, the Earl of Clancarty. There is considerable intimacy between Lady Dunlo and Mr. Isidor Wertheimer, it is true, but I will prove by evidence that she has *never* been his mistress.

"I ask you, gentlemen of the jury, to listen well to my client and believe her, when she will state under oath the real facts of this case. I ask you not for charity, gentlemen, but for justice. As you have seen, little charity or mercy were shown to Lady Dunlo by those who sought to have her marriage dissolved."

Mr. Lockwood turned to Belle and had her state her names, before and after marriage. "And how long have you been on the stage, Lady Dunlo?"

"Since I was fourteen years old; I performed on occasion at Aldershot and in Farnborough. My sister and I—that is Flo, or Mrs. Seymour—have a double act: the Sisters Bilton."

"And when you were enceinte with the child of Mr. Weston, did you perform then?"

"No, after a time, I could not. And because my engagements ceased, my sister's were much reduced."

"I see. And when did you first make the acquaintance of the co-respondent, Mr. Isidor Wertheimer?"

"I believe it was spring 1888."

"And he took the house at Maidenhead for you shortly after meeting you, is that correct?"

"Yes."

"But you were still attached to Mr. Weston, were you not?"

"I was. Somewhat."

"And I believe you refused to engage yourself to Mr. Wertheimer?"

Belle glanced at Isidor; he smiled, a small push of encouragement. "Isidor—Mr. Wertheimer, that is—he was not serious about marrying me. He said it as a lark. We both knew it was not something that would happen."

Mr. Lockwood frowned. "I have not asked you the question before, Lady Dunlo, but was there any intimacy between Mr. Wertheimer and yourself?"

"No, there couldn't be. I . . . he . . . No." Belle stopped herself from saying more and kept her eyes on Mr. Lockwood.

"When you lived at Turnagain Lane was there intimacy between you then?"

"No."

"And Conduit Street?"

"No."

Judge Hannen waved his hand with impatience and Belle looked over at him: "Have you ever been his *mistress?*" the judge said.

Though alarmed by the gruffness of His Lordship's intrusion Belle answered clearly: "I have not."

Mr. Lockwood nodded to the judge and resumed. "Did Lord Dunlo know that Mr. Wertheimer had offered to marry you?"

"Yes, I told him so."

"Let us move, now, to the days following your marriage to Lord Dunlo. Where did you reside?"

"William and I took a room at the Victoria Hotel."

"And how long were you there?"

"A few days—until my husband left for the antipodes."

"Did you know he was leaving you?"

Belle glanced at William, but he kept his chin dipped to his chest. She looked at Mr. Lockwood. "The night before my husband went away he was strange in his manner. After we had dined he told me to go to bed and said he wanted to take a walk alone to think. I was not alarmed—everyone likes to be solitary at times, myself included. But still, I asked him not to go; his demeanor had unsettled me. He went out to walk anyway and returned at about half past five in the morning. He woke me to tell me he would not go abroad; he complained about his father."

"Was he agitated?"

"Somewhat."

"I asked him what was I to do if he *did* go away and he inquired if I could keep myself. I was then earning five guineas a week at the Empire Theatre, so I said I could. He kept repeating that his father wanted him to go; he seemed unwell. Unhappy and disturbed. I fell asleep and when I woke William was sitting on the bed in outdoor clothes. 'I'm going,' he said. I begged him to take me with him, but he said he could not. He showed me two letters from his father, one of which contained money. He said he had to leave or his father would cut him off. My husband promised he would come back in December, when he was of age. Then, he said, his father would give him an allowance with which to keep me. But if he stayed, his father would give him nothing and have nothing to do with him." Belle gulped, her voice losing itself as she swallowed. "I implored him not to go and again he said he would not; he said he loved me and could not stand to be apart from me. He got back into bed beside me and we slept. When I woke, about nine o'clock, he was gone."

Belle winced to recall the exquisite stab of opening her eyes to find William absent, of searching the Victoria for him before flying to his rooms in the Burlington to sit in the hollowed-out atmosphere there. Why, she wondered, did the pain of that memory have a sweet tinge to it? Surely that should not be the case. Perhaps it was William's lengthy prevarications that night, the fact that she knew he was confused and sad; that his reason had been tampered with by his father. She could not, somehow, think of those conversations without compassion; his father's grip on him was so strong William did not know his own mind when pressured by the earl.

Mr. Lockwood strode on. "Lord Dunlo left you—his wife—at the Victoria Hotel in Hampstead without money and without a marital home. He simply sailed away."

"Yes."

"What did you do then?"

"I left the Victoria Hotel and returned to my room in Conduit Street, but the landlady had begun to object to me staying because she did not care for the singing of my canary."

Titters from the gallery.

"How came you to go to Sixty-three Avenue Road, to live there?"

"Mr. Wertheimer offered me his house as a friend. He wished to help me."

"Mr. Clarke, the detective, says he saw Mr. Wertheimer in your bedroom, at the window, on the sixteenth of September. Is there any truth in that?"

"None whatever."

"There is no truth in the suggestion that Mr. Wertheimer was in your room or that he struggled with you or that he kissed you?"

"None."

He went over the fact that Wertheimer had come to Manchester at Christmas to see the pantomime, making sure to point out they had stayed at separate hotels, but also saying a Mr. Lumsden, a hotel employee, reported witnessing "certain familiarities" between Belle and Wertheimer. Piano playing, close conversation and so forth.

"We played the piano together, but there it ends."

"You told us that no provision of any sort was made for you when Lord Dunlo went away. Have you had from your husband, since that time, a single halfpenny?"

"No."

"Since your marriage has Mr. Wertheimer ever kissed you?"

"He has not."

"Has he kissed you before?"

"On one occasion at the Corinthian Club. He thought he might go to live in America and said he intended never to return. The kiss was meant as a good-bye. He had been drinking."

A man at the back of the court guffawed. Judge Hannen rose in his seat and roared, "Get that man out of this court. I will not have any signs of amusement exhibited here. I wish this to be distinctly understood: certain feelings are manifested by amusement at the indecent which cannot but affect those who observe it. An opinion outside the jury is sought to be created. I will not have it."

An officer of the Crown removed the laughing man and Belle took the opportunity to look to Flo. Her sister's vigorous smile told Belle she was acquitting herself acceptably. She would surely be permitted to step down soon.

Mr. Lockwood looked to Judge Hannen and when he nodded, he turned once more to Belle.

"Lady Dunlo, since your marriage has Mr. Wertheimer always treated you with respect?"

"Always."

"He has expressed a stronger affection for you than yours for him. That is, you did not return his feelings about the prospect of marrying him, for example?"

"That is so."

"Has there ever been familiarity of any description between you, besides that which you have alluded to just now?"

"Never."

"No further questions, my lord."

Belle watched Mr. Lockwood retreat with regret for she knew that Mr. Russell was about to step up and he would not gentle her as Lockwood had done. Mr. Russell began by going over everything about Belle's acting history, right back to her start performing for the militia. He asked about Weston, of course, and Belle answered succinctly.

"How did you make the acquaintance of Mr. Wertheimer?"

"Major Noah asked me to dinner after Mr. Weston's trial—that was February 1888—and Mr. Wertheimer was there. We were seated together at table and we talked all evening." Belle paused. "Shortly after that meeting, realizing my predicament, Mr. Wertheimer said he would do anything he could to help me. But I was not on intimate terms with him; we became solid friends very swiftly, that is all. He had taken the house at Maidenhead and by May I had moved there."

"So there was a certain amount of intimacy?"

"No, not intimacy, friendship. We lunched, dined and supped together frequently. Invariably we saw each other every day. But my sister Flo was often there and her husband, Mr. Seymour."

"Miss Bilton, did Mr. Wertheimer buy your clothing?"

Belle answered indignantly. "He did not."

"Did he buy clothing of any sort?"

"He bought things for the child. And he paid the household expenses."

"Let us move forward now to August of last year, to Sixty-three Avenue Road, another house taken by Mr. Wertheimer and occupied by you. Mr. Wertheimer had a bedroom in this house?"

"That is correct. He kept evening dress there."

"He, in fact, lived there?"

"No, he did not."

"But he told you when the arrangement was made that he would require a room there?"

"Yes, he did."

"What did you think your position was there?"

"Everyone knew what my position was."

"Everyone? Did your father and mother know?"

"No."

Mr. Russell shook the paper in his hand and glanced at the jury. "Now, you are a woman of the world. You have heard of men keeping mistresses?"

"Yes."

"You know how they live?"

"Yes."

"Did you not think it strange that Mr. Wertheimer should spend so much money on you? Did you not think it looked as if you were living as his mistress? Particularly in a place such as St. John's Wood?"

"No, I had nothing to do with him in that way." *How much simpler it would be to say* he *would want nothing to do with* me *in that way. Yes, sir, Mr. Wertheimer loves women but when it comes to it, he would rather lie with a man.* Belle searched for the right words. "We know the ways we conducted ourselves, Mr. Russell; we know there's no stain on our own behavior."

Mr. Russell moved on and began to ask about her first meeting with William, about his many proposals, about Belle's caution because of the Le Poer Trench family's likely feelings on the matter.

"So, at the time you were entertaining Viscount Dunlo, you were still on intimate terms with Mr. Wertheimer?"

"Isidor Wertheimer and I were firm friends; we saw each other a lot; there was no intimacy. Mr. Wertheimer has been good to me since the day I met him. Better than any other."

"And after your marriage, when your husband had gone abroad, it was true you lived under the protection of Mr. Wertheimer. You say that?"

Belle flexed her fingers. *Why does he keep repeating himself? Is he trying to trick me?* "Yes, I agree with that."

"You mean you were living as his mistress."

"Certainly not."

"You mean to say that stating that you were living under his protection doesn't convey to your mind that you were living as this man's mistress?"

"No, Mr. Russell, it does not. Mr. Wertheimer was protecting me."

"While Lord Dunlo was away, Mr. Wertheimer proposed marriage to you, did he not?"

Belle was growing weary. "Mr. Wertheimer loved to talk about marriage, but he never meant it." If only it were possible to explain, without retribution, that Isidor only spoke of it because it would be a way to save him, to shield him from the world's castigation, from prosecution.

"Did Mr. Wertheimer at one stage cable a proposal of marriage to you, Lady Dunlo?"

Why, Belle had forgotten about that. It was a joke—one of Isidor's silly drunken gags. "Yes."

"Did you cable back?"

"Yes."

"What did you say?"

"That I would not marry him; I reminded him I was already married. We were sporting with each other."

"Do you have this cable?"

"No, I do not keep letters or cables."

"But you kept Lord Dunlo's letters?"

"Yes, all of them."

What Belle did not say was that most envelopes and letters she received were cut up for privy fodder. She squashed the thought in case it brought forth a smile.

Mr. Russell pushed on. "You spoke to Lord Dunlo about Mr. Wertheimer?"

"Yes."

"And about Mr. Weston?"

"Yes. William knew everything."

"Mr. Wertheimer came to you on the day your husband went away?"

"Yes."

"Once ensconced in Sixty-three Avenue Road, you became aware you were being watched?"

"Yes."

On and on he went, outlining dates and meetings. Belle did not deny any of what Mr. Clarke had reportedly seen of her walking or talking with Wertheimer. She had nothing to conceal.

"Was Mr. Wertheimer on sufficiently familiar terms with you to abuse your husband?"

"Abuse him?"

"Did he approve of him, like him? Or was there disapproval in his attitude?"

"He seemed to like William well enough. But as the months wore on, when Lord Dunlo stayed away, Mr. Wertheimer raised doubts about my husband's constancy."

"Did he make you cry when he spoke of him?"

"Yes." Belle glanced at Wertheimer. "But once only."

"Why did you not go to live at your sister's house instead of Sixty-three Avenue Road, at the end of August last year?"

"Flo had no room for me—her lodgings were small."

"You wrote to Lord Dunlo and said you would be staying with your sister, did you not?"

"I thought I might go there, but Flo was unable to accommodate me. I also wanted my husband to see that he had put me in a sorry position. Flo's quarters were small and he knew that."

"You also wrote to Lord Dunlo that 'W' had called on you, but you did not see him as you were alone."

"Yes."

"Yet this was the man in whose house you were living and with whom you were constantly going about."

"Yes."

"Did your sister urge you to come stay with her?"

"She asked me to stay once she had found a larger house."

"And you intended to do that?"

"Yes."

"Presumably this 'larger house' would have been neither as ample nor as luxurious as Avenue Road?"

"That's correct."

"Miss Bilton, did you habitually see Mr. Wertheimer in the morning, did you habitually see him in the evening, and did he accompany you home from the theater at night?"

"No."

Mr. Russell sighed. "You saw him, however, nearly every day?"

"Yes."

He returned to his notes and began, once again to go over Mr. Clarke's sightings. He outlined date after date when she and Wertheimer had met and Belle confirmed each one.

"Is there one single incident deposed to by Mr. Clarke, excepting that one occasion about the window, which you can swear was not correct?"

"Yes."

"What is it?"

"He has sworn that I was often alone with Mr. Wertheimer. I was not. The page boy, Jacob, and the maid, Rosina, were present. If not them, then my sister was in the house with me."

"When you went to Manchester, was there one week out of the thirteen weeks you played there that Mr. Wertheimer was not present?"

"He came three times to Manchester."

"Why did he come?"

"He came to see me perform. As friends often do."

Mr. Russell shifted on his feet. "Miss Bilton, were your letters to Lord Dunlo candid?"

"Yes."

"Did you tell him Mr. Wertheimer came to see you in Manchester?"

"No."

Mr. Russell nodded grimly as if satisfied he had heard in that moment exactly what he had come to hear. "No further questions, your lordship," he said.

Belle unhooked her hands from each other; her fingers ached from being squeezed. She looked around to find Flo, and her sister nodded and patted the seat beside her. The judge told her to step down, and Belle returned to Flo.

Wertheimer looked almost tranquil as he took the stand. He had clearly given himself an early night, for his skin did not have its customary pearlescent sheen; the red carnation in his lapel caused a radiance in his cheek. He came across as a man contained and checked, disciplined in a way that Belle admired.

Mr. Gill—Wertheimer's solicitor—examined him first and he went through how Isidor and Belle had met, how he supported her when Weston was at the Old Bailey et cetera. There followed a lesson in London geography while Mr. Gill named Belle's various addresses and if and when Isidor had visited her at these places.

"During this time, Mr. Wertheimer," said Mr. Gill, "you conceived great admiration for Miss Bilton, did you not? You were greatly attached to her?"

"I think admiration is the correct term."

"You had asked her to marry you?"

"Yes, on several occasions."

"Have you always treated her with respect?"

"Yes, I have always done so."

"When you took the house at Avenue Road, did you retain a bedroom there?"

"Yes."

"And you stayed there from time to time?"

"I sometimes changed from morning into evening dress there."

"And there was no impropriety between you and Lady Dunlo, as she then was?"

"Absolutely none."

"Why did you threaten to go away?" Mr. Gill consulted his notes. "To America, I believe?"

"There were many things—a quarrel with my father over my grandfather's property, chiefly."

"Around that time, did you cable a marriage proposal to the lady?"

"Yes. I remember almost the exact words."

"Which were?"

"I said: 'Come away with me and marry me. We will both be free!'"

"She replied, refusing you again?"

"Yes."

"Although she again and again refused you, you hoped that someday she would marry you?"

"Yes." Wertheimer dipped his head. "I thought that we would get along all right."

Belle felt as if she were listening to a stranger. Yes, Isidor had offered her marriage but it was in jest, one of his giddy jokes. The bats in the barn knew that!

"Did you ever give her money?"

"No, never."

Mr. Gill talked on about the comings and goings at Avenue Road. Was he ever alone with Belle? How often did he go upstairs?

"Is there any truth in the statement by Clarke that you were at her bedroom window? A window that overlooked Norfolk Road?"

"Not an atom. It is an absolute lie."

"Have you ever put your arm around her waist when driving with her?"

Wertheimer paused, plumped for no, though he knew many who would contradict him. Including Belle.

"Have you ever kissed her?"

Oh, what is this? thought Belle. *Are Isidor and I not firm friends? Are friends to keep the length of a barge pole between them?* How she wished to upturn the rigid norms of society where affection—even that born of ardent friendship—was for private rooms only. How freeing it would be to embrace and hug and laugh in the street. Had Wertheimer kissed her? Why, yes, he had.

"I kissed her on one occasion—at Maidenhead, before her marriage. She was distressed about her child and I comforted her. And perhaps once more, in the Corinthian Club, when I thought I might go away; a brief, farewell kiss."

There had been a hundred more kisses than that, certainly, of the type friends share, but none perhaps as lingering as the one at Maidenhead after the baby was born. Hadn't everyone been in an exhausted muddle that day? Mr. Gill plowed on, through Manchester and Christmas, through Belle's return to London for Mr. Harris's *Venus*.

"Up to the present time, has there ever been any familiarity between you and Lady Dunlo?"

"Never. On any occasion."

"Did it ever occur to you that you were placing her in a position that people would suppose her to be your mistress?"

"Well, there is this to be said. I knew her former life had not been un-impeachable. I would have married Belle if she had desired that and it would have been our own affair. I knew I should not insult her and that was more than could be said for Lord Dunlo and his so-called friends."

"You knew Lord Dunlo's friends objected to the marriage?"

"No, nothing of the sort."

"Did it not cross your mind that it might compromise her in the eyes of Lord Dunlo's family if you were about with her so much?"

"Lord Dunlo's family did not enter into my consideration. I do not live my life according to the decrees of the aristocracy; I make my own way. You see, I merely wanted to help a friend in distress; I did not need to think how it might affect the sensibilities of everyone else in London."

"Did your own family know where you were, all the hours you spent with Miss Bilton?"

"No, they never had the impertinence to ask. I am beyond the age of tutelage."

"Why did you spend so much time at Avenue Road?"

"The fact is number sixty-three is a beautiful house and I like it there. Further it has a fine garden and I enjoy its air. And nothing gave me so much pleasure as to be in Lady Dunlo's society. Nothing in the world. On Sundays we often drove about together—nearly the whole day."

"So, you went to Avenue Road for society and fresh air?"

"Yes."

"I shall ask you again, did you enter the lady's bedchamber, as Mr. Clarke has reported?"

"It's an infamous lie."

"Have you ever said to her that Lord Dunlo wanted brains and other things?"

Wertheimer winced. "On one occasion, I think I did so; I was angry with him. It seemed to me that he did not treat Lady Dunlo as well as she deserved."

Mr. Gill turned to Judge Hannen. "Nothing further, Your Honor."

Flo squeezed Belle's hand and stood.

"I shan't be long," Flo said.

She was right. Mr. Russell did not squander time rehashing old details.

"From first to last," he said, "Mr. Wertheimer was wanting to marry your sister?"

"Yes. I made a bet with him about it."

"You made a bet? What was that? When was it?"

"Oh, it was about a year or so before she married William. Lord Dunlo. It was when we first knew Wertheimer."

"What was the bet?"

"I bet him that he would never marry my sister."

"Did your sister know of this bet?"

Flo flicked her eyes in Belle's direction. "She did not."

"And is the bet still running?"

"Yes."

"Why would you make such a bet?"

"I knew my sister would marry only for love. Wertheimer is a good fellow, a wonderful friend and support, but she doesn't *love* him, not in the marrying way."

"Did you not think it wrong that your sister should live at Mr. Wertheimer's house at Avenue Road?"

"No, he was a loyal friend to her through her difficulties. And I was often there and my husband, too. And the servants have always been very visible in that house, very *present*."

"Were you aware that your sister received valuable gifts from Mr. Wertheimer?"

"I know they exchange gifts—they have a strong friendship."

"Mrs. Seymour, have you ever seen any objectionable relationship between your sister and Mr. Wertheimer?"

"Never."

A Summing-up

Judge Hannen sat and waited for absolute silence before he embarked on his summing-up. He put Belle in mind of the brown bear at the zoological gardens. In truth, he had no ursine qualities, but the quizzical way he lifted his head to study people reminded her of Hector, the bun-scoffing bear. The animal watched patiently and swung his head from side to side, when he thought more goodies might come to his waiting mouth. Judge Hannen was watchful in a similar way, but his movements were subtler than Hector's. He was quietly fearsome like the bear, though not as contained, for his pit was the bench and his zoo the courtroom.

The court went still. Judge Hannen tilted his head and began.

"This suit, we must remind ourselves, was instituted not by Lord Dunlo but by his father, the Earl of Clancarty." He addressed the jury directly in a solemn tone. "The suit was prepared and prosecuted by Lord Clancarty."

Belle listened to Judge Hannen's words and felt her anticipation swell: everything might turn out right. She shifted in her seat and inclined toward the judge to better apprehend his meaning.

"Lady Dunlo," he continued, "has been on the stage from an early age. I need not enlarge on the dangers of that profession—the present case illustrates them. We have heard in detail the evidence as to the relations between the co-respondents, Mr. Wertheimer and Lady Dunlo. Gentlemen, under ordinary circumstances the evidence is such that you might be justified in believing these parties were living together. The difficulty and danger, however, is that we are dealing with an entirely different life from that of ordinary people. We are dealing with actors and antique dealers, gentlemen. Young bohemians, you understand, and their rules are not necessarily our rules. Miss Bilton—or Lady Dunlo, if you prefer—would not have governed her actions in precisely the same way as ordinary persons. Do not do the lady an injustice by applying ordinary views to matters so different.

"I think it extremely unlikely that Mr. Marmaduke Wood, for example, is the best or most competent judge of a woman's character or life. His view would not be the correct one to take. Do not believe, gentlemen, that everyone on the music hall stage is immoral. Neither can every woman who has given birth to an illegitimate child be purchased. You know these things, do you not?"

He paused; the jury foreman nodded his head, a servant on behalf of his fellows. Belle puffed up, elated. The judge was appealing to the jury's sense and to their better natures; they might listen to him. Even if they were against her, it intoxicated her to think that the old bear Hannen was with her. He was gloriously on her side!

"Remember that Mr. Gill has told you that his client, Mr. Wertheimer, has nothing to gain from this case one way or another. Gentlemen, you must decide if the relations between Mr. Wertheimer and Lady Dunlo were improper after the marriage. It is not—*not*—the time anterior to the marriage of Lady Dunlo you have to consider. Excepting this: how the lady's conduct then would bear on her conduct after her marriage. If she were Wertheimer's mistress before her marriage, it would be more reasonable to suppose they resumed their relations after it.

"But ponder this also: it is a very serious thing for a woman to be deprived of the protection of her husband. Lord Dunlo married this lady, then promptly absented himself from her life. The letters Lady Dunlo wrote to her husband while he was abroad were a credit to her—they were affectionate, not coarse. To my mind it is despicable that Lord Dunlo signed the divorce petition while writing to her, his *wife*, that he did not believe any statements against her. He showed an utter want of appreciation of an oath on his part. The case, however, does not depend on what Lord Dunlo said or thought or did. He was a mere cipher, a puppet in the hand of his father and the men employed by him. The case must depend not on Lord Dunlo's conduct but on the impression which you, the jury, have of the evidence."

Judge Hannen nodded and the jurymen were accompanied out of the courtroom to consider their verdict. Belle and Flo sat still in their seats, hands clasped; Wertheimer came and sat by them. Sweat steamed under Belle's clothes and her breath came short. She reached for William with her eyes, but he kept his head hanging down and stared into his lap. Belle willed him to lift his chin and seek her out, but he did not. Soon she would know if she was to be exonerated. Soon, too, she would know if William meant to be the husband he *should* be.

"How long will it take?" Belle whispered.

"It could take hours," Wertheimer said.

But just fifteen minutes after they retired, the jury filed back in and took their places. When Judge Hannen was seated and silence reigned, he turned to the foreman.

"What say you?"

"Your Honor, we find that the respondent and co-respondent are not guilty of the charge of adultery."

An excited "halloo" broke from the public gallery, followed by applause and more shouts of triumph. Flo embraced Belle and they laughed. Oh, the hallowed relief.

"Felicitations, Belle," Flo said and kissed her sister's cheeks over and over. "Well done, my darling."

Wertheimer and Belle shook hands warmly and laughed. "Jolly good," Wertheimer said.

The noise from the gallery rose; there was foot stamping and clapping, people shouted Belle's name.

"Silence!" Judge Hannen banged his gavel. "The petition is dismissed."

Belle strained to see William through the crowd that milled before her. He was still seated, but he looked over and smiled. She pulled the gold heart from inside her collar and kissed it; William put his hand to his breast and tapped. Belle's tears streamed freely and she lost sight of William as she was whirled from the courtroom in a mill of bodies.

When she emerged onto the Strand, a scrimmage began: people rushed forward to greet and congratulate her. Cries of "Brava, Belle!" and "Well done, Flo!" went up. The sisters shook hands with their well-wishers and signed cabinet cards that some had brought with them. Every few moments Belle looked around for William but could not see him. A gray-clad figure stood to one side and Belle apprehended that it was her mother. She thanked the people gathered around her for their support and broke free.

"Mother." She stood before her, the glee of the win subdued by her mother's taut expression.

"So you triumphed, Isabel," Mrs. Bilton said.

"It would appear so." Belle's stomach felt as though it was lodged in her windpipe and she longed for a nip of gin to wash it back down into her belly.

"You will be a lifelong bread-and-honey eater, Isabel. I always knew it would be so."

"I'm not sure I take your meaning, Mother."

"Things always go the way of people like you, in the end," Mrs. Bilton turtled her lips and leaned in. "There was ever something grasping about you. From an infant you wanted more than anyone could provide."

"Certainly more than you could, Mother." Mrs. Bilton's marmoreal exterior remained—she was cold to the core, despite the apparent thaw of their last meeting. "Good-bye, Mother. I shall embalm you in my memory, for I doubt we'll meet again."

Flo came and their mother made a show of ignoring her. Flo hooked her arm through her sister's and pulled her back. "Come now, Belle. Our cab is waiting."

Belle allowed Flo to lead her to the hackney. The driver helped them both in, then got up onto his seat and drove on.

Flo turned to Belle. "What did Mother have to say?"

"She wanted to chide me, of course."

"What else could she want?" Flo tucked herself into Belle's side. "*Do you love him?*"

"William?"

"Wertheimer."

"Isidor? No!"

"Funny, I thought every woman loved the man who saved her."

Belle put her hand on her sister's arm. "But I do love my savior, Flo. His love saved me. And mine for him. I love William."

Even before Flo took to the stage at the Royal Trocadero, everyone in the shilling balcony and the sixpenny pit vied with each other to welcome her with a gust of appreciation. They stamped, clapped and yelped when Flo's name was announced as the next act. But many eyes turned upward to Belle once they realized she occupied a box. The clamor increased and the men waved hats and the women their handkerchiefs. Belle bowed and waved back, pleased with the ovation. When Flo finally walked on to do her turn, it took several minutes for the din to die down. Flo curtsied deeply before beginning her song and threw her arm upward to indicate Belle, in case anyone might have missed that Lady Dunlo was present, though the courtroom door had shut only hours previously on her victory. The crowd whooped again and Flo began to sing, chaste and large-eyed:

> "*Lost his way, poor boy, lost his way, poor boy,*
> *He cried and made a fuss, lost his train and lost his bus,*

And lost his way, poor boy, lost his way, poor boy,
He wept some more, made a fuss, lost his train and lost his case . . ."

The entire theater erupted and Belle laughed as loudly as any of the pit boys who were now standing, tossing cheeky hand kisses to her. Once her sister had finished, Belle bowed once more and slipped from her box to go backstage so that she and Flo might travel to the Café Royal together.

Throughout the day crowds had waited for them, and the Café Royal was no different. When the two sisters entered the foyer of the hotel, they were greeted by a throng. They shook hands with several people and Belle accepted their congratulations. She recognized a newsman from the *Pall Mall Gazette.* He stepped forward with the usual impertinence of his profession and, without even offering a greeting, began to question her.

"What verdict did you anticipate, Lady Dunlo?"

Belle turned and looked him straight in the face. "Why, the verdict that was given, naturally. I knew I was innocent of the awful charge that had been trumped up against me."

He scribbled down her answer and continued. "Do you intend to continue your theater engagements, Lady Dunlo?"

"I've had no time to consider the matter, sir. I'm not really sure." It would, of course, depend on William, and his relations with his family, but she was not about to divulge that to a newsman.

"What is your opinion of the judge"—the man checked his notebook—"Sir James Hannen?"

"Well, of course I find him a dear man." The crowd who had jostled closer to hear what Belle was saying, laughed. "Oh, but I really mean that about him, I feel it keenly," she said, looking around at their faces. "His lordship is a dear and fair man."

"And were you satisfied with the advocacy of your learned counsel, Lady Dunlo?"

"Why, yes. I was delighted with Mr. Lockwood." Belle smiled. "And Mr. Wertheimer's man, Mr. Gill, well, he has been a brick, truly. They have done us proud."

"And your opinion of the counsel on the other side?"

"Mr. Russell did his utmost, his dead level best, in a very bad case. I feel a little sorry for the man." Belle slid her arm through Flo's. "Now, you will excuse us, ladies and gentlemen. The court case has given us an appetite and we're ready for our supper."

The crowd parted and further compliments were given:

"Brava, ladies."

"Congratulations, Miss Bilton!"

The sisters launched forward arm in arm toward the gilt and crimson of the café. Perhaps, Belle, thought, William will be within; her gut lurched. Since they had left the court she had hoped that every corner she turned might reveal him. He would come forward to stand before her and they would embrace. She would want to admonish him, but she would hug and forgive him—of course she would, if only he would show himself. Belle sighed and Flo gathered closer to her side. As they neared the café door, Wertheimer walked through it and stood before them; he offered a broad smile. A fresh carnation was pinned in his lapel.

"Victorious red," Flo murmured.

"Isidor," Belle said.

"Belle."

He beamed and held out his hand, which she pumped gratefully. They stood and looked at each other, their hands still clasped.

"Oh, lord," said Flo, "are we going to stand out here for the night? My stomach is doing a tarantella; I will capsize if I don't eat soon."

"Shall we?" Wertheimer said, offering an arm to each lady.

"We most certainly shall," Belle said.

The two sisters flanked Wertheimer and the trio entered the precious, promising sanctum of the Café Royal.

A Reconciliation

When William arrived at Avenue Road, the day after the petition was dismissed, Belle's first words to him were, "How can I trust you, William?"

"Please find it in your heart to, Belle," he said. "I beg you to have faith in me, my darling."

Rosina had let William in, for Jacob had disappeared after his day in court. Wertheimer waited for him to turn up and resume his duties as page boy, but Belle knew they had seen the last of Master Baltimore. Belle tried to reprimand Rosina with a glare when she announced William, but the girl refused to look at her.

Belle agitated her skirts now and stood before her husband. "Have faith in you? But, William, you're someone who does not do what you say you will do. I don't like that kind of person. That kind of man."

It was strange to have him in Avenue Road, his tall frame filling the smoking room. His hair was wet from the rain and when he came closer, she could see that his coat was quite soaked, as if he had walked the two and a half miles from Burlington Street. All the way from Mayfair in a torrent, to speak to her. Well, well. Maybe she *could* forgive yesterday's blasting silence. Forgive all of it. He moved even nearer and put both hands on her waist.

"You *must* have confidence in me, my darling," William said. "I'm much changed."

"If you are, William, why did you not come to me yesterday? Would that not have been the courtly thing to do? The proper action? A way to manifestly show these great changes that have come over you?"

She pulled his hands from her waist and walked to the window. Belle surveyed the street; wind and rain were making a rackety day of it and, she found, it matched her turmoil.

"My love," William said, "please listen to me. It was all a frightful mistake: the petition, everything. I was much addled while abroad, my thoughts so very disordered. Remember I was ill. Godley Robinson wore me down, on my father's instruction. I was utterly befuddled. I'm in no such state now. My mind is as clear as can be, as is my heart."

Pritchard flitted mightily in his cage—was he pleased or upset by William's voice? Belle couldn't decide.

"Belle, won't you try to understand? Won't you accept that I am deeply sorry? You must hear me, Belle. I cannot apologize enough. For the case and everything about it."

"It's hard for me to know what to think about it all. When you continue to act in odd ways, how am I to believe your remorse or discern changes in you?"

"Mama said yesterday she sees nothing but difference in me this past year." His look was mournful.

"You saw your mother?"

"Yes. She came to tell me that my father is determined to dispossess me of whatever he can. He has begun to sell off his assets in Ireland. Mama says he is selling Garbally's furniture and paintings at Christie's."

"I see. And does Lady Adeliza mean to help you?"

"I believe so. She was much saddened by the trial, by my father's actions."

Rosina brought tea though Belle had not requested it. They drank in silence and ate Little Cupids, Belle wondering if the girl had purposely served those particular cakes.

"The weather is unsettled," she said.

"Yes, it has been changeable of late."

William's look was mesmeric when she spoke, as if Belle were inventing language as it fell from her tongue. He asked after Flo, Seymour and Wertheimer, and Belle gave brief reports. But their eyes traveled over each other's faces and bodies, and they sucked at every word the other said, thirsty for a trickle of feeling to match their own. *Is he as churned up as I am?* Belle wondered. She wanted nothing more than to drop at his feet and clasp her arms around his waist. Did he want that, too? He had come looking for forgiveness—did he want everything that might accompany that?

"William, do you mean for us to go on?"

"Go on?"

"As husband and wife, William. Are we to be united now?"

William pushed the tea table to one side and fell to his knees on the rug. He took her hands and jostled them with his own.

"Of course, Belle, of course. That's why I'm here. I love you with every idiot inch of my head and my heart, with all of me. I want to be with you more than I want any other thing. I want to show you that I can do this right."

Belle whimpered and leaped into his lap. They kissed and it was the most natural thing, to feel William's tongue hot and swollen in her mouth. Tears slipped from her eyes and mingled with their spit; they laughed and cried. Within minutes they were buried under the coverlets in Belle's bedroom overlooking Norfolk Road, attempting to swallow each other whole, while they hatched plans for their combined future.

SUMMER 1891

London and Galway

A Death

Ten months after reuniting with Belle, having not seen his family at all, William was summoned by Lady Adeliza to his father's bedside in London. Belle knew better than to ask to accompany him. That he failed to arrive before the earl expired troubled William greatly. He had traveled to Berkeley Square from Plymouth where Belle was performing.

"His body was still warm," he said to Belle, when he got back to her later that May evening, as if trying to fathom how that could be. He missed his father's death rattle by mere moments. "I took his hand in mine and the heat had not yet left it. The skin was soft, his fingers pliable in my own fingers. My sister, Katherine, said I was lucky not to have witnessed the end; she said it was 'not smooth.' When I questioned her for more, she fell silent. Whatever her opinion, I should have liked to look Papa in the eye one last time."

Belle took him in her arms. "If you could allow yourself to weep, it might peel back some of the pain of the past months."

"I wish I could but no tears will come." William sighed. "I wish I had made things equitable between Papa and me, I would like to have been able to do that. To assuage my guilt, I suppose."

"Now, now, my love," Belle crooned. "What do you have to be guilty about? Your papa chose his own path with regard to you."

He lifted his head from her shoulder. "Mama reports that he does not want to be buried in Ireland, in the family vault at Saint John's. I confessed my surprise. Now, why should he not want to be interred there, Belle? He loved Garbally, and Ballinasloe, as I love it."

She looked at William and wondered at his naïveté. "It may be because he was afraid I may end up in the tomb beside him, my love. Your papa did not want his earthly remains cheek by jowl for eternity with a peasant countess."

William sighed and pulled at the black tie Belle had knotted for him that morning.

"I hope I did not hasten his death with my outburst in court. With everything afterward. My neglect."

"Your father was gravely ill, my love. He attended court against the will of his doctor, remember?"

"Yes, you're right." He stayed his hands. "And I needed to say what I said that day. For my own sake."

"You did, my darling. He saw, then, that you had become a man."

William sighed. "I wonder if the men of our generation can ever call ourselves *men*? Papa and his ilk were a different breed to us; they grew up quicker. Their fathers were perhaps stricter and would not countenance bad behavior. Papa had to put up with mine." William tugged at his tie, loosening it. "Mama said that he wished for an unostentatious burial. He shall have it in London, I suppose."

"He could surely have had that in Ballinasloe, too?"

"Indeed." William slipped the tie from his neck and worked his finger behind his collar. "Though perhaps not if he wanted a *very* quiet burial. My grandfather's funeral there was rather a grand affair. His coffin stood on a catafalque in the picture gallery at Garbally; I was brought to pay my respects, but I was young and too loudly I asked Mama if Grandpapa meant to sleep all day. I was bustled outside to the procession beyond the portico. Two hundred children stood there waiting for the coffin. The boys wore armbands of crepe, the girls black rosettes; the tenants had bands and veils of black on their hats. They looked festive and I wanted very much to march with the boys, as I saw it. But I was stuffed into a carriage for the solemn trot to Saint John's. The town felt eerie that day— no shop or business was open, the shutters were closed on the houses. It was as if my dead grandpapa had cast a sullen spell. I did not like it. As the carriage made its way up Church Hill, the tenants formed a cordon right and left. I waved to the gamekeeper, a man I liked because of his even temper; he was always patient with me. When Mama saw me wave, she slapped my hand and I entered Saint John's with tears dripping down my cheeks. All the old ladies condoled with Mama and Papa, and cried even more at the sight of my wretched face."

Belle helped her husband out of his jacket. "Your papa loved you, William."

"Did he, Belle? We both know that he was disappointed with me. Always. We never fitted properly together, he and I."

"His pride was damaged, for sure, when you went behind his back to marry me, but he loved you well."

"You know it was said once that Papa had all of Grandpapa's prejudice and none of his ability. I wonder, Belle, how can you be so kind about my father when he treated you so ill?"

"He didn't know me, William. It's true he didn't care to remedy that, but it's easy to feel animosity toward a person who's not real to you, whose eyes you never look into. If he'd taken the time to get to know me a little, perhaps he would have found things to like about me."

"Maybe your greatest fault was aligning yourself to me. It was *me* he disliked."

Belle took him in her arms. "Parents are odd creatures, William. They don't always behave in rational or generous ways. Perhaps they even act selfishly in order to preserve themselves. But I do believe your papa was on your side. Despite everything."

A Beginning

As they approached Dublin's Broadstone railway station, William told Belle that the bridge their coach was crossing had been an aqueduct until recently.

"It used to carry the Royal Canal," he said.

Belle nodded in appreciative interest, for she knew William was proud of Ireland and she wished him to know that she was willing to be great hearted about the place.

"The railway station is a fine-looking place, to be sure," she said.

"Neo-Egyptian in style," William said, as if he were architect and builder, both. "The Midland Great Western Railway Company is run by visionary men."

He sighed and took Belle's gloved hand in his own and she could sense a settling down in him, a belonging to it all that had begun on the sea crossing on *The Lady Martin*. But, no, it had started before that, when Lady Adeliza informed William that he was not to be disinherited entirely. It was then that William had grown, before Belle's gaze, into the man she knew he could be. On the crossing he grew larger, more Irish, more resolved. When they had approached Waterford, William's itch to disembark ran through him like electricity. He dragged Belle to the ship's rail—despite the fog that made the deck slippery—so that she should enjoy the first glimpse of his homeland as soon as he did.

The steamy curtain meant, of course, that the land was obscured. The mist was not the brown, smoke-choked fog of London; rather it was a scarfy vapor that seemed to amplify the sound of *The Lady Martin* breaking through the water. Gulls keened like the bereaved, the nearer the ship got to the coast. The boat and birds together made some cacophony, but Belle saw that William reveled in it. Her stomach surged with the movement of *The Lady Martin*, but she didn't let the sickness overwhelm her. When the yellow gleam of the Hook Lighthouse shone through the mist, accompanied by the long, lonely burr of the horn, William almost keeled over with excitement. To Belle, he was once again the boy who had been lost during the machinations of the trial and all that happened after it: their reunion, his ostracizing by his father. William giggled; he grinned; he jigged with the anticipation of finding his feet once more on Irish soil. For herself, Belle was quietened by the sea and its over and back between the two islands, ferrying its freight of fish and men, reinventing itself with every sandy shift. To what new life did it carry her? She had left the stage once Lady Adeliza secured her and William's future. It was a wrench, but Belle had known the day would come. And she would dance at parties and balls, and everyone loved to hear a song well sung, did they not?

Now seated on the train in Dublin, waiting for it to lurch forward to Ballinasloe, Belle began to settle, too. William sat opposite her in their compartment, readying their accoutrements for travel: his *Irish Times*, Belle's *Women's Penny Paper*, and a bag of lemon drops to ease queasiness. He laid these things on the seat beside him and sat back, a man in charge of himself and his life.

Belle ran her hands over her mourning silks; they made a pleasing rustle when she smoothed the skirts. In style it was a restrained gown, but the jet buttons and Limerick lace trim lifted it, Belle felt, from the ordinary to the rather grand. William had ordered the silk crepe de chine from a mill in

Lyons. He had it fashioned into gowns by his mother's favorite London seamstress and it pleased Belle that he went to such pains. She also wore a black enamel brooch with a gold repoussé border, containing who knew whose hair; it had been an early gift from Wertheimer when she had admired it in his Maidenhead home. Belle was glad to be the finest in attire; Lady Adeliza, she knew, had worn Parramatta silk and Lady Katherine, her sister-in-law, just bombazine. William himself looked august in black gloves and cravat, and a new suit from Henry Poole & Co.

"Should I move Pritchard's travel cage to the overhead rack?" he said.

"Leave him be," Belle said. The cage sat on the seat beside her and she lifted the edge of the black cloth that covered it to peep in at her pet. The somber material made it seem as if Pritchard, too, was in mourning. The cage was small and she fretted that her canary did not have enough room to exercise his wings and legs; he was perch bound and sulky looking, his feathers puffed out. "Do you think he's well? He's awfully still and quiet. Entirely unlike himself."

"I'm sure the little fellow is tip-top," William said. "But you could sing to him, darling. How about 'Fresh, fresh, fresh as the morning'?" William sang the line softly, one of Belle's old tunes that he liked to resurrect to cheer her. She leaned across, put her hand to her husband's cheek and kissed his lips.

She turned to Pritchard and sang:

"We're fresh, fresh, fresh as the morning,
Sweeter than the new mown hay,
We're fresh, fresh, fresh as the morning,
And just what you want today."

The canary cocked his head for his mistress and offered a few notes in return; Belle smiled.

"See?" said William. "Your birdy friend is up to snuff, as ever." The train chugged out of the station. "Westward ho!" he said, rubbing his hands together.

"Indeed, my love."

Belle shivered, wondering again what awaited her in County Galway; none of the family would be there, of course; Berkeley Square was their permanent home now. But she would have ample staff to deal with and William would be much occupied with the affairs of the estate. How would she fare alone, without Flo? Who would tell her how to do things?

William had tried to prepare Belle for her new life, but some of his proclamations about what she might expect only increased her anxiety.

"The Irish like to be agreeable," he had told her, "but there always seems to be a bubbling dissent in them, too."

So what could she look forward to—congeniality or contention? She tried to dredge up Flo's advice about going in "with heart and mind un-barred." And something else, what was it? Oh yes, "Keep your feet firmly planted."

"Feet firmly planted," Belle murmured.

Belle hoped to make acquaintances among the local gentry, but would they accept her? William had assured her she would make friends, that the Irish of all classes were ebullient and welcoming, despite their natural discordance. There would not be a friend like Wertheimer among them, of that she was certain. Dear Isidor. He offered fulsome forgiveness to William for dragging him into the whole court debacle. And he promised to write to Belle frequently now that Ireland had claimed her and they would no longer see each other so much. She resolved to write to Wert-heimer the moment she landed in Ballinasloe to lure him from London to Garbally to visit; Galway surely had plenty of pleasant diversions that would amuse him.

The train shunted forward, leisurely at first while it shook off the city and gathering speed as it pressed on toward Mullingar and Galway. Their compartment was as fine as any on a train in England, Belle was pleased to apprehend—finer, perhaps, for being newer. She stroked the nap of the maroon seat and admired the polished wood of the racks.

"There are beds in some of the carriages, Belle. Got up like steamer berths. A lot of the cattlemen are wealthy fellows and they like to down some grog, then take their rest as they travel between sales." Belle nodded her encouragement and William carried on, determined to lay before her, it seemed, the best of everything Ireland had to offer. "There is a ladies' carriage also, for women traveling alone or with children."

"So they can avoid the cattlemen, no doubt."

Belle looked out the window at the passing landscape—the banks to the side of the tracks swayed with tall flowering stems and the plants' pink spears nodded as if greeting each passenger one by one. The babe wriggled beneath Belle's gown. Already she had had to switch to a featherbone corset; and it was a blessing that she was in mourning, for none of her old bodices would fasten across her enlarged bosom. This baby was making a mountain of her long before little Isidor ever had. She thought of her son. He was amply provided for, she had seen to that, and Sara, she knew, would do well by him. One day, she hoped, he might come to Garbally, too, if it could be arranged. Not as her son, perhaps, but as an esteemed and welcome guest. Maybe one day, when he understood the circumstances of his birth, he would see why she had had to do what she did. Belle put her hand to her middle. Maybe the child growing inside her now would be the baby girl she longed for; William, of course, hoped for a boy. This pregnancy was easier, she found, perhaps because the babe was loved already. Poor baby Isidor, he had had such an inauspicious start.

William leaned forward and placed his hand over Belle's stomach. "How is the sixth earl today?" he said.

"Awriggle, as always," she said.

When they lay in bed together William liked to talk of the baby and imagine his future. He put his cheek to Belle's abdomen, as if the infant might announce pertinent information about itself to its papa's ear. They would not know whether it was a boy or a girl until Christmas, of course, and Belle's confinement. "It seems a devilish long wait," William said often. Their baby, if a boy, would also hold the title Lord Kilconnell and William told Belle about Kilconnell, the place. "A dainty town, an area of trees and small lakes, a few miles distant from Ballinasloe." They would ride out there soon, so Belle could cast her eye over it, her yet-to-be-born son's domain.

Being enceinte had made Belle sluggish and hungry; all she longed to do was sleep or eat, and already she wondered whether the restaurant car would bring food to their compartment, rather than her having to walk there.

"Might they have sago pudding on board, dearest? I do so fancy something sweet and milky."

"I shall find out for you," William said and rose from his seat.

"No, no. Perhaps I am too sleepy to eat. Sit, sit. Let me close my eyes for a spell."

The rickety-rackety jaunt of the train lulled Belle into a doze where every sound—voices, track noise, the opening and closing of doors—became part of the same far-off, liquid thrum. She woke as the white girders of the bridge at Athlone cast shadows across her eyes through the window. The Shannon had burst its banks after a heavy rain and the river threw its skirts wide to cover fields where swans threaded the hems. Belle shook herself awake to better appreciate the scene.

There was romance to Ireland, it seemed. Yes, it was green like England, but it was less tangled somehow, with its spilling riverbanks, low stone walls and squat houses. There was something flung about to the landscape, a not-quite-togetherness that she thought might suit her. She would fit in, surely; she would find ways to make friends even if it took some time.

"I don't want you to fret about being lonely, Belle," William said, sensing her anxieties. "As I've said, society is not so pronounced in Ireland—even less so in the west. You can expect to mix with all. People are not so inclined to be hierarchical."

Belle wondered if this was fancy on his part—wouldn't the son of an earl always have been treated with deference by ordinary people? Might

William have long mistaken respectful submission for friendliness? What would they know of *her* in Ballinasloe, she mused, and what would they make of her?

The train slowed and she looked out. "Little could be amiss with a place where trees grow in the middle of lakes," she said.

"It's a turlough, my love—a temporary lake."

Sure enough, when Belle peered closer she could see the stone walls bounding the lake, which seemed to shimmer under the sun.

"But it's so beautiful—a tree in water. The branches are mirrored roots."

William reached across and pressed her hand. "Are you happy, Belle?"

"Yes, William, very happy. And hungry. Ever so hungry."

The train shunted on and, in no time, it puffed into the station at Ballinasloe; the door to their compartment swung open from the outside as soon as movement ceased. How did the stationmaster know they were within? A hand was thrust forward to Belle and she took it and stepped down. William emerged behind her, throwing greetings like confetti to various people.

"Hullo, Flanagan! Ah, Mr. Burke, it is good to see you. Very good, indeed!"

All was gray. The platform, the limestone buildings that made up the station, the sky, the faces that loomed around Belle with unbridled interest.

"How do you do, gentlemen?" she said.

"Come now." William was suddenly officious and commanding. "Leave the countess some space to walk."

Belle took William's arm. "Countess" still felt somewhat like a sobriquet to her but she enjoyed growing accustomed to it. Since she heard that Lady Adeliza did not mean to deny William his due, a great peace had descended into Belle's mind. It engulfed her now, this confident, tranquil feeling, and it was tinted with excitement, for now she knew that her life was beginning anew. This was not like moving to London; her days would be ordered here and she would have a position.

Though all about was gray, it pleased Belle that the air smelled sweet: peat smoke drifted from the station chimney and a strong floral smell came from a stand of lilac that swayed beside the pedestrian bridge. This was a place that held promise.

William walked forward along the platform and Belle glided beside him; they gained the arched entranceway to the building. The name of the station, "Ballinasloe," hung in black letters on a white sign. It suddenly struck Belle how odd it sounded: Ball-in-a-sloe. Later she would ask William to explain it to her. For now, she only wished to get to Garbally Court, the place she had heard so much about, so often, to see it for herself.

The carriage made slow progress from the station to the gates of Garbally, affording Belle time to glimpse something of the area from the window. She saw rows of squat thatched buildings that released smoke skyward; William assured her that there was a proper town with streets of shops and that she would see it once they had settled. He looked out at the passing scene with contentment and Belle sat back and watched him, glad that he was glad.

When they arrived at the entrance of the estate, which lay at the top of a gentle hill, the gates were locked. William alighted from the carriage to see what could be done and, after a spell, Belle joined him. The driver said he would go to one of the groundsmen who lived nearby to see what was what. While William and the coachman made arrangements for the keys, Belle pulled up her skirt and hitched as much of its silk into her waistband as would fit. She climbed the black gates—her pregnancy had not yet made a complete indolent of her—and in seconds was at the top, over and down the other side. She began to walk the path through trees that would surely lead to the house.

"Come on, William," she called, not looking back.

She soon heard the rattle of the gates as her husband scaled them. He jogged up behind her, and they walked through the trees and out into parkland. Bees stumbled in a drowse from meadowsweet to buttercup in the grass that bracketed the long track, and the echo of a woodsman's ax traveled pleasantly to them from among the trees. There were these small sounds and no others; a great peace thrummed up from the earth and descended from the large sky above Ballinasloe.

When the carriage rolled up behind them—a key evidently located—Belle and William chose to continue to walk the rest of the way. It would delay the moment when William could lay the house out before her, and it afforded Belle a more gradual taking in of at least part of the estate she had heard so much about. And it felt glorious to stretch her limbs after being so long seated on the train and let the Galway sun take her in its embrace.

A Home

Belle heard a clock strike an early hour, three, maybe, or four. Was it the clock tower at Saint John's Church in Ballinasloe town, or some nearer one on their land? William had told her over dinner that Ballinasloe meant "the mouth of the ford of the hosts," and she repeated the meaning to herself, wondering who would concoct such a convoluted appellation. And what on earth might it mean? Oh, William had tried to explain, but he was being as complicated in his account as the reasons behind the awkward name. It was perhaps an Irish trait to be oblique and circuitous; Belle would ask him when he woke.

She sighed and ruffled her toes under the covers. Sleep did not come easily to her when the babe within wriggled at night. It fluttered against her skin and the movement meant she lay awake most midnights, and beyond, feeling the ticklish kicks, her head a mishmash of thoughts. Her hands traveled now over her hips, onto her thighs and buttocks—all was fleshily soft. William loved this new pillowiness in Belle's form; she found she did not mind it as much as she had the first time she carried a child. Everything was different now.

She poked her nose above the coverlets—the bedroom air was keen and cold. She must become accustomed to brisk rooms again, she realized, after the always-warm comfort of Avenue Road, the muggy heat of a string of hotels and, later, Flo and Seymour's cozy home where she and William had lodged for a while.

It had been difficult to leave her sister to cross the sea—they had been fast companions since Flo was fresh from the womb. It would be hard to have only letters for a time—Flo was not a keen correspondent. But Flo would visit her in Galway and Belle would spend almost half the year in England. Flo and Seymour were tight these days, thankfully, but Flo was a little alarmed at Belle's move to Ireland.

"Must you go, Belle?" she said. "You're no hand at provincial life. Remember Maidenhead? You almost went barmy with the drabness of it! No, you will return to bask in London's stink and clatter within a month, I guarantee it."

"We mean to come back and forth," Belle had said, "but Garbally will be our main home."

"Ireland!" Flo said, with a moan. "It's such a rough, drenched place. And the people are ugly and dull, by every account. I worry you will not thrive there."

"With William beside me, all will be well."

Flo softened. "I'm sorry, dearest, I shouldn't say such things. It's just that I won't know what to do without you, old stick."

"You'll get along, Flo," Belle said, but she was as gut punched as her sister at the idea of their separation. It was the only cloud that obscured what she hoped would be a bright onward march.

Belle put thoughts of Flo aside and rose from the bed where her husband made a long, comforting hump. By thin moonlight she descended the staircase of Garbally Court; the place was hushed, the marble of the steps felt wintry underfoot. Mildew draped its heady scent over everything. Still, this was a palace. The finest house Ireland had to its emerald name, perhaps. William had already shown her the throne room and the seat where no king's rear end had ever been comfortable—nor any queen's for that matter.

"It waits for royal posteriors still," he'd said and lifted Belle into it. "There now, it has one."

The baby squirmed again.

"Time, time," Belle whispered, putting her hand to her stomach as if that might soothe the child. "There is plenty of time."

Once at the bottom of the stairs, she made her way to the ballroom, where she opened some of the long window shutters. Under crepuscular light, she viewed the portraits of William's ancestors. They were as portraits of the nobility usually are: stern and condescending. She could divine William in some of their faces and their stances. But her husband, it appeared to her, had not his forbears' arrogance. Belle wondered if likenesses of her own children would hang there someday, if her own portrait might also grace the wall.

Leaving the ballroom, she slipped out the front door and under the portico. This path to the left would lead to what was called the broad walk, William had told her. He would take her in the morning around the grounds to see his favorite oak grove, the icehouse, the forty steps that led to nowhere, the stables and the farmyard. Everything she had not seen on her walk down the avenue from the gates.

Belle stepped farther out and crossed the path so she could stand and look at the house, at its long bank of top-floor windows—eleven glinting panes. One day, she hoped, the face of a child might peer from each one. The grass felt alive under her soles. What joy this place would bring. What joy it had already brought; she and William had spent hours in torsions of ecstasy in their new marital bed. William seemed to find his best erotic self here and they had kissed and plunged and caressed as never before for, it seemed, hours on end. William had kissed Belle in places she didn't know she liked to be kissed: her thighs, her inner arms, the small of her back. She had sat astride him and rocked slowly, then faster until he gasped and cried out. Sated and exhausted they then slept, tangled limb on limb around each other, until the baby's usual nocturnal fluttering woke Belle and propelled her out of bed to her nighttime wanders.

Dew doused Belle's feet now; she wriggled her toes and rose high on them, ever the dancer on the edge of performance. She settled the gold heart on its chain at her throat, then threw her arms wide. Garbally Park held two thousand acres. Two *thousand* acres. This was more land than her mind could even fathom. And it was her home.

"Home," she said to the facade of the house. "Home," to the oaks that flanked it. To the yellowing sky she said it and to the sharp Galway air. "Home," she said to her dawn companions: the owl, the bat, the badger. "I am home."

Author's Note

The characters in *Becoming Belle* are almost all based on real people. Some newspaper reports of the divorce case contradict each other and many display the journalist's personal bias but, by and large, I stuck to the reported facts of the case. The British Newspaper Archive was a valuable resource, as were the National Archives at Kew and the National Portrait Gallery in London. Brian Casey kindly allowed me to read his PhD thesis on the Clancarty estate. Thanks are due also to Damian Mac Con Uladh, who shared useful information and photographs relating to the Le Poer Trench family, and to my sister Aoife O'Connor for archival help. Any mistakes in fact are my own.

BELLE BILTON (aka Countess of Clancarty) gave birth to twin boys in December 1891, Richard and Power. Power died two years later. She had three other children with William: Beryl, Roderic and Greville. Belle died of cancer on New Year's Eve 1906 in Galway, age thirty-nine. She is buried in the grounds of Saint John's Church, Ballinasloe, County Galway.

WILLIAM LE POER TRENCH (aka fifth Earl of Clancarty) was declared bankrupt in 1907 in Ireland and moved to England, where he was bankrupted in 1910. In 1908 he married Mary Gwatkin Ellis. They had three children: William, Power and Sibell. He died in 1929, age sixty, and is buried in England.

ISIDOR WERTHEIMER was declared bankrupt in August 1891. In 1892 he "very quietly" married eighteen-year-old Mary Hammack. He died in his mother's house in January 1893, after catching a chill on a horse ride in Rotten Row while in recovery from typhoid. However, it has also been suggested he died by his own hand. He was twenty-nine. There is no evidence to suggest that Wertheimer was gay.

FLO BILTON lost her husband William Seymour in 1894; she remarried that same year. Flo died in 1910, age forty-two.

KATE MAUDE PENRICE BILTON died in 1930, age eighty-seven. Her husband, John George Bilton, predeceased her in 1905; he was sixty-three.

ALDEN CARTER WESTON (baby Isidor's father) disappears from records in 1891 (while serving seven years for fraud).

ISIDOR ALDEN CLEVELAND WESTON (baby Isidor) joined the Canadian Expeditionary Force in 1915. He married Ida Duchon-Doris in London in 1919. He died in Oregon, age eighty.

PRITCHARD, Belle's canary, is an invention. In fact, she owned a Saint Bernard dog.

GARBALLY COURT and its parkland were sold to the diocese of Clonfert in 1922. It became the home of Saint Joseph's College, a Catholic boys' secondary school, which exists there to this day.

ACKNOWLEDGMENTS

Thanks to my family, as always, for myriad supports. Especially my husband, Finbar, who acts as sounding board, buffer and all-round good guy.

Go raibh míle maith agat ó chroí to my gorgeous agent, Gráinne Fox, for kindness, wisdom, strength and fun in abundance. Gratitude also to Veronica Goldstein and all at Fletcher & Co for continued hard work and cheerleading.

Enormous thanks to my editors, Tara Singh Carlson and Helen Smith, and forensic copy editor, Martha Schwartz, who painstakingly shepherded Belle into becoming the Belle she needed to be. Many thanks also to Helen Richard and Deborah Sun de la Cruz for valuable input and support on the journey with the novel, and to all at G. P. Putnam's in New York and Penguin Canada in Toronto for their continued amazing work.

Biggest thanks, and a huge brava, to Isabel Maude Penrice Bilton herself for being a courageous, determined, creative woman, willing to swap the lights of London for the delights of rural Galway. This novel is my salute to you, darling Belle.